Hot and strong . . .

"Chérie." He lifted his hand and cradled the back of her head, bringing her face down to his. "Kiss me."

She sighed into his mouth before she kissed it, and her breath warmed his tongue. She smelled of apples, but she tasted of honey and almonds. Thierry watched her eyes close, felt her thighs tighten over his, and then the liquid heat of her mouth melded with his.

She kissed him as she had moved, graceful but cautious, a little cat finding its way in the dark. He had never felt anything like it. His need for her blood pounded inside him, demanding more than soft lips and silky tongue, and he used his hand to tilt her head.

Inside, where it cannot be seen. Where it will be her secret, and mine.

When Thierry sank his fangs into the soft flesh inside her lower lip, she groaned.

Her blood flooded his mouth, hot and strong, the pulse of life that hummed in her veins pouring into his. Thierry drank from her lips, warming with each swallow, intent on taking only what he needed. The wounds in his belly and sides itched as they began to knit and close, the signal that he had had enough of her. Yet she kept kissing him, giving him her tongue as well as her blood.

PRIVATE DEMON

A NOVEL OF THE DARKYN

Lynn Viehl

A SIGNET ECLIPSE BOOK

SIGNET ECLIPSE
Published by New American Library, a division of
Penguin Group (USA) Inc., 375 Hudson Street,
New York, New York 10014, USA
Penguin Group (Canada), 90 Eglinton Avenue East, Suite 700, Toronto,
Ontario M4P 2Y3, Canada (a division of Pearson Penguin Canada Inc.)
Penguin Books Ltd., 80 Strand, London WC2R 0RL, England
Penguin Ireland, 25 St. Stephen's Green, Dublin 2,
Ireland (a division of Penguin Books Ltd.)
Penguin Group (Australia), 250 Camberwell Road, Camberwell, Victoria 3124,
Australia (a division of Pearson Australia Group Pty. Ltd.)
Penguin Books India Pvt. Ltd., 11 Community Centre, Panchsheel Park,
New Delhi - 110 017, India
Penguin Group (NZ), cnr Airborne and Rosedale Roads, Albany,
Auckland 1310, New Zealand (a division of Pearson New Zealand Ltd.)
Penguin Books (South Africa) (Pty.) Ltd., 24 Sturdee Avenue,
Rosebank, Johannesburg 2196, South Africa

Penguin Books Ltd., Registered Offices:
80 Strand, London WC2R 0RL, England

First published by Signet Eclipse, an imprint of New American Library,
a division of Penguin Group (USA) Inc.

First Printing, October 2005
10 9 8 7 6 5 4 3 2 1

For Katherine Rose,
my small demon.

Where a faint light shines alone,
Dwells a Demon I have known.
Most of you had better say
'The Dark House,' and go your way.
Do not wonder if I stay.

—Edwin Arlington Robinson, *The Dark House*

Chapter 1

*B*itch in a Lexus. *Awesome.*

Todd Brackman watched the silver SUV swing around the corner. The lane lights reserved for account holders only had switched from green to red an hour ago, when the bank had closed, but the ATM lane's light still glowed green.

Green for the green. Brackman wiped the sweat from his face onto his sleeve. *Come to get me some cash.*

Driving into the city and setting up for this job had taken hell near forever. Brackman had put up with the sweats, shakes, and fever, watching every car, knowing it would work only one time. He'd spent half the day out of sight, hiding behind the bank's Dumpster.

Now here she was. *My bitch. Awesome.*

She wasn't actually Todd's, but he knew her sort. Beauty-parlor babe, coming home after having her nails polished. Driving too fast, yammering away on the phone as she dropped by to tap the account for more cash. Didn't this one have a phone pressed to her head and a rock on her married hand he could see even this far away?

High-maintenance twat, Todd's old uncle George would have called her. *All bucks, no bang.*

Something metal crashed into metal, making Brackman tense. The wind must have slammed shut the Dumpster lid he'd opened earlier to shade himself from the sun.

Brackman forgot about the noise and watched the SUV. He guessed she would check him out, so he worked on the tree. Being sweaty might have given it away, but here it actually made him look like he was on the job.

As if he'd ever hump his ass like a landscaper.

Todd thought about his uncle George, who had humped plenty. The old man had had barely enough to eat, a Chevette that farted smoke, and a decrepit single-wide on a back lot in the Lake View Trailer Park. Seemed like heaven when Todd came to live with George after his parents had kicked him out, but then he'd watched his uncle eating mac and cheese four nights a week and never having more fun than getting snot-faced on Wild Turkey every weekend. What had it gotten old G? His heart crapped out, right in front of the drill press he'd run since Kennedy had been assassinated.

The crank Brackman had squirted in the old man's coffee thermos the morning he died had helped, but after George threatened to throw him out, what else could he do? The single-wide was only big enough for one, anyway.

Brackman had dreamed of his uncle when he'd been snoozing behind the Dumpster. Old George had been pissed as always; not about Todd spiking his Folger's, but about the plan. He'd told him not to touch anyone or their green. But the old prick had talked and smelled funny.

It didn't make sense: George had been a sad-ass ancient fart, but he'd have cut his own throat before he turned faggot and started wearing perfume, the way he had in the dream.

Brackman concentrated on the tree again. Screw George. This was a sweet idea, truly awesome, and if nothing went nuts-up, a guaranteed score.

Sweat soaked the front of his O'Malley's Lawn and Tree Service uniform shirt. The name *Bobby* had been embroidered over the pocket because Todd had stolen it from old George's neighbor. That and some shit from the work trailer hitched to the back of Bobby's rusted-out El Camino. He'd thought about boosting the car, but the nosy assholes at Lake View would have seen and called the cops.

Lousy job for picking up any tail, Bobby had said once when they'd been sharing a little weed after a paintball match. *Won't look at me twice when I'm working.*

Bobby's too-big uniform hung on Brackman. Last year Bobby had stopped playing paintball and turned into a lazy fat fuck. He'd even had to pay that skank, All-Night Lisa, for sex.

Brackman thought renting pussy when you had a working hand was like burning hundreds for the heat.

Bobby lost his respect for Todd, too. *Why you keep saying "awesome" and "freaking" all the time? Sounds retarded.* Bobby wouldn't play p-ball anymore, and he'd acted pissy after George had croaked. Bobby had even refused to lend him what he'd needed for this job.

That was why Todd didn't feel bad about sticking Bobby with one of the old man's steak knives that morning.

The bitch pulled up to the ATM and put the SUV in park. Brackman glanced over without moving his head. Phone down, arms elbow-out while she dug through her purse. Two cars sat waiting on a green light a block south.

Perfect. Freaking awesome.

Brackman moved around the trunk of the tree to get closer. He reached in his pocket for the paintball and found it wringing wet. He was sweating buckets; once the bitch put out he'd have to link up with his supplier.

The driver's-side electric window silently zipped down and a tanned hand fed the ATM a debit card. The autoteller's cheerful recorded voice welcomed the bitch to the Anytime Money Service Center and asked for her PIN.

Brackman squeezed the thin plastic ball so hard that he thought for a second it might explode. *Wait for it, dude, wait for it.* The ATM made a series of four same-tone bleeps as the woman's fingers tapped the number keypad.

The account services menu appeared.

Brackman ran up to the driver's side, reached around the edge of the windshield, and slammed the paintball against the glass. As the thick white paint exploded and the bitch shrieked, he grabbed her wrist and pressed the fourteen-inch blade of the chainsaw against her forearm. The chainsaw's little gas motor blatted as it idled.

Her eyes nearly popped out of her head, though, as he leaned in. "Move," he told her, pressing the hot, dirty blade into her skin, "and I'll cut it off."

"Please." It came out on a choked whisper. "Don't. Please."

Brackman used his thumb to put in a one and five zeroes on the ATM number pad. While the console processed his request, he worked the big-ass diamond ring off her bony finger. "Take off the freaking jewelry."

She used one hand to pull off her earrings, the movement jerky-fast. "Won't give you that much."

"You'll give me whatever I want." He heard the autoteller whine about something and glared at the console. "Where's the cash? Why ain't it coming out?"

"Won't give you a thousand. The daily cash limit is two hundred." She gulped air, her little tits heaving under her blouse.

Two hundred? That wouldn't get him more than four hits, much less out of the county, and he for sure couldn't hang here. He peered in the Lexus, squinting as a strong, flowery odor burned his nose. "What else you got on you?"

A fist out of nowhere knocked the chainsaw away from the bitch's arm and out of Brackman's grip. A big bum dressed in black hauled him backward. Brackman's face slammed against the paint-covered windshield.

"Connor." The bum used Brackman's face like a dishcloth to wipe a hole in the paint before he jerked him back. To the bitch, he snarled, "Flee."

Tires squealed as the bitch took off. Brackman spit paint, swiping and clawing at the bum and his own burning eyes. Even when he could see, the asshole's face was hidden behind a mop of filthy, tangled hair.

Wino on a bender. Brackman started to swear, and then the bum seized him by the front of the neck. "Ay . . ."

The bum's fingers stopped crushing his throat, but he didn't let go. In his other hand he held a knife with a weird blade.

"I got no"—Brackman coughed—"grief with you, man."

"The woman?" Hot, burning eyes glittered. "Your grief with her?"

The asshole sounded funny. The knife he slid back into a sheath clipped to his belt—it wasn't silver, but some darker metal. Brackman couldn't see any other weapons. Maybe the bum wasn't packing anything else.

"Owed me money." He wrapped his fingers around the steak knife, still sticky with Bobby's blood, in his pocket. "You hurting, am I right?"

"Hurting." The bum's roof-beam shoulders hunched.

Brackman spotted the chainsaw, now in pieces. "Aw, what'd you do?" The stench of perfume was making him sick. "Get off me, man; you freaking *stink*."

The huge hand released him. "Flee, Connor." When Brackman didn't move, he shouted, *"Run."*

"Sure." Brackman turned his body to hide his hand as he pulled the steak knife from his pocket. He'd cut the nosy fuck's throat, and then what? Bitch was gone; chainsaw was ruined. Maybe his supplier would fence some of Bobby's stuff. "Awesome work, man."

The bum swung away.

Brackman jumped on his broad back and ripped the serrated edge of the steak knife across his neck. Hot blood sprayed Todd's hand. Once he'd sliced him wide, he rammed the blade into the side of his neck. The man stopped moving and stood frozen, a domino about to topple.

"Sorry you messed with me now?" Brackman said against his ear, twisting the knife a half turn.

"We."

Grimy fingers closed over his hand. Brackman shrieked as three of his fingers snapped, and then he was upside down, tucked under the bum's arm, and everything was moving. No, they were. The bum carried him across the lot and with a single toss threw him into the Dumpster.

The bags inside the Dumpster acted like a thick cushion, blowing out and breaking Brackman's fall. He hardly felt it. *But I cut him. I freaking* cut *him.*

Holding his broken hand against his chest, Brackman tried to sit up, but the bags under him shifted. Tears of frustration swamped his eyes, and his nose clogged. Asshole ruined his plan, broke his chainsaw, and wouldn't die. How freaking fair was that?

"Why you messing with me, man?" he shrieked at the opening above him. "I got nothing. Nothing, and you go and *break my freaking back.*"

The Dumpster rocked as the bum jumped in and landed to stand over him. Todd looked up, and hot wetness soaked the crotch of his pants as he pissed himself.

The steak knife was still sticking out of the side of the bum's neck. There was no gash across his throat. The dirty skin on his neck looked as if it had grown around the base of the knife.

"Wait." This guy was like *Dawn of the Dead* or something. Brackman could talk his way out of this, bribe him. *Old George's supply of Wild Turkey.* His broken fingers and the nice, sweet smell inside the Dumpster made it hard to get the words out. "Booze. You want some booze? I got a lot back at my place."

The bum yanked the knife out of his neck. "No." The steak knife fell from his hand onto Todd's chest.

"Come on and help me, then, man." Brackman hunted for the knife with his good hand. "I'm really hurting here." He curled his hand around the plastic handle. "Help me."

The big man hesitated, and then reached down for him.

"Shithead." Todd shoved the steak knife into his belly, once, twice, three times. "Now you freaking die."

"Known, Connor." Beneath the tangled mess of dark hair, the bum's cracked lips parted, and something long and sharp glittered. "I'm already dead." He bent down.

At last Todd Brackman saw exactly what the bum was packing, and screamed.

"Ms. Shaw?" Thomas, the youngest of the security guards at the Shaw Museum, called out as he wheeled in a handtruck bearing a large wooden crate. He looked around the lab.

Jema Shaw put down the ancient double-handled jug she was dating and came around the worktable. "Right here, Tom."

"Oh. Hey." The guard eased the crate into an upright position. "Man to see you. Want me to take him to the clean room or storage?"

"Storage, please." She saw a small tear in the latex covering her palm and pulled it off to replace it with a fresh glove. "I'm not unpacking anyone new until I finish the Sogdies." She went back to the jug.

"Good thing he's dead, then, huh?" Thomas came to peer over Jema's hunched shoulder. The flannel-covered table held an assortment of soft-bristled brushes, picks, and testing vials.

A large lens clamped to an extending-arm vise magnified the dull orange of the clay jug, which was cracked but intact, but for a broken lip. "I thought the museum was for Greek stuff, not the Saudis."

"Sogdies, short for Sogdians," she corrected him. "They were rebel Greek tribes who occupied the mountains north of Afghanistan." Jema used a small brush to remove some sand grains embedded in the pot's side etching. "Where Uzbekistan is now."

"Uzbekistan." Thomas frowned. "Right."

"One of the Sogdian rebel leaders, Oxyartes, held off an invasion force led by Alexander the Great. He couldn't be beaten and wouldn't surrender until Alexander agreed to marry his daughter. This might have belonged to Oxyartes's war master. His mark looked like this." She traced a fingertip in the air over the stylized animal figure etched into the side of the jug.

Thomas leaned closer, squinting. "That a wolf?"

"A wolf, or a large dog. It may also represent one of the war master's personal gods. I don't think he was a native. Sogdians were very tolerant about religions outside their own, too. An incredibly progressive culture, for their time." Jema gave the confused young guard a sideways look. She'd lost him at Uzbekistan. "Would you like to hear about life in the war master's garrison at Kurgan-Tepe? I've got a couple dozen spear shafts and arrowheads to date and catalog next."

His eyes widened and he shuffled back a step. "Wish I could, Ms. Shaw, but I gotta make my rounds." He adjusted the set of his belt over his skinny hips and nodded toward the clock above her workbench. "Kind of late for you to hang out here, isn't it?"

Jema glanced at the time, 6:57 P.M., which meant that the museum had been closed for three hours and dinner at Shaw House had been served fifty-seven minutes ago. *Damn.* Had her mother invited anyone important over tonight? "Yes." *If she had, she'd have called by now to chew off my ear.* "I'll finish up now."

"One more thing," he said, his young face serious, "you shouldn't stop at any drive-through ATMs on the way home."

It was such an odd request that Jema almost laughed. "Why not?"

"This mugger? Used a chainsaw to rob a lady when she stopped at an ATM." He named a bank two blocks from the museum. "She got away okay and all, but next one might not be so lucky."

Jema swallowed. Tom's warning conjured the image of a dark round face, beautiful hazel eyes, and a shy smile. Luisa Lopez, who had worked part-time on the museum's house-keeping staff, had been the victim of an equally brutal assault during a home invasion a year ago. Luisa had not been lucky enough to get away okay, and was still in the hospital, recovering from injuries that should have killed her.

Luisa didn't have a shy smile anymore, but the doctors were gradually replacing the skin that had been burned off her face. They would eventually get to perfecting her new lips.

Jema went to visit Luisa every week, but the young woman rarely spoke or acknowledged her presence. Bandages covered the hazel eyes while the new lids that had been grafted over them healed, but Luisa, blinded by the fire set to kill her, would never see anyone again.

"Have a good one," Thomas said. He wheeled the crate into the corridor leading to the antiquities storage area.

Jema set thoughts of Luisa back into memory as carefully as she repacked the Sogdian jug. She placed its box on her in-progress shelf before going to phone home and make the necessary excuses.

Originally Jema's office had served as a supply closet, and still held the lingering odor of floor wax and wet mops. At nine feet by seven feet, it was barely large enough to qualify as a prison cell, but it had enough space to accommodate her desk and shelves for her personal reference books. She didn't have to impress anyone with her office—no board members or visiting dignitaries came down here. That was her mother's job. Jema's territory was the lab, where she currently spent her time dating and cataloging the museum's acquisitions.

You're delicate, Meryl Shaw had said when Jema had suggested moving out of the underground level to help the museum staff with the exhibits and tours. *You can't risk exposing yourself to the general public.*

Jema switched on the small black-and-white TV she kept on her credenza and turned to the late edition of the news. She hated the loneliness of working in the museum's basement, but she did love her desk, a fussy little antique writing desk at which some Victorian lady had once penned invitations to teas and balls. Rather than facing the door, she had turned the desk around toward the wall. She had no window, but beneath a six-by-nine return air vent hung her diplomas, awards, and certifications, along with her favorite painting, framed in plain black wood.

On the television, a reporter was standing in front of a small bank building and finishing up his live report. "The body of the suspect, Todd Brackman, was found in the bank's Dumpster. Police are presently conducting a massive search of the area for an unidentified man who may have acted as Brackman's accomplice. Brackman's neighbor, Robert Pechowsky, an employee of O'Malley's Lawn and Tree Service, was also found stabbed to death earlier today. We'll bring you updates as this story develops. Spencer Holt, Channel Five News."

Jema turned off the set and rubbed her tired eyes, trying not to think of Luisa. As she turned back to her desk, she saw the receiver sitting on the blotter and groaned. She must have forgotten to hang it up after getting a call earlier from the events coordinator. *I've got to stop doing that.*

The tiny red voice-mail light on the telephone console blinked on and off, so she replaced the receiver, put the phone on speaker, and pressed in her retrieval code.

"Good evening, Shaw Museum com-mailbox user," the automated system's computer-generated voice said. "You have one new message from"—there was a pause for the caller identification, which a far colder voice gave as—"Jema, you're late." After a second pause, the automated system continued with, "To play the first mess—"

"That's okay." Jema punched the speaker button. "I'll hear it soon as I get home."

She finished tidying up the lab and stopped in the tiny lavatory to give herself an injection of insulin. She was glad she was able to take her shots at the same time every day; many diabetics didn't have a stable condition and were dependent on constant blood-sugar monitoring. Jema had been on insulin therapy since birth, so needles were no big deal, but she hated the thought of never knowing exactly when she would need one.

Jema walked upstairs and into the museum's main gallery. Although her father, James Shaw, had commissioned the Shaw Museum built to house artifacts recovered from a lifetime of overseas digs, Jema had never really liked the enormous building. The polished imported marble and towering Grecian columns were massively dignified, but they reminded her more of a mausoleum than a museum.

In a sense, the museum had killed her father shortly after Jema was born.

She stopped in front of the security guard office, where the night-shift supervisor was initiating the computerized security system from the main monitoring console. "Good night, Roy."

"Ms. Shaw." He swiveled around, startled. "I didn't know you were still here."

Did anyone, besides her mother? "See you tomorrow." She smiled before heading for the side exit.

"Let me walk you out." Roy's thirty extra pounds had him wheezing a little by the time he reached her. "You hear about the shi— ah, incident over on Grandview?"

"Tom mentioned it." She waited as he unlocked and held the door open for her. "That poor woman. She must have been terrified."

"She was lucky. Chicago's overrun with junkies and homeless." Roy trotted beside her down the short flight of steps to the employee parking lot. "Police should save our tax dollars and just shoot them instead of arresting them."

"You don't mean that," Jema chided.

"Good thing they don't let *me* carry a gun." Roy peered into the windows of Jema's Mercedes convertible before watching her unlock the door. "You head straight home, Ms. Shaw."

Did everyone think she was helpless? Jema thought of her mother and her temper ebbed. "I will, Roy, thank you."

The drive from the museum to Shaw House usually took

twenty minutes, but Jema didn't rush. She needed to practice her excuses before she got home.

"Sorry I'm late, Mother," Jema told the steering wheel. *No, that's too breezy.* "I'm so sorry I'm late. Late again. Forgive me, Mother. Forgive me for missing dinner."

Jema wouldn't have missed much. Keeping her blood sugar under control required a strict diet, and their cook prepared her meals separately from those she served to Meryl Shaw and her guests. It didn't really matter what she ate or if she ate anything at all; her mother simply expected her to be at the table. In Meryl's view punctuality was a courtesy, tardiness a deliberate offense.

I know you don't intend to be deliberately ill-mannered, Jema, her mother had said the last time she had come home this late, *but you should consider my feelings. When you don't arrive on time, I worry that something has happened to you.*

"I got caught up in work— No, don't mention work; she hates that," she muttered under her breath before she resumed the rehearsal. "It was inconsiderate. *I* was inconsiderate. Of you. I'm sorry I was so inconsiderate of you, Mother." She scowled. "I sound like I'm twelve. I'm *acting* like I'm twelve."

Jema didn't know why she felt compelled to rehearse her apologies before she delivered them. Whatever seemed sincere and acceptable in the car always came out sounding completely inadequate in front of Meryl Shaw's impassive face. Still, each time she did something thoughtless, Jema tried to express remorse that at least *sounded* genuine. She knew she was an enormous disappointment to her mother; she didn't need to add insult to injury.

"Maybe if you meant it," Jema told the dashboard as she drove up to the black wrought-iron gates that kept out the curious and the misdirected, "she'd believe you."

She looked toward the house and caught a partial reflection of her face in the rearview mirror. An oval-shaped slice of eyes and forehead. Gaunt, pale, pathetic, but at least it was there. She turned away before she saw any more. She hated mirrors.

Acute diabetes had been sucking the life out of her since the day she was born, but now it seemed it was gulping.

"I'm not sorry." Jema felt hot and dizzy, and leaned forward, resting her forehead against the cool leather encasing the steering wheel. "It's my life. Let me live it."

Saying that to Meryl, who had kept Jema alive for the last twenty-nine years, would be the same as kicking her in the abdomen.

Self-pity was not an option, so Jema straightened, pressed the remote clipped to her visor, and drove through the wide iron gates when they opened. She parked to one side of the garage where her mother's stately Rolls-Royce was kept, and went into the house through the kitchen entrance. The cook had already tidied up and left, but Jema could hear two voices coming from the direction of the sitting room, and followed them.

"I am not interested in your opinions, Daniel. I employ you as our physician," Meryl Shaw said, her voice matter-of-fact. "Not the family therapist."

Jema stopped outside in the hall and listened.

"Would you like me to tell you how mental stress affects the physiology?" Dr. Daniel Bradford sounded equally calm and controlled, but affection made his tone warmer than Meryl's. "You can't imprison Jema. She needs her work and a certain amount of freedom."

"I decide what Jema needs," Meryl stated flatly. "Not you, not anyone." She coughed several times. "I'm having chest pains."

Here come the chest pains. Jema leaned back against the wall and closed her eyes.

There was a stretch of silence, and then Dr. Bradford spoke, far more gently this time. "You know it's your ulcer, not your heart. This anger only aggravates it. No," he said as Meryl muttered something, "you're not. Drink this to settle your stomach, and then I'll take you upstairs."

The pager set on silent that Jema carried began to vibrate— an angry bee trapped in her pocket. She checked the display, but she already knew what it said. The other, secret part of her life beckoned.

She glanced at the door, pocketed the pager, and walked away from the sitting room.

As Jema drove away from the estate, she didn't look back.

She never saw the hunched shape of the man who stepped out of the darkness as the gates of Shaw House slid closed.

The man lifted the radio in his hand and spoke into it. Light from the gate lamps made the polished black cameo ring he wore sparkle. "Miss Shaw has left the premises."

The reply was immediate and terse. "Follow her."

Chapter 2

Valentin Jaus swung his *langenschwert* up and over his head, placing the blade behind his back. His opponent and seneschal, Falco Erhart, circled left rather than taking advantage of the opening. In the long mirrored wall beyond them, their reflections moved, a tall, dark Goliath battling a short, fair-haired David.

Although Jaus was the master of Falco, Derabend Hall, and everyone who watched them, he was not the Goliath of the match.

"*Zornhau,*" the dry voice of Jaus's *tresora,* Gregor Sacher, said from the sidelines. The training area, known as the lists, was so large that any voice echoed—whenever clashing steel didn't drown it out. To the teenage boy standing beside him, he murmured, "Note how the master engages the Spaniards' *arrebatar* technique, which permits a *feichmeister* to cut with the whole arm."

"Falco does not move in to attack the opening, Opah." Wilhelm Sacher watched both men with wide eyes. As a *tresora* in training, he was permitted to observe most aspects of Jaus's life within the walls of Derabend Hall. "He goes to the side."

"An experienced swordsman cannot be baited," Sacher advised the boy. "Falco uses the *ueberlauffen* to move out of reach of an attack and exploit whatever weakness the attack opens."

Jaus would have completed the movement and used the flat of his sword on Falco's shoulder, had his seneschal been careless enough to fall for the ruse. Indulging clumsiness defeated the purpose of practice matches. Falco, however, rarely made mistakes, and knew Jaus better than any man among the *jardin*. He also had the physical advantage of superior size and reach, and used it.

Despite this, Falco had never beaten his master. Jaus dominated in their matches not because he was stronger, but wiser. His experience was ten times that of his seneschal's.

Losing battles was also not something Valentin Jaus permitted himself to do anymore.

As the second son of a prosperous and influential baron, Valentin had been sent all over Europe to train with Spanish, English, and French masters. Over time his fighting style had absorbed much of their techniques. His original training in Austria had begun with the classic *drey wunder,* the three principal attacks of the German masters, but he had never limited himself to them. There was much to be learned outside the European schools of swordsmanship as well; in his time Jaus had traveled to places like Russia to train with Cossacks, and Japan to learn from the samurai.

It helped that Jaus was not human. Nor was any man present in the lists except Sacher and Wilhelm, who wore the black cameo rings of *tresori,* the humans who served the Darkyn.

"Why do they fight with copper-tipped swords, Opah?" Wilhelm asked. "You said that it is the only metal that can pierce the skin of the *vrykolakas* and poison their blood. Would it not be safer to use plain steel?"

"Our master uses the same weapons our enemies do," Sacher said. "To train with anything less would be to face them ill-prepared. There are ways in which plain steel and other metals can be used to injure the Darkyn, but we will discuss those later."

Falco paid no attention to the exchange between the *tresora* and his grandson. His focus remained on Jaus, and attacking from the left—which he did with lightning speed—which should have created a second, indefensible opening. Anticipating the counterattack, Jaus used the parrier-dolch to trap Falco's sword with the quillions of the dagger in his left hand.

"*Spada e pugnale,*" Sacher called out before he murmured to Wilhelm, "Now the master will use his *kriege.*"

Before the old man finished speaking, Jaus had used his

parrying dagger to disarm his seneschal. As Falco's sword skidded across the polished oak floor, Jaus pressed the very tip of his blade against the seneschal's bare chest, denting the pale skin but not drawing blood.

"Nachreissen; am schwert," Sacher spoke loudly again. "Point, *oberhau,* and match."

The men on the sidelines who had remained silent and motionless during the match now relaxed. Some, knowing they would eventually take Falco's place and serve as Jaus's opponent, exchanged dispirited looks. The seneschal was a bold and efficient swordsman, but the suzerain of their *jardin* fought as if his veins ran with ice.

Jaus maintained his stance but drew the sword away from the other man's heart. "Your tempo was off tonight."

"I did not hunt earlier." Falco took a sudden step forward, impaling himself with an inch of copper-clad steel. As Jaus jerked his wrist to remove it, the seneschal rubbed his hand in his own blood and displayed it for the observers to see. *"Was sehrt, das lehrt."*

Suffering tutors us.

"So does practice." Jaus watched until the wound on Falco's chest closed before as he handed his *langenschwert* to Sacher and accepted a dark blue linen robe in exchange. He noted Wilhelm's pupils, which had dilated, and his mouth, which hung open slightly. "Wilhelm?"

"Camellias," the boy murmured, staring at Jaus. "So many."

Jaus shrugged into the robe, which masked some of *l'attrait,* the flowery, hypnotizing odor his body produced. "Hans, take our young friend outside for some fresh air."

One of the men came and guided the unresisting teenager through a nearby exit.

"Excuse the boy, master," Sacher said as he used a white handkerchief to wipe the blood from Jaus's blade. "He has not yet acquired a tolerance."

"Perhaps we should invest in some nose plugs." To the men of the *jardin* watching the match, Jaus said, "Use *hart und weich*—weakness against strength, strength against weakness—and you find the balance that gives control."

Sacher pressed a hand to the side of his head, covering the

small earpiece he wore, and then murmured to Jaus, "A call from Cyprien in the main house."

Jaus had not spoken to his old friend and adversary Michael Cyprien since Richard Tremayne, high lord of the Darkyn, had named Michael seigneur over all of the American *jardins*. He had given Michael his oath of loyalty before the instatement, and would keep it no matter what the cost.

Knowing Michael's determination to bring the Darkyn out of the Dark Ages and into the twenty-first century, Jaus suspected the cost might be considerable.

"This will take time," Jaus told his seneschal. "Drill the men on their forms until I return." He walked with Sacher and his guards out of the lists and across the compound to the main house. "Aside from low tolerance to *l'attrait,* your grandson seems to be adjusting well, Gregor."

"If well means asking me a thousand questions about the Darkyn each day, yes, he is," Sacher said. His smile faded. "He reminds me so much of Kurt at that age."

Kurt Sacher, Wilhelm's father, had lived and worked in Jaus's household since boyhood. As was customary with *tresori,* Gregor had been training his son to assume his place. Kurt had grown up with the Darkyn and had been quite willing to serve the *jardin.* Then came the terrible night when Kurt had not returned from a trip into the city, and the police had come to tell Gregor that his son had been shot during a robbery attempt. Kurt's wife, Ingrid, fell into a depression, and three months after Kurt's funeral took an overdose of sleeping pills.

The sudden loss had devastated Sacher, a widower with no other living family. For a time Jaus thought he might lose his most trusted servant as well, and had offered to release Sacher from his *tresoran* oath so that he might escape any painful memories caused by living among the Darkyn. But it had been Kurt and Ingrid's orphaned son, Wil, who had kept his grandfather from withering away in despair, and Gregor would trust Wil's future to no one but Jaus.

I cannot look after him forever, master, Sacher had told Jaus when he brought Wilhelm to Derabend Hall. *This only you can do.*

On the way to the main house, Jaus noticed that the elderly

man's right hand was wrapped in a flesh-colored bandage, and recalled the minor kitchen accident that had caused the wound. "That burn has not healed."

"No, but it will, master." Sacher tucked the offending hand out of sight in his jacket pocket. "Give an old human time."

Jaus wondered how much of that they had left together. Gregor had served as his *tresora* for seven decades, ever since losing his parents to the Nazi occupation of Austria. Tresori pledged to serve the *jardin* until death, but at a certain age retirement usually became a necessity.

Had the time come so soon?

Jaus paused and rested a hand on the old man's shoulder. The scent of camellias filled the night air. "Why have you not seen your doctor?"

"My doctor wears braces on his teeth," Sacher said mildly. "I am not quite sure he has finished passing through puberty yet. Such things do not inspire my faith in his judgment." He glanced down at Jaus's hand. "You had only but to ask, master."

"Forgive me. I worry about you." Jaus removed his hand to input the pass code on the entry door's keypad, releasing the electronic lock. One of the four bodyguards escorting them opened the door while two took position on either side of it. "It is a pity Cyprien's leech remains with him in New Orleans. She is a gifted healer."

"That woman." Gregor sighed and shook his head. "She frightens me more than the doctor with braces." He checked his watch. "I will have Wilhelm come in and attend to his schoolwork now. I hope his head is clear enough to cope with calculus, for mine, I fear, will never be." With a bow, the elderly servant left Jaus.

Valentin walked through the cool white lights and stark shadows of his home. He had commissioned three different construction firms to demolish the decrepit eighteenth-century mansion that had formerly occupied the lakefront property and had Derabend Hall built to his own exact specifications. The loss of the historic landmark house at first scandalized the city along with his wealthy neighbors, until its replacement rose from the ashes. Derabend Hall, a towering castle of black granite and gray slate, dominated the landscape. The finished product caused Valentin to be hailed as an architectural renegade and visionary by Chicago's elite.

No one realized he had simply reproduced a modern version of his family's fortress in the Austrian Tirol. The original, Schloss Jaus, had long vanished, reduced to ruins by Napoleon's forces and then dust by succeeding wars and time.

Bright colors, cheerful patterns, and most of the clutter of the modern world annoyed Jaus, so he commissioned an interior design firm to furnish his new home sparingly in solid black, white, and silver. One of the designers published photographs of Derabend Hall's stark rooms, which set off a minimalist, colorless trend in interior design that swept the nation. It was then that Jaus stopped employing humans outside the *jardin* to indulge his preferences, as the exposure made his already nervous *jardin* rather paranoid.

The only color indulgence Jaus permitted himself was the midnight blue used in his bedroom and office. The latter was a large and efficient workspace with the very latest in information processing and storage technology. His computer database, a prototype designed personally for him by a billionaire software mogul, collected data from a hundred different sources for analysis, and could track the whereabouts and activities of anyone he chose to monitor.

Information was the shield of the modern man. The more one possessed, the better protected one fought.

Jaus pulled up his mainframe screen at the same time he picked up his phone and connected to the line that had been placed on hold. "Seigneur Cyprien, this is an unexpected honor."

"Suzerain Jaus, the honor is mine," Michael said, "but time, alas, is not."

"We shall move directly to business, then." Jaus sat down in his favorite leather chair. "How may I serve, my lord?"

"One of Jofferoin's scouts spotted Thierry Durand in Memphis six days ago. The scout tried to track him, but lost him in Copley Square." Michael paused. "Evidently he is using the homeless and unfortunate as camouflage."

Jaus remembered Cyprien's description of the injuries inflicted on Durand by the Brethren, an organization of former priests who had been hunting, torturing, and killing the Darkyn since they first became *vrykolakas*. "He is still in such a condition? I had thought Dr. Keller's treatment successful."

"She repaired the damage to his body, but not that inflicted upon his mind," Michael told him. "Thierry came to clarity briefly when he discovered, as we did, that Angelica was the traitor among us. I fear his wife's betrayal may have since finished what the Brethren started."

"If he can use cover and evade a tracker, then he is not completely mad." Jaus pulled up a map of the United States and drew a line from the city of New Orleans to Memphis. The direction was unmistakable. "You believe he travels here, to Chicago."

"When Thierry left New Orleans, he took with him the file of data that you collected on the men who attacked Alexandra's patient, Ms. Lopez," Michael said. "He perhaps seeks vengeance."

Jaus, who had fought alongside Thierry Durand more times than he could count, sighed. "He never would tolerate anyone who threatened or harmed a female. Even in the times when swine were regarded as more valuable than women. I've always admired that about him."

"As have I." The seigneur's voice changed. "He must be taken, Val. Taken alive and brought back to New Orleans. I will send you a supply of the drug Alexandra has developed. It will render him helpless."

"The Saracens attempted to do the same, many times. Do you remember it?" Jaus sat back and rubbed his eyes. "They always sought to capture the largest and strongest of us on the battlefield. How often did we watch Durand cut them down where they stood?"

"I cannot say."

"He was like a scythe through new wheat." Jaus gazed at the only photo in his room, a snapshot framed in crystal. It was the only photo that existed of Valentin Jaus. In it, he sat in a rocking chair, with a dark-haired toddler sleeping in his arms. "He will do the same to the police, or anyone who tries to drug him."

"Agreed, but we are the only ones who can stop him. The tranquilizer will help."

Jaus didn't have confidence in Cyprien's leech or her drugs, but with the proper precautions, he might lure Durand into a trap. "It will be as you wish."

"Use whatever you need. If it is mine to give, you have but to ask." Cyprien sounded rushed now. "I must go, old friend, but keep me apprised of the situation. *Adieu.*"

Jaus hung up the phone and called in one of his guards. "Have Falco report to me as soon as he is finished with the men." When the guard left, he picked up the phone and called the newest of the American suzerains, one whose council he trusted as much as Michael Cyprien's. It was the only thing, however, he trusted about him.

"It is Jaus. I need some advice." He explained the situation. "You brought him out of Dublin. How will it be?"

"I had to swaddle Durand in copper chains simply to remove him from the Brethren's playroom. They'd broken his legs, crushed his feet, and cooked him in more than a few places, and still he tried to tear off my head." Lucan, High Lord Tremayne's former chief assassin as well as Michael Cyprien's oldest adversary, smothered a yawn. "We have all seen the magnificent work performed by Cyprien's lovely little surgeon. Durand will now be very healthy, very strong—and mad as Monte Cristo."

"Yes."

"You need no advice from me, Valentin," Lucan said. "You already know what you must do. Kill him."

Jema stopped at a pay phone to call the coroner's office, and after receiving the details sat for a few minutes, debating whether to return to Shaw House or continue on to her night job. Meryl would be in bed now, and Dr. Bradford never waited up for her. The usual confrontation would be delayed until the morning, when her mother would interrogate her over the breakfast table.

Where were you? Meryl often checked with the museum to learn when Jema had left, so she wouldn't be able to answer that one honestly. *How late did you arrive home?* That would have to be tailored to match Jema's first response. *Have you no consideration for the feelings of others?* That would be her cue to apologize for causing her mother to worry, which would not satisfy Meryl, but was still expected.

Jema wished she could tell Meryl about her secret life. *I work for the coroner's office, Mother. I process crime scenes at night. I collect and identify unusual trace evidence. I make reports to the police. In a way, I help them catch the killers.*

Meryl's reaction would certainly be swift, negative, and inescapable. *You're a Shaw. Shaws do not work for anyone.*

Feeling disgusted with herself, Jema drove downtown to the crime scene, a private courtyard park maintained for the residents of an exclusive condominium. Showing her ID helped her past the uniformed officers securing the perimeter, but it didn't impress the homicide detective supervising the forensics team.

"Shaw? You took your sweet time getting here." Detective Stephen Newberry held out a hand for her ID. His bland face and spare, narrow frame might have belonged to an English teacher, but the hard blue eyes were all cop. "Get caught in rush hour?"

"I just got home from my day job, Detective," she said, handing him the badge issued to her by the coroner's office. He studied it with an insulting thoroughness. "I came here as soon as I received and confirmed the page." *After an internal debate of no more than ten or fifteen minutes,* she amended silently.

"We've been waiting twenty minutes for you," Newberry told her. His short, copper hair drained the color from his pale face, while the deeply etched lines around his eyes and mouth added ten years to his age. "Maybe you could drive a little faster next time. I'll mention it to your boss."

"I'm an independent consultant contracted by the coroner's office, Detective, not a county employee," Jema said as she put on protective shoe covers and the plastic garment shroud that would keep her from depositing fibers near the body. "If you want to get me in trouble, you'll have to speak with the owner of Shaw Museum. Would you like my mother's telephone number?"

"That's okay. I've got too much foot in my mouth right now." Newberry escorted her through the gauntlet of forensic techs and crime scene investigators until they reached the body. "You already worked a few of these, right?"

"Yes." Jema smiled a little. "I was initially consulted by the Chicago coroner's office when an importer was found murdered. The killer had stabbed him to death with what appeared to be an ancient Spartan dagger. I identified the weapon as a fake, but I also found an archaic Greek symbol traced in the blood near the body. That led to the arrest of a well-known collector. Apparently the importer sold him several fakes."

"Being able to identify old blades doesn't get you a job with the coroner's office," Newberry said.

"No, but having a degree in forensic science and being willing to work part-time at night does." She stopped as she saw the victim.

The nude body of a man lay facedown on the brown grass. The back of the head bore a depression wound so severe it had distorted the entire skull, and the rest of the body showed signs of an extended, ruthless beating.

Jema dealt with death on a daily basis while cataloging artifacts, many of which were funerary objects found in graves and tombs. Yet the dried, brittle femur of a nobleman's household retainer, ritually sacrificed a thousand years before the birth of Christ, did not in any way compare to seeing the brutalized body of a man who had been alive only a few hours ago.

It was real. It was hideous. It could not be reasoned away.

"I'm told constant exposure eventually enables one to maintain an emotional distance," she said, clenching her hands in her pockets. "How long does that take?"

"About fifty years, give or take a couple of decades," Newberry said, his mouth tight. "It helps if you drink."

Jema pulled on a pair of latex gloves and removed a paper evidence bag from her packet. The detective stayed back as she first walked around the body, and then paused and looked intently at the grass and soil. "There isn't enough blood. He probably wasn't killed here."

"That was our take." Newberry gestured toward a number

of small evidence flags planted in a patch of soil three feet from the body. "No footprints from the tire tracks. Maybe dumped from the back of a pickup truck that came through the maintenance entrance." He sounded vaguely surprised, as if he hadn't expected her observation.

"Did he work or live near here?" Jema knew murders were often committed close to or inside the victim's place of employment or home.

"He managed a convenience store six blocks over." Newberry came closer. "His night-shift clerk was the last one to see him alive, two days ago. He left the store at ten P.M. and never made it home."

"The body landed faceup; it was turned over." Jema pointed to patches of soil on the back and legs. "They wanted him facedown for some reason." She crouched and used a pair of tweezers to extract a minute amount of short brown hair from the tangle of grass near the still right foot. "This could be animal hair. Anyone walking a dog through here tonight?"

"No. The building doesn't allow pets. We'll double-check when we canvass the building, see if anyone's been breaking the rules." Newberry took the evidence bag from her, marked it, and handed it off to a waiting tech, to whom he said, "If the photographer's through, let's get some guys over here to lift and bag him."

Jema eyed the arrangement of the limbs, the condition of the fingernails, and the patches of scalp showing through the thick dark hair. "He fought back while he could, but he was tied up at some point. The marks on his wrists indicate they used rope or cord." As the technicians flipped him, Jema looked at the victim's face. It was Asian, young, and badly swollen and lacerated. "Dear God."

A knife had been used to carve a swastika into the victim's face. The cuts were so deep that bone showed through.

Light flashed as the scene photographer snapped several stills of the victim's facial wounds. Newberry got on his cell phone and began to pace as he reported to his superiors. Jema concentrated on inspecting the front of the body, but her eyes kept straying to the terrible symbol that had been cut across the young man's face.

"You finished?" the detective asked her after finishing his call.

"Almost." She found bits of tissue in the grass and carefully retrieved them to give to one of the techs. "I'd check it against the wounds on the inside of his mouth."

Now Newberry looked dumbfounded. "How do you know that?"

"The teeth marks present on the outer lip. He bit it repeatedly, and probably did the same to his tongue and the sides of his cheeks. He was trying not to scream." She bent down and removed a few more hairs from the front of the man's battered chest. "These match what I found in the grass, but they aren't dog or cat hair; they're too coarse and thick, almost like wool."

"We'll send them to the FBI labs," Newberry said, although he didn't sound happy about it. "They should tell us something in a week or two."

"I know a local anthropologist who specializes in identifying faunal remains. She can compare these to her database and determine what species they are, as well as run DNA," Jema offered. "The turnaround would be a day, maybe two."

The detective looked at the body. "I'll clear it with my captain first. If we use your expert, we'll need copies of all the reports, and the samples will have to be returned to the SOC unit." Detective Newberry handed her a clipboard with a form, which she signed, showing that she had been present at the crime scene. "You said he tore up his mouth, trying not to scream. Why?"

She'd said too much. "It's only an observation, and I could be wrong."

"But?"

"I worked with a number of Asian college students on summer internships at the museum. One dropped the end of a heavy crate on his foot and broke three toes, and yet he didn't make a sound." She watched the morgue orderlies lower the victim into an open body bag. "Some Asian cultures consider a show of pain demeaning."

"They beat him to death, but he bites through his lip to keep from crying out, because that's worse?" Newberry sounded incredulous.

Jema tried not to flinch as the morgue body bag was zipped shut. "If you knew you were going to die, Detective, wouldn't you hold on to whatever pride you could?"

"I'd rather shout and get someone's attention, so I didn't have to die. Not like this." Detective Newberry gave her a narrow look. "You talk about death like you've got some kind of personal experience."

She would, soon enough. "The dead are my business."

Chapter 3

Thierry Durand knew he was mad.

His derangement didn't frighten him. It made a place in the world for him, and gave him purpose. No battle was ever won by wholly sane men. Every great family had a bat or two in the attics; every village had an idiot. He had never been defeated by anything, not the Saracens, not the Brethren, not the crazy woman he had loved. He would not surrender to madness.

Surviving it . . .

He thrust a hand under the shredded remains of his shirt. Blood no longer oozed from the wounds in his belly and ribs, but they were not closing. They were too many and too close together. If he did not wish his insides to spill out and drag along the street, he would have to hunt.

Hunt, when he was the hunted.

He had put enough distance between him and the dead thief to feel relatively safer, but he could not roam this part of the city covered in blood and garbage. The whirling red and blue lights of police cars had sent him into the shadows of this alley to hide, and within a few moments there were more. That was when he discovered the alley had no exit, and he was trapped. As he braced himself against one wall, prepared to defend himself, the police sped past. It took a moment for him to understand that he was not their object.

Once the street cleared, Thierry edged down the wall to have a look. The black-and-white cars, lights still flashing, had congregated outside one of the tall, elegant buildings on the opposite end of the street. It had to be a serious crime for so many to come, but they were not here for him. Some of the patrolmen were setting up barricades, others walking up and down the street to speak to the humans who were coming out of other buildings.

If he stepped out of the alley, he would be seen. They would not question him. They would see him covered in gore and filth, and they would try to take him. Or shoot him. He couldn't risk being challenged by humans, not in his present state.

He would have to wait until they had gone.

Thierry settled behind a stack of flattened paper boxes and watched the rats as the light drove them to find sanctuary. That was what he truly needed now: a house or place of business where he could wash, rest, and not be seen by human eyes. But here, in Chicago, the people of the city lived like every day would be their last, never opening their doors, never unlocking their windows.

The city was a fist, squeezed too tightly against him.

Light-headed and cold, Thierry closed his eyes and put a protective arm over his belly. With his other hand he drew his dagger. His hand felt empty without the blade, and he could never rest unless he held it ready. He had owned many daggers during his long life, but this one was special to him. It had been a gift from Tremayne, who had shown him how to use it two hundred years ago, after Thierry and Michael had helped him escape Rome.

If you are taken and there is no hope of escape, thrust it here. Thierry could still feel the brush of Tremayne's distorted hand on the back of his neck. *One quick stroke, to cut through. It is the same as losing your head.*

Thierry would have done so when the Brethren had come for him in France, but he had been sleeping with his wife, Angelica, and that was the only time he went naked of clothes and weapons.

She had known this. She had told them.

Coming to Chicago and hunting the men who had harmed Luisa Lopez had kept him from drowning in his madness. He could read English and had understood what had happened to the girl as soon as he had opened the file. Luisa had been tortured by the Brethren. Cyprien would not know this; he had not witnessed the sadistic ways the monks worked on humans. Thierry had. So he had set out on the journey, certain that this would serve as his penance for attacking Alexandra, who had only tried to help him, and to pay back the Brethren, who had destroyed his life as well as his body.

A light-colored convertible drew parallel to the alley and parked across the street from it rather than going farther down to the crime scene. His attention sharpened when he saw the human female who stepped out alone in the dark. She was young, thin, and dark, a little cat of a woman. From the way she moved, she was out of her territory, alert for danger. She had her gaze fixed on the police lights, however, and was ignoring everything else around her.

Like him.

I could walk up and take her now. Thierry rose, his hand tightening on the dagger as he scanned the area around her. That she was so close to him when he was in need made him more angry than hungry. He was not the only predator out tonight. *Has she no one to look after her? To keep her home, safe from things like me?*

The woman didn't spare him or the alley a glance, but walked down to the crime scene and, after showing one of the officers her wallet, disappeared into the building.

Thierry sank back down behind the crushed boxes. He was as good as a walking sieve, and she was too small. Women of any size were the worst of temptations. But if he did not hunt soon, he would be too weak to do more than crawl deeper into the alley filth and hide. Then he would have to wait until someone came close enough to grab.

Not the woman. Not any woman.

His loneliness had become harder to bear than his madness. He could not bring himself to hunt a woman, not after what he had done in his madness to Alexandra, so he had been feeding exclusively on males.

Hunting on the streets of Memphis had been Thierry's greatest mistake.

He had not meant to stop in Memphis; the car he had stolen developed an engine problem, and forced him to leave the interstate, where there were too many state troopers who might stop and offer help. The car's engine had died in the very heart of the city, where there were few places to hide.

The Darkyn hunter who had crossed Thierry's path had picked up his scent, but more important, he had recognized and pursued him. That was when Thierry knew that he was being hunted, and no one else but Cyprien could have issued orders to capture him.

If he was to find his salvation, he would have to outwit his oldest friend and elude his own kind.

Time passed. Minutes, then hours. Thierry reached for the strength he would need to rise again. It had always been there when he'd needed it, but now it eluded him. Without it he felt dry and withering, a husk beginning to crumble. He had not fed enough during his journey to this city; his reserves were exhausted. So, too, was his spirit. Finding the men who had hurt the girl had been the torch in a long, lightless tunnel. His failure to do so would snuff it out, and then there would be nothing but the dark.

He could not survive the madness without some light to guide him. Had he not earned a little?

"Hello?"

He opened his eyes and peered over the top of the boxes. Incredibly, the woman from the convertible was standing just outside the alley, looking in.

"Is someone in there?"

Is she mad, too? Thierry dared not blink or breathe, and then something uncurled inside him, something stronger than his fear for her. His scent, always intense when he was wounded, changed.

"If you're hurt, I can call for help." She was actually moving into the alley, looking at the ground and then from side to side. Tracking like a hunter, but she was not Kyn.

Thierry looked at the ground in front of the boxes. A wide, winding ribbon of blood spatters darkened the asphalt. That was what had drawn her; he must have trailed blood from the street to here. He couldn't believe he'd been so careless.

Stand up. She is right there. Take her.

"It's all right," she said, her voice a caress. "I work with the police." She stopped in front of him and stared at the boxes concealing him. "I can help to get you to the hospital."

Her scent was very light; he almost lost it in the flood of his own. But no, there it was, the smell of her skin like warm, ripe apples. It was such a wholesome and ordinary scent that it disconcerted him. Modern women did not smell of orchard fruit. They doused themselves with costly perfumes. Angelica had hated her body's scent and did everything she could to erase it. This woman smelled of nothing else.

Her blood will taste of it.

"I know you're afraid," she told him as she took a step closer, "but I won't hurt you."

Thierry had held out until that moment, but she had drawn too near him, and the need became agonizing. It bargained with him: *Only a little. Only enough to heal the wounds.*

If he did not take her blood, he would not leave this alley. "Come here."

The sound of his voice, harsh from not being used in so long, startled her. For a moment he thought she might bolt, and part of him prayed she would. He watched her breathe in deeply, and her eyelids grew heavy.

Disgust with himself could not stop him from commanding her again. "Come here. To me."

The little cat moved around the boxes slowly, deliberately, drawn and drugged as she was by *l'attrait*. Thierry's had always had a particular effect on women.

She was more delicate than he'd supposed, thin-skinned, with fragile-looking limbs. Hollows and shadows marred the alabaster oval of her face. He lifted his hand and drew her down to him, entranced by the shape of her mouth, the lush curl of her lashes. Her garments were plain, a simple blouse and trousers, but beneath the ivory silk small breasts rose and fell.

She smelled of apples but she was made of moonlight.

Thierry held her by the waist as he positioned her to straddle his lap, intending to keep her weight from pressing on his wounds. The stiff arc at his crotch filled the notch in hers, and he flinched, unaware until that touch that he had become aroused in other ways.

Thin fingers brushed his hair back from his face. "Golden,"

she murmured as she stared into his eyes, fascinated. "They're golden."

Thierry's fangs shot out into his mouth, eager for her flesh. He had not touched a woman since he'd nearly killed Alexandra Keller, but he could no more set her away from him than he could cut off his arms.

"So are yours." A dark gold, rimmed with brown so dark it looked black. She might be as small as Alexandra Keller, but at least her eyes did not remind him of her. "Unbutton your blouse, *chérie.*" It was silk, and he did not wish to mar it with blood.

No, that was far from the truth. He wanted to see her.

Slowly she unfastened the pearl buttons nestled in the silk, opening the edges slowly. She did not wear anything to hide her breasts, small and firm, taut and flushed. Hard little apples, each barely enough to fill his palms.

A silent howl went up inside him. *Father in heaven, have you not done enough to torment me?*

Thierry did not dare put his mouth to her perfect breasts; his hunger would have him tearing at them. His gaze moved up, following the line of her throat to once again fix on her mouth. Like her breasts, the little cat's mouth was small, her lips pale pink. It was not the tight rosebud of a child, however, but the full, graceful curve of an American beauty just beginning to bloom.

He would not savage her, but he would taste her. He would use the dagger on himself if he did not.

"Chérie." He lifted his hand and cradled the back of her head, bringing her face down to his. "Kiss me."

She sighed into his mouth before she kissed it, and her breath warmed his tongue. She smelled of apples, but she tasted of honey and almonds. Thierry watched her eyes close, felt her thighs tighten over his, and then the liquid heat of her mouth melded with his.

She kissed him as she had moved, graceful but cautious, a little cat finding its way in the dark. He had never felt anything like it. His need for her blood pounded inside him, demanding more than soft lips and silky tongue, and he used his hand to tilt her head.

Inside, where it cannot be seen. Where it will be her secret, and mine.

When Thierry sank his fangs into the soft flesh inside her lower lip, she groaned.

Her blood flooded his mouth, hot and strong, the pulse of life that hummed in her veins pouring into his. Thierry drank from her lips, warming with each swallow, intent on taking only what he needed. The wounds in his belly and sides itched as they began to knit and close, the signal that he had had enough of her. Yet she kept kissing him, giving him her tongue as well as her blood.

Thierry discovered that he could not take his mouth from hers.

His wife had never liked to kiss, preferring to use her mouth more directly when they were intimate. Thierry used human women for blood only; loving his Angel had kept him from taking more. Oh, there had been moments. Women so beautiful they seemed to glow beneath his hands. But he had been a man of his word, and after rising to walk the night, he had clung to his marriage vows as the last of his honor.

Now he clung to this human woman, helpless, suspended in her passion.

The hands on his chest curled tight, and her thin body trembled, moving her against him in small, shivering waves. At last he felt her pulse slow and found the strength to tear his mouth from hers, panting with the heat and life she had given him, feeling the hateful ravenous beat surge up inside him, the killer within that demanded this and more and everything she had—

"Enough." He pushed her back, holding her as she swayed.

Had he taken too much? He could feel the old, forbidden madness grinding inside him, demanding the rest of her. How simple it would be to give her rapture as she enthralled him. There was more to be had from her than the blood in her veins. Her trousers were flimsy; he could have them off her in seconds. No one would stop them or see them here. Like this, she would refuse him nothing.

Like this, he would kill her. "Enough."

"No." As lost in *l'attrait* as Thierry was in her kiss, she reached for him again. "More."

In that moment he nearly put her on her back, for there was nothing in this world or the next he wanted more than to bury his cock and his teeth in her flesh.

"Chérie," he whispered, desperate now. "You must stop or I will not. Stop, please."

Her hands fell to her sides, and she looked down at him, her eyes wet. "Please."

It was good that he was insane, or she would drive him to it. "You must leave me now," he told her, dragging in air as he fought for control. "You will forget me."

"I will forget you." A single tear slid down her cheek. Another chased it to her chin.

"You will go home and sleep." He stood and brought her to her feet with him. There was blood on her lips, and he bent down and quickly licked it away before it could drip on her blouse. The second taste of her nearly undid him. "In the morning, what you remember of this will seem like a dream."

"A dream." She smiled a little. "Remember."

He buttoned her blouse and put his arm around her to guide her to the edge of the alley. It took everything he had to remove his hands from her. He looked for oncoming traffic and anyone who might see her. The street was deserted, the police gone. He found her keys in her pocket and pressed them into her hand. "Go now, little cat. Drive straight home. Sleep." He couldn't help adding, "And dream of me."

She nodded and walked to her car, moving like a small robot. By the time she drove around the block *l'attrait* would disperse, but its lingering effects would ensure that she followed the instructions he had given her. She would dream of him, but he would never see her again. That was as it should be.

His savior turned her car around to drive away. Thierry would have retreated into shadows again, but he could not. Not when he saw the vanity plate on her front bumper.

JEMA'S BENZ.

"Hold still."

Dr. Alexandra Keller planted one hand between Arnaud Evareaux's bare shoulder blades to keep him from rising from the exam table. With her other hand, she adjusted the overhead lamp shining down on the lower half of his torso. Mysterious bumps of various sizes bulged beneath Arnaud's otherwise flawless skin. Two light scents, much like lavender and parsley, tinted the air.

"It burns," he complained.

"It should." Alex selected a small bump, lanced it, and quickly dug out a metal pellet shaped like a small freshwater pearl. The scent of parsley became more intense. The pellet made a clinking sound as she dropped it in her discard tray. "Next time you decide to go trespassing in the moonlight, pick a property whose owner doesn't shoot first and ask questions later."

Arnaud turned his head to give her a one-eyed glare. "I would have pried them out myself, had the coward not shot me in the back."

She plied her scalpel again. "Given the scatter radius, Arnie, if the coward had shot you in the front, you'd be prying this stuff out of your groin." She smiled as Evareaux groaned and closed his eyes. "Or I would."

It took another thirty minutes to remove all the buckshot from Evareaux's lower back and buttocks, but his Darkyn physiology healed the lance wounds almost instantly, so once the last pellet hit the tray, all Alex had to do was sponge him clean and hand him his clothing.

"I mean it, Arnaud," she warned. "Stay away from those farmers' daughters. The next one might blast you in the face."

"You were able to heal the master's injuries," he said as he stepped into his pressed trousers.

"The master had his face beaten off. He didn't have little bits of metal lodged in his brain." She went to the sink to wash up. "So how long have you been part of the garden gang?"

"I have served the master for six hundred fifty-four years." Arnaud sounded huffy.

"What sort of talent do you have?" She didn't think he'd tell her, but the Darkyn had mental abilities that gave them some form of power over humans. Cyprien could erase memory, while his seneschal could compel humans to do things physically. According to Cyprien, every Darkyn's talent was different and unique to the individual.

Alex had a talent, too, but she didn't like hers.

"My gift is none of your business," the vampire told her, his voice growing colder.

"Is it something more embarrassing than me picking shot out of your ass?" When he said nothing, Alex's lips twitched. "Okay, we'll let that be your little secret. How long have you been a *vrykolakas?*"

He fiddled with his tie. "I was cursed after the master returned from England."

She stripped off her surgical shroud, balled it up and tossed it in the dirty linens hamper. "You were not cursed. You were infected with something that caused your DNA to mutate." She saw his expression. "God does not hate you, Arnaud. If He exists." Personally she wouldn't put money on it.

"I violated my holy vows." He shrugged into his jacket. "I became a creature of the night who feeds off the blood of the living."

Alex thought of her brother, John, a Catholic priest more devoted to his God than his only living family. John had lived more piously than the pope. She pulled off the mask hanging from her neck. "What did you do before that?"

"Excusez-moi?"

Alex rolled her eyes. "What did you do to earn the Almighty's wrath *before* you became a blood-feeding night creature?" Arnaud appeared confused, so she added, "You'd have to do something pretty rotten, right? So what was it? You were a Templar. A priest with a big sword. Did you forget to polish your armor? Skip some rosaries? Play hooky from the last Crusade? I need some details here, Arnaud."

"You do not understand." He made the same gesture that Cyprien did whenever Alex got on his nerves. "You are only a child among us." He stalked out of the treatment room.

"Wait, I wanted to ask you—— Damn it." Alex kicked her instrument cart, sending it flying across the floor to collide with the table. Both fell over and made a gratifying amount of noise.

The Darkyn were really starting to piss her off.

Moments like these made Alex miss her former life as a busy, successful reconstructive surgeon in Chicago. The patients she'd treated took a lot longer to heal, but she'd been able to make a difference in their lives. Okay, so she hadn't had the world's greatest relationship with her brother. When they were kids, John had protected her, cared for her—hell, he'd been her whole life. It was only after becoming a priest that he'd tossed her away and gotten sucked into the church. *We might have settled things between us,* she told herself. *Eventually.*

Until Michael Cyprien had sent his men to kidnap Alex and bring her to New Orleans, and the world had turned upside down.

Most of what had happened in the six months since that fateful day in the garage at Northeast Chicago Hospital still seemed surreal to Alex. Cyprien had snatched her because she was one of the few surgeons in the world fast enough to successfully operate on him. He had abducted her, and then convinced her to restore his face. After the surgery was when things had gotten out of hand, and Cyprien had nearly killed her in a mindless lust for blood. Alex had later woken up back in Chicago with no memory of what had happened. In time she had learned that Michael had saved her life by giving her his own blood, but in the process he had also infected her with it.

To top off everything, they'd fallen in love with each other.

Alex bent down and began picking up the instruments from the cart, now strewn like bizarre confetti around the fallen table. The office she was using at night to treat the Darkyn belonged to a dermatologist who practiced there during the day. He was one of the many humans who served the *vrykolakas,* but he wouldn't want to see his treatment room looking like a biker gang had ridden through it.

"I don't want to be a vampire," Alex muttered. "Vampires are snotty. Vampires are pigheaded. Vampires are chauvinistic, narrow-minded, idiotic cave trolls."

"You forgot inconsiderate, thick-skulled, and high-handed," a low, deep voice said from behind her.

She smelled roses but didn't stop working. "That too." Once she had filled a basin with instruments that would now have to be sterilized again, she turned to face her lover. "Did he tattle on me, or was it the noise?"

"I woke up and you were gone."

Michael Cyprien was the epitome of the tall, dark, handsome man. Only the strands of white hair framing his face reminded her of their first meeting, when his head had been reduced to a blind mass of horrific scar tissue and healed-over pulverized bone.

"Next time I'll remember to say good-bye before I leave for work." She made a mental note to give Arnaud a barium enema when he came in for his follow-up. "I'll ask Phillipe to look into a punching bag for my office."

"A wise alternative." Cyprien looked around the room and spotted the buckshot. "You were able to help Arnaud?"

"Physically. Aside from the fact that *l'attrait* in his case makes him smell like a garnish." She righted the table and sat on it, dangling her feet from the edge. "Mentally? He's just like all the others. Gloom and doom. Convinced he's damned to eternal vampiric life for some horrible sin he committed." She eyed him. "You know the guy, right? Tell me the truth. What's the worst thing Arnaud ever did?"

Cyprien thought for a moment. "He joined the Templars so that he would not have to marry the woman his father chose as his betrothed. It was said that she had vast holdings and an impressive dowry."

"So he's . . . enormously stupid?"

"His betrothed also had boils and the pox."

"Whoa. Nice dad. But see what I mean?" Alex propped her forehead against her hands. "How am I going to come up with a viable treatment if no one will talk to me about the genesis of this thing? I'm not going to risk going to any human experts, not after what happened to Leann." Leann Pollock, an old Peace Corps friend of Alex's who had offered to get her access to the CDC disease archives, had been tortured to death because of her involvement in Alex's research.

"Be patient." Cyprien came to stand in front of her, and stroked one of his long, sensitive hands over her messy mop of curls. "Secrecy is how the Darkyn have survived all these centuries. You cannot undo seven hundred years of experience with a single conversation."

"They don't trust me." Alex brooded for a moment. "It's because I took longer to wake up, isn't it? They don't think I'm for real."

"The fact that you took seven days to make the final change concerns many," he admitted. "But you are the first human to become Darkyn since the fifteenth century. We have no basis of comparison." His eyes, light turquoise rimmed in gold, fixed on hers. "What are you keeping from me this time, *chérie*?"

Too many things. Like her talent.

"You know I don't need as much blood as you do." She noticed a new scratch on her palm and showed it to him. "Evidently I don't heal as quickly, either."

He cradled her hand between his and studied it. "How long before it heals?"

"If it's the same as the last one, it'll disappear in an hour. Maybe two." She poked him in the ribs. "Stop looking at me like *I* have boils and the pox."

Cyprien didn't laugh. "You have been feeding only on human blood? You are not experimenting on yourself again?"

"Grade A, type O whole units, fresh from the private stash." She tried not to think about the fact that he had bought a blood bank to serve as her caterer. "All I've done is tap my veins for a few blood samples." When he started to protest, she shook her head. "This is nonnegotiable. My mutation is not progressing the same as yours did. I could have some kind of modern immunity that's interfering with it."

He didn't like that. "You are Darkyn—"

"—but am I immortal, like the rest of you?" Because she didn't know, and couldn't bear the look in his eyes, she slid off the table and into his arms. "You're in charge now. You've got the Brethren, Tremayne, and every secret vampire club in America on your plate. I'm the doctor. Medical has to be my baby."

"So it seems." He rubbed his thumb across her lips. "You are done for the night?"

"Yeah." She grinned. "I forgot to tell you the good news. I've found a way to help Jamys." She slipped out of his loose embrace to grab the folder of research from her desk.

Alex showed Cyprien the data and diagrams she had gleaned from different medical journals that published the latest in reconstructive surgical techniques. "The first time I examined him, I thought the Brethren had torn out his whole tongue, but on my second check I found a stump with muscle tissue still intact. This is what it looks like now."

"Could it grow back?" Cyprien asked, looking through what she pulled from the folder.

"No, the Darkyn's regenerative powers don't stretch that far. The good news is I can make him a new one." She lifted her arm and made a circle with one finger on the inside, near her wrist. "It'll take two patches of muscle, harvested from this area. I'll fold and graft them onto the remnant muscle."

Cyprien nodded. "This has been done before?"

"To vampires, no. To humans who have lost their tongues to cancer or massive oral injuries, yes. It's a very successful procedure, too. Most patients who undergo it regain their ability to swallow and speak." She showed him several before-and-after photos of patients who had undergone the origami-like reconstruction. "They've also done successful whole-tongue transplants as well, but that isn't an option for us. The only tissue Jamys's body will accept is his own."

"Have you spoken to him about this?"

She thought of the last time she'd talked with the young Darkyn. *I have to stop thinking that way. Jamys may look seventeen, but he's got six hundred years on me.* "He wasn't very interested. I think he's worried about his dad. Has there been any word on Thierry?"

"I have scouts looking for him." Cyprien studied one of the surgical diagrams of the harvest site. "Will transferring muscle in this fashion cause Jamys to lose use of his arm?"

Why was he changing the subject so fast? Alex made a mental note to talk to Phillipe, Cyprien's seneschal, about Thierry. "The grafts won't be that deep or extensive. Remember how small the tongue is." She stuck hers out at him.

Cyprien set the papers aside. "I do not remember," he said, his voice deeper, his accent heavier. "Show me again."

Invisible roses filled the room.

Alex felt a sudden dull ache between her legs and swallowed. "We can't have sex in my office," she said, bracing herself against the edge of the desk. "It's unprofessional. It's unethical."

"I won't report you to the authorities." Cyprien pulled her

up against him, holding her there with one hand splayed over her bottom. "Do you know, I haven't touched you in fourteen hours."

"You count the hours?"

"The hours." He bent his head and skimmed his lips over hers. "The minutes." His hands were under her shirt, his fingers pulling aside the cups of her bra. "The moments."

Alex felt another ache, harder and hotter, inside her mouth as her *dents acérées* emerged from the holes in her palate. Her fangs had formed soon after Cyprien had infected her with his blood, but she'd never used them.

"I want to kiss you," she muttered, "and I want to jump on you, and do terribly personal things to your body. But why the hell do I want to *bite* you?"

"Because it feels good." Cyprien scraped the side of her throat with the tips of his own fangs, so delicately that he didn't break the skin. "Aren't you curious to know how it is, *chérie?*"

"I haven't fed." She would not beg. She would tremble, moan, and shimmy against him like a lap dancer, but she refused to beg. "If I bite you, you'll ruin my dinner."

"I taste better than the plastic-bag blood." He kissed her, hard and fast and so deep their fangs met. Alex's were smaller and shorter, and the tips fit just inside Cyprien's. He lifted his head and tore his collar open. "Try me."

Alex stared at the smooth skin on the side of his neck. Her own *l'attrait* drenched the air around them with lavender. "What if I take too much?"

Drinking too much blood put the Darkyn into a mindless bloodlust they called thrall, after which they remained unconscious for several days. Thrall also induced something in humans that the Darkyn called rapture. Rapture somehow destroyed the mind of the victim before they died of blood loss.

"You cannot, unless you bite me many times or feed quickly." He caught her lower lip between his teeth, released it. "We heal too fast."

"Okay." She could hardly believe she was saying this, agreeing to *do* this. Injections of blood weren't sustaining her anymore, however, and there was nothing else she could digest except blood, water, and a little wine. "This doesn't mean I hunt. I do *not* hunt."

"I will hunt for you." Cyprien lifted her off her feet and carried her five steps to the exam table.

They're going to fuck. Satisfaction, urgency, caution. *Light it now.*

Alex stiffened as she saw Cyprien carrying her inside her mind, but through a window, as if she were standing outside. A black-gloved hand picked up a red can and hurled the liquid in it against the office's front door. "Michael, wait. Put me down."

Two cans oughta do it. Trotting around the building, splashing more liquid. *Take the interstate. Get back before dawn, keep my alibi together.*

"I am." Cyprien was laying her out on the table.

"No. Someone's outside." Alex pushed his hands away and jumped from the table. Strong gasoline fumes made her eyes water. "Can't you smell it?"

He comes out, I gotta pop him. The thought was as cold and hard as the gun the man removed from his jacket. Checking the clip. The dark gleam of bullets. *Head shots. Only head shots.*

The man was a hired assassin.

Alex knew because it was her talent—the ability to read minds of killers. She seized Cyprien's arm. "We have to get out of here. Someone's been sent to kill you. He's outside, splashing gas around the building. He's going to burn down the office. If you walk out, he'll shoot you with bullets made of copper. I don't know what they're called but they explode inside a body."

Cyprien picked up a scalpel. "Go to the tunnels."

A match, lit and tossed. Another. *God, this stuff catches fast.* Huge, black-smoking flames burst from the gas-soaked walls. Caught up in the vision, Alex nearly shrieked.

"Alexandra." He was shaking her. "We must go, *now*." He dragged her out of the treatment room.

The Darkyn had tunnels all over the city, which they used to move from one location to another. It permitted them free access to areas during the night where they otherwise might be stopped and questioned by police, who like the rest of New Orleans believed the water table was too high to build anything underground. It was one of many successful myths the Darkyn had used to mask their existence.

The dermatologist's tunnel access was hidden beneath heavily stacked shelves in his storage room. Cases of Botox and Retin A went flying as Cyprien tore the shelf away from the floor and entered the code into a tiny keypad disguised as an air-conditioning thermostat on the wall beside it. A panel of linoleum slid to one side, revealing a dimly lit tunnel.

Alex looked over her shoulder. "Wait. He's a professional arsonist, so he won't stop burning until he's caught. We have to call the cops on this guy." Smoke was seeping in the narrow crack beneath the closet door, and Alex felt the heat that came with it. She then remembered what she had left behind. "My blood samples—"

"No time." Cyprien pushed her toward the opening in the floor and climbed down in after her, waiting only long enough to close the panel behind them.

Cyprien led her through an unfamiliar section of tunnel, with other keypads and panels to open and close. There were too many for Alexandra's liking.

"What if the fire comes in here?" she demanded as they passed over the third threshold. "Or the firemen find the panel up there burned away?"

"The doors and panels are fireproof. No one will enter the tunnels." Cyprien turned a corner and Alex saw they were in the tunnel that led to La Fontaine, his mansion in the Garden District. He pulled down the steel ladder leading up into the lower level of the house and then glanced at her. "How did you know the assassin was an arsonist and carried copper bullets?"

"I saw him watching us. I heard his thoughts." She scowled. "It's my little bonus, okay? I can see inside someone's mind, but only if they're a killer."

"He was not Kyn." Michael seemed to take comfort in that.

"He could have been. I did the same thing with Thierry." Alex saw his expression shift. "What? I didn't ask for this. The evil Darkyn fairy stuck me with it."

"You could read Thierry's mind."

"Loud and clear. The whole time he was here, he was think-

ing about killing everyone in the house, the city, the state, etc."
She sighed. "Couple of times I was ready to help him."

Michael put his hands on her shoulders. "Alexandra, Kyn
talent works on humans. Only humans. That you can read the
mind of a Kyn in a killing rage . . ." He didn't seem to know
how to end that sentence.

"So we'll know when Phillipe really gets sick of your bull-
shit." She shrugged. "I don't see the problem."

"You will tell no one of your talent."

"Let me think." She consulted the upper dome of the tunnel.
"Nope, I'm still going to do whatever I damn please. I'll let you
know when that changes." Now he'd yell in French, or shake
her, or say something stupid about being her master, and she'd
have to clock him.

"I give you nothing but unwanted gifts." Michael leaned
over and pressed his mouth to the line between her brows. "I
am sorry, Alex. It cannot be a pleasant thing for you. But it
would be better if you told no one."

"It saved our asses tonight. Stop being understanding only
so you can get me to do what you want. I hate that." She
climbed up the ladder and into the house, where Cyprien's
seneschal was waiting for both of them.

Alex could have built a replica of Phillipe out of LEGOs; he
had the same blocky, solid dimensions. When they'd first met,
she'd hated him, and he'd probably looked forward to tossing
her out of the mansion. Over time, however, keeping Cyprien
alive had made them allies. Now Phillipe and Alex shared a
constant, if sometimes exasperated, affection for each other.

"An assassin tried to kill us at the doctor's office," Cyprien
told Phillipe. "Double the guards and summon the hunters. He
was carrying copper bullets. If he can be found, I want him
taken alive."

"Master, there is something you should know." Phillipe
handed him a folded piece of paper, upon which something was
written in French.

"What is it?" Alex asked.

"Jamys." Cyprien folded the note in half. "He has gone to
Chicago to find his father."

Chapter 4

Where you say you were going, my friend?"

Jamys Durand looked at Hal, the man driving the vehicle in which they rode. He had not said, naturally, but he again took out the folded map from his jacket and pointed to Chicago.

"Right 'round the corner." Hal's head bobbed up and down. "I'll drop you, then head over to Fort Wayne. Got me a honey there. Always puts me up for a night, makes me breakfast. Waitress, but she works lunch shift."

Jamys imagined a pot of honey and Hal hung from a pole before he sorted out the expressions. Most of what Hal said required thoughtful deciphering. Jamys's English was not very good, and he had only himself to blame. His uncle Gabriel had warned him that he would need to know the language someday.

Hal talked a great deal, but seemed to require no response from him. Which was agreeable to Jamys, who could manage only a grunt at best.

Hal's voice became part of the drone of the engine as Jamys stared out into the night. They would be in Chicago soon, and he would have to do more than point at maps and grunt if he was to find Thierry.

I'm coming, Father.

Hal was the seventh human Jamys had met since leaving New Orleans. The first day of his journey, Jamys had concerned himself only with getting some distance from Cyprien and the *jardin*. In America, crossing a distance he could manage; remaining undiscovered, hunting and feeding, and finding shelter for the coming day proved quite a challenge.

Jamys knew he had to be careful in this country, so unlike France, his homeland. He'd also had his doubts about walking among humanity so openly again. He didn't trust humans. He didn't trust anyone anymore.

Did Thierry feel like this? Was that why he had run away?

His father had to know he was being hunted. Thierry knew Michael Cyprien; knew he would discover the missing file on Luisa Lopez. Without question, he would know that Cyprien would trace Thierry's movements from New Orleans north. *Why* Cyprien was hunting him, Thierry might not understand. There were other reasons Jamys had decided to go to Chicago. Jamys had to reach his father before Cyprien did, or many more Darkyn would die. He was also not sure what Cyprien intended to do to his father if he captured him.

Surely an archer did not pry a shaft from a wounded lion only to draw a bow against him anew.

His father and Michael Cyprien had been friends since they were boys. Thierry often told tales about how they had trained and fought and taken their vows together. They had gone to Castle Pilgrim to hold the last of the Holy Land against the heretics. They had even died and risen to walk as Darkyn within days of each other.

Cyprien cannot kill him if he cannot find him. Jamys didn't need the Darkyn to get Thierry out of the country. With his talent, he could use humans.

"You follow baseball, son?" Hal asked him, and this time gave him an anxious look that indicated a need for an answer.

Jamys shook his head. He found modern athletic competitions pale, pathetic imitations of true sport.

"I'm a Cubbies man, myself," Hal told him, and went on to explain why for the next thirty minutes.

Jamys knew his father was likely mad, as everyone said, and that made him dangerous. Still, his father's body was healed, and he was free; perhaps that would help him come back to his senses. Then Cyprien would not have to put him back into the cell in the floor, or keep him in copper chains, or "decide what to do with him."

Fear for Thierry traveled with Jamys, a cloak that was sometimes light, sometimes smothering.

His father's madness was as much Jamys's fault as it was Angelica's. Part of him could still not stomach the fact that his mother had turned against his father and their kind. Even when he had heard her promising to hunt another Darkyn for the Brethren, Jamys had been paralyzed with disbelief, sure that it was some horrible jest. But to preserve her own miserable skin, his mother had sent him, his father, and the rest of the Durands to die slowly in the secret dungeons of the Brethren.

How many other Kyn had his mother handed over to be tortured by the Brethren? Why, when Jamys had learned she intended to hurt more of their kind, had he not warned his father?

"My cousin follows the Red Sox, the poor sumbitch," Hal was saying. "One year he got so agitated, he carried the TV out in the yard and put a sledge to it."

Jamys was glad his mother was dead. Seeing her decapitated by Cyprien's *sygkenis,* Alexandra Keller, had made part of this wretched situation right again. The human doctor had done so much for them. Now it was his turn. He would save his father, and redeem Thierry and himself in the eyes of the Kyn.

Hal's car was a wide, comfortable luxury sedan. After that first, long night of walking, Jamys had used cargo trucks that occupied the roads every hour of the day as his central means of transportation. He climbed onto the top of the first at an all-night diner just outside Baton Rouge.

When the trucker pulled off the road to sleep for several hours, Jamys had climbed down and used *l'attrait* to discover the driver's route. Later, just before the truck turned west, he got off and walked until he found another truck, another driver who had stopped on the side of the road to sleep.

Hal, whose job was to assess damages to property his employer insured, had pulled off into the parking lot of an all-night restaurant to grab a quick meal before continuing on the next leg of his "route." Jamys had intercepted him on the way back to his car and used his talent to convince him to give him a ride.

He could convince any human of anything simply by touching them and thinking what he wanted them to believe. Jamys was only sorry that his talent didn't work on the Kyn.

During the trip north, Jamys had learned that Hal was one of the rare humans who were completely content with his situation. He enjoyed his life without guilt, shame, or a need for more than he had. His desires were limited to drinking a great deal of ale, obtaining the signature of a famous pitcher, and having sex with two identical twin human females at once.

Aside from the "twins" scenario, which Jamys thought rather odd, he envied Hal. Hal's mother was still alive, and judging by how reverently he spoke of her, was much beloved by Hal and his six brothers and sister. He would wager Hal's mother had never maimed and killed Hal's family, friends, or employers.

"You look sick, boy," Hal said. "You want me to pull over for a bit?"

Jamys placed his hand on Hal's neck. *I am not sick.* He couldn't erase Hal's memory as Michael could, but he could plant any suggestion in the human male's mind. He wished he could talk to him this way. To say something like: *I am worried about my father. A man who was his friend is chasing him.*

"Some friend," Hal said, reacting as if Jamys had spoken out loud.

You can hear me like this?

"Sure." Hal gave him an amiable grin. "So what's the story on this guy after your dad?"

He is a great strategist. Jamys didn't think Cyprien was evil, but he was not sure how becoming seigneur had changed his father's friend. *The type who makes plans atop designs within schemes.*

"Your dad and him couldn't talk out whatever pissed him off?"

Maybe that was why Cyprien was pursuing him; Thierry had nearly killed his *sygkenis*. Jamys remembered how Thierry had reacted once when his uncle Gabriel had simply shouted at his mother. *He made a bad mistake. A great insult.*

Or perhaps now that he was the American seigneur, Cyprien had set aside all thoughts of friendship. As their leader, he might see Thierry only as a Darkyn gone insane—one of the most dangerous creatures on the face of the earth.

Hal frowned. "Can't your dad just apologize, make it up to him?"

It may be too late for that. Cyprien would send men capable of killing Jamys's father who would find Thierry before him. It would take many of the best hunters; his father was fast and lethal. What if Thierry wanted to die? What if he died before Jamys could reach him?

Jamys was angry with Cyprien, too. If he had wanted Thierry dead, why had he let him escape from New Orleans? Why had he not killed him there, quickly, cleanly, mercifully? Was this some penance he wished Thierry to make for being oblivious to Angelica's crimes? Where was the justice in this?

"Coming up on Chi-town, my friend," Hal said. "Where do you want me to drop you?"

Jamys saw a cluster of small houses beyond the interstate, within walking distance of the city. He would need to make some preparations before he hunted Thierry. *That is where I wish to go, Hal.*

"You got it," the man said, shifting over to the exit-ramp lane.

Ten minutes later, Hal was driving off to meet with his waitress in Fort Wayne, and Jamys was walking down a suburban street, checking the small spaces between the houses. He soon found what he was looking for.

A bath first, to mask his scent.

Jamys checked the windows of the house before he leaped over the closed gate and walked across the yard to the dark oval of water. Now as he set aside his satchel and descended fully clothed into the chlorinated water, he plotted his next move.

Cyprien might assume Thierry was acting out of madness, but Jamys thought his father's journey had been one of his saner decisions. Luisa Lopez had not been the victim of a random attack. Alexandra had talked about Luisa, and he knew, as Thierry likely did, that she had been tortured. Cyprien and Alexandra had not yet realized that Luisa's injuries were consistent with an interrogation by the Brethren.

During his captivity, Jamys had been witness to the monks doing the same thing to his father's *tresora*. Familiar as he was with the delights of the rack, the strappado, and the whip, there was no mistaking the wounds they had left on the human girl.

But why would the monsters brutalize Luisa? From the way Alexandra had described her, she was barely more than a child. She did not serve among the *tresori*. What could she have done to attract their vicious attention?

The water around him turned darker as the water lifted days of dirt and dust from his skin and garments. When satisfied that he had soaked off the worst, Jamys surfaced and climbed out. A potbellied man in a flannel bathrobe stood on the deck. He looked angry, and seized Jamys by the arm.

"What are you doing in here?"

I needed a bath, he told the man. *You have a very nice pond.*

Jamys's scent enveloped them, and the man's eyes turned dreamy. "It's a pool."

I have probably muddied it. Jamys pulled some of the paper money he carried—wet now, like his clothes—and offered it to the man. When he didn't take it, he pressed the soaked bills into his hand and added a suggestion. *Use this to have it cleaned.*

"You took a bath." The man sounded like a sleepwalker who had been roused too quickly. "In my pool."

I was very dirty. Jamys looked around him but saw no one else. *I am leaving your property now. I will not return. You should not summon the police. You should forget I was here.*

"Thank you."

Jamys caught the man as he pitched forward and eased him the rest of the way to the deck. Some humans could not bear too much exposure to his talent and fainted like this. He put a hand on the pudgy neck to check his pulse, and then tucked the money into the man's front pocket before he jumped back over the fence.

Now to find shelter.

Farther down the street Jamys began seeing the same colorful paper stapled to every signpost and telephone pole, and stopped to see if he could make out what it said. There was a picture of a badly dressed boy and girl on it.

RUNAWAYS—NEED A PLACE TO STAY? DON'T GET LOST ON THE
STREETS—FIND SHELTER AT THE HAVEN.

"Cops are all over it." A foot nudged him. "You hear me,
Bri? They found him."

Brian Calloway looked at Blaze. He'd told the other boy a
million times to call him by his gang name, Decree, but when
Blaze got the shakes he still forgot. "So? They wanted him
found."

"So I'm just saying." Blaze, whose real name was Troy
Ogilvie, paced like a hungry dog. "Raze knows we chiseled the
little gink, right? You called him."

"I called him, and he was real happy about it." Decree settled back in the red-and-brown-plaid armchair he and the other
boys had snatched from the back of a moving van in the middle of being unloaded. "Said the money'd be coming in a couple days."

"A couple of days?" Blaze looked ready to puke.

Decree knew the other boy was an addict, but he'd thought
money from the last job would have tided him over. "I've got
cash if you need a loan."

"That's good. That's great." Blaze scrubbed a hand over his
mouth and chin. "So I ditched the truck in niggertown, like you
told me to. We gonna ever buy one?"

"Raze says we can't be throwing around a lot of money.
Cops see one of us driving a brand-new ride, they're gonna
pop us." Which Blaze should have remembered; they'd all
been there when Raze had explained their new direction.

Two more boys came in, ducking under the roll-down door
of the storage bay. One of them held up a six-pack of beer, a
trophy of success.

"Bring that shit over here." Decree pulled on his T-shirt and
felt his scalp. Three days of stubble prickled against his palm.
Damn, it grew back fast; he'd have to get Pure to shave him
next time he went to see her.

"They had his parents on the news," one of the boys said as
he passed around the beers. "Little fuck's father was a white
man. Guess his dick's too small for anything but gink pussy."

More boys came into the storage bay. Some brought beer,

others subs, chips, and candy. All had clean-shaven heads and wore a uniform of black jeans and T-shirts, combat boots and bomber jackets. Most had elaborate tattoos and piercings. Two or three of the older boys wore white suspenders instead of belts, with names written in indelible marker on the straps.

Someone switched on a boom box while the beer and food were shared. Decree listened as the others egged one another about the job. As the night came on, the noise level died down, and by unspoken agreement the boys formed a circle around Decree and the armchair.

"We did good," he told them. "Raze is real happy with us. Cops don't know what the fuck, as usual."

The boys, some of whom were already a little drunk, laughed and jabbed each other. Decree held up a hand for silence.

"We gotta keep it level now. No showing on the street. You go home, go to work, go to school. Like nothing happened. Anyone pops you, you know the number and story." He looked at Blaze, who was rocking a little. "Questions?"

Bull, a thick-bodied jock with bruised hands, caught his eye. "When's the next hit?"

"Raze'll phone it in. He says these guys are good for steady work." Decree saw Blaze, who looked ready to puke, shake his head at the offer of a beer. There was always someone who couldn't handle the fallout. "Okay, that wraps it. Be out here on Friday, and bring your working clothes."

The boys picked up their cans and garbage, dropping them into an open barrel on their way out. When Blaze went to leave, Decree stopped him. "Hang out for a minute, man. I got something for you."

Blaze licked his dry lips. "Something good?"

Decree checked his watch. "Yeah, a delivery. Should be here any minute."

"That's great, man." Blaze circled the bay restlessly. "I was telling my old lady, Jude, how great this gig is. She's been bitching and complaining, you know?"

"You tell her about the job?" Decree asked.

"No, man, I wouldn't." Blaze shook his head. "She can't

keep her yap shut; tells her mom everything. I didn't even tell her I was back in with the boys. Her mom'd call the cops."

Decree heard steps outside the bay. "That's good, Blaze. Business is better without the bitches getting involved."

"Hey, you got a little on you, man?" Blaze released a wretched chuckle. "I'm truly squeezed."

"I got a stash outside in my ride. Hang here."

He walked out and pulled on his jacket. Nights were getting cold and long; he'd have to steal something warmer soon. For him and for Pure.

Raze came out of nowhere, as usual. The first time he'd done it, Decree had nearly passed out. Now he was used to Raze's magic tricks, or he told himself he was. His balls still shrank a little every time he looked into those eyes. Raze had the unblinking black eyes of a cobra, ready to strike.

Tonight they weren't frightening, only intent. "All went well?"

"The boys are tight, but I think Blaze has been talking to his bitch and her mom. He gets chatty when he runs dry." Decree nodded toward the bay. "I told him I'd give him a little."

Raze smiled, and that was worse than looking into his empty eyes. "Let me."

Father John Keller had grown up on the streets of Chicago. For a number of years he had also lived on them, a time he considered his primary education. The Department of Children and Families had eventually caught up with John and his young sister, Alexandra, and placed them in foster care with the Kellers, a wealthy, kind couple with no children of their own who had eventually been able to adopt John and Alex. John had gladly exchanged his freedom for a home and a life of security for Alex, but he had never forgotten the lessons the streets had taught him.

The street kid inside John hadn't wanted to come back to Chicago.

John had spent the last six months in limbo, moving through a series of cheap hotels and using up what little savings he had while he'd tried to decide what to do. The money had run out faster than his doubts and fears. He had used the last of it to return to the city of his birth with only one clear purpose: to officially leave the priesthood and confront his mentor, Archbishop August Hightower. Hightower had to answer for the events that had finished John as a priest and caused the slaughter of a hundred more just like him.

That decision John had debated long and hard, for the bishop had played a significant part in what had happened in New Orleans, and was still a member of the *Les Frères de la Lumière*, the Brethren of the Light. He might throw John back to the wolves rather than tell him why these things had happened. Hightower also knew about the sadistic practices the order of former Catholic priests used to pursue their mission. The bishop had been the one to show a videotape of them to John.

The Brethren's mission, Hightower had claimed, was to prevail in a centuries-long struggle against another secret society of vampirelike demons called the Darkyn.

What John could not convince himself of was that Hightower was entirely aware of just how murderous his secret order had become, or that they were using Darkyn to hunt other vampires. *I'm not sure I believe everything I saw in that church.*

He had called Hightower before coming to Chicago. The bishop had sounded appalled and relieved when John had called him. *We thought you had been killed in New Orleans.*

I survived, John had told him. But had he? *I have to see you.*

The bishop immediately advised against meeting in his offices or anywhere near a church. *There is a bakery around the corner from the* Tribune. *Meet me there tomorrow at two. I will be wearing street clothes. Sit outside.*

It was at a small table outside the bakery that John now sat, staring through the window at the rows of fancy cakes and fruit pies, watching the cream-laced tea that had been served to him in a delicate porcelain cup grow cold. He could see his faint reflection in the window, his dark hair hanging past his collar; his skin, which had acquired a yellowish cast from spending too many hours indoors; the short beard he kept meaning to shave away but couldn't bring himself to do more than trim.

I look like I'm on the edge, he realized. *The way I used to when Alex and I were living on the streets.* John had turned his back on everything he had learned during his childhood to better himself. Now he was slowly reverting back to what he had once been. The skinny, angry kid he had despised. *All I need is a shave and a job.*

"Johnny." Hightower appeared as suddenly as a three-hundred-pound man could, and came around the small table to embrace him with both arms. "The Heavenly Father has heard at least one of my prayers. Welcome home, my son."

"Your Grace." John looked over the older man's shoulder, expecting to see Hightower's assistant, Father Carlo Cabreri, hovering behind him. The bishop was alone. "You came by yourself?"

"Under the circumstances, I thought it best." Hightower lowered his bulk to perch carefully on the small wicker chair across from John. Once the waitress had served him tea, he said, "Six months, Johnny. Six months I thought you dead, and not a single phone call to alleviate my suffering. Was that to punish me for my part in this?"

"No." John had never been comfortable with the bishop's affection for him, or the amount of insight he had into John's character. Hightower had also been the one to convince him to join his order. "Six months ago I watched Cardinal Stoss and one hundred of his followers attack a group of Darkyn in a church. The Brethren were slaughtered. All of them."

"We suspected as much, but we have no eyewitness reports, and no bodies were ever recovered," the bishop told him. "Please, if you do nothing else this day, tell me precisely what happened that night."

John recounted the events as they had happened, leaving out only the part Alexandra had played in them. Hightower might react worse than John had if he learned that Alex had become one of the Darkyn.

What he wanted now was the truth. "After it was over, Cyprien told me that the Templars had never been Brethren. He said that he and the others like him *were* the Templars. The same ones who had escaped the church when it tried to exterminate them in the fourteenth century. He said they had been cursed, or maybe brought back something from the Holy Land that had turned them into vampires."

Hightower frowned. "An incredible story. You must have been terrified. You didn't believe him, of course."

"After what I witnessed in that church, Your Grace, I don't know what I believe." John drained the cold tea from his cup. "Cyprien told me other things, such as the fact that my training in La Luchemaria was simply another form of Brethren torture."

"Stoss took things too far in Rome; that much is true," the bishop said. "We had no idea he was abusing novitiate brothers in such an outrageous fashion. Stoss used his position in the order to do many things that we would never have condoned. I knew him, John, and he was once a good man. Perhaps he fought the demons too long and lost sight of what we are trying to do. I can assure you that Stoss was an exception, not a rule, among the Brethren."

"What about Cyprien's claim that *they* are the Templars?" John asked softly. "It does fit the history. Warrior priests, already wealthy beyond imagining. Add immortality to that, and even the pope wouldn't be able to resist making them outlaws, to be hunted down and tortured for their secrets."

"No, you're wrong," Hightower said, his gaze open and steady. "Cyprien lied to you. The Templars who were exterminated by the old church were not vampires. They were only the last of the Crusader priests, wealthy and powerful men whose treasuries tempted a greedy French king and a corrupt pope. The few who escaped torture and death swore that no innocent would ever again have to suffer such unmerited persecution. That is why we became the Brethren and took up the fight against the *maledicti*, John. If we do not hold them back, they will sweep across this world like a plague to exterminate the human race."

Hightower sounded convincing, but he was one of the most persuasive men John knew. When motivated, he could probably make someone believe that the sun came out at night and the moon was made of Brie.

"I don't believe you." John took perverse pleasure in saying the words that had burned inside him since watching the

Darkyn systematically execute Stoss and his monks. "They still wear the white tunics and carry banners bearing the Beaucent. They have no reason to wipe out humanity—"

"You speak of these creatures as if they were still human and possessed their souls. These are demons sent up from hell itself to torment mankind." Hightower removed a thick envelope from his jacket and tossed it onto the table. "They use whatever they can to manipulate us, to turn us against each other. Look inside."

John didn't want to open the envelope. He didn't want to be sullied with any more knowledge of the Darkyn or the Brethren's dirty secrets about them. Still he reached for it and took out the photographs inside.

The light was poor, but the images were clear enough for the two people in them to be identified. One was Angelica Durand, the shape-shifting vampire who had come to New Orleans to kill Alexandra and Michael.

The other was John Keller, drugged and crazed, in the process of raping her.

"The Darkyn have already infiltrated the Brethren," Hightower said, his round face pale now. "We took these from one of the priests they had operating in Rome. Read the letter with them."

The letter was only half a page, quite short and to the point. The Brethren were to release the Darkyn being held in custody, or the photographs would be sent to every newspaper in the world.

"Have they sent them?" John found enough voice to ask.

"No. We were able to recover the negatives and what copies their operative had made. I have them all here, John. I have kept them safe until I could give them to you personally."

The bishop's sympathetic gaze appalled him almost as much as the photographs. "Is this how you intend to bring me back to the church? By blackmailing me?"

"Good God, is that what you think of me?" Hightower gripped his arm. "I'm giving them to you—all of them—so you can rest easy. I think you should destroy them, John, but whatever you do, don't make the mistake of thinking that this will be the end of it. The *maledicti* have targeted you now, and they won't rest until you are back in prison."

"Why?" John felt more tired than he had when he had walked out of the prison in Rio so many years ago. "I pose no threat to them. I'm not part of the Brethren. I'm finished being a priest. As of today, I'm a private citizen."

"Then why did they take your sister?" Hightower countered. "What possible reason could they have had for killing her?"

He almost didn't bother to correct the bishop. It was better that the Brethren think Alexandra was dead. "My sister is still alive. She's with Cyprien now." He wouldn't say she was one of them, because he didn't quite believe it. Could his sister really be a vampire?

"For God's sake, then, come back to us, John," Hightower urged. "I'll explain how Stoss and Cyprien manipulated you between them. If these creatures have Alexandra, then the Order is the only thing that can keep you safe now."

"I know what the Order can do." John shook his head and rose to his feet. "I'll take my chances."

"How much money do you have?" Hightower removed a slim wallet and opened it.

"I can't accept—"

"You said you're done being a priest, Johnny. As soon as I file the paperwork, which to respect your wishes will be today, your income will stop. The maledicti won't permit your sister to help you, and if you try to lay claim on her estate, they will make it vanish." The bishop held out a handful of bills until he saw that John wasn't going to take them. He grimaced and put them back in his billfold. "You can't do this on your own."

"I can." John expected to work, and he wasn't too proud to take any job. He couldn't afford to stay in hotels any longer, but there were efficiencies, and even homeless shelters. He didn't have to live on the streets again.

"Let me help you." Hightower lumbered out of the chair and rested a hand on John's shoulder. "I won't try to push money on you or talk you into coming back to the Order or the priesthood. I've made enough mistakes, my son. From this point forth, I'll support whatever decisions you make."

"Why?"

"You're the closest thing to a son that I'll ever have," Hightower said simply.

John didn't trust the bishop entirely, but Hightower had come to meet him on his own, and he had never condemned John for his actions. The fact was, he would need some help to make a new start. "What did you have in mind?"

"Dougall Hurley is looking for help at the Haven," Hightower said. "Hurley manages the place, and he's an ex-priest, but he has no connections with the Brethren. The Haven is a shelter for runaway teenagers. The church provides some of the funding for it, but that's our only involvement. Hurley handles the place on his own with a small staff, but he needs more help for the kids."

John knew of the Haven, which was located a half dozen blocks from St. Luke's, his former parish. It had been in operation for more than twenty years, and had an excellent reputation. "I have no experience working with runaways."

"You took a couple of psychology courses in the seminary, and you've worked with troubled children in the past. These youngsters are desperately in need of guidance." Hightower sighed. "Dougall does well with the practical side of things, but he needs someone to provide quality counseling. You would be a godsend, John."

The last time he had followed Hightower's wishes, he had been imprisoned in Roman catacombs, drugged, tortured, and driven to rape.

It has nothing to do with the Brethren, John thought. *If it doesn't work out, I can walk away.* "All right," he told the bishop. "I'll go see Hurley and apply for the job."

Chapter 5

A soft, polite tapping on the bedroom door dragged Jema from an exhausted sleep. "Yes?"

"I'm sorry to disturb you, miss," Micki, the upstairs maid, said from the hallway, "but your mother would like to see you downstairs."

The clock on her bedside table read 7:02 A.M., a full hour earlier than the alarm Jema had set to get up in time for work. *She must be ready to read me the riot act.* "I'll be down in five minutes, Micki," she called out, wincing at the rasping sound of her own voice.

"Thank you, miss." Footsteps retreated quickly.

She sat up and tried to yawn. "Ugh."

Someone had cemented Jema's tongue to the roof of her mouth, which tasted as if she'd been sucking on a dirty penny. Because she often experienced nosebleeds during the night, she checked for stains.

Five small reddish-brown spots marred the ivory case, right where her head had dented the pillow.

She felt her nose with cautious fingertips, but something made her lower lip throb. The source turned out to be two deep, small gashes on the inside of her lower lip. They only began to sting the second she discovered them with the tip of her tongue. Her chin itched; she scratched and looked at her hand. Flakes of dried blood were under her fingernails; streaks of the same reddened her fingers and palm.

That accounted for the spots, but not the mess on her hand. *I must have bitten my lip and rubbed my face in my sleep. That* the victim she had examined at the crime scene the night before had done virtually the same thing made her shudder.

He was trying not to scream.

Dream of me.

Something about last night was . . . fuzzy. Unable to decide what, Jema rolled out of bed. Maybe she'd had a bad dream. She couldn't remember her dreams, which vanished like fog the moment she woke, but she had the feeling last night's had been a doozy. As for her cut lip, there couldn't be a connection to the murdered man. It was some unhappy coincidence, produced by a restless subconscious.

Dream of me.

Her muscles protested as she walked across the floor and into the adjoining bathroom. She felt battered and exhausted, and wondered if she'd tensed while sleeping. *Is that why I'm so sore and tired? Did I have a nightmare?* The unexplained cuts on the inside of her lip voted yes.

She eyed the shower. Because Meryl Shaw disliked hot showers, Shaw House's water heaters were set to a low temperature. In the morning it took forever for the shower to heat up. An icy shower would probably wake Jema up like nothing else, but the prospect made gooseflesh rise on her arms. She turned on the water in the sink to rinse the revolting metallic taste from her mouth, but before she bent down the visage in the mirrored medicine cabinet gave her a horrified look.

A grotesque mask of dark red streaks covered her face.

Water filled the sink as Jema stared. *That can't be me.* The image reached up and tugged at her lip to look at the cuts on the inside. Had it bled this much? They were deeper than she'd imagined, like punctures instead of cuts. The sound of the sink drain trying to gurgle down the water made her bladder swell and ache.

There has to be a reasonable explanation. Okay. She breathed in deeply, clearing her head. *I rolled off the mattress and smacked my face on the floor. My front teeth cut my lip. I crawled back into bed without waking up or remembering—*

Golden eyes. She'd dreamed of them. He'd told her to.

Dream of me.

She glanced down at the water filling the sink and saw the

distorted reflection of her bloodstained face. A gasp burst from her as a sharp pain burned at the back of her head, in the same place the victim's skull had been crushed. Where his hand had cradled her head.

What's happening to me?

It took a moment for Jema to realize that pain was caused by a piece of her hair tangled around the collar button of her nightgown. Moving her head strained at the roots just above her nape. She fumbled with the button and tore the hair free, swearing under her breath as several strands parted from her scalp and fell into the sink.

If you knew you were going to die, Detective, wouldn't you hold on to whatever pride you could?

Unbutton your blouse, chérie.

Jema jerked down her panties and dropped onto the toilet. Just in time, too; fear had punched her in the belly with a quick jab. The urine burned as it came out, and she closed her eyes, rocking a little as she forced her cramping bladder to empty.

Please, God, not my kidneys.

She felt better as soon as she saw her urine was only cloudy, not tinged with more blood. The last time her kidneys had caused major trouble, her urine had looked like cherry 7UP for three weeks. There had also been the raging yeast infection the antibiotics Dr. Bradford had prescribed to cure the kidney infection had caused.

I need a pot of coffee. Coffee always clears my head. It might also chase away the dull throb of the headache that was now forming behind her right eye. She remembered that her mother was waiting for her. *Maybe two pots.*

Jema scrubbed her face and hands clean, took her morning injection, and quickly dressed. Before this last year, she'd always waited until after breakfast for her first shot of the day. That was no longer possible. The downside was that the insulin ruined her appetite, so she ate less after the injections. If she didn't stop losing weight soon she was going to look like a skeleton.

Breakfast at Shaw House, like every meal, was held in the formal dining room. Meryl Shaw had redesigned the former reception room, ripping out the nineteenth-century olive-green wallpaper along with the antique Colonial banquet, table, and faded Persian rugs. Tall panels of burled walnut and molded brass wainscoting now bordered the room. The floor, a glossy jasper, had curious brown and green patterns within the stone that formed paisleylike patterns. Being stone, it was always cold.

The centerpiece of the room was the dining table, an endless expanse of dark oak that had once graced a castle in England and could comfortably seat fifty. The fussy crystal chandelier that had once filled the with room with its glittery, frivolous light had been banished to the attic. Recessed spotlights in the walnut veneer of the ceiling now provided more distant, anonymous illumination.

Jema didn't like the dining room—the windows, hung with ostentatious burgundy satin curtains, were always drawn—and she thought all the deep colors were depressing. At the same time, she knew why her mother gravitated toward dark, heavy decor.

Meryl Shaw knew how to work a room.

The owner of Shaw House sat at the very end of the table, a living ghost in the dark room. Jema's mother wore nothing but the iciest of white, which matched the colorless, ruthlessly cut cap of hair framing her pale face. Her eyes, as cold and clear as green marbles, delivered everything from disinterest to contempt with a single glance. Her thin lips, the only spot of color on her face, were carefully outlined with the same rose lipstick she had worn all her life.

"Good morning, Mother." Jema dutifully went to her place at her mother's left hand and sat down. A maid appeared to pour coffee and set down a bowl of oatmeal and a small plate with a bran muffin. She picked up her glass of water and drank half before her thirst eased a bit.

Meryl did not immediately reply, concerning herself with adding some cream to her tea. She did not offer the tiny pitcher to Jema, who along with being diabetic was also lactose intolerant. "Did you sleep well?"

The cut inside her lip stung as she finished her water and started on the black, unsweetened coffee in her cup. "Yes, I did."

"I did not." Meryl picked up her fork and cut a small piece from her French toast. "Bradford had to give me a stomach treatment, and then I tossed and turned until dawn. Where were you last night?"

Jema accepted another glass of water from the maid and glanced at her. "Are you feeling better?"

"That is not the point." Meryl set down her fork. "I had thought the rebellious stage occurred only during adolescence, but your behavior indicates otherwise. What is next? Body piercings? Tattoos? Loud music played at ridiculous hours?"

"I'm twenty-nine," Jema said. "Too old for navel rings and Kid Rock."

Her mother sniffed. "Thank heavens."

"I wouldn't mind a tattoo, though." Jema held out her forearm and pretended to study it. "Maybe a little parrot on the inside of my wrist."

"I'd rather see Daniel amputate your arm," Meryl snapped.

Dr. Daniel Bradford walked into the dining room, where he stopped and looked at both women. "I hate walking in late on a conversation like this," he joked. "Especially when it involves me dismembering someone."

Jema smiled at Daniel, whose round, sturdy form, pleasant features, and silvered hair and beard made him look more like an off-duty Santa than a physician. "Mother was just giving me her opinion on tattoos."

"Disgusting, filthy things." Meryl gave him a cutting glance. "Sit down, Daniel."

"We were just talking about why I didn't get home on time last night. For which I am sorry, Mother," Jema tagged on quickly. She quickly drank some water from her refilled glass. "It was inconsiderate of me and it won't happen again."

"You didn't answer my question," Meryl snapped. "Where were you?"

Now she would have to lie again. "I went for a drive down by the lake after work. I left late, and I thought you would be in bed by the time I got home." Jema stared into her eyes and kept her expression guileless. "I'm sorry." She drained the rest of her water.

"There, Meryl," Daniel said as he took his place across from Jema. "It won't happen again."

"Of course it will. This is the third time this month. Did the two of you think I wouldn't notice?" Her mother picked up her teacup and then placed it back on the saucer, hard enough to make the china clink. "It's a man, isn't it? Why are you hiding him from me? Is he someone unsuitable? Someone you met at the museum?"

"No, Mother."

They all fell silent as the maid came in to serve Daniel and refill Jema's water glass a second time. *We can bicker all we like in private,* Jema thought, *but God forbid we say anything in front of the servants.* Sometimes she hated her life so much she could cheerfully run away from home.

Where would you go? The snide voice of her reason demanded. *What would you do? Live in a trailer park? Work at McDonald's? How would you even pay for your insulin?*

"I've never stopped you from inviting anyone to the house," Meryl said, picking up the conversation as soon as the maid retreated back into the kitchen. "I'd like to meet him. I can arrange a quiet dinner for us—"

"There is no man in my life, Mother."

"You two need to eat before it gets cold," Daniel said, picking up his own fork. "This French toast looks marvelous. It's always better with powdered sugar and strawberries, isn't it?" He made a face at Jema. "I'd share, but it would knock your blood sugar through the roof."

"I'm not a fool," Meryl said, completely ignoring the doctor's attempt to redirect the conversation. "My marriage to your father may have been brief, but I remember what it's like to be in love." She pursed her lips and at last dropped her gaze to fuss with her napkin. "I don't understand why you'd waste your time, but that's your affair, of course."

Jema closed her eyes for a moment. "I'm not seeing anyone."

"Would either of you like some juice?" Daniel broke in with forced heartiness. "I think you could manage a small glass, Jem." He eyed her water glass, which she had emptied a third time. "Unless you'd like to keep doing your excellent imitation of a camel about to cross the desert."

"No, thanks, Dr. Bradford. I don't know why I'm so thirsty." She tried to smile at him, but her mother's basilisk gaze had fixed on her again, and this time it was impossible to escape.

It was time for another of Meryl's lectures. Jema guessed it would be yet another version of "They only want you for your money."

"These men pay attention to you for only one reason," Meryl said, not disappointing her. "Your money. When I'm gone, you'll be one of the richest young women in the country." Meryl's expression didn't soften, but her voice did. "Have you told him about your condition? Mentioned anything about how it's deteriorating?"

Daniel's smile faded. "Meryl, I hardly think this is the time or place to—"

"Be quiet, Daniel. Jema, don't you see how that is the only thing they find attractive about you?" Meryl's voice became strained. "The fact that you'll be dead before you're forty—"

"There is no man." Jema couldn't stand another moment of this, and pushed out of her chair. "I was late getting out of work. I went for a drive. I came home from there. That's all it was. That's all it ever is."

Daniel got to his feet, his expression filled with something more immediate than sympathy. "Did you already take your morning injection?"

Jema was sick of being questioned. On the other hand, too much insulin could cause an adverse reaction, and Daniel was simply doing his job by asking.

"Yes." She picked up the bran muffin to tuck it in her pocket. "I'll eat this on the way to work, to be safe." She faced her mother. "I apologize for being late last night. You're right: It will probably happen again. Maybe it's time I made arrangements to get my own place."

"That isn't necessary, as you know." Meryl Shaw pushed away from the table as well. She could not rise, because an accident at a dig in Greece thirty years ago had left her paralyzed from the waist down. She used the switch on her battery-powered wheelchair to come closer. She lifted her chin. "I understand your need for . . . privacy." She said it the same way she would *prostitution*. "I know I can be demanding at times, but it is only out of concern for your welfare."

That was the only way her mother ever expressed her affection for Jema, and it preserved the distance between them like nothing else. Jema had tried to change that, but Meryl's emotions were too well guarded. *She lost her heart with my father*, she reminded herself. Once it had been enough to make Jema feel a helpless love for Meryl, but love had to be returned or it dwindled into misery.

All she had left was pity for her mother, and a sense of obligation that was becoming as weighty as her loneliness. It didn't help that most of what Meryl said was true.

No man would ever love her for who she was. All she could offer was her inheritance, and a disease that would ensure he could spend it with another woman while he was still young.

Dream of me.

There was no one for her to dream of. No one who would dream of her.

"I have to go to work." She left quickly, before Daniel or her mother could see her face, or guess how much she hated herself in that moment.

Chapter 6

JEMA'S BENZ. Jema.

Thierry tried to explain it away. Many women in Chicago could be named Jema. A dozen? A hundred? A thousand?

He knew only one.

Jema was the name of the woman he sought. A name had been listed in the list of people interviewed in Cyprien's file. Jema Shaw, an anthropologist who worked at the Shaw Museum, the same place the girl had been employed at night. This Jema Shaw was also the only daughter of James Shaw, the founder of the museum. She might know someone or something that could help him find the men responsible.

He could not tell if his little cat was the same Jema. There were no photographs of her. The only other information in the file about her had been an odd notation, written in a dark, heavy script: *Jema Shaw has acute diabetes and her health is presently in decline. Any contact with the Kyn must be first approved by Suzerain Jaus.*

Perhaps the warning had been made because of Jema Shaw's position in society, or to safeguard her from being casually used as nourishment. And he had used her, fed upon her, taken her without a second thought.

Had he harmed her? Was she even now being rushed to a hospital, where she would die from blood loss? He was sure he had stopped in time—but she was ill. Ill and he had fed on her.

The only woman who might be able to help him, and he had used her as if she were no one, nothing.

Thierry's thoughts curled like snakes in his head, alternately hissing and striking, from dawn until sunset. As soon as the sunlight had disappeared, Thierry left the alley and searched until he found a car with an ignition system he knew how to cross-wire. He did not like stealing vehicles, and he hated driving on the wrong side of the road, but a car would provide a faster means of escape if he encountered trouble in the city. Also, he could not go to the Shaw Museum too late; if Jema Shaw worked there, she might leave after the museum closed.

If his Jema from the night was Jema of the museum, and he had not harmed her, she would know him the moment he came near her. Through *l'attrait,* her body would recognize his.

Then, too, there was the matter of his appearance. He was not in any state to walk openly among humans, not with his stained, tattered garments and unkempt hair. They would think him one of the unfortunates who haunted their roadways and parks, and hurry away or summon their police.

He could not risk being challenged. Not when his shame over what he had done to Jema might send him into another bout of thoughtless, uncontrollable rage.

Thierry knew where the museum was, thanks to a folded paper he had found in one of the tourist kiosks located around the city. Even in France, he hadn't approved of the modern "information age." In his view, it was too much. One did not build a castle only to hand out plans of how to breach its walls. Yet the paper offered many details, including a simple street map, which guided him from Michigan Avenue through the side streets up to the very steps of the place itself. He parked in an alley a block away and walked down to it.

With each step, he looked for his little cat of a woman, praying she would not be Jema Shaw.

If one did not have the paper or know that the Shaw Museum housed Greek and Roman antiquities, one only had to look at the outside of the place. It was miniature replica of the Parthenon in Athens.

While he had been waiting in the alley, Thierry had taken time to read the entire pamphlet, grateful that he had been taught to speak, read, and write English during his years in the Temple. From the information offered, it appeared that the Shaw Museum had been created to house the artifacts recovered by James Shaw during his many archaeological digs in the Mediterranean.

Jema's father had done almost exactly as Lord Elgin, who had brought back statuary that eventually became known as his "marbles" from Greece. Indeed, Shaw had made more than two hundred forty trips to Greece and the surrounding Mediterranean to explore obscure sites and retrieve what the paper named "time-lost treasures." After shipping the artifacts back to America, he had commissioned a team of experts to restore and preserve what he had recovered. The museum had been built to display the fruit of the combined efforts.

Thierry, who had spent centuries admiring the vast collections in his native Louvre, found Shaw's efforts rather odd. Americans were endlessly fascinated with themselves, and took far more interest in their own rebellious, pithy history than that of the rest of the world. Why had Shaw gone to Greece and Italy to dig through theirs?

The museum offered three collections of Greek, Roman, and Etruscan art, whose ages spanned six thousand years of the respective civilizations' histories. Much of the artifacts apparently were unusual statuary, temple and ritual pottery, and other religious and iconic objects. The paper assured him that all of James Shaw's findings had been analyzed with more care than any that had ever been recovered in the history of his field, and that the museum was now regarded as one of the finest privately owned collections of Mediterranean antiquities in the Western world.

Perhaps the man had been seeking some proof of God, Thierry thought as he reconnoitered the building. Whatever James Shaw had been pursuing, he had left no ancient stone unturned in looking for it.

His sharp eyes caught the sight of a petite, dark-haired woman walking to the front of the museum. It was her, the little cat from last night. She went past two men in uniforms standing by an open door. Neither man glanced at her.

Jema Shaw.

Thierry paralleled her movements as she went from one side of the lobby to the other, retrieving papers from different offices. She passed directly in front of a woman vacuuming the carpets, and stepped around a young man emptying the trash cans. Like the guards, they gave her no notice.

Thierry frowned. These people were not ignoring her. They were behaving as if they didn't see her at all. Yet it was natural, even for humans, to look at anyone who came within a certain proximity. Jema was Shaw's daughter; she owned this property, and employed all these people. Where was their deference?

He could not enter the museum to speak to her; according to the paper it had closed twenty minutes before his arrival. There were phone numbers printed for museum admission and administration, and although Jema's name was not listed beside them, he decided to try calling the one for administration. The phone would enable him to make contact with her without inflicting *l'attrait* on her again.

Seeing the grandeur of the Shaw Museum also helped Thierry understand the notation in the file a little better. Jema Shaw was a woman of wealth and consequence. The Kyn were always careful to avoid such people. Fame and fortune drew too much attention to those who possessed them, and by extension, anyone around them.

The Darkyn could not afford to stand in the spotlight.

In America a pay phone waited on virtually every corner, and Thierry found one in a shadowy spot across from the museum. He was not familiar with American coins, so he fed a handful of them into the slot provided for payment before he dialed the main administration number. It rang four times, and then a male voice answered, "Shaw Museum security."

"I would speak with Jema Shaw," Thierry said quickly. "This is Henri Dubeck from France." The Dubecks had been in service to the Durands; Henri had been the cousin of the Durand family's *tresora*. He had first introduced Thierry to the Louvre, where he had worked as an assistant curator.

It had been four hundred years ago, so Thierry felt safe using Henri's name.

"I'm sorry, Mr. Dubeck, but Miss Shaw has just left for the evening," the man told him at the exact moment Thierry saw Jema exit the building through a side door. "May I take a message?"

He had to speak with her.

"Non, merci." Thierry hung up the phone and trotted down the block after Jema Shaw. He would have caught up, but an odd feeling made his steps slow. Watching her from behind gave him a strange, uncomfortable sense that he had done so in the past.

It was not possible. He knew he had never seen her before last night.

The fenced parking lot behind the museum had a gated entrance and exit with an EMPLOYEES ONLY sign posted between them. Jema walked into the lot and took one of the three vehicles left in it, an all-too-familiar Mercedes convertible. His final doubts vanished as she drove up to the gate and he saw the vanity plate on the front bumper.

JEMA'S BENZ.

Thierry went around the corner to retrieve his stolen vehicle, and used it to catch up with the Mercedes as it turned toward the immense lake just to the east of the city. Naturally that was where Jema would live; where there was water, there were the wealthy, with their large private houses and secured estates. Her father was dead, but there was no mention of her mother. Perhaps Jema lived with her. His little cat might even have a husband.

A husband who should be whipped for permitting her to wander through the city alone at night. Perhaps before he spoke to Jema, Thierry would speak to her husband.

Thierry was not surprised when the Mercedes drove up to one of the largest and most affluent-looking homes, or that high brick walls and electronic gates prevented him from following her onto the property. He drove past and took a short tour of Jema Shaw's neighbors. Nearly all of the homes showed signs of occupancy except the one bordering the north side of the Shaws' property. That house, a smaller but opulent contemporary mansion, had all of its windows shuttered. The wealthy often possessed more than one home; even during his human lifetime Thierry's parents had rarely spent more than a few months at Château Durand before retreating to their estate in Marseilles or the great house in Paris. There was a very good chance that no one presently resided in this one, and would not for some time.

Mansions had many rooms and furnishings; a thousand places where Thierry could conceal himself and no one would be the wiser. As shelter, it would serve him far better than an alley or a Dumpster.

The other bonus was that this house had not been gated or fenced in. The only thing that divided the two properties was the six-foot brick wall surrounding Jema Shaw's home. He could jump the wall with little effort, and find his way into Jema Shaw's bedchamber.

Once there, Thierry could find out everything Jema Shaw remembered about Luisa Lopez and him. She would never be the wiser, because he would do it all in her dreams.

August Hightower did not like surprises, but when Cardinal Stoss's replacement showed up at the diocese, he had no choice but to welcome him. One did not refuse to see the Lightkeeper, a man who held absolute power over Hightower and four thousand other Guardians of the Faith.

Cardinal Francis D'Orio had left the Vatican after the recent death of the pope. Like all Brethren, he was not a member of the Catholic Church or the priesthood, but like August Hightower, he pretended to be both in order to collect information and influence Rome to better serve the order. D'Orio had been so adept at his role-playing that he had quickly risen through the ranks of the church. Had Stoss not died in New Orleans, he and D'Orio might have given the new pope more competition during the selection for his office.

No Brethren had ever yet been elected pope, but there were many men like D'Orio and Hightower. Then, too, the Catholic Church had been plunged into its darkest era since World War II, and the new pope was a very old man.

Sometimes August liked to imagine himself on the throne in Vatican City. He felt sure that he would make an impressive Vicar of Christ. D'Orio, on the other hand, had taken over active leadership of the Brethren as their Lightkeeper and was now out of the running.

"Your Grace," Cabreri called him from the reception office

the morning after he had seen John Keller. "Cardinal D'Orio is here."

Hightower almost choked on the raspberry bear claw he was nibbling. Quickly he brushed at the crumbs that had fallen on his chest. "I'll see him in five minutes."

"He cannot wait, Your Grace," Cabreri said. "I am escorting him back to your office now."

The Lightkeeper arrived with an entourage of priests, monks, and bodyguards in discreet businessmen's attire. D'Orio entered Hightower's office with the silent confidence of one to whom doors were never closed, and after his men scouted the room, came out of the cluster of cassocks. He did not wear the traditional red of a cardinal, but affected plain Benedictine black. Only his black skullcap and his weathered, swarthy features, the latter of which Hightower had seen in photographs, identified him as the most important man in the room.

With them came Hightower's assistant, Father Carlo Cabreri, who smoothly performed the formal introductions. "Your Eminence, may I present Archbishop August Hightower. Bishop Hightower, Cardinal D'Orio, Lightkeeper of the Brethren."

August came forward and bent over D'Orio's proffered hand, pressing his lips with reverence to the older man's ring of office, a diamond cut into the shape of an hourglass. "Your Eminence, we are blessed by your presence."

"Such optimism. You've got crumbs on your mouth." D'Orio turned to the entourage, "Go count some candles." He glanced at Cabreri. "You too, Carlitto, and no listening over the intercom." As soon the bishop and the cardinal were alone, D'Orio sat down. "You're fatter than I thought you'd be. Have you tried the Atkins diet?" Before Hightower could answer, he gestured toward the nearest chair. "Sit, August. I have a lot to do on this trip, so we need to make the most of the next seven minutes."

Hightower didn't know whether to feel cheered or dismayed as he sat down. "You're an American."

"Born and raised in Brooklyn. My first parish was in Chinatown." D'Orio smiled, showing excellent dentures. "I'm older than you think, too. I was a priest when you were in diapers. Men in my family usually live past ninety with all their brains and most of their parts still working."

"I'm glad to hear it," Hightower said cautiously.

"I'm glad one of us is getting good news." D'Orio settled back in his chair and folded his hands over his sunken belly. "I'm told you met with Father John Keller yesterday. What I want to know is, why didn't you deliver him to us?"

"John Keller was my protégé," August said. "I've been bringing him along for nearly thirty years. When Cardinal Stoss decided to use him, I asked that he not be wasted. Stoss ignored my counsel, used him in an atrocious manner, and proceeded to throw him away."

D'Orio's laugh had a faint, metallic ring to it. "So you played catcher." He made a casual gesture. "You know how this works. Whatever the boy was to you, he's a threat to the Order now. Have him brought to the facility for processing."

"Please, Your Eminence." Hightower felt sweat bead on his face. "John Keller is the only connection we have left to his sister, Alexandra."

"The plastic surgeon."

"Precisely. You must know that she has gone over to the *maledicti,* and her talents will interfere greatly with our mission." Hightower chose his next words carefully. "Alexandra has also become the lover of Michael Cyprien, the one we believe will be Tremayne's successor. John Keller led Stoss and the Brethren directly to his sister and Cyprien in New Orleans. If Stoss hadn't planned the attack so poorly, we might have captured all of them alive."

"You would use your own protégé as bait." D'Orio's eyes glittered. "You've got very cold blood running through those veins, August."

"I am loyal only to the Order, Your Eminence, and for the Order I would do anything. You say that John no longer has any value to the Order." Hightower shrugged. "I disagree."

D'Orio nodded slowly, and turned his head when a gentle knock sounded on the door. "That is my two-minute warning. Where is Keller now?"

"I've arranged a counseling position for John at one of our recruitment shelters. He has no money, and no other sanctuary, so it is as good as a holding cell." The bishop tried not to let the relief he felt show in his voice. "Once he's settled in, he will want to make contact with his sister."

"He'll be monitored around the clock?"

August nodded. "Naturally."

"All right, August. I'll let you fish with a live worm." D'Orio stood as another knock sounded and the office door opened. "If Keller doesn't produce something in the next eight weeks, he's finished." He held out his hand.

It was less than Hightower had expected, but any reprieve was better than none. He had bought more time for himself and John. "Thank you, Your Eminence." He bent over and touched his lips to the diamond hourglass.

Father Carlo Cabreri returned to Hightower's office as soon as he had escorted the cardinal and his men to a limousine waiting outside. "His Eminence is not what we expected."

"His Eminence is a tenement boy from Brooklyn." Hightower rang the kitchen downstairs cook and ordered lunch be served an hour early. "That he came to see me personally is what concerns me now."

"You must be highly regarded in Rome," Cabreri said. "It is perhaps a show of appreciation for your many contributions to the mission."

"I am unknown in Rome," Hightower corrected him. "What's more, I have worked very hard to stay that way. This fiasco of Stoss's has ruined more than my plans for the Kellers."

"We have another, more immediate problem, Your Grace," Cabreri said. "Luisa Lopez has undergone eye surgery. A corneal transplant, and it seems it was successful."

"What?" Hightower glared. "Why was I not informed of this?"

"It was privately arranged by the mother. Our people in the hospital knew nothing about it until after the procedure had been performed." The bishop's assistant looked uneasy. "Jema Shaw has also become actively involved in Lopez's case."

"Jema?" Hightower went from furious to astounded. "What in God's name is she doing in the middle of this?"

"The museum job you obtained for Lopez," Cabreri re-

minded him. "While the girl was working there, apparently
Shaw became friendly with her."

"Jema Shaw, friends with Luisa Lopez? Hardly."

"Jema Shaw has also been moonlighting as a forensic consultant for the coroner's office," Cabreri told him. "Last week
she requested copies of all the Lopez case evidence reports.
Our men in the department have managed to stall the paperwork, but he can't shuffle it forever."

"How many lambs must I sacrifice, Lord?" August muttered. "How many hopes must I burn?"

Jema was part of another of August Hightower's special
projects, although she had never offered much promise. Jema
Shaw had come to his attention after her famous father's death
in Greece; August had hoped to make use of her once she had
come of age. Her poor health kept her from being of any con-
structive use as a breeder for the Order, but her inheritance
would have certainly enriched the Brethren's treasury—as
well as his own.

"Our people could make an anonymous report and lead
the police to the grave sites," his assistant suggested. "Once the
bodies are recovered, they will be quickly identified and the case
closed."

"Not if the police show Luisa mug shots," Hightower said
flatly. "She won't identify them as the men who attacked her."

"She has always refused to give a description to a sketch
artist," his assistant pointed out. "Perhaps she does not know."

She knew, August thought. "Luisa will never give the police a description, but she won't identify the wrong men, either." He paced for a few moments, turning over the
possibilities in his mind.

"I've never understood why you permit Lopez to live," his
assistant said, rather bitterly. "She has caused us nothing but
trouble since they pulled her from that fire."

Luisa Lopez was August Hightower's personal insurance
policy, but he would never tell Cabreri that. "You don't have to
understand, Carlo. You merely have to assure that the girl is
not touched."

"What about Jema Shaw?"

When God demanded a sacrifice, He wanted the best, not

the most convenient. August sighed. "She is expendable. Arrange it."

"There was an inventive fellow who used a chainsaw the other night," Cabreri said, almost cheerful now. "He's dead, but his accomplice is still at large. We have a description of him."

Hightower shook his head. "Too dramatic. Make it something simpler, so that it will not attract undue attention. A traffic accident."

Chapter 7

Valentin Jaus waited by the seawall that bordered his compound, as he did every evening just after dusk. More often than not he stood watching the private, empty stretch of rock that hemmed Lake Michigan, and used the time to sort out his tasks for the night. Occasionally he would walk a few yards down the uneven shoreline, always looking at the charcoal-gray water, never at the houses beyond the seawall.

Pride kept Jaus from doing many things another, weaker man might not be able to resist.

The *jardin* bodyguards did not accompany their suzerain to the lakefront, but remained near the house within earshot. The *jardin* did not usually take such chances with their leader, but Jaus had insisted on spending this interval each day alone. He was not foolish, and he was never unarmed, but he needed the space and opportunity to think. More so now that there was a chance he need never be alone again.

If it is as she says, my lady can truly be mine.

Cyprien had told him of Alexandra's determination to prove the Darkyn were not under a curse. The surgeon believed their condition was some sort of genetic disorder, originally caused by, of all things, a viral blood infection. It seemed incredible—unthinkable—but if she proved correct, it could mean that the centuries of hopelessness were over.

Hope, after so many years of accepting that there would never be any, was a kiss to the soul and a dagger to the heart.

Alexandra Keller was also seeking answers as to why she herself had survived exposure to Cyprien's blood and had become Darkyn. If she discovered how, and more humans could be safely changed, the Kyn could grow stronger. They would have to. If the Brethren discovered that the *vrykolakas* could once more breed, then there would be nothing to prevent a full-scale war between the ancient enemies.

Jaus had a more selfish reason for wanting Alexandra to succeed. A safe method to change human into Darkyn would not only give him a future with the woman he loved; it would save her life. And there, now, as if summoned by his very thoughts, his lady appeared, moving through the half-light toward the water. Jaus tensed the moment he saw her, and yet he felt a deep relief.

Unlike so many others, this night he would not spend strangled by his solitude.

She walked down the wooden steps from the edge of her property to the cluster of large stones that formed a natural ridge bisecting the two hundred yards of shore in front of her home. As always, she went to the rocks and perched on the largest and flattest of them, and looked out at the water.

It was her favorite place, which was why he came out here each night on the pretense of needing time to think, in order to watch it.

Jaus had never set out to fall in love. Human women provided nourishment and sex, but their short life spans made anything else inadvisable. Jaus had never been expected to love, either; he had been born and raised to manhood in a time when men did not feel such emotions, not toward their wives or even their mistresses.

Men loved their horses, their swords, and their liege lords, usually in that order.

Many men of his class married women. It was an expected duty, performed to obtain property, produce heirs, and secure family fortunes. His contemporaries regularly took mistresses to give their delicate lady wives relief from the physical demands of holy matrimony, and to enjoy sex with a ripe, willing woman. Women had never tempted Jaus beyond a few hours of sweaty pleasure, so he did not regret forsaking them when he took his vows and became a knight of the Temple.

Would she think differently of me if she knew I had been a priest for fifteen years? An inane question, that; he thought of her as his lady, but suspected she rarely thought of him, if at all. *Would she share my life if I find some way to save hers?*

He had a terrible suspicion that he was not above using her gratitude, or blackmailing her with it, to get what he wanted.

Jaus climbed over the short seawall and made his way toward the rocks. Despite all his caution and longings and endless inner debates, this was when he felt most ridiculous. He had come to this country to acquire power. A man in his position had thousands of responsibilities, and no time to indulge such useless pursuits. He also knew nothing would come of going to the rock and speaking to his lady. He never dared to do anything else.

Still, he went to her, as helpless as a storm-tossed ship driven to shoals.

"Good evening, Miss Shaw," he said as soon as she noticed him approaching.

"Mr. Jaus." She turned and smiled. "How have you been?"

"Very well, thank you."

Their conversations rarely varied from the polite, impersonal greetings exchanged by passing acquaintances. Before and after such meetings, Jaus often thought of many clever remarks he might have made, but whenever he spoke to Jema, none of them would come out of his mouth.

It would help if she gave him permission to use her given name, but she never had, and the rigid manners he had been taught as a boy prevented him from using it without her leave. Thus they had remained Mr. Jaus and Miss Shaw. It made Valentin want to dash his own head against the rocks. No, that was not precisely true. It made him want to scoop her into his arms and carry her back to his house.

There he would show her how he had been for the last twelve years. There he would teach her exactly how he wished her to say his name.

His eyes studied Jema's calm, thin face. She had not the faintest idea of what he wanted to do to her, or how often he had fantasized about it. How much he wanted to peel the dull clothes she wore from her body and worship it with his hands and mouth. How without a qualm he would hand over his *jardin* for a single night in which he could kiss her, and touch her, and fuck her until dawn—

This need was turning him into a mindless fiend.

The shame Valentin felt over his lust for Jema did nothing to banish it. The thought of having her caused his fangs to slide out of the twin holes in his palate, fully extending, aching with need. He breathed in deeply, willing his cock not to do the same thing.

I am not an animal at the mercy of my needs. I am a man, an honorable man, and this is my lady. I will conduct myself accordingly.

"I think it might snow this weekend," Jema said, tilting her head back to look at the sky. "Then we'll be stuck indoors until April."

Here he was, literally shaking with desire for her, and she was speaking of the weather. She was brilliant and charming and entirely engaging, and he loved her with a passion that left him speechless, but she was also, as the American saying went, totally clueless.

"Are you ready for winter?" she was asking.

Jaus hated the long, cold months, because they deprived him of these chance encounters. So did her disease, which was draining the life out of her year by year with slow, relentless cruelty. The reminder of the little time they had left together made his fangs retreat, but for the first time, hope would not permit him to bid her good night. "Would you care to walk with me?"

She gave him a short, startled glance, and then suddenly jumped down from the rock. "Lead the way."

Jaus did not lead her, and in fact slowed his steps so as not to hurry her. His first walk with Jema was going to last as long as he could make it.

Why did I not ask her to do this before tonight? He sensed the scant inches that separated them, a bare handbreadth of air. His insides clenched. *Before tonight I had more sense than to draw this close to her.*

Jaus had never dared touch his lady. His curse, and his talent, made it too dangerous.

"I love the lake at night," Jema said. "It's so quiet, and I can always sleep a little better after I've walked down to look at the water. It's hypnotic or something." She glanced at him. "Is that why you come down here, or are you more into the exercise?"

He came down for her, of course. He couldn't have her, and he refused to touch her, but that didn't stop him from seizing a few minutes in her company.

I am a fool, Jaus thought as he watched her hips move as she walked, and imagined them welded beneath his, framed in the blue satin of his bed linens. His fingers digging into the slight curves as he sank into her. *A fool, and a masochist.*

She was waiting for him to answer.

"It is very tranquil," Jaus said. "I find it relaxes me." This close to her, he could see new changes that were not evident from a distance, and he focused on them instead of the siren song of her hips. "Are you feeling well? You seem more slender than the last time we met."

"Skinny, you mean." Jema made an adorable face. "My appetite has been terrible. I never feel like eating anything. I just force it down because I know I have to."

He could sympathize, but he doubted she would appreciate his dietary difficulties. No, if she knew what he needed to live, it would send her screaming into the night.

She gave him the same swift scrutiny. "You, on the other hand, never change. You always look like you just came from the gym."

The gym. Jaus groped for the meaning of the word. *Some sort of sports facility?* Was his hair disordered? Were his clothes wrinkled? "I am not certain of your meaning."

"You're so fit." She gestured toward one of his arms, the forearm exposed by his sleeve, which he had rolled up to make his appearance more casual, more human. "You must work out every day to keep in such good shape."

Now he understood the reference. "I am fortunate to have a . . . happy metabolism." He could smell blood on her breath when she spoke, and it was terribly distracting. Had she cut her lip, or had a tooth pulled? No such matter had been reported to him. "I wonder if I might impose upon you."

"Impose?" She stopped and turned to him, her expression openly curious.

It reminded him of the first time he had seen Jema. Now, standing here and staring into her face—they were exactly the same height—Jaus wished he could go back in time to that moment. If he could, he would not have let her go. He would have abducted her, taken her out of the country that very day. Over the centuries he had reclaimed his family's vast holdings and influence in Austria; no one would challenge him there.

Fantasies of having Jema to himself had filled many of his lonely hours.

It would never happen. Jaus's obsessive desire for Jema was too dangerous. Such primal, reckless lust was just the sort of thing that sent the Kyn into thrall. Wanting her to this degree made her automatically off-limits to him.

He would not risk killing the only woman he would ever love.

"Mr. Jaus?" Jema was saying. "Is something wrong?"

Her voice shook him out of his thoughts as a hard hand might drag him from slumber. "Forgive me; I was gathering sheep," he lied.

"Wool." At his blank look, she added, "The expression is 'woolgathering.'"

"Ah, yes." He had mastered her language but not its idioms. Yet another reminder of how different they were. "Miss Shaw, each year I hold a masque for my friends and business associates. I would like it very much if you were to attend."

"A masque." She sounded puzzled. "Is that like a Mardi Gras thing?"

"A little, perhaps." He inclined his head. "One wears a costume and dances to music. It is to be held on the night of October thirty-first."

"Oh, a Halloween party." She laughed, delighted. "I forgot it was so close." Her happiness abruptly ebbed. "Is it just for couples? I'm not seeing anyone, so I'd have to come alone."

He would have to go carefully now. "I, too, am presently unattached. Perhaps you would consent to having me serve as your escort as well as your host?"

"I guess." She sounded puzzled. "Are you sure? I mean, I've seen some of your girlfriends. They're all so beautiful."

Girlfriends? She was speaking of the women Sacher procured for his nourishment and occasional entertainment. What excuse could he make? "None of them are available."

"Okay. I might as well celebrate my last night in my twenties; I'll be thirty the next day." She gave him a wry look. "But you already know that."

Each year on November first, Jema's birthday, Jaus sent a bouquet of camellias he had raised himself to Shaw House. It was a long-standing tradition.

"Yes." He smiled. "I have been saving a special birthday gift for you. Perhaps you will like it better than the flowers."

"Oh, but I love the ones you send," she assured him. "It wouldn't feel like my birthday without them." She gave him a mischievous glance. "What could be better than your beautiful camellias?"

"Something that will always make you think of them," he assured her.

"I can see her; she's down by the lake," Daniel Bradford said, looking through the window facing the dark lake. "I think your neighbor is talking to her. The short, blond fellow, the one whose name I can never remember."

"Valentin Jaus. Of course it would be him. He trots after her like a dog whenever she goes down there." Meryl sipped a dainty measure of bourbon from her glass. "He's walking her to the steps, isn't he?"

"He's not chasing her around them." Daniel chuckled. "I've seen the man from a distance, mostly in his car when it comes and goes, but I never realized how short he is. He's the exact same size as Jema." His voice grew thoughtful. "Is he interested in her?"

"He's nosy and pushy," Meryl told him. "That's all."

He might have been more, but Meryl had taken steps long ago to assure he never would be. She despised Valentin Jaus as much she had as his pompous ass of a father. Valentin Sr. had harassed her for years, calling to check on Jema when she was younger, offering his help where it wasn't wanted, and sending his ridiculous flowers to the house every year on Jema's birthday. It was as if the older Valentin had been trying to taunt Meryl: *Happy birthday to your daughter, Jema. If not for me, she'd be dead.*

Meryl had been overjoyed when the old man had died during a trip to Europe. Then his son came to take possession of the estate, and picked up right where his father had left off.

"You're brooding again," Daniel told her, coming over to take the glass of liquor out of her hand. "You're also drinking too much."

"You're right. What do I have to worry about? She'll probably live forever. You two can bury me." Meryl heard the soft buzz of the zone alarm as a door opened and closed at the back of the house. The sound had a Pavlovian effect; she instantly relaxed.

"There, you see?" Daniel patted her hand. "She's home, safe and sound."

"Don't patronize me." Keeping Jema safe and whole had been one of the two greatest torments in Meryl's life. Every day was precious; she held on to them and Jema with tight, unyielding determination.

Jema's job at the museum was an unnecessary risk. However, the situation had been unavoidable. It had been the result of the professional indiscretions of a renowned anthropologist in Germany, who had been forced to retire after allegations that included botching and falsifying the carbon dating of historically important specimens; every reputable museum in the world was reexamining their inventories.

Meryl Shaw had resisted the idea of having her husband's artifacts subjected to reexamination, but in the end was forced to concede to the board of directors. That they had offered the job to Jema only added insult to injury.

"Your father sacrificed his life for the museum," Meryl had told her. "A man doesn't do that to perpetuate fraud. Refuse the position."

Jema, who had followed the international uproar over the counterfeiting of antiquities, had defied Meryl. She felt there were too many sites around the world "salted" with artifacts of dubious origin in order to attract archeological teams, and she saw the job as a way to keep her father's name and reputation from ever being questioned.

The irony was that Jema had no idea that her father had committed one very large professional indiscretion. One that, if it became public knowledge, would ruin his name forever.

At least now I can get some work done. Meryl flicked the switch on her wheelchair and maneuvered it over to her desk. "Leave me alone, Daniel."

He replaced the stopper on the crystal liquor decanter. "No more bourbon, Meryl. Your ulcer has taken enough abuse this week." He bent as if to kiss her cheek, and then thought better of it and straightened. "I'll see you in the morning."

Meryl waited until Bradford had left before unlocking her desk drawer and removing the inventory files. In them were detailed lists of every artifact that James Shaw had brought back from his digs.

"It has to be in the last lot from Athos." She shuffled the lists and studied the one marked LOT A-G240. "But where?"

The Athos dig had been the last she and James had worked together before his death. When he had first proposed the site, she had thought it a complete waste of their time.

"We won't find a village; it's in the middle of nowhere," she protested when her husband had shown her the position of the find. "Maybe some exile set up a goat farm, but there was nothing else even built there."

James insisted they go to Athos anyway. He had found a mention of the village charged with a sacred duty in a prayer scroll taken from another, more prestigious dig. The scroll hinted that the villagers bargained each year with the gods to win the gift of immortality. James also became convinced that there was an object involved, and after many comparisons to other ancient texts, he began to regard it as a Greek version of the Holy Grail.

"They were told to make this tremendous climb up a mountain every year, just after the harvest. Once they reached the mountain's summit, they presented the homage to the gods. If the gods were pleased, they would transform the homage into a powerful icon that granted one of the villagers immortal life." He laughed at her expression. "Yes, I know to you it's nothing but a myth. But the homage was real, material. Even Hesiod wrote of it, describing it when transformed by the Gods as a source of great power and beauty."

"It sounds like an early version of the Prometheus legend," Meryl said, trying to hold on to her temper, "with immortality instead of fire. What happened to this homage? Why did the ritual stop?"

"The usual: greedy gods versus greedy mankind. Too many immortals were made," James said. "The king of the gods became angry at the power they wielded over other humans. So he made the homage turn immortals' blood into poison, and cause their touch to be deadly to ordinary men."

"I suppose their hair became snakes, and their faces so ugly that to look upon them would turn you into stone?" Meryl demanded. "For God's sake, darling, listen to yourself. You're a scientist. You can't seriously start believing in fairy tales now."

"You'll see," was all James would tell her after that.

From the beginning, the Athos dig had a series of disasters. They had difficulty finding men willing to work the deserted mountainside site, as it was regarded by the locals as a combination of holy ground and the gates to hell itself. The men they could hire worked at a snail's pace, walking off the site at twilight and never returning. Then there was James's insistence on searching every cave they found no matter how small or insignificant; the mountain was riddled with them.

Meryl had refused to go back to the States when she discovered she was pregnant. Her family had disowned her the moment she'd announced her engagement to James, so they would have nothing to do with her. James was an orphan, so there was no one on his side to help her with the birth. Going back to Chicago would mean sitting in an empty house for the next seven months.

No, James had put this baby inside her, and Meryl was determined to stay with him until it was born.

"Women all over the world work up until the minute they give birth," she told her husband when he argued with her about remaining at the site. "Besides, this is going to be our life. Our child will go where we go."

It was toward the end of her pregnancy that Meryl noticed

her husband was slipping away several nights during the week, waiting until he thought she'd fallen asleep before sneaking out of camp. She had tried to follow him more than once, but James always seemed to sense it and would circle around to come back to camp, acting as if he'd gone for nothing more than a pleasant evening stroll.

James had a new woman on the side, of course. Meryl had never enjoyed sex, so she didn't resent the other women. She had ignored them; she could ignore this one. And she had, until the day James found the Phaenon Cave.

Meryl stared down at the inventory list in her hands, her eyes wide and unseeing. Everything that had gone wrong in her life had started the moment James broke through the seal of the cave. She should have never stayed with him. If she had listened and come back to Chicago, she wouldn't be in this wheelchair, or this mess.

"This is it, this is the one," James had said as soon as the men had cleared the brush back from the rough slabs of slate rock that had been stacked and crudely mortared together to seal the entrance. "I knew it."

Meryl had been in a terrible mood. Her back had been killing her ever since she'd dragged herself out of her tent at dawn to accompany James to the dig. Because she had never had a child, she hadn't recognized the constant ache as labor pain.

"It will be just like the fifty other caves we've unsealed on this godforsaken rock," she warned him. "I'm beginning to think someone in nine thousand B.C. had a very twisted sense of humor."

Unlike the other caves they had explored, this one presented a unique set of problems. When the top half of the sealing stones were removed, so was the support for the soft soil above them, which immediately began to crumble. A support beam and struts had to be hastily fashioned and wedged into place before the entrance could be completely cleared.

Then there was the smell. Meryl was used to subterranean gases, but this one was particularly vile, as if the interior were filled with sulfur and something that had drowned and rotted in it. Every man who tried to enter the cave grew sicker with every step; after a few feet their eyes began streaming and they began to choke. Even James couldn't bear the stench.

"At last," Meryl said as she sourly observed the workers rushing into the brush to vomit, as she had every morning for the first three months of her pregnancy, "there is some justice in the world."

James refused to leave the site unexplored, and fashioned a mask for himself out of a cloth soaked in water and a pair of protective goggles.

"I'll send for a set of scuba gear if I must," he told Meryl just before walking in the cave, "but this should get me in far enough to see what's back there."

Unable to recall another moment of the worst day in her life, Meryl picked up the phone and called the museum.

"Yes, Dr. Shaw?"

"Roy, I need lot two-forty taken out of storage and brought over to the house tomorrow," she said. "I'm having a small get-together for some museum board members and I'd like to set up a temporary display. Pack it the usual way and have it here by seven."

"I'd like to help you out, Dr. Shaw, but the head curator told us nothing was to be removed from storage until the inventory and cataloging was finished," the security guard said.

Meryl forced a laugh. "Roy, I own the museum and its contents. I'll take whatever I like out of it."

"That's something I've been meaning to talk about with you." Roy's tone changed. "The curator and I've been talking about things, and I asked him some questions. Lately I've been taking a lot of things out of here for you, so I wanted to cover myself. Just in case I was doing something that might get me in trouble."

Meryl's hand tightened on the receiver. "That's really none of your business."

"The curator set me straight about a bunch of things," Roy continued smoothly. "Things nobody around here seems to know. Like who really owns this place. You understand what I'm saying, Dr. Shaw?"

She understood that she'd been an idiot to trust a security guard with a ninth-grade education. "What do you want?"

"A little appreciation would be nice," the guard told her. "You could start showing it when I bring this lot over."

Meryl opened the second drawer to her desk. Inside was a strongbox with the cash she kept for household use. Next to the box was a .22, small enough to tuck under the fold of her lap blanket. "I'll have it waiting for you."

Chapter 8

The owners of the property bordering Jema Shaw's home had installed a very sophisticated alarm system on their mansion, one that prevented anyone from breaking into the house. They also had many conveniently located decorative trees among their artful landscaping. Once Thierry discovered how extensive the security system was, he selected a tree, climbed it, and broke off a suitable branch. When he allowed the branch to fall, it struck one of the windows on the side of the house; not enough to break the glass but with adequate force to set off the motion sensor attached to it.

Modern humans regarded drawbridges, guardhouses, and moats as archaic, but Thierry could not think of any that had ever been defeated by a mere stick.

Predictably, the police came two minutes after the branch struck the glass, followed by a truck from the security monitoring company. A technician in pristine overalls stayed at the gate while the police checked the house. Once they had determined the house had not been entered, the technician discovered the cause and reset the system.

"I'll call the Nelsons from the office; they're over in Australia until January," the tech told the two uniformed officers. "This kind of thing happens all the time."

Thierry, perched in another tree that concealed his presence and gave him an unobstructed view of the exterior alarm system control pad, waited until everyone had left before dropping down to the ground and entering the pass code to disarm the system.

That left entering the house. He was tempted to break the

window, but shattered glass or a missing pane might be noticed by the groundskeepers or neighbors. Also, it would allow any-one else access to the mansion. Instead he climbed to the top of the house, where he found an attic vent large enough for him to squeeze through. Once inside, he replaced the grille, worked his way downstairs, and reset the alarm system.

The Nelsons had filled their home with modern, rather ugly furnishings, but they had thoughtfully kept the water as well as the electricity on. Thierry went first to the largest bath and spent an hour in the enormous shower, scrubbing himself clean.

The layers of dirt and dried blood on his body turned the water black, then brown, until it finally ran clear. The stab wounds on his torso had closed, but the areas were still tender to the touch. Also, the brief amount of effort breaking into the mansion had exhausted him.

He would have to hunt tonight.

Thierry dried off with one of the thick, salmon-colored tow-els left hanging in the bath chamber and walked naked into the next room. It apparently belonged to the lady of the house, who possessed an incredible amount of cosmetics, perfumes, and toiletries. Among them Thierry found a pair of sharp scis-sors and used them to trim the hair that had grown over his eyes. He didn't have the skill to give himself a proper haircut, so he trimmed the rest to what he considered a reasonable length and bound it back with an elastic band. Unless it grew suddenly, which it sometimes did without warning during the daylight hours, he would pass as a normal American male.

He was like most Darkyn and did not grow facial hair, so shaving was unnecessary. He was glad, because using the elec-tric beard cutter the man of the house had left behind was be-yond him.

Clothes presented the next problem. Thierry was not a small man, and Mr. Nelson, while almost the same height, ob-viously weighed fifty pounds less. After trying on several gar-ments, Thierry found a pair of trousers with a pleated front that were not skintight on him, and a dress shirt that he could but-ton up to the center of his chest. He covered these with one of Nelson's knee-length Armani coats. It was too tight across his shoulders, but with the colder temperatures no one would question it.

Half the day had passed by the time Thierry turned out the lights and stretched out on the too-soft bed in the Nelsons' master bedroom. He nearly jumped out of it when he saw his reflection staring down at him from the mirror fixed to the ceiling. Why the devil did they have that up there? Did they dress on their backs?

So they can watch themselves, my love, Angelica's ghost purred in his mind. *Remember how much I wanted one? Seeing yourself while you're having sex is erotic.*

Thierry rolled out of the bed and dragged the thick coverlet from it, laying it out on the floor well out of sight of the mirror. He needed to rest, not think of her. He had to plan how to get into Jema Shaw's house. There was no time to indulge his madness.

What will you do after you find the girl's attackers? Where will you go? Who would welcome a madman into their society?

Michael should have killed him while he was his captive. It would have put a proper end to this miserable life of his.

Thierry closed his eyes, curled his hand around his dagger, and thought of Jema Shaw. He knew nothing of her except what he had shared with her in the alley. She was wealthy, ill, and had befriended Luisa. That indicated she probably had a kind nature. The fact that he had already fed on her underscored the need to be very careful with her.

He could not take her blood again, under any circumstances.

At dusk he left the Nelsons' and walked to where he had hidden his stolen car, and drove back to the city in time to enter the museum. It had begun snowing outside, so Thierry did not remove his coat once inside. A young man sitting at a desk in the lobby was the only one to speak to him, and he simply asked for five dollars.

"You do not have your own money?" Thierry asked him, perplexed.

The clerk frowned. "It's the price of admission, sir."

One had to pay, of course. Thierry forgot this was one way in which humans made their living. Fortunately he had sorted out what money he had left back at the Nelsons', so he handed over one bill marked with a five.

"Thank you." He offered a folded paper, much like the one Thierry had found in the tourist kiosk. "We're closing in an hour, sir."

He examined the paper with interest. This one showed the layout of the interior. From the lobby he was evidently free to wander the open areas and special exhibit rooms.

"Is Miss Jema Shaw here?" he asked the clerk.

"No, this is Miss Shaw's night off." The young man gave him a tentative smile. "Can I call someone else to help you, sir?"

What an accommodating lad. Thierry shuddered to think of allowing him to guard his family and treasures, and then was overwhelmed by another realization. *My family is lost to me. Jamys, Liliette, Marcel. All lost.* "It isn't necessary."

Thierry was in no mood to admire six thousand years of sculptures, pots, and relics, but he had to admit the collection was as impressive as the museum that housed it. Only a man who appreciated the world's best classical art forms could have aspired to such a feat. Only a man with a great fortune could have made it happen. Shaw had indeed left behind a remarkable legacy for his daughter.

But will she live long enough to enjoy it? Thierry wondered. He knew almost nothing about diabetes, but had gleaned enough from television campaigns and newspapers to know that it was a scourge without a cure.

Ill, and I fed on her.

He noted the three security guards posted at various positions throughout the museum, and the cameras that tracked back and forth, sweeping the areas around the exhibits. Jema Shaw's office was not marked on the paper, but there was a notation about a lab, storage, and offices on the basement level that were not open to the public. An employee elevator was located near the lavatories, however, where there was only one security camera. When the lens turned away from him, he slipped around the corner and took the elevator to the basement.

The museum's lower level contrasted sharply with its upper

exhibit rooms. Here everything smelled of dust, paper, and soil. The air was so dry Thierry could imagine himself back in Palestine, crossing an arid plane. No cameras here, either, something he thought rather stupid. There were as many treasures here as above, if not more. Why were they not better guarded?

He wandered through two rooms until he found a tiny office with Jema Shaw's name marked on the door. Inside he found a cramped, horrible space with a faint, unpleasant chemical odor and an exquisite little desk facing a wall.

Americans. They should be physically restrained from decorating a place of business. What sort of office was this? Why had she been given such a dismal corner? There was hardly enough room in this place for a cat. He could barely pick up her scent here.

His gaze was drawn to the painting over the desk. It did not fit the room any more than the desk did, but the more he stared at it, the more it captivated him.

Or would have, if a security guard had not stepped into the room. "Excuse me, sir, but what are you doing in here?"

Thierry turned and sized the man up. He was older, heavier, and unarmed. Healthy enough, although he smelled of fear. "Forgive me," he said, deliberately assuming a bucolic look and deepening his accent. "I was looking for the lavatory, yes?"

The scent of gardenias permeated the air.

"It's not here, buddy." The guard breathed in deeply, and his expression became confused. "That's nice. I mean, you'll have to come with me."

"Of course, *mon ami.*" Thierry smiled, not moving. "But you are looking tired. You should rest for a moment before we go upstairs."

"I should." The guard almost did, and then rubbed a hand over his face. "I'd better . . ." He tugged a radio from his pocket and stared at it and then Thierry. "I'd better . . ."

"Sit down," Thierry suggested.

"Yeah." The guard wandered to the chair at the desk and sat down. "Why am I so tired?"

"It is a difficult thing, is it not?" Thierry rested a hand on the man's thinning hair. "Working this late when you should be sleeping."

The guard nodded heavily, his eyes half-closed. He tried to yawn, but couldn't. "Hate my shift. Always makes me . . ." His head sagged forward.

Thierry picked up the man's arm and unbuttoned the cuff of his shirt. His pulse was slow but strong. He waited a short time, willing his own need to ebb, before he used his fangs on the man's wrist, and then only to take a small amount of blood.

Drinking blood directly from the source was always dangerous. The Kyn had discovered that it was better to separate the blood from the human and then drink it at a distance, to prevent any chance of inducing thrall and rapture. He had no time to do so, however, and nothing in which to put the blood.

Thierry found a box of plasters in Jema's desk and used two to cover the punctures he had left in the guard's arm. He also found a box of sugar-free lemon drops, a bookmark made of lace, and beneath a heavy text on geology, a small stack of novels. Some were classic literature; others were modern novels. All were stories of love.

Are you a romantic, little cat? He found the fact that she hid the candy and the books in her desk rather endearing. He had even read one of the books—*Pride and Prejudice*—although he had thought many of the heroine's problems would have been solved if someone had simply strangled her mother.

Forcing himself to attend to the matter at hand, Thierry turned to the guard and placed a hand on his neck. With such contact, he could rouse the man's sleeping mind long enough to hear and accept a suggestion. "You hurt your arm on nails sticking out from a packing crate. Seeing the blood made you feel dizzy. You put on the plasters before you sat down. There was no one in Miss Shaw's office."

Hurt my arm, the guard's mind responded. *No one in Shaw's office.*

After glancing at the painting again, Thierry left the sleeping man and hurried upstairs. A guard waiting by the lobby desk began to say something, until Thierry was only a few steps away. Then he and the lobby clerk seemed to become instantly, completely bewildered.

"Good night," Thierry said, and was out of the doors before their expressions cleared.

The snow was falling more rapidly now, and the night had turned bitterly cold. Thierry returned to the lakefront, where he concealed the car and walked through the snow-covered lawn at the back of the Nelsons' property to the wall that stood between it and Jema Shaw's home. He jumped the wall easily enough, but locating her in the enormous house was going to require some effort. She had a security system, although this one was not nearly as sophisticated as the Nelsons'. There were also French doors all around the house, and they were the easiest to open from outside.

Thierry had no idea why they were called French doors. His native countrymen weren't stupid enough to put them in their homes.

He climbed up one corner of the house, using the deep depressions between the decorative rock casements as hand- and footholds. The roof was peaked, but not sharply, and the eaves extended out far enough to allow him to hang over and look into the second-story windows.

He had looked into three before he saw a patch of snow beyond the roof glitter with light. Quickly he drew back until he saw the source—a window with a balcony at the back of the house. He leaned over to look down, in time to see Jema Shaw closing the curtains inside. A few seconds later, the light in the room went out.

There she is. He waited five minutes, and then ten, hoping that was enough time for her to drift off. He did not want to waste this opportunity.

Thierry jumped down from the roof and landed on the small, rounded balcony outside Jema Shaw's bedroom. The French doors here had none of the security devices attached to them, as on the first and second floors. Only a brass hook-and-eye lock stood between her and the rest of the world.

Rather than feel grateful, he became angry. *Does no one in this place care for her safety?* He took out his dagger and inserted the blade in the seam of the frame, and then hesitated. *If she is awake, she will see the window open. She will cry out.*

He could not jump from here to the ground without risking

broken bones. Alex, Cyprien's doctor, was far away in New Orleans. There would be no one to heal his wounds this time. Only hunters probably looking to take his head, or the monsters who would put him back on their racks . . .

Cyprien might call off the hunt, but there would always be Brethren waiting.

Fear's many long teeth bit into him. *Never again.* He tightened his hand around the hilt of his dagger. As long as Thierry had the blade, he was safe.

The lace curtains had been drawn and the lights switched off, but that did not guarantee that Jema Shaw was sleeping. He listened for movement from within but heard nothing. Silently he pressed one hand against a frost-whitened pane of glass, closing his eyes to block out the snow falling around him.

Where are you, little cat? He had not used his talent to search for a human unknown to him since New Orleans. There he had been so deep in the madness that he could not remember reaching into the minds of the priests. Jema was not like the other humans he approached; her illness made it vital that he not hurt her. *Are you sleeping? Do you dream now?*

When Thierry's talent first touched a human mind, he saw color in his own. A glimmer of silver appeared inside his head when he found her, deep in slumber but not yet dreaming.

There. For the rest of it, he would need to touch her.

The blade slid easily into the seam. Thierry lifted the lock's hook up from its eye catch, and then eased the door open an inch. Now he could hear the whisper of her breathing, the slow beat of her heart. He shrugged out of his borrowed coat, leaving it and the snow covering it out on the balcony, and slipped inside.

Unlike the rest of the mansion, this room had none of the trappings of wealth. Jema had been given but a few cast-off pieces of furniture, their paint scratched, their wood scarred and stained with age. Two squat oil lamps, the sort he had not seen in a century or more, sat as dark and cold as the room. He could smell that she had burned a few candles, pitifully scented to imitate the fragrance of real flowers. No wood in the fireplace; no comforting blaze to warm her. Even the lace of the curtains appeared yellowed and old.

The shabbiness of the room angered him. *This is how they treat the great Dr. Shaw's daughter? Like a poor relation, banished to a garret?*

Thierry walked over to the bed. It was too small, and all that covered the sleeping girl was a sheet and a faded, patched blanket. She huddled beneath them, motionless but for the slight rise and fall of her chest. One hand lay open-palmed next to her cheek, the other tucked with a fold of the blanket under her chin.

She even sleeps like a cat. Tenderness flooded through him as he reached down to draw back the edge of the coverlet. She wore a nightdress of soft material printed with tiny blue flowers. One tug on an ivory ribbon released the collar and bared the slim column of her throat to his gaze.

There, beneath the delicate skin, the pulse of her lifeblood danced.

The sight caused Thierry's *dents acérées* to emerge, and his hunger swelled. Before he had taken Jema in the alley, he had not touched a woman in weeks, not since losing control with Cyprien's *sygkenis*. He no longer trusted himself, so human men provided his sole nourishment during his journey to Chicago. There was no temptation of thrall with them.

Having tasted Jema brought back what it felt to have a woman under his hands. To hear the sounds she made as he took what he needed from her. To give her what little he could in return—

That was charade, darling. Angelica's ghost patted his cheek. *All part of the torture.*

Thierry would never trust a woman again. *But Jema is human, not Darkyn. And she is ill. As long as all we share are dreams . . .*

Thierry pressed the tips of three fingers to the side of her throat. When he closed his eyes, the silvery color of her mind was there, glowing like the moon on water, deepening as she responded to his talent and moved across the dark borders and into the realm of dreams.

Thierry followed her and waited until her dream took form,

for only then could he become a part of it. Colors and light flooded his mind, forming and shaping themselves to Jema Shaw's specifications. It was always disconcerting at first, to be so completely immersed in the dark and then find himself—

In Jema Shaw's bedroom.

Unlike the dreaming girl, Thierry was still fully conscious and aware of his physical reality, so it was as if he had become his own twin. Yet in the dream, he saw Jema's room quite differently. Everything that he considered worn, worthless, and insulting to the daughter of the house was actually held in great affection. Jema treasured the old things around her; had in fact collected them carefully over the years. Her prize possession was the ancient blanket under which she slept, something she regarded as priceless as a museum artifact. More so, for it had been cut and sewn and sandwiched together by the hands of her father's mother, a woman who had died before Jema's birth.

Not castoffs, he thought, trying to understand what he saw through her eyes. *Antiques. Heirlooms.*

In the real bedroom, Jema slept on. In the dream realm, she sat up and looked straight at him. "Hello. Who are you?"

Questions in dreams had to be answered with caution. The wrong words could cause the sleeper to awaken suddenly. Thierry did not want Jema to fear his presence, or anything about him. If she did, she would never tell him that which he needed to know. Before he moved out of the shadow concealing him, he conjured a hooded cloak out of the dream realm and drew it around him[LC6], so that she could not see his face. "I am whoever you wish me to be."

She laughed. "That's convenient."

Thierry sat down on her bed—her two-hundred-year-old Colonial American bed, another much-cherished acquisition—and took her hand in his. "Perhaps I could be someone you trust. Someone for whom you care."

Jema's smile faded. "No. I don't want you to be anyone like that. If you are, you'll leave." The colors and shapes of the room rippled like the surface of a clear pool struck by a heavy stone. "I know I'm not here to be loved, but I'm tired of being alone."

He touched her cheek. Her skin felt hot and damp, the way it might after she wept. "I won't leave you. I want to know everything about you." He might have to risk some questions, in order to coax her into telling him about Miss Lopez and the hall of artifacts.

She drew back and her voice turned cool. "Why?"

Why, indeed? Thierry suddenly realized that he had no business here, not with this lonely, neglected little cat. Her illness was serious, and what few months or years she had left to her should be lived to the fullest. All he could give her was madness and pain. He should slip out of her dream, out of her bedroom, and out of her life. He saw himself doing so, quite clearly. "I need you."

Jema reached up and touched the edge of the hood covering his face, but did not try to push it back. "What are you? Are you Death?"

Thierry could not speak. Could not deny what he was.

"No, not Death," she murmured. She picked up one of his hands and examined it. His nails had grown long again, thick and pointed, like talons. "You've come from the painting over my desk."

The painting. Thierry remembered it now. The same nightdress, the same silky ribbons had adorned the figure of the sleeping woman. His cloak was not unlike the shadow cast over her bed; the form of a man whose hands were not those of a man. . . .

Now he understood her dream. *We have become the painting that she loves.* "Yes."

"I'm glad." She brought his hand up and pressed her cheek against it. "I've waited so long for you. Will you come back to me again?"

He closed his eyes, almost breaking from the dream before he gave in to temptation. "Yes."

Chapter 9

"You'd be the archbishop's problem priest," a harsh voice said.

John turned from studying the cork bulletin board in the Haven's entrance hall to see a thin, big-eared man staring at him. The man was wearing a carpenter's jeans and Union Jack flag T-shirt. His orange-dyed hair fell in thick dreadlocks that reached his shoulders. If all that wasn't enough to chisel an impression, white letters on the shirt spelled out BUGGER OFF IRAQ.

"I'm John Keller. I'm here to see Dougall Hurley about the counseling position you have available." John wondered if Union Jack here would be his first client. He had the right clothes, but his face was on the weathered side for a teenager.

The dreadlocks swung forward and back as small blue eyes inspected him. "You'd be a wop, a spic, an Oreo or a Twinkie. Which is it?"

John despised racial slurs about as much as he did white men who affected dreadlocks. "I wouldn't know. I was adopted."

"Oreo'd be my guess. More cream than coffee. I'm Hurley." He didn't offer his hand. "You don't like my hair."

"Your hair is immaterial," John said. "I don't like your language."

"Irish were the white niggers in this country. Still are," Hurley informed him. "I'm just embracing my cultural heritage. "You really looking for a job, Keller, or a place to lie low?"

What, precisely, had Hightower told this man about him? "I'm applying for a job." Which he had no intention of accepting, because he didn't work for racists, so he'd make this fast.

"More mouth on you than what he usually dumps on me."
He jerked his head toward the office at the end of the' hall.
"Come on, then, let's have a go."

Hurley's office was a hodgepodge of scrounged furnishings
and file piles. Antiwar posters almost covered the stains and
holes in the Sheetrock walls. A bumper sticker plastered to the
front of his desk read NAMES CHANGE, SKIN DON'T. An ancient
coffeepot sat cooking the molasses-colored brew inside its
carafe to an even murkier black.

"You don't want the coffee," Hurley told him when
he caught John looking at it. "Turns your insides African-
American."

"I can drink anything," John said mildly, "but I prefer tea."

"Aren't you the bloody cucumber." Hurley sat down in the
rickety-looking chair behind his desk. "As it happens, former
Father Keller, we don't do tea here."

He nodded. "I'll bring my own." To another job. Any other
job but this.

"We also don't harbor fugitives unless they're under eighteen and haven't copped to a major felony. I'm the only broken-
down priest on the premises, and most of my time is spent
trying to keep the kids from dealing, turning tricks, and making
funny-colored babies." Hurley raised his orange brows. "Jump
in anytime you'd like to tell me how I should piss off."

It was good practice for other job interviews. "I've completed several courses in psychology and child management,
and I have practical experience with feeding and counseling the
homeless, including their children." It was hard to recite what
credentials he had without sounding defensive. "I'll need some
direction, but I'm a fast learner. I believe I can handle whatever
the job entails. Your racism offends me."

"Good. I'm an equal opportunity bigot. I hate every-fucking-
one." Hurley tucked his hands behind his head and kicked back,
making the chair beneath him creak. "Right. Let's say Melissa,
little not-quite-white girl, who's built like Beyoncé but can't
walk and chew gum at the same time, comes to you. She wants
to know what she should charge her boss at the diner for a hum-
mer. You'd counsel her to do . . .?" He spread out one hand.

"I'd suggest other ways she can make extra money." John

kept his face bland. "Or, if she had her heart set on it, I'd find out the blue book on Hummers and help her sell the car."

Hurley uttered a single, sharp laugh. "You come with a little sense of humor, former Father Keller. His Graciousness didn't mention that."

His Grace hadn't mentioned a lot of things. Such as how a bigot like Dougall Hurley had ever been ordained.

"Look, *former* Father Hurley," John said, "I don't want to be here, but I've nowhere else to go. Neither do these kids. Frankly I don't care if you call me John, Keller, or Snickerdoodle, but call a kid a racist name in my presence and then you'll see me pissed. Avoid that, find a hairdresser, and we should all get along fine."

"What about your sheet?" Hurley's gaze moved over him. "You've got one. Overseas and sealed, so I can't get a copy, but I know it exists."

He thought of getting up and walking out. But he would not run from his sins, or this man. He was done with that. "I was charged in Rio with solicitation. I did nineteen months."

"Solicitation." Hurley whistled, then pulled out a fax and tossed it onto his cluttered desk, where it curled into a tube. "That sounds so much nicer than 'banging a spic working girl,' doesn't it? While you were in uniform, no less."

"You already knew."

"Call it a test of honesty." Hurley's lips thinned. "All right, here it is, Don John. You eat, sleep, and work here. No private sessions, no special privileges."

"You're offering me the job?"

"Shut up; I only do this once. You take your turn scrubbing toilets and peeling potatoes like everyone else. I can't pay more than minimum wage, but I'll toss in your room and board. I find you with your hands on any part of my clients, for any reason, you'll go back to jail." He gave him a genuine smile. "What's left of you."

It was not what he had hoped for, but it was more than he had. "Accepted."

"Christ, you're stupider than I thought." Hurley pulled his feet off the desk. "I'll show you around the zoo."

John expected to hear a continuous stream of racial jokes

and slurs out of Hurley's mouth as they walked the narrow corridors of the Haven. The shelter manager instead gave him a precise and informative minilecture on runaway children.

"A million and a half kids live on the streets in this country," Hurley told him as they went through a restaurant-size kitchen with incredibly ancient appliances. "Every day fifteen hundred more run away, are abandoned, or become homeless with their families. Five thousand of those will be murdered, kill themselves, or die out there in a year."

John learned that the shelter's clients had been on the streets anywhere from a few days to years, and two-thirds of them were girls.

"Fifteen-, sixteen-year-olds get the hard grind," Hurley said as they walked up the first of the resident floors, which John expected to be deserted. Instead it was packed with teenagers coming in and out of rooms, loitering in doorways, sitting in the halls. All eyes turned to him and Hurley as soon as they came into sight. Oddly they reminded him of the hamsters he'd once seen in a pet store: terrified, resigned, handled by any number of rough hands. "They're too young to get jobs and apartments, too old for foster-care placement. That's why I lost our state funding: no max stays, no forced placements or reunifications."

"I don't know those terms." John was trying not to stare at a stick-thin girl whose older, pregnant companion was lacing a leather thong through the two rows of steel rings pierced at half-inch intervals down the length of her arm. The girls glanced at John through thick rings of black eyeliner. Both might have been thirteen or fourteen.

"Max stay means predetermined length of residence," the shelter manager said. "Most shelters have a max stay of one month before they turn the kid back out on the street. Forced placements mean being shoved into foster-care homes; reunifications are the court-ordered family reunions. Most of these kids run because something's wrong at home. You don't heal a mauling by throwing the baby back to the pit bulls."

As Hurley showed him the infirmary, which was kept under triple dead-bolt lock, he told him of the wide variety of problems the children who came to the Haven brought with them. Many had drug or alcohol dependencies, had suffered physical, mental, and/or sexual abuse, and had moderate to serious health issues. Before being admitted to the Haven, the children were required to have a physical exam.

"About half of the girls are pregnant on admission," Hurley said. "Most can't afford abortions, and we don't fund them, so they go full-term. State takes the babies and I don't stop them; they've got a better chance in foster care. The boys are thieves, gangsters, or hustlers; they come in pretty banged up. We fix what we can. Anyone with AIDS goes to a shelter in Kenosha that handles clients with HIV. This is one of the common rooms; we've got one on every floor."

The area was set up like a family living room, with several couches, chairs, and lamps. Everything had a Salvation Army–reject air about it. Most of the sitting spaces were taken up by motionless teens. A decrepit television crackled as it showed a snowy rerun of *The Honeymooners*. Despite clearly posted NO SMOKING signs on every wall, the smell of cigarette smoke lingered.

John noticed one boy sitting beside a girl with white-bleached hair with black roots. They were squashed together by the confines of the love seat they shared, and the boy was dozing. "Brian?"

Brian Calloway's eyelids lifted and then closed. "Decree."

"Brian, it's John Keller." He wouldn't have recognized Christopher's brother, except for the diagonal scar on his forehead. Brian had received it during a street hockey game, when he'd taken a stick to the head. "Do you remember me? I came to see you in the hospital. Your brother Chris was one of my altar boys."

"Decree is his name," the girl sitting beside Brian told John. She had a voice to match her sweet smile. "Mine's Pure."

"It's a pleasure to meet you." John was intent on Brian, who appeared to be falling asleep again. "Brian—Decree—do your parents know that you're here?"

Brian Calloway got to his feet, stretched, and yawned. "Fuck off." He bent over to kiss Pure before he strolled out of the room.

"Decree's folks kicked him out," Pure told John as she rose. She was taller than Brian and wore clothes so washed-out and tattered that John blinked. A silver belly ring winked back at him from her navel. "You working here now, John?"

"Yes." He wasn't used to being addressed by his first name, especially by a young person. *Stop thinking like a priest.* "Where is Brian's room? I'd like to go and talk with him."

" 'Fuck off' doesn't sound like an invitation," Hurley advised him, "but you can't. He doesn't live here."

"Decree has his own place." Pure bent down to pick up a plastic grocery bag that appeared to be filled with bananas, oranges, and plums. "He just comes to the Haven to visit me."

"Visit." Hurley's dreadlocks swayed. "There's a new word for it. Like minks, they are."

"Haven't caught us yet." Pure's round cheeks dimpled. "See you around, John." She left the room.

John stared after her. "That girl is how old?"

"Fifteen, she thinks. She was born in the projects, but her mother never got around to filing her birth with the state, or celebrating her birthday." Hurley walked over to one of the other teens and held out his hand. "Open a window next time, pinhead."

The boy's features soured as he produced a crumpled pack of cigarettes, which Hurley pocketed.

"You're telling them how to break the rules," John said as they left the common room.

"They already know," the shelter manager assured him. "I only remind them." He took out the cigarettes he had confiscated and shook one out. "Menthol." He grimaced as he took it out and lit it before offering the pack to John. "You?"

"I don't smoke."

"You don't drink, you don't smoke, what do you do?" Hurley sang as he trotted up the next flight of stairs.

John had a feeling the shelter manager would need more counseling than his clients. After weaving in and out of more clustered teens, he asked, "How many kids have you got here?"

"Officially? One hundred and fifty, our state-approved capacity." Hurley took the cigarette out of the corner of his mouth, sniffed the air, muttered, "Fuck me," and went to unlock a supply closet. "Unofficially, about three hundred or so. Always doubles up after the first snow, when the little darlings discover they can freeze to death sleeping out there. We roll out blankets and sleeping bags in the common rooms for the extra bodies."

"Isn't there somewhere else they can go?"

"There's the state-funded shelter, but they don't take druggies, sex offenders, or fire setters unless they undergo psych treatment and have a spotless sheet for one year prior to admission." He rummaged through the closet, looking for things. "A couple of halfway houses will take knocked-up girls, but no boys. The adult homeless shelters will take anyone willing to take a beating and rape after lights-out."

Hurley took out a mop and bucket and handed the mop to John. In the bucket he put a large bottle of commercial floor cleaner.

"What's this for?"

"Your first counseling job." Hurley dropped his cigarette and ground it out under the toe of his grime-grayed sneaker. "Very sensitive one. One of our more artistic souls. Follow the smell."

John followed Hurley down to one of the bathrooms, where the door was propped open. He smelled the odor four feet from the bathroom. "You have septic problems?"

"Nope," Hurley said, gesturing for John to precede him.

John stopped just inside the bathroom door, where a pile of clothes had been dropped. A heavy young woman occupied the center of the room. She was naked, on all fours, and carefully coloring a line of grout between two tiles. If not for the smell, John would have thought she was doing so with a large Tootsie Roll. About half the tile had already received similar treatment.

Hurley came to stand beside him. "John, meet Beanie. Beanie, sweetheart, this is John."

The girl turned her large head, showing a face rounded and distorted by Down syndrome. "Hi, John," she said, her voice loud and hearty. "How are you? I'm fine." She went back to her art.

"Beanie?"

"She picks out the names herself and uses them until she gets tired of them," Hurley said as he retrieved the girl's clothes and handed them to John. "Last summer she was SpongeBob. Tell John what you're doing, Beanie."

"I'm making writing," the girl said. She moved back to sit on her haunches and admired the floor. "See? Just like Doogie." She frowned and reached over to brush at one side of the line.

"She thinks I have pretty handwriting. Why are you using shit for your art, Beanie?" Another, stronger odor permeated the air as Hurley emptied half the bottle of cleaner into the bucket and took it over to the sink to fill it with water.

"Warm and squishy. Make my own paint." The girl eyed John. "You know what it says?"

"No, I'm sorry," he said, not knowing whether to vomit or weep. "I don't."

She smiled, showing badly decayed teeth with several gaps between them. "It says, 'Beanie is beautiful. Beanie is great. Beanie is . . . Beanie.'" She went to work again.

This child had no business living in a runaway shelter. "Hurley."

"Don't waste the breath." He thumped the bucket down in front of John. "Beanie baby here showed up about two years ago, looking for food and a place to write her shit in peace. We ID'ed her through fingerprints. The kiddie nuthouse she grew up in kicked her out soon as she turned eighteen. She's too old now to go anywhere but the state hospital, and they've got a retard waiting list." He put on a pair of yellow gloves. "So Beanie lives here with us. We try to guess when she's due for a number two, but it's a bitch. She can hold it for days."

"What's her real name?" John asked as he immersed the mop in the bucket.

"She doesn't have one." Hurley went over to the girl. "Her birth certificate is blank. Her mom and dad probably argued over it. You know how brothers and sisters fight." He bent down and put a hand on her arm. "Time to clean up now, Beanie girl. After your bath, you can have a nice long talk with John here about all your shit."

The girl beamed up at him. "Beanies don't stink."

*   *   *

"This is a waste of time," Alexandra told Cyprien as she climbed out of the car that had brought them from the airport to Derabend Hall. "What can this Jaus guy do that we can't?"

"Valentin Jaus is suzerain of this region." Michael noted the heavy guards present around the car and in front of Jaus's house. Something had his old friend worried, and he hoped it wasn't his arrival. "He has controlled the city of Chicago since World War Two."

"So he's the Darkyn Al Capone." Alexandra checked the horizon, saw the sun had set, and removed the dark sunglasses protecting her eyes. "I still think we should take your guys and hit the streets."

"That is why I am in charge, and you are not." Before she could reply, he rested two fingertips against her lips. "We agreed that Kyn business is my baby. We will be safe here, *ma belle.*"

"Safe from what?" she demanded.

"Many things." Including the arsonist in New Orleans whom his men had still not caught, and Alexandra's own determination to find Thierry and Jamys, which had given her a recklessness that might be equally as dangerous. He saw a familiar figure emerge from the house. "Here is Jaus. Be polite."

"Polite how, exactly?" She took off her coat. "Be polite as in kiss his ass, flutter my eyelashes at him, do the demure little woman thing, act all master-whipped—"

"I mean shut up, Alexandra." Cyprien stepped forward to exchange formal greetings with Jaus, who had guards following but not flanking him. "It is good to see you again, Valentin. My *sygkenis,* Alexandra Keller."

"The delight is mine." Jaus bowed, then offered his hand. "I only wish I had happier news for you, seigneur." He turned to Alexandra, executed a second, more elaborate bow that included kissing the back of her hand. "Valentin Jaus, at your service."

The scent of camellias surrounded them and blended with the smell of roses and lavender.

Alexandra's scowl deepened when Cyprien eyed her. "Oh, I can talk now?" She faced Jaus. "Dr. Alex Keller. Services occasionally provided, but only if I like you." She frowned for a moment, as if she hadn't meant to say that.

Jaus's shrewd gaze moved over her. "I will endeavor to win your regard, then, madam."

"Try finding our friends," she told him. "That would up my estimation in a huge way."

Jaus refrained from a formal staff presentation and merely introduced his seneschal, Falco, and his *tresora,* Sacher.

"Welcome to Derabend Hall," Falco said to Cyprien. His dark eyes flicked toward Alexandra, and his mouth compressed for a moment. "May I greet your *sygkenis?*"

Alex saw Cyprien's nod and planted her hands on her hips. "Does everyone have to ask before they talk to me?"

"Only if they are Kyn," Cyprien said, "and only if they belong to another *jardin.*"

"Great." Alex huffed out some air. "More rules to remember."

Falco performed a proper, rather chilly bow before he returned to his place behind Jaus. Sacher, who was not required to adhere to such formality, greeted Cyprien warmly, and charmed Alex by presenting her with a nosegay of pale apricot tea roses.

"These are lovely, thank you." Alex buried her face in the blooms. "My favorite flowers."

Sacher gave Michael an amused look. "I had an inkling they might be."

"How is your grandson, Gregor?" Cyprien asked him.

"Growing out of his wardrobe. Every time I look at the boy, he has shot up another inch." The old man's smile became that of a fond uncle as he added, "I offer my congratulations on your elevation to seigneur. The high lord could not have made a better choice for this country."

"Shall we go inside?" Jaus asked. "I expect a call from Ireland shortly."

Cyprien glanced at Sacher, and then at Alexandra.

"May I show your lady our beautiful gardens?" the *tresora* asked, picking up the subtle hint. "I think Dr. Keller would enjoy seeing them before the light is gone."

"Of course." He would have to see to recruiting a new *tre-*

sora for himself when they returned to New Orleans. Sacher was a treasure.

"Maybe I don't want to see the gardens," Alex muttered as Sacher took her arm in his and expertly steered her away from the men. "Maybe I want to hang out and hear what the grown-up vampires talk about."

"Very dull stuff," the elderly man said as he led her down the walkway. "I always find myself nodding off in the middle of it."

The scent of lavender gradually faded from the air.

"She is clever and beautiful," Jaus said. "Not quite what I had expected, however. Does she always speak so . . ." He made a diplomatic gesture.

Cyprien nodded. "Always."

"Tremayne once said that you would meet your match someday." Jaus's hair caught the last of the light as he shook his head. "I thought he meant on the battlefield."

Cyprien thought of his convoluted relationship with Alexandra. "There are many fields of battle, my friend."

After he directed his hunters to join the *jardin*'s and prepare for a night on the streets, Cyprien went with Jaus into his office. "There has been no word of either Durand?"

"One sighting of Thierry, none of Jamys." Jaus offered Cyprien a chair and handed him a copy of the homicide report on a thief found dead in a Dumpster. He went around the desk to sit down while Cyprien skimmed it.

"Heart attack, broken fingers, but no signs of feeding or stabbing." Cyprien looked up at him. "The drugs he was using were determined as the primary cause of death. Thierry didn't kill him."

"He tried to kill Durand," Jaus said. "According to my people in the coroner's office, he had Kyn blood all over him. We've substituted human blood for what was in evidence, so there will be no question of exposure."

"This weapon he used." Cyprien resisted the urge to crumple the report in his fist. "A steak knife."

"Also covered with Kyn blood, so I had it replaced with a duplicate as well." Jaus removed a plastic bag from a drawer and offered it. "A very cheap steel blade with no copper content."

"That tells us that he hasn't been feeding properly." Only when weakened could a Darkyn be vulnerable to metals other than copper. "Why would he be in such a state?"

"He's mad, Michael. If his wounds have not yet healed, he'll be even more dangerous." Jaus nodded toward the door, outside which his seneschal waited. "Falco has crossed swords with Thierry in tourneys, and he's by far my best tracker. He's been taking the hunters out every night, but we've yet to find a trail."

"Gabriel Seran, Angelica's brother, taught Jamys to track," Cyprien warned. Gabriel had been the finest hunter in France, and his skills had only increased when he had risen to walk as Kyn. "So, where you find the father, you will find the son. I don't want the boy hurt, Val. Like his father, he's suffered enough."

Jaus nodded. "Tremayne is waiting for your call." He dialed a number on a line Cyprien knew was encrypted and secure, and put the phone on speaker.

"Dundellan Castle," Cyprien's former tresora answered the line. "Éliane Selvais."

Jaus gave him a thin smile. He knew that Éliane had in part prevented many Darkyn from dying in New Orleans, but she had also been planted in Michael's household as the high lord's spy. "Valentin for Richard."

There was only a fraction of silence. "One moment."

Although Éliane had only remained with him to serve as a conduit to Richard, Cyprien sometimes regretted losing his *tresora*. She had been cool under pressure, kept his household extremely well organized, and carried out his orders without question. Phillipe was doing his best to fill in until he found a replacement, but he had yet to fathom computers and the extensive paperwork involved in Cyprien's empire.

"Michael, Valentin." Distance and telephone equipment only partially reduced the power of Richard Tremayne's voice, which could bespell a human with a few whispered words. "I trust all is well on your side of the Atlantic?"

"As well as can be expected, my lord," Cyprien answered. He moved his chair a little closer to the desk so he could be heard clearly, and saw the framed photo of Jaus holding an infant. "How may we serve you?"

"The good Brothers have elected D'Orio to replace poor Stoss," Tremayne said. "He was in Chicago a few days ago to meet with Hightower. He then went to New Orleans to put his seal of approval on the new cell there. Thoughts, impressions, gentlemen?"

"After Stoss's attack on my *jardin*, I am not surprised," Cyprien said carefully. The picture of Jaus and the baby distracted him; Darkyn did not allow themselves to be photographed. "They send their hunters wherever there is prey to be had."

"In the four hundred years since our kind came to America, no one knew about New Orleans." Tremayne's tone changed. "This fallen priest, John Keller, exposed your *jardin*, Michael. He led the Brethren practically to your front door. Yet he remains at large, free to do things such as meet with Hightower just before the archbishop received the Lightkeeper. In your city, Valentin."

Jaus rested his head against his hand.

"John Keller was a victim of the Brethren." Cyprien had little love for Alexandra's brother, and John had created an enormous amount of trouble for them. His annoyance did not stop him from feeling pity for Keller. The man had been manipulated and tortured; his faith abused, so much so that his life would never be the same. "He is no longer in a position to harm or expose us."

"I am sure it is as you say," Tremayne told him, "but I do not gamble on whether a man will or will not remain worthless. Find John Keller and kill him."

Cyprien almost agreed, but then remembered that he and Richard were, in essence, equals now. "Are you giving me an order, my lord, or a suggestion?"

Tremayne laughed, and it was a beautiful, horrible sound. "I am giving you three days, seigneur."

The call ended there.

"If I ever wish to be elevated to your position, Michael," Jaus said, "I hope you will talk me out of it."

"When you did not do so for me?" Cyprien rose. "I had better go collect Alexandra. Do not speak of this to her, Val."

One of the guards directed them to the kitchen, where Alex and Sacher were sitting at a table. Alex had retrieved her medical bag from the car and was gently cleaning a festering wound on the back of the old man's hand. Neither of them noticed the two Darkyn standing and watching them.

"You do not put butter on a burn," Alex was telling Sacher as she discarded one stained gauze pad and applied a new one to the raw-looking wound.

"It is part of the salve I make, a remedy from the old country." Sacher grimaced. "It feels better than this."

"This is antiseptic, to kill all the little germs that have been breeding in your homemade salve and infecting your wound." Alex inclined her head toward a discarded bandage. "You've been keeping it wrapped up and damp. Wounds like these needs to dry out and form a scab. No more bandages and absolutely *no more butter.*"

"It is unsightly," the old man explained. "I do not wish to offend the master's eyes."

Alex snorted. "He's a big, strong vampire; he can deal with it. Or would you prefer to answer the phone and sort the mail with a hook?"

Jaus moved to the table. "I do not think a hook would be very becoming, Gregor."

The elderly *tresora* started, and then sighed. "You said this would be done before our masters were finished."

"Your master. My boyfriend. I didn't know how bad it was until we got the bandage off." Alex finished and collected the used gauze. "Don't get it wet and don't wrap it up. I'll have another look at it in the morning." She turned to Jaus and dumped the dirty material in his hands. "You know where the garbage can is; I don't." She walked past him to stand before Cyprien. "You ready to hit the street with the hunters?"

Cyprien looked over her shoulder at Jaus. "Alexandra, we need to talk."

Chapter 10

John heard water running overhead. From the direction, it sounded as if someone was using the showers on the third floor. He looked around the common room. "Has anyone seen Beanie?"

The kids gathered around for his first encounter discussion group answered the same way they had to his discussion topic: grunts and sounds, all negative.

"Keep talking, and pass this around," John told them, handing the bowl of microwave popcorn he'd made to one of the kids. "I'll be right back."

Hurley had left John in charge of the Haven so that he could make the rounds of the few charitable organizations willing to share some donations of food and clothing with him.

"No showers, partying, or raiding the pantry until I get back," the shelter manager had warned. "That goes for the kids, too."

John had forgotten about Beanie, whom he was sure he would find in the midst of another artistic session. It had taken two hours to clean up after the last time, and that had been with Hurley's help. *I'll tell her to stop and take a shower while I mop the floor. I'll make it a game of some sort. See how fast she can wash herself.*

The sound turned out to be coming from the girls' showers, but the door was locked from the inside. John had Hurley's master key ring, which unlocked every door under the roof. He didn't make the mistake of knocking—Hurley had also told him that when startled, Beanie would often throw her fecal matter in defense—but released the dead bolt and walked in.

The warm, humid air inside the shower room was lightly scented, but with floral soap instead of feces. The girl standing under the center shower had her back to him, but she wasn't thick-bodied or entirely naked. Not until she reached down and stripped off the wet, transparent pair of pink bikini underwear covering her hips. Water had turned her bleached hair a dark yellow, and there was an eighteen-inch-wide, wing-shaped black tattoo above the cleft of her bottom. A fist-size bruise marred the peach curve of one buttock.

It was the dark roots beneath the bottle-blond hair that identified her for John, who turned around and faced the door. "You're not supposed to be in here, Pure."

"Oh, John." She laughed. "You scared me." A shower tap squealed, and then the sound of spraying water dwindled to a leaky trickle. "You can turn around. I don't care if you see me."

"I do," he told the door. "No showers during the day; you know the rules."

"Rules." She blew a raspberry.

"I can't take one, either," he assured her.

"Dougall said you weren't a priest anymore." Her voice echoed against the tile, and wet feet made small splashes as she came closer. "That means you can be like everyone else is. Everyone else would look at me naked, John."

"I'll wait outside for you." He went to open the door and found her wet hand on top of his. Warm water from her body soaked into his shirt and trousers as Pure pressed herself against him. She'd washed her hair with a shampoo that smelled almost like papaya or mango. It was so strong in that moment he could almost taste it. "This isn't appropriate. Please step back."

"Have you ever had sex with a girl?" Pure asked as she pressed her cheek to the center of his back.

I raped a woman once. John closed his eyes. "That's none of your business."

She chuckled. "I'll be your first, if you want. I've never been with a guy virgin. I think it would be kind of neat. I bet it doesn't hurt you."

"Pure." John reached down to remove her hand from his fly. "You don't have to use sex to get what you want."

"If you're a priest, I guess not." She brought her other hand around to stroke his hip. "But outside church, Holy Daddy, everyone fucks each other."

"I'm not here for that," he said through clenched teeth, willing himself not to get hard. "I'm here to help you make a fresh start."

"My uncle picked me up one night." Her voice went low and soft. "I thought he was going to take me home to live with him and my aunt. You know? To stop me from turning tricks. He took me to this fleabag motel. Said he'd always wanted to do me, and how I should, like, give him a family discount."

"I'm sorry." He turned around and took her by the shoulders. "He had no right to do that to you. I know it was a terrible experience, but not every man who cares for you will behave that way."

She smiled up at him. "Terrible? Are you kidding? My uncle is hot. I fucked him blind." She slid out of his grip, catching his hands and trying to put them on her breasts. "I bet you've got a nice, big dick. It'll feel so good when you push it inside me. We can do it here, on the floor."

He closed his hands into fists and pulled them away. *She's not Sister Gelina. She's a traumatized kid using the only thing she knows.* Why would she come on to him; that was the question. "Was this your idea or Brian's?"

Her dark brows drew together. "Huh?"

"You don't give it away for free, I know. Do you need money? Or did Brian tell you to do this, to get even with me for something I did?"

Pure folded her arms. "I just wanted to fuck you."

"You've got Brian coming here every day for sex. It's not for that." He was onto something; he could see the fear and resentment in her eyes. "Did Hurley turn you down? Did he say you had to leave here?"

"Shut up." She strode over to the wall rack and yanked down the threadbare towel. "You don't know anything. You probably like boys. I know, I'll ask Brian if he wants a blow job next time he comes around. He might give you one, too, if you pay him enough."

"I can't help you if you won't tell me what's wrong," John said as gently as he could. "Sex isn't the answer to everything."

"I'm pregnant, okay? For, like, the fourth fucking time." She wrapped the towel around herself. "It costs three hundred dollars to get rid of it, and they won't do me anyway 'cause I still owe them a hundred bucks for the last one."

"Brian's the father?"

She screwed up her face. "Yeah, Brian's the father," she mocked.

John picked up her clothes from the bench near the sinks and handed them to her. "What does he have to say about this?"

"It's not my fault the rubber broke, you know? I told him to take it easy, but did he listen? No, he's got to drill me like fucking was gonna be outlawed next week." She pulled on her jeans and T-shirt. "He's gonna be so pissed."

"You could stay here, have the baby, and put it up for adoption," John suggested. "We'll talk to Dougall about it."

"Decree doesn't want me here. He hates me being here."

Just how much control did this boy have over her? "Brian isn't having a baby. You are."

She sighed and regarded the slight, round curve of her belly. "I hate abortions. Not 'cause I'm Catholic or anything; I just hate . . . killing it." She looked up at him. "I thought if I fucked you and told you it was yours, you'd help me. I'm sorry."

"I'll help you anyway," John told her. He opened the door. "Clean up in here and come downstairs. I'm having an encounter group with some of the long-term residents."

Pure's lips formed a reluctant curve. "Is that like for close encounters, or what?"

John felt somewhat damp but considerably better as he went back to the common room. Getting the truth out of Pure was real progress, for her and himself. He'd tell Hurley all the details of the incident, including the offer of sex, just in case Pure said something to one of the other kids. The last thing he needed was Hurley thinking he was going after the female residents while they were bathing.

John opened the door to the common room and walked in. "Sorry, everyone, now where are—"

The popcorn bowl sat on the coffee table, as empty as the rest of the room.

*   *   *

"I'm not happy with you, young lady," Daniel Bradford said as he removed the pressure cuff from Jema's arm. "Your blood pressure is off, and it's not simply the weight loss. How many injections are you taking each day? Three, I hope?"

Jema knew she shouldn't have skipped dinner after coming home from work. Going directly to her room always brought Dr. Bradford up to check on her. But she'd been so tired, and in no mood to hear another hour of her mother's complaints about how she looked, talked, ate, and breathed.

"Three most days, but sometimes I need four." She flexed her arm and sighed. "Yesterday I took five."

"Jema, you know that's too much insulin. You're not eating enough to balance it out." The doctor placed his stethoscope in his medical case and sat down on the side of Jema's bed to tie a rubber strap around her upper arm and fill a syringe with clear liquid from a small vial. "I'm going to give you a B-12 shot, but you need to pick up the slack here. I want you to eat full meals, three times a day, and keep to your injection schedule."

"Two meals." She turned her head and winced as he injected her. "I can never manage three."

"Two, and a large snack." He pressed a cotton ball to tiny wound the needle had left in her skin and bent her arm up to hold it. "Jem, I know this is hard on you, and your mother doesn't make things easier, but I can't wave a magic wand here. If you don't eat, you run the risk of going into insulin shock."

Insulin shock had put her into a coma once for a week, an experience Jema would rather not repeat.

"Two meals and a huge snack." When he would have risen from the bed, she touched his arm. "Dr. Bradford, can I ask you a really personal question?"

"With as many as I've asked you all these years?" He chuckled. "Fire away."

"Why did you come here to live with us?"

He looked puzzled. "Because Meryl hired me to; you know that."

"No, that's not what I mean." She wasn't sure what she meant. "Didn't you ever want to set up your own practice, or get married, or not be around my mother for a few decades?"

"Ah, I see." He took her hand in his. "I'll tell you a secret about me, honey. I had all those things once upon a time. Good practice in the city, great wife, and I only saw your mother in the newspaper. She's much nicer in print, by the way." His smile drooped a little. "I don't know how to put this any other way but the truth. I made a mistake with a patient, Jem. As a result, the patient died, and I got sued. My second mistake was that I tried to cover it up. They let me keep my license, but they took my house and my practice, and what was left my wife took in the divorce."

He had never spoken of any of this to her. "I'm so sorry, Dr. Bradford. I shouldn't have asked you—"

"This was long before you were born, Jem. You weren't even a twinkle in your parents' eyes. I got work as a doctor for a private home health care service. A few years later your father hired me to examine your mother when she was flown back to the States. It was a couple of weeks before his accident in Greece."

"I think I was only a month old," Jema said. "Why did he leave us like that?"

"There was nothing James could do, and he felt he had to go back to Greece and close off the dig." His gaze grew distant. "Meryl was just beginning to improve when she received the telegram from Athens saying that your father had been killed. She was so distraught after that, I thought I might lose her. Then there were all the problems you were having; by then I knew you were diabetic. You both needed full-time care."

"So you took on the Shaws," Jema guessed.

"Actually, I refused the job twice. I was afraid I might make a mistake again and hurt one of you." He smiled at her. "You were the one who changed my mind. Your mother couldn't take proper care of you, naturally, and with your condition a nanny wasn't enough. You were such a pretty baby, and so good." He reached out and brushed a lock of hair from her cheek. "Even when you were deathly sick, you hardly ever cried. I wish James could have had more time with you."

Jema had always considered Daniel Bradford rather like a kind if somewhat distant uncle. Seeing the affection in his eyes brought home how much she and her mother meant to him. "I

know my father would be grateful for everything you've done
for me and Mother."

"Thank you." He looked oddly ashamed. "I hope he would
feel that way. I could never fill James's shoes, Jem, but sometimes I fool myself into thinking I'm sort of the man of the
house here." He bent over and kissed her forehead. "Now, get
some rest and let that shot do its magic. I'll see you at breakfast. Bring some appetite." He rumpled her hair exactly as he
had when she was a girl, picked up his case, and left.

Another reason for Jema's bad mood was the hair sample
taken from the young Asian murder victim. Detective Newberry had obtained approval to send it to her colleague, Dr. Sophie Tucker. Sophie had called her when she had finished
testing the specimen, but she couldn't identify the source.

"I've ruled out every breed of dog, cat, and domesticated
mammal in North America," Sophie told her over the phone.
"I'm sending samples out to faunal experts I know in Europe,
South America, and Asia, but it's going to be a week, two
weeks maybe, Jema."

Detective Newberry hadn't been very receptive to the news
either, and when Jema called him he told her that he was sending a sample to the FBI. "I don't have time to sit on my hands
while these experts scratch their heads, Miss Shaw. You understand."

Jema rolled over and scrunched her pillow up under her
head so she could read for a few minutes before turning out the
light.

> *Till Elizabeth entered the drawing-room at Netherfield, and
> looked in vain for Mr. Wickham among the cluster of red
> coats there assembled, a doubt of his being present had
> never occurred to her. The certainty of meeting him had
> not been checked by any of those recollections that might
> not unreasonably have alarmed her.*

Poor Daniel, she thought as her thoughts wandered from the
page. To have lost so much and ended up with her and Meryl.
She'd have to make an effort to gain back some weight. She

really didn't want to end up in a coma again, and anything that improved her health made Daniel Bradford very happy.

Someone in this house should be.

She never grew tired of reading the adventures of the intrepid Miss Elizabeth Bennet and her sisters, but as the description of the ball at Netherfield went on, the words began to run together and blur. Jema felt hot for some reason, too, and pushed back her quilt as she set the book aside and reached to turn out the light.

"Sweet dreams," she murmured as she closed her eyes.

The darkness was only a corridor, and Jema crossed it easily. She entered the drawing room at Netherfield, and looked in vain for Valentin Jaus among the cluster of blue coats assembled there. That he would not be present had never occurred to her; they had a date. The certainty of meeting him was absolute; he wouldn't show up now with one of his tall, beautiful blondes.

Is there something wrong with my gown? She had dressed with more than usual care, disdaining the drabness of her wardrobe for a high-waisted gown the color of blood. All the other women were in white, ivory, and soft gold, so Jema stood out like a stop sign, but she remained in the highest of spirits. *Mr. Jaus said he didn't have a date for the ball, and this way he can see me in the crowd.*

"Good evening, Miss Shaw." A pleasant-looking young man with wavy brown hair sketched a short bow before her. There was an orange rabbit with purple eyes peering out of his jacket pocket at her. It nodded and disappeared.

"Good evening, Mr. . . . Denny." Jema didn't know his last name. "The ball appears to be a great success."

Denny viewed the room with approval. "That it does. My rabbit is quite overcome. I daresay it will be the talk of his hutch for hours and hours." His happiness ebbed abruptly into formality. "I am sent to convey the regrets of my friend, Mr. Valentin Jaus, as he has been obliged to go to town on the bus, and has not yet returned." He offered her a significant smile and added, "I do not imagine his bus would have whisked him away just now, if he had not wanted to avoid a certain gentleman here." He lifted a carnival glass to his eye and peered through its rainbow flutes across the room.

Jema followed his gaze. A tall, handsome man dressed in snow white and midnight black stood on the opposite side of the room watching them. "Darcy."

Darcy waited until Denny had taken his leave before weaving through the assembly toward her. He moved with great care but insufferable surety, and her acquaintances dear and casual parted to form a path for him as if he were royalty.

He was altogether too tall, too broad, and too dark for such an assembly as this. That bronze skin, those dark eyes, the gleaming hair—someone had polished it with a silk cloth—all completely unacceptable.

Jema engaged her friend, Miss Lucas, to give her an excuse to turn a shoulder against the odious man. Any attempt on her part to give attendance, show forbearance, or have patience with Darcy was injury to Jaus. She wanted to kick the man in the shins, but she simply resolved not to engage in any sort of conversation with him. That would save her slippers and her toes, and prevent Mr. Bingley's lovely parquet floor from being scuffed.

"Miss Lucas, Miss Bennet." Darcy bowed in an odd fashion, bringing his head close to hers. "You are not formed for ill humor, Jema," he murmured.

How dare he. All of her prospects for the evening had been destroyed, thanks to him, and now he used her Christian name without her leave? "Mr. Darcy."

"May I have the honor of the next dance, Miss Bennet?" Darcy asked.

She had vowed never to dance with him. On the other hand, her cousin Mr. Collins was hovering nearby, a fat spider prepared to snatch her from the floor and spin her stumbling over his misplaced feet and wrong-way turns. The first two dances her cousin had commanded of her had brought her nothing but mortification, and had terrified the rabbits. The moment of her release from Mr. Collins had, in fact, been ecstasy.

As dancing with Darcy will be.

He smiled a little, as if he could pluck her thoughts from her head. "It is only a dance."

Without quite knowing why, Jema accepted. He walked to the other side of the room at once, leaving her to fret over her temporary insanity. "I hate that man. Hate him. More than oatmeal. More than B-12 shots. More than puce-colored rabbits. Rather more than Mr. Collins."

Miss Lucas offered some consolation. "I daresay you will find him very agreeable, Jema. He pays you a great compliment by singling you out, and he carries no rabbits on his person."

"I should hope not." She hoped he danced quickly, too. Mr. Jaus might yet return from town to make an appearance. Buses ran from downtown all hours of the night.

"You're being a simpleton," Miss Lucas whispered as the present set ended and Darcy walked to the dance floor. "Don't let this supposed date with Valentin make you unpleasant toward a man ten times his size."

"He isn't *that* tall," Jema snapped as she walked over to take her place in the set. She would be dignified and ignore all the astonished looks from her neighbors, who doubtless had heard of her vow never to dance with Darcy.

As unseen musicians began to play, Darcy reached down and took her hand in his. He wore black gloves, as she did, and laced his fingers through hers. Jema danced, grimly intent on matching the perfection of his steps. He paid her no compliments and in fact said nothing as he took her through the first turns.

She wanted to make him suffer, as he had made so many suffer. Perhaps the greater punishment would be to make the ever-silent Darcy speak.

"There are a great many rabbits in the room tonight," Jema said. It was the truth; nearly every gentleman sported one hiding in his pocket or under his hat.

Darcy looked down at her with a frown but did not reply.

"It is your turn to say something now, Mr. Darcy," Jema informed him with a pert look. "I talked about the rabbits, and you ought to make some sort of remark on the size of them, or the number with orange fur."

He regarded the insubstantial figures dancing around them. "Whatever you wish me to say, I will."

"Very well. That will do for the present. Perhaps by and by

I may observe . . . I may observe . . ." Jema frowned. The music had gone low and soft; she should be able to concentrate better. "I can never remember what I may observe."

"Private balls are more pleasant than public ones," Darcy told her. The other men and women dancing around them faded away, like the music, and he turned her in his arms, holding her closer than was strictly polite. "But we can be silent for a time."

"One should speak a little, you know, or we will look odd. . . ." She saw that the drawing room was empty but for her and Darcy. "Now we may have the trouble of saying as little as possible. There is no one to see us. Is that your doing? You're always chasing people off with your proud, disagreeable manner."

"No." Darcy whirled her across the floor and out through one of the windows onto a wide balcony. A banana-colored rabbit hopped quickly into the dark beyond the stone balustrade. "This is your fantasy."

"I do not think this even a prudent idea, sir," Jema told him in her chilliest tone. "So it cannot be my doing."

"Are you consulting your own feelings," Darcy asked her, "or do you wish to gratify my own?"

"Both. I don't want to be with you. You're going to ruin everything. I wish you would go away. I wish this night could last forever." Jema moved out of his arms and pressed a hand to her heart. Her gown was open and her skin felt damp with sweat. Ashamed, she turned away from him, facing the darkness. "I am speaking off my head. I beg you let me return to the house." If only she knew where Longborne was.

He came up behind her and rested his hands on her shoulders. His breath whispered against her skin. "Why do you want the ball to last forever, Jema?"

"It's when it happens," Jema turned around and faced him. "Here, now, while we are dancing. Do you feel it?"

He stared down at her, and his black eyes glowed with golden light. "I feel only your sadness."

"Oh, that. Well, terrible things are going to happen very soon. My family's reputation will be destroyed by a terrible scandal. My sister . . ." Jema felt a deep, wrenching anguish.

"Someone wants to carry off my sister and do wicked things to her. My father is out looking but he cannot find her."

Darcy put his arm around her waist. "Is that what happened to Luisa?"

She frowned. "My sister's name isn't Luisa. It's something else. I'll remember it in a moment. May I ask to what these questions tend?"

"Merely to the illustration of your character," he said, tracing his finger along the curve of her brow. "I am trying to make it out."

"No. I'm supposed to do that." She glanced down as a half dozen balls of fancifully colored fur hopped onto the balcony. "Why are there so many rabbits at Netherfield? Do you think Mr. Bingley a terrible shot?"

"Jema." He nudged her chin until she met his gaze. "Do you remember what happened to Luisa?"

The rabbits jumped over the balustrade and clung to the black velvet sky beyond, where they turned into tiny stars, forming a ring around the tunnel that led to Luisa. That was a very long, very small tunnel, and there were things inside it that Jema hated.

Luisa was trapped inside.

Frightened, she buried her face against Darcy's dark jacket. "Please don't make me go. Please."

"Will you look at me, *chérie?*"

Jema lifted her face. His eyes were different now, and what she saw in them made her heart constrict. "I know you. You're the golden-eyed demon. I can't remember when, but I know I've dreamed of you."

"You are dreaming of me now," he murmured. "Don't be sad, Jema. I will not make you say or do anything you do not wish to. Perhaps someday you will trust me." He paused, and smiled. "What do you think of books?"

"I don't want to talk about books," she said, lifting her hand to touch his face. "I am sure we never read the same ones."

"You would be surprised." He turned his head and pressed his mouth to her palm. "We could compare our different opinions."

"I can't talk of books when you touch me like that," Jema

said. "My mind is full of something else." She drew his head down to hers. "Is yours?"

"Your mouth." He brushed his against it. "How it tastes. Will you give it to me again?"

"Again?" Heat poured through her body, burning it from the inside out. "Have we kissed before?"

"Once." He kissed her again as if he couldn't help it.

"You're Darcy. You're the demon." Jema closed her eyes as he took down her hair. "Which is it?"

"I will be," he murmured against her ear, "whatever you wish."

"Man, don't you do anything but sleep all day?"

Jamys opened one eye, expecting sunlight to pierce it. The glow filtering through the window was fading, however, and with the coming twilight he could feel his body rousing.

A boy with a shaved head perched on the end of Jamys's cot. "You don't talk much. I like that."

Jamys wondered if the boy was going to offer him sex. Nearly everyone, male and female, had since he'd come to the shelter. He sat up, wary now, and pulled the worn sheet up over his hips.

The boy laughed at him. "Shit, you are new here, aren't you?" He leaned over and held out his hand. "I'm Decree."

The contact enabled him to reply. *My name is Jay.*

"Jay, right." Like all the other humans with whom Jamys had used this new aspect of his talent, Decree reacted as if he had spoken out loud. "You run with anyone, man?"

Jamys shook his head.

"With that hair, I didn't think so." Decree pulled out a card and a pen and wrote a number on it. "This is my cell. You need something, you use it."

Jamys accepted the card. He couldn't use a phone, but it was a kind gesture.

"You know my girl, Pure?" Decree nodded toward the doorway, where a tall female with bleached hair was waiting.

Jamys had seen her around the Haven. She had a face like a Botticelli Madonna, and she was one of the few females who had not offered him sex. He nodded toward her.

"There's this new faggot working here who used to be a priest," Decree said. "Guy named John. He knows my family and wants to do good—you know the type?" He didn't wait for an answer. "If she's got any shit with him and I'm not around, you mind taking care of it for me?"

Jamys shrugged. He had no love for priests, but he wouldn't attack a man for trying to help someone.

"Jay's out most of the night, Decree," Pure said. "Like you. And John hasn't bugged me."

The boy gave him a sharper look. "You going out tonight, man?"

Jamys nodded and glanced at the girl.

"No, she's not going anywhere. I don't let my girl work the streets no more." Decree went to Pure and kissed her. "He seems okay if you want to hang here. I'll swing by in the morning." He walked out, leaving the girl alone with Jamys.

Pure smiled at him. "He's worried about me. Lot of dickheads around here."

Jamys pulled on his trousers and got out of bed. As he did, Pure came in and closed the door. He watched her as he finished dressing, but she seemed to be content to lean against the wall and smile at him.

"You really don't talk much." Pure walked over to him, lifting her hand toward his face. When Jamys went still, she frowned. "I'm not going to hit you, Jay. Your tags are sticking up." She reached behind his neck and tucked it the two bits of cloth protruding from his collar. "Mmmm. You smell great. Like a forest. What is that?"

The contact made Jamys's *dents acérées* slide into his mouth, and his scent intensified. He didn't feed before he went to hunt his father; hunger kept him sharper and more alert. It was tempting, though, with this girl here. The door was closed; no one would come in.

As if she knew his thoughts, Pure's face whitened. "Shit, shit." She started to sway, and he caught her with one arm before she fell.

Pure, he thought as he put her on the bed. She was completely limp. *Wake up.*

She opened her eyes a few seconds later. "Where the fuck—

Oh." She relaxed back against his pillow. "I hate when I do that." She pressed a hand to her flat stomach and grimaced at him. "Sorry."

Jamys was torn. Obviously she was ill, so he couldn't use her for blood. He needed to leave and hunt Thierry, but he didn't want to leave her like this. He touched her cheek. *I'll go get someone.*

Pure snuggled against his pillow. "Can I stay here in your room? Everyone's afraid of you, so they'll leave me alone if I'm in here."

Everyone feared him? Jamys had not realized. Occasionally humans reacted that way to Darkyn—as if on some level they sensed they were only food to them—but he had not consciously tried to instill fear in anyone. *Are you sick? Do you need a doctor?*

"Not right now." She closed her eyes and a few moments later fell asleep.

Jamys pulled the sheet over her before he left the room. On his way down to the first floor, he noticed the other residents of the Haven moving out of his way as he walked down the hall. In varying degrees, every boy or girl showed some fear of him. But why? Jamys was sure he'd done nothing to create such wariness.

At the bottom of the stairs he saw a man sitting with the large-headed girl who always smelled like a well-used privy. He had dark hair, so he wasn't Hurley, the man whom Jamys had met his first night at the shelter. He started toward him until the man turned his face and Jamys saw his profile.

It was John Keller.

Jamys turned quickly away before the priest saw his face. Alexandra's brother had been used by the Brethren to find and attack Cyprien. What was he doing here? He couldn't risk staying and finding out. There might be Brethren watching the Haven, or working here. Wherever John was, they were sure to come.

"Hey." John was looking at him and standing. "Wait."

Jamys ran.

Chapter 11

Alexandra Keller had often entertained fantasies of killing Michael Cyprien. Not unusual, considering the fact that he had almost killed her once and, in fact, had killed her after declaring his love for her. Well, perhaps not technically—she was still alive, or as alive as one could be in a highly mutated inhuman state—but it was close enough.

Michael had brought her to Chicago to help her find two of her Darkyn patients, so when he had vetoed the idea of letting her join the hunt for Thierry and Jamys, that had ticked her off. Hustling her off to the executive bedroom Jaus had provided for them hadn't resulted in sex, something that might have distracted her, and for that she was grateful. She hated it when Michael tried to railroad her. Instead, she'd almost been ready to kick back and let the boys handle things when he dropped the bombshell about her brother John.

He hadn't minced around the words, either. "The high lord holds your brother responsible for the Brethren infiltrating New Orleans," Michael said. "He has ordered me to kill him."

"Excuse me?" She was sure he'd just said . . ."Was that *kill* my brother?"

"John was seen meeting with a known Brethren operative a few days ago," he told her. "Tremayne is angry over the exposure." He caught her arm as she went to the door. "Do you remember what Tremayne did the last time you saw him angry?"

Alex had seen the high lord angry exactly one time, in the church in New Orleans where the Brethren had tried to kill her, Michael, and a lot of other Darkyn. Tremayne had removed the mask he wore and had beheaded a former Catholic cardinal.

"Yeah." The image of the high lord's face was permanently etched on her brain cells. "I remember."

"Alex, look at me."

It was amazing how furious she could be with Michael and not attack him with a blunt instrument. Well, there were all those hours she'd put into rebuilding his face; she hated the idea of ruining her best work. Although this might do it: choosing between the brother she'd worshiped and now despised, or the lover she'd despised and now worshiped. "What?"

"I am not going to kill John."

All the strength went out of her legs. She'd been so sure— John, Michael, and Tremayne formed an ugly triangle—but there . . . there was the truth in his eyes. He meant what he said.

"Thank you." She staggered over to sit down on the bed. Jaus had given them what appeared to be the honeymoon suite; it was all white. Or maybe it was the room for crazy vampires. She certainly felt like straitjacket material. "I really appreciate you not killing my brother."

He came and sat beside her. "We will work it out, Alexandra. I swear it."

"That's good." She rested her head on his shoulder. "In case you change your mind, if you touch one hair on his head, I'll cut yours off."

"I know you will." He pushed her back onto the bed and rolled on top of her.

"Hang on." She stared up at him. "You tell me the king of pain has ordered you to waste John, you scare the living shit out of me for the ten seconds I'm thinking you're going to do it, and now you want sex?"

"I wanted you before that." He smoothed her chestnut curls back from her face. "I wanted you in the kitchen, on the table where you were working on Sacher. I wanted you in the car on the way from the airport." He bent down and bit her chin. "I wanted you in the plane—"

"You *had* me in the plane," she reminded him. "Twice."

"I wanted you three times. I want you all the time, day and night, here and now, everywhere." He rested his forehead against hers. "I want to wear you on me."

"Like a bull's-eye?" She didn't want to smile, but her lips weren't cooperating.

His hands tugged at her clothes. "Like my skin."

Making love with Michael had been a revelation for Alex. She'd enjoyed men since she'd gotten rid of her virginity in high school, but medicine had been the only lover she'd been faithful to. Sex had usually been a relaxing romp to release tension, but it had never been a priority.

Until Michael, who only had to look at her to make her wet, and make her feel as if she might weep. "I love you."

He drew back a little and gave her a hello-stranger look, as if seeing her clearly for the first time.

"What are you to me?" he murmured, his voice dropping into a softer, deeper register.

Those words. Everything became clear to her, the things she hadn't understood, the nameless worries that she'd shoved aside because he'd needed her more than she'd needed reassurance. There was so much she loved about him: his long body, the beauty of his hands, the way being close to him made every inch of her skin hum. How his scent changed subtly when he wanted her, roses and wine and sun-warmed sheets. But she didn't know him, and most of the time she still didn't trust him.

"I don't know," she heard herself say, just as quiet and low. "We'll find out."

He muttered something indistinct and attacked her mouth.

There were moments that night when Alex thought Michael Cyprien might kill her. Something had changed; something that he had held back from her before. She knew because there was a lot she had in reserve.

He could do the sweet romance-novel stuff, but he didn't try to sweep her away in a wave of passion. He came at her like an avalanche and fucked her brains out. Up, down, sideways, with her on her knees, then straddling his face, then bent over and holding on to whatever she could grab. Once, when he was hammering inside her, she turned around and bit him, drawing blood. He yanked her head back and returned the favor.

It was hard to tell who did the most damage. Cyprien healed too fast, and she wasn't interested in looking at herself.

By dawn they were both exhausted, hungry, and huddled together, a couple of boxers in the fifteenth round. She lifted her head from his neck and saw love in his eyes. Love, and helplessness.

She knew she had to let him in sooner or later. Sooner had just arrived.

"When I was ten, John started getting religious on me." The words were going to come out of her whether she liked it or not. She looked up at the canopy they'd torn sometime during the night. Streamers of shredded white netting swayed faintly in the stream of air from the supply duct. "Mom thought it was great, because she had pretty much figured out by then that *I* wasn't going to be a nun."

"*Souer* Alexandra." Cyprien shook his head.

"Yeah, right?" A laugh escaped her. "Anyway, for Christmas Mom bought Johnny this expensive stereo and all these tapes of religious music. She got a really good set of headphones for him, too, so he could listen to it whenever he wanted. I think she was afraid he'd get into the Sex Pistols or something if she didn't do the parental-guidance thing. And John loved it. He'd sit in his room with the headphones on and listen to those tapes all night. Instead of telling me bedtime stories."

Michael trailed his fingers over the bruises that were disappearing from her breast. "Were you jealous of his music, or his faith?"

"Both. I wasn't allowed to touch his stereo, so I was pretty green about that. He started chasing me out of his room, or locking the door to keep me out. Now I know he was probably shaking down the suspect"—she saw Cyprien frown—"that means masturbating—but I didn't get that talk for another four years, so I didn't understand."

"You thought he didn't love you anymore." He tucked her against him.

"Bingo. One night I had a bad dream and went to his room. Even then, I'd always go to him when I was frightened. I liked the Kellers and all, but Johnny was the one who killed the monsters who lived under my bed." Her lips twisted. "He had his headphones on, but he must have seen how upset I was, because for once he didn't chase me out. He let me sit next to the stereo, and he even put the headphones on me. The tape he was listening to was a recording of *Jesus Christ Superstar* on Broadway. Have you ever heard it?"

He nodded.

"I listened to these strong, amazing voices singing this stupid Bible story that I never liked. I always thought Jesus should have kicked ass instead of letting himself get nailed to the cross. But listening to that tape, hearing the story in words I could finally understand, I got it." She swallowed. "Then the tape played the scene where Jesus is whipped. It was horrible. It sounded so real I thought they were really doing it—really whipping someone. I know I was crying halfway through it, but John didn't turn off the tape. He just picked me up and held me on his lap. And he made me listen. I didn't understand why he did that, either. Not for a long time."

"Alexandra." Cyprien brushed away a tear clinging to her lashes.

She looked at him. "My brother is a jackass. I can't stand to be in the same room with him. I will die before I let anyone hurt him."

"Then he is safe, *mon amour,*" Michael told her, "because I will kill anyone who tries to touch you."

Alex snuggled with Cyprien until he fell asleep. The Darkyn actually didn't sleep as much as hibernate, but she could tell from the moment his pulse dropped from low to non-existent. Hers wasn't going to do the same, so she eased out of his arms, dressed, and tiptoed out of the room.

The only other souls awake in Derabend Hall were Sacher and his grandson, Wilhelm, who were having breakfast in the kitchen. Alex tried not to drool at the sight of the big, fluffy waffles with golden syrup steaming on their plates. She was still struggling with the fact that she was on a liquid diet for the rest of eternity.

"Dr. Keller." Sacher got to his feet and introduced his grandson before asking, "Is there something you require?"

"I need to borrow a car, Sach." She knew where she had to start looking for John. "I'd like to drive across town to the hospital and see a former patient of mine."

"The sun has already risen." He nodded toward the window. "Perhaps you could visit tonight?"

"It's okay. I'm not as sluggish as the other vamps." As it happened, she could tolerate sunlight much better than Cyprien or Phillipe, another difference in her mutation.

Sacher sent Wilhelm to bring one of Jaus's cars around to the front of the house, and while she waited Alex checked the elderly *tresora*'s hand.

"This looks a lot better this morning." She was pleased to see that the tissue inflammation had shrunk and a scab was forming. "We'll clean it up again tonight, but keep it dry and uncovered today."

"You are very kind," Sacher said. "Are you certain I cannot drive you? All I would need to do is drop Wilhelm off at his school on the way."

"It's okay." She smiled. "I grew up in Chicago, and I'm kind of sick of being driven places."

Alex had never driven a Porsche, but once she had gone zero to sixty in the time it took her to blink, she decided that she could get used to it. The dark-tinted windows kept the sun from irritating her eyes, so she didn't have to put on her shades until she reached Southeast Chicago Hospital.

She checked in the lobby to make sure Luisa was still on the burn ward and then took the elevator to the fourteenth floor. The four million dollars Cyprien had paid Alex for fixing his face and not dying of rapture and blood loss had moved Luisa into a private room and afforded her the best physicians Southeast had to offer.

Alex bypassed the nurses' station and went directly to Luisa's room. The young girl was out of the burn cradle and in a bed with an adjustable mattress that could be reconformed daily to prevent bedsores. The preliminary skin grafts that had been performed on her face and neck looked healthy, but her eyes were covered with a thick band of gauze. From the rise and fall of her chest Alex could tell she was awake.

"Hey, stranger." She took off her jacket and hung it over the back of one visitor's chair. "Long time, no see."

Luisa's head turned toward her voice. "I know you?" Her voice still sounded deep and husky from the damage to her throat, but repairs the reconstructive surgeon had made to her mouth had greatly improved her enunciation.

"I'm Alex, your old doctor. Remember me?" She went to Luisa's bedside and touched her hand. The fingers that had been fused together were now separated and covered with tiny skin grafts. "I was in town for a couple of days, so I thought I'd stop in and see how you're getting along."

"Dr. Killer. I remember you." Luisa turned her head away and moved her scarred hand out from under Alex's.

"It's Keller, actually." Alex sat down in the bedside chair so she could study the work that had been accomplished. Luisa's skin grafts were the color of dark chocolate, a perfect skin match. "Your face looks good, sweetie. They really grew some nice skin for you."

"Wouldn't know."

Alex had expected bitterness—Luisa had been through a continuous tour of hell, and the ride wasn't over—but the apathy was more disturbing. "Is there anything I can do for you while I'm in town?"

"Isn't it a little late to be asking her that?"

Alex turned to see a short, dark-haired woman with folded arms glaring at her. "It's never too late to be helpful. Who are you?"

"Jema Shaw. Luisa and I worked together." She came to stand on the other side of the bed, rather like a bodyguard. "Luisa gets tired very easily. You should go."

"You should butt out." Alex turned to Luisa. "Has my brother been to see you? He's the priest who came to read from the Bible to you when I was treating you here."

"No." Luisa's voice tightened on the word. "No priests."

"You've got some nerve, lady," Jema said. Her pale face flushed pink with anger. "You walk out on her in the middle of her treatment, and now you come back just to see if your brother's been around praying over her?"

"She gave my mother a lot of money," Luisa said, sounding very tired now. "Leave her alone, Miz Shaw."

"I apologize, Luisa. I didn't realize she'd left some conscience money for you." Jema stalked over to the window.

Alex imagined shoving the other woman through the plate

glass for a delicious moment, but then she saw how thin and
frail-looking Jema was. *Probably another patient who got dis-
charged.* "I'll come back to see you another time, sweetheart."

"Good," Jema said without looking at them. "Make it next
Christmas. That's when they expect to discharge her. You can
wave good-bye and Luisa might see it this time."

God, what a nasty little bitch. "You take care, okay?" Alex
touched Luisa's forehead, just as she had in the old days, and
found scarred fingers around her wrist, urging her down. She
bent close.

"Don't come back," Luisa whispered in her harsh voice.
"Don't you never come back here." She shoved Alex's hand
away from her face.

"All right." With one last glance at Jema Shaw, Alex picked
up her jacket and left the room.

She should have expected Luisa to be upset, Alex thought
as she rode the elevator down to the lobby. She had abandoned
her at a critical point in her treatment, when Luisa had been
fighting everyone and everything except Alex. John had done
the same thing to her, leaving a wound that would never heal.
It didn't matter that in Alex's case it hadn't been by choice, and
that her mutation made it impossible for her to treat humans
anymore.

Luisa had counted on her, and she'd bailed.

I could treat humans. Alex walked out of the elevator and
smiled wanly at a security guard. *I treated Sacher's hand without wanting to sink fangs into him. All I'd need to do is feed
well before I saw any patients—*

Kill this bitch quick.

Alex staggered to one side, almost blundering into a new
mother being wheeled out to the valet parking area. The
woman shrieked, clasping her newborn close, while her husband tried to get between them.

"Sorry." Alex stumbled away, groping for a handhold, finding the security guard. "Sorry."

Black jacket. Red rose corsage.

"Miss? Are you all right?" Hands tried to steer her.

The flood of murderous thoughts pouring into Alex's mind
prevented her from responding. The thoughts weren't obses-

sive or out of control. They were as precise as sculpted ice, formed and formulated, a glistening tower of controlled hatred ready to shatter and fall like a hail of glassy razor blades.

"I need to sit down," she said. "I . . . I'm pregnant."

"Right here, ma'am." She was guided to a chair and helped into it. "I'll get a doctor."

"No. I'm just a little dizzy. It'll pass." She directed a blind smile toward the voice. She wanted to smash her hands to the sides of her head, but she held on until the guard retreated.

Nausea and reaction had her trembling like a leaf. The emotions she sensed were never good ones, but this killer was consumed by hatred. It was all he felt—hatred for his target, hatred for himself, hatred for life—and he reveled in it. He was a machine running on evil.

Hit her once. Back over her.

He was going to use a car to do it. Alex's mind shrank, not wanting any more, not another single thought, not another split second of—

Could take her back. No one there now. Images of a basement, and other women screaming and writhing on the filthy table in it flashed across Alex's wide eyes. He'd used power tools, knives, electrical current, anything to inflict maximum pain. *Slice her, dice her, do her up nicer . . .*

Across the lobby, a tall, broad-shouldered man walked through the main entrance. He wore a shirt and tie and carried a jacket, but Alex would have known him anywhere.

"John?" She fought through the killer's thought stream and got on her feet and raised her voice desperately. "John."

Her brother heard his name and looked over at her.

Pop it like a balloon. The killer was imagining his target's head bursting under the rear wheel of his car. Black car, late model, specially outfitted. Trunk lined in plastic. He was going to take the body. Even after they were dead, he toyed with them. He liked fucking the dead.

"Get out of my head," Alex whispered.

He was looking at his reflection in a car's rearview mirror. Not his face, but his eyes. An arrow-shaped stud set with three diamonds pierced the center of his right eyebrow. He'd taken the stud from one of his victims. He'd ripped it out of her—

Alex felt her fangs emerge and used them to bite her tongue, hard. As her own blood filled her mouth, the thoughts and images retreated—just in time for her to see her brother make an about-face and stride out of the hospital.

"No. No, John, wait." She jerked on her jacket and hurried after him.

She couldn't see outside; the sunlight nearly blinded her. She fumbled in her pocket for her shades, swearing when she found the pocket empty. She must have left them in Luisa's room. If she squinted, she could see well enough to get to the car, and she'd just drive around until she could spot him. She stepped out into the circular valet drive.

"Alexandra!"

Something knocked her off her feet, and she landed under it. Wind, black rubber and a roar rushed past her head, only an inch away from it. Michael was on top of her. A car was screeching to a halt.

"Get up." Michael hauled her to her feet and dragged her behind a wide cement pillar, just as the back end of a black car rammed into it. Plaster and cement chips scattered around them, and there was an ominous cracking sound overhead.

Smoke from the squealing tires wafted into Alex's face as the driver of the car took off. Before she could do more than cough, Michael hurried her away from the pillar and into a waiting limousine.

"What are you doing here?" Alex asked as soon as they were inside.

"Sacher told me you had left alone. Jaus has GPS locators on all of his vehicles," he told her. "Why did you come here?"

"To see Luisa." Alex slumped back against the seat. "I saw my brother on the way out. I was trying to get to him—and then that car came out of nowhere."

"He tried to kill you." Cyprien's composure was absolute. "I will find him."

She looked down and saw the red rose corsage on her lapel. "He didn't want me."

"I watched him try to run you down," he shouted, not so calm now. "Twice."

"I heard his thoughts. The sick son of a bitch came to kill

the woman wearing this jacket." She tugged at the lapel. "But it isn't mine. It belongs to someone who was visiting Luisa." She glanced over her shoulder. "We have to go back. I have to warn her."

"No." Cyprien picked up a phone. "Jaus will take care of it."

Jema stayed with Luisa for an hour, but after the visit from the obnoxious Dr. Keller, the girl didn't say a word.

"I'll be by to see you in a couple of days." She always waited for a farewell, but didn't get one. "Take care, Luisa."

The front lobby was crowded with people and police, and Jema saw there had been some sort of traffic accident right in the valet parking area. She changed direction and left the hospital through the emergency room entrance, which was directly across from the visitors' parking lot.

She thought of all the work waiting for her at the lab, but for some reason she had no ambition to go in and dive into it as usual. The huge breakfast Daniel Bradford had insisted she eat wasn't sitting well on her stomach, either. By the time she'd driven three blocks from the hospital, she had to pull off the road and hurry into the nearest restaurant, a Wendy's, so she could use the restroom.

The only stall was empty but reeked of cheap pine cleaner. She knelt down on the dark brown tile, holding the wall with one hand.

It couldn't be food poisoning. Was her blood sugar too high? It never felt like this. She'd left her injection kit in the car—

The first surge slammed up Jema's throat, and she bent over quickly, vomiting into the toilet. That was followed by another, and another, until her stomach emptied. Still she heaved, spitting out saliva when nothing else would come up.

She leaned back against the side of the stall and gulped air. She was too sick to go to work, too sick to stand up. She needed to go home, and rest, but Meryl would get upset. Maybe she could lie down on her couch in the office for a few hours. Hardly anyone came downstairs; no one would know. She was Meryl Shaw's daughter; no one would care.

"Hey, lady." A pair of ankles above dirty sneakers appeared next to the gap under the stall door. "You okay in there?"

"Yes." Jema jerked some toilet paper from the big plastic-cased roll and wiped her face before she groped and flushed. As she stood, she was relieved to see that she hadn't puked down the front of her clothes. She only smelled like she had.

She opened the door and met the owner of the sneakers, a pudgy teenage girl with huge metal braces on her teeth and the most gorgeous thick curly red hair Jema had ever seen.

"Here." She gave her a pretty smile and held out a small yellow cup filled with a clear soda and lots of ice. "Diet Sprite. It'll help."

"Thanks." Jema went over to the sink for a wash before she tried a sip. It did help, and she looked at the girl in the mirror over the sink. "I guess everybody out there heard me, huh?"

"Yeah. I think the people over in the McDonald's next door did, too." She joined her at the sink and handed her some brown folded paper towels. "My manager's pretty cool, though. If you want to sit for a while, you know, till your belly quiets down, he won't chase you out."

"No, thank you. I've got to go to work." She dug some bills out of her pocket, but the girl only shook her head.

"I know how you feel." She chuckled and touched the front of her uniform smock, and then it dawned on Jema: She wasn't pudgy; she was pregnant, probably eight months along. A mother-to-be at barely sixteen, if she was that old.

Jema thought she saw the girl's smock move a little. "Is the baby kicking?"

"Oh, yeah. He does this Jean-Claude Van Damme thing in there sometimes and I nearly pee my pants. Not so bad this morning. Here, feel." She took Jema's hand and rested it against the basketball-size bulge under her sternum.

Jema felt a weird nudge against her palm. It was tiny but it was solid and strong. That hidden, straining sign of life mesmerized her. "Wow."

"Rocks, doesn't it? Take care, lady." Another sweet smile framed her braces before she slipped out the door.

Jema looked at her tingling palm. She didn't want to go to

work, or back to Shaw House. She wanted to follow the girl, and ask her a million questions, and feel the baby move again.

Depression kicked in, a mule with sharp hooves. *You will never be pregnant.* It was the reason Meryl had Daniel started Jema on the pill as soon as she had her first period, so there could be no possibility of pregnancy. Even if she'd been married and willing, the strain on her kidneys would kill her. *You'll never know what it feels like to carry a child.*

The air turned freezing. It became so cold so fast that Jema wouldn't have been surprised to see snowflakes start drifting around her. Hallucinations seemed logical, given the way her morning had gone.

She waited and sipped Diet Sprite until she felt steady enough to drive, and left the restaurant. There were three voice-mail messages waiting for her at the museum, all from Detective Newberry.

"I've got to go do some interviews, so I won't be in," Newberry said after leaving two messages for her to call him. "The FBI would like a copy of the report you get from your expert. Seems they can't identify the hair either. We need this hair to substantiate a tentative ID on a couple of suspects, though, so it's become vital to the case. Leave me a message or call me after three P.M. Thanks."

Jema contacted Sophie Tucker, who was still in the process of collecting reports from her overseas contacts. "We've ruled out Europe and Asia," Sophie told her, "as it doesn't match any animal sample in their database. I should have South America's report by tomorrow. Strange how it doesn't match anything."

"Well, if it does, call me. This detective really needs the information to help with an arrest warrant," Jema told her.

The rest of the day continued to be problematic. She had difficulty concentrating on her work, and she was terribly clumsy. She nearly dropped a krater on loan from a central dig in Pompeii, which would have cost the museum's insurance company several hundred thousand dollars. Thomas couldn't find the next lot she had on her inventory list, either.

"I don't know where it is, Miss Shaw," the young guard told her. "I checked everywhere. I think Roy might have moved it when we got that last shipment in from Venice, but he called in sick today."

"That's all right, I was going to quit a little early." Jema gave him a wry smile. "Leave a note for Roy to see me in the morning about it."

On the way home, Jema debated whether or not to tell Daniel about her morning purge session at Wendy's. He'd be upset with her again, and she was sure it was just caused by forcing down so much food. Her stomach had obviously shrunk. To her surprise, neither Daniel or Meryl was home when she arrived, and one of the maids told her that they'd gone to see a specialist in the city.

God, don't let my mother go downhill now, too, Jema thought as she ate an early dinner alone in the gloomy dining room.

Daniel and Meryl still hadn't returned by dark, and Jema decided to make an early night of it. She'd been sleeping like a rock lately, and woke up feeling rather wonderful in the morning. She still felt hot, however, even after a cool shower, so she pulled down the quilt and decided to forgo her nightgown. After a moment's hesitation, she stripped out of the bra and panties she had put on after her shower.

She rarely slept naked, but it wasn't as if anyone would see her.

Chapter 12

Thierry was glad he was already damned to hell for his sins as a human, because if he was not, what he was doing to Jema Shaw every night would sure send him to burn at the devil's right hand.

Each night he swore he would go and hunt and stay away from her. He would go, and he would hunt, but he always ended up on her balcony a few hours from dawn, feeling with his talent to be sure she was asleep, sliding the lock open with his dagger.

He couldn't stay away from her. He couldn't get enough of her.

Even as Thierry now walked into her room and went to stand over her sleeping form, he tried to discipline his mind. *Only do this to gain her trust. Only go into her dreams to find out who hurt Luisa.*

He was sure she knew; there was some terrible secret her mind held locked tight from him. After entering three of her dreams he knew she was hiding it from herself as well. Jema Shaw knew something so terrifying that she wouldn't let herself remember it.

Her dreams could be the key to his salvation. The problem was that they were destroying him.

Angelica had never been like this. She had made a pretense of wanting him all the time, but Thierry could look back now and see how he had been played for a fool. He had loved a woman who had shaped her personality as easily as she had her body. She had played a role that appealed to his desires while never showing her own.

Oh, there had been hints of the truth, so obvious now in hindsight. Her eagerness for sex had been constant, but only when he had been rough with her had she grown truly excited. Her petulance when he refused her something—the few times that he had—had always been edged with anger, as if she wanted to strike him instead of pout.

Had she wished him dead, all the years they had been together? Had the love he had thought he had seen in her eyes been only a clever mask for her hatred?

Angelica had even used his trust in her to carry out her revolting work for the Brethren. The way she had convinced him to permit her to travel by herself, laughing at his worry that she would be taken by the monks. *I am Darkyn; they are human,* she had said once. *They can do nothing to me.* Such confidence, but that had been one of the few truths she had told him. The Brethren would never harm their most talented hunter and interrogator.

Thierry wished Alexandra Keller had not killed his wife so quickly. Angelica had not deserved such mercy. *But if she had not, I would have my Angel's blood on my hands.* His love for her was dead, but even so he was not sure he could have killed her. She had been the traitor of their kind. She had been the mother of his child.

That duplicity shamed him as much as Angel had.

Only thinking of his son, Jamys, could dispel Angelica's ghost. Yet with those thoughts came even more intense guilt. Fearing in his madness that he might harm the boy, Thierry had abandoned him.

He is safe with Cyprien. Perhaps in time, Jamys would even forgive him for the part his father had played in his suffering. Yet Jamys would never be able to tell him either way. Angelica had done that, too.

She carried our son in her body when she was human. She told them to turn him into a mute. She suckled him at her breast. She watched them torture our son. My son. My boy. Thierry ground his palms into his eyes, as if he could shove the madness farther back, to some place where he could cage and chain it. *She would have seen us all murdered. She said that she had watched the torture. She enjoyed it.*

How could he have not seen this? How could he have loved such a monster?

Thierry looked down at Jema's sleeping face, and knelt beside the bed. She had never hurt anyone in her life; he sensed that. She would rather suffer herself than see another in pain. It was one of the weapons her clinging mother used on her—her guilt, and her love.

If he woke her and told her everything, would she feel sorry for him? Would she take him into her bed as openly and affectionately as she had welcomed him into her mind? Or, facing the real demon, would she scream?

He brushed his hand over her cheek, tucking a piece of wayward hair behind her ear. Then he cupped the long curve of her throat and closed his eyes.

It became easier each time he touched her.

Tonight he found himself in a wide, open field covered with small purple and white wildflowers. One building stood before him, and it appeared to be a small, rather dismal-looking tavern. As he walked toward it, snow began to drift down from the perfectly clear blue sky.

Jema was standing outside the tavern's entrance door. She was dressed in abbreviated clothes; a silvery shirt that ended just beneath her breasts and a black leather skirt that hugged her hips. Her small feet were shod in glittering red shoes with heels so high he feared she would do herself an injury trying to walk in them.

Her face was painted with makeup, far more than she ever wore. Red lips parted and pursed as she inspected him. "Why did you come back?"

The snow picked up, changing from a drift to a steady fall. Over the last several nights he had learned that asking her questions did not startle her awake, as it did most humans. "Why are you dressed like a harlot?"

Jema brought forth a sword, one fashioned in a time long before Thierry had walked the earth as a human. She lifted the sword and brought it straight down, burying the tip of it in the deepening snow. It made a smooth thunking sound that went up the back of Thierry's neck. The hilt quivered a little after she took his hand away. "Isn't this what you wanted?"

"No." The sword confused him. Jema's dreams were playful, even erotic, but they were never about battle or violence.

She smiled. "Good." She sauntered over to him and tucked her arm through his. "Come in and buy me a drink."

"It would be my pleasure." He walked in with her, circling around the sword in the snow. "Is this from a book, Jema?"

"I don't read books." She gave him a seductive smile before releasing his arm and strolling over to the bar.

Thierry stopped inside the door and let his eyes adjust to the dim interior. All of the stools at the bar were filled, but none of the men there bothered to turn and look at him. Behind the bar, the short, stocky Hispanic was topping off a mug. He looked at Thierry and nearly dropped the beer.

"Hey." Jema curled a finger at the bartender, who hurried over to look down the front of her blouse. "This is my friend Jack. Jack and I are going in the poolroom, and we don't want to be disturbed."

Now heads turned and everyone had a look at Thierry. Everyone swiveled back to hunker down over their drinks, muttering things to each other.

"You won't be, Miss Jem," the bartender said, grinning and showing a gold tooth. A pink stone shaped like a rabbit adorned the tooth. "Have a good time."

Thierry strode over. Two men got off their stools and made a space for him. He leaned on the edge of the bar and saw that the little bartender had the rag in his hand twisted into a tight knot. All the other men showed him their backs.

"A bottle of champagne for the lady," he said to the bartender.

The bartender gave him a doubtful glance and came over to whisper, "The lady don't drink." His breath smelled of peppers and onions. "She's not in . . . you know"—he winked—"the mood."

"I'm getting bored," Jema announced as she adjusted the black satin band around her upper thigh.

The two men sitting on either side of the empty stools beside Thierry flung some bills on the bar and left. "Where is the poolroom?" Thierry asked.

The bartender jerked a thumb to the left.

Thierry straightened and turned toward Jema. The air grew colder with every step he took. She was standing half in shadow, half in the blue-and-white light from a sign that read COORS in looping script.

Before he reached her, Thierry drew on the dream realm to adjust his own appearance. Faded jeans, a black T-shirt, scuffed boots. He didn't change his hair or features; in this place he looked right at home.

"You have," Jema said, walking up to him, "without a doubt, the best chest I've ever seen." She ran her hand across it. "Big, wide, well developed. Muscles on top of muscles. Better than Brad Pitt's, and he has the number one spot on my perfect-pecs list."

He had no idea who Brad Pitt was, but he went along with her play. "I'm glad you like it."

"I'd like it better naked and sweaty." She leaned in, balancing on one foot. "I could make you sweat, you know. All night long. Take off your shirt."

One part of Thierry wanted to put his hands on her shoulders and push until he had her on the floor under him. Another part wanted to shake her until her hair tangled. "Why are you behaving like this?" It reminded him too much of Angelica.

The bartender and the rest of the patrons suddenly ran for the door, fighting to get through the door until Jema and Thierry were alone.

"Just like a western movie," she told him. "All we need are some guns to draw on each other."

She's furious. Now Thierry could feel the emotion raging inside her mind, manifesting in this dream. "I'm not going to shoot you." As she sauntered back toward a wide pool table, he followed her. "What happened that made you so angry? Talk to me."

"Is that what you really want me to do to you with my mouth?" She tapped her scarlet lips with a finger. *"Talk?"*

That stopped him in his tracks, about a foot and a half away from her. He had kissed her, and fondled her, but the eroticism of her dreams never went beyond that. Tonight was different. "I'm not here for that."

"Cute. You said you'd come back. You said you'd be whatever I wanted you to be." She leaned back against the bar. "I want you. You do realize that. You've been teasing me every night this week."

His eyes narrowed a fraction. "Me, or will anyone do?"

"Good point." She treated him to a long, insulting smile. "You have to go."

"No." He crossed the space between them and saw her garments had become shorter, tighter, as if they had been painted onto her skin. He refused to let them distract him. "You know me. You know why I'm here. I want you to trust me." Nothing was between them now but two inches of icy air. Snow was piling up around them, as high as his knees now. Inside, he was scalding. "I will do whatever you want, but talk to me. Tell me what you want."

Jema grabbed his belt loops and pulled his hips against her belly. "I want you naked, inside me."

"Why?"

She glared up at him before she pressed her hand to his crotch. "Why do you care?" She moved her palm up and down, dragging her fingernails against the rough fabric. "You'll like it. You liked everything else."

"I did." He bent down. "I do. But what we do together isn't what makes you angry now."

Pain flashed over her face, and she stepped back. Her mouth trembled, and then tiny diamonds appeared on her dark lashes.

"I want a life."

"You have—"

"I want a *life*." She hit him with one small, hard fist. "I want a husband, and a house, and a baby."

"Jema." He caught her wrist before she could hit him again. Wind howled through the tavern, whirling around them, pelting their faces with tiny sharp ice crystals. "You can have whatever you want here. I'll give it to you."

She took in a sharp breath, and the snow and wind disappeared. "Even if I puke up my guts like I did at Wendy's?"

"Even so." His breath wasn't coming out in white puffs anymore; the perspiration on his face wasn't freezing. "You are stronger than the anger. I think you are stronger than me."

"I'm not. I'm dying." She looked down. "Could you let go

of me now?" When he saw how tightly he was holding her, she added, "I have enough bruises from the last time."

He turned her right hand over to see livid marks his fingers had left. On the other side of the dream, he was doing the same thing. "Forgive me. I didn't realize I was hurting you." He took his hand away. "I cannot come into your dreams anymore, little cat. I cannot protect you."

"I can take care of myself." She looked down at herself as if puzzled. "Be great if you could tell me what all this is about, though."

She was emerging from the dream, ready to wake. He had to keep her with him, if only for a few more minutes. That meant making her desire to dream more urgent than her desire to wake.

"This is about you and me." He picked her up in his arms and carried her over to the billiards table, sitting her down on the edge of it, spreading her legs to step between them. He eased her back against one arm and pulled up the edge of her blouse with the other.

"Wait." She sounded shocked, but she didn't struggle. "What are you doing?"

"What I want, and what you want." He stroked her small breasts with his hand, cupping them, squeezing them until she made a soft sound. Then he deliberately reached under her skirt, expecting to find panties to pull out of the way.

He found her instead, and pushed two fingertips inside her.

"Look at my hand," he told her. "Watch what I do to you." He shifted his hand so she could watch him work one finger into her sheath while he rubbed his thumb where her folds met. She was so soft and slick that she drenched his fingers.

Jema reached down to cover his hand, as if she couldn't bear to watch the erotic way they were joined. He brought her hand back up to rest it against her breast, and then pressed his gleaming fingers against her lips.

"Open for me, *chérie*." When she did, he gave her a taste of herself, spreading the silky fluid on her lower lip, teasing the tip of her tongue with it.

Her eyes were huge as his fingers left her lips and she looked up at him. That was when he thrust his hand back down between her thighs, cupping her sex and using the heel of his hand on her, doing with his fingers what he wanted to do with his cock.

She convulsed, releasing a cry so sweet it made his head pound. Then her eyes closed, and the darkness pressed in around them.

The dream, at least for tonight, was over. Thierry left her mind as gently as he had entered it, and came back to himself, kneeling by her bed in her room, alone with her sleeping form. At first what he saw didn't make sense, because the dream world wasn't real, and never intruded upon reality. But there she lay, the sheet pushed aside, her slender body naked to his eyes.

His hand, resting on Jema's bare thigh.

Thierry looked at his hand, and closed his eyes for the space of a heartbeat. Then he brought his damp fingers to his lips, and tasted her.

When Valentin heard about the hit-and-run attempt at the hospital, he summoned every hunter and tracker in his region and gave them what description of the killer Alexandra had been able to provide.

"I want the driver found. Do whatever you must to locate him and bring him to me. Alive." He could barely get the words out, so great was his rage.

That someone would dare attempt to assassinate the seigneur while he was in Jaus's territory was a blatant sneer at his authority, and he would not tolerate it.

"I don't believe the attack was meant for Alexandra or me," Michael told him once they had left the *jardin* briefing in the lists. "It may be a case of mistaken identity."

"I don't understand."

"While she was at the hospital, Alexandra picked up another woman's jacket by accident. This woman, Jema Shaw, was the intended target."

Jaus stopped. "Jema Shaw. You're sure about the name?"

"Yes, she was visiting Ms. Lopez while Alexandra was in her room, when the mix-up happened." He hesitated before adding, "Alex's talent enables her to sometimes read the minds

of killers. She knew the man's thoughts as he was waiting outside the hospital. She didn't connect them to Miss Shaw until
after the incident. If you would be so good as to help us locate
her, she should be warned that her life is in danger."

"You have only to walk four hundred feet and you may
knock on her door." Jaus gestured to Shaw House. "Miss Shaw
is my neighbor."

"I see." Michael glanced at the house. "Perhaps this has
more to do with you and Miss Shaw than me or Alex."

Jaus managed to dodge the rest of Cyprien's questions and
excused himself on the pretense of contacting Jema. He tried
her office at the museum first, only to be told that she had called
in sick for the day. When he called Shaw House, one of the
maids answered, and asked him to hold while she checked to
see if Miss Jema was taking calls.

"Mr. Jaus," Jema's voice came over the line unexpectedly.
"Is something wrong?"

He realized that he could not say someone was trying to kill
her, or demand to know why. "No, Miss Shaw, I was only calling to . . . confirm that you will be attending the masque at my
home on the thirty-first. I have heard that you have not been
well."

"I'm feeling a little blah," she admitted, "but I think I should
be back to normal in time for the party. I'm so glad you called."

She was *glad* to hear from him. *Glad* he called. He sat down.
"You are."

"I needed to ask you a question."

*Do I love you? Yes. Do I need you? Yes. Yes to everything and
anything you ask of me. Yes, yes, yes.* "Please do."

"I'm not sure what sort of costume to get for your party,"
she said. "Frankly, I've never *been* to a costume party. Would
you be able to steer me in the right direction, tell me where I
can find something suitable?"

He rubbed the back of his neck. "I can. In fact, I have just
the costume in mind for you." He knew nothing of costumes;
Sacher took care of such matters. "Would you permit me the
liberty of hiring it for you and sending it to your home?"

There was a brief silence. "I couldn't impose on you like that."

"It would be my pleasure," he told her, "and I could assure

you that our costumes complement each other. Or perhaps you think me vain for suggesting that."

"No, I think it's a lovely idea. I'll reimburse you, of course."

He almost laughed before he remembered modern females were very insistent on paying for things themselves. "As you wish."

"Terrific. Then I will see you on the thirty-first. Thanks for calling and checking on me."

"Until then, Miss Shaw." Jaus ended the call and cursed himself for being nine kinds of an idiot.

"Boy, I wish I spoke German. Or is it Austrian?" Alexandra Keller closed the door to his office behind her. "That sounded very sincere."

"It was." Jaus spared her a glance. "How may I serve, my lady?"

"You must not have seen how we wrecked the bridal suite upstairs." Alex dropped into the chair in front of his desk. "Point is, I'm not a lady. So you can drop that right now." She took the framed photo from his desk and studied it. "Cute baby. Can't be yours. Anyone I know?"

"No." He took the photo from her and put it inside his desk. "What can I do for you, Dr. Keller?"

"You can tell me how Jema Shaw relates to the Kyn. I already know she lives next door, and you've been sending her flowers on her birthday for thirty years." She smiled when he stared. "Sacher didn't say a word. The kid did."

"You take a great interest in my personal business," Jaus snapped.

"I take a great interest in anything that almost gets me squashed like a tomato thrown off the Sears Tower," she told him.

He should have had this woman killed when she was still human enough to die. "Miss Shaw and her mother have been my neighbors for thirty years. I send a bouquet on Miss Shaw's birthday out of courtesy."

"You send flowers to a funeral out of courtesy." Alex smiled. "You send flowers to a beautiful woman on her birthday to tell her you care. How much do you care for Jema Shaw, Valentin?"

He had never told anyone. Sacher had probably guessed—
the old man was remarkably intuitive about Jaus's feelings—
but no one knew. Jaus had no intention of telling anyone, until
he heard the words coming out of him, spilling into what should
have been a dignified, lofty silence.

"It happened on her first birthday, late in the afternoon," he
told Alex. "Jema's nanny had brought her outside to play on the
lawn and had then fallen asleep in the shade of one of the massive
oak trees. Jema wandered away. At the time, the brick wall surrounding Shaw House had not yet been built. Somehow that child
slipped past my guards and onto my property. I found her in the
garden, crying. She had knocked over one of the tables, and the
glass top shattered. She was sitting in the middle of the shards."

Jaus remembered how loudly Jema had screamed, and the
state in which he had found her in his camellia garden, her
hands bloody, and her small face wet with tears and mucus. The
moment she saw him, she held up her small arms. It had struck
him like a fist.

No being, human or Darkyn, had ever held out their arms to
Valentin Jaus.

"I didn't know Jema at the time, and I had no idea that she
belonged to my neighbor, Mrs. Shaw. All I knew of Meryl was
that she was wheelchair-bound, and that an accident in Greece
had killed her husband."

He told Alex how he had rescued baby Jema from the mess
and brought her into his pristine, child-free home. How he had
picked the shards out of her hands and cleaned the cuts, and
arranged fresh clothing, a bath, and a bottle of warm milk.

"I wouldn't let anyone else care for her or take her from
me." He was still not sure why he had been so adamant about
that. It may have been the alarming size of her—she was no
bigger or heavier than his lightest dagger—or the way she
curled up against him, her cheek pressed over his heart, her
small thumb tucked into her mouth. "While Sacher notified the
police, I fed Jema the bottle and rocked her to sleep. I refused
to put her down so that my *tresora* could take a photograph of
her for the *jardin* files—we photograph all humans we come in
contact with—and that is how I ended up in the picture."

"You must have given her to the police."

"It was terribly hard to do that, when they came to collect her. I'd never held a baby, and I felt so possessive of Jema. That night, the police informed me that Jema had been identified as the daughter of my nearest neighbor. Imagine my surprise." He felt a bitter amusement over the memory. "When they called, I had started working out how I might adopt her as my own daughter. I felt as if someone had stolen her from me."

Alexandra sighed. "Oh, shit."

"A good description of how I felt." He rose and walked around the room. "It was much easier when Jema was a child. I know what you are thinking, but I only felt the most distant and paternal-minded of affection for her."

"I get that." She nodded. "Then she grew up on you, and wham."

"Wham indeed. I began to see her not as a child, but as a woman. I don't know why. Jema has a lovely face, but she is no way robust, or anything like the women I prefer."

She rolled her eyes. "Yeah, us skinny, dark American chicks can't compete with those zaftig, blond Austrian babes."

"I couldn't see the attraction, and then it was so simple and clear to me. She is not like any woman I have ever known." He gave her an ironic look. "I have known my share."

Alex grinned. "I bet you have, Valentin."

"That was when I began collecting moments I shared with Jema. In the last thirty years, I have spent at least an hour in the simple honesty of her gaze. I have heard perhaps ten minutes of the sweet cascade of her laughter. I have watched the elegance of her hands dance for I know not how long. They always make me forget the time." He made a face. "I make a poor poet."

"What are you talking about?" She rested her hand against her cheek. "I think *I'm* in love with you now."

It felt ludicrous to laugh, but what else was his situation?

"Once I knew my feelings would not change, I became disgusted with myself for a time and eliminated all possibility of contact between us. I told myself over and over that she was a child, a fragile, often gravely ill child, and I had no right even to think of her in such a way. Then, too, came the time when I had to pretend to die and return to Derabend Hall as my 'son.' The Kyn who stay in one place must do so regularly to prevent suspicions among the locals. Thus Jema will never know that the man who found her in his garden, the man she thought was my father, was in fact me."

"You're breaking my heart here, Val." Alexandra shook her head. "Isn't there some way you two can be together?"

"Jema doesn't know I love her. She's dying. Juvenile diabetes." He came to stand beside her chair. "There is one way, but I never considered it. We have not been able to change humans for the last five hundred years . . . until you, Alex."

Her expression changed. "You're not talking about . . . oh, no." She got up from the chair and held up one hand. "I don't even know *why* I survived being infected, and my mutation isn't the same. Kyn blood kills every living thing that I've exposed to it. Before you ask, no, I am not experimenting on humans."

He felt confused. Cyprien had told him how diligently Alexandra had been working on fathoming the origins of the Kyn. "But Michael said that you're studying us. He said there was a possibility—"

"I'm looking for a *cure*. A way to turn us back into human beings," she told him flatly.

Despair turned into disbelief. "Why would we wish to be human again?"

"We're still human. We're just really powerful and our diet sucks. Excuse the pun." The humor left her eyes. "Let's be clear on this. If I did discover how to change a human into Kyn without killing them, then I'd never tell anyone. I am not restocking Tremayne's army of darkness."

"Then Jema and I can never be together." He turned away from her and went to the window to look at the gardens.

Alex tried to placate him. "You still have her human lifetime to share. You could make it work."

"Jema's thirtieth birthday is next week." He knew which flowers he would send to Shaw House. "I have spoken with doctors, and thirty years is far beyond what was predicted for her life expectancy. Her decline cannot be reversed. The next time I send her flowers, it *will* be for her funeral."

Chapter 13

The antique clock Jema kept by her bed told her she had woken up fifteen minutes late for work. The more dependable LED alarm clock behind it confirmed the time.

"Nice going, Shaw." She shoved her face in her pillow so she wouldn't have to see the evidence of her extreme laziness.

It was his fault again. Golden Eyes.

Over the last week she'd woken up each morning remembering a little more of her dreams. The first day it had been only a fragment; she recalled something about a ballroom and dancing with a tall, dark man with golden eyes. The second morning came with a vague recollection of a conversation she'd had with the same man. She'd been in a precolonial muslin gown; he'd been dressed in buckskins. They'd been standing under a waterfall lit from the outside with torches, and she remembered feeling cold and miserably wet. He'd told her that she would have to endure it, as he endured . . . something. The dream evaporated from there.

Yet as each day passed, less of her dreams vanished when she woke. None of them was recurring, but she became convinced that the men in them were all the same man. His appearance and clothes varied from one night to the next, but at some point in the dream, his pupils would contract into thin, dark lines like a cat's, and the irises would turn to gold.

Jema remembered most of the dream she'd had last night. "I can't believe I picked him up in a bar, or let him do that to me. On a *pool* table." She wrapped her arms around herself and giggled like a girl. "Too bad it didn't last long enough for me to . . . oh, I am depraved." She pulled back the covers and laughed again when she realized she was naked. "Completely, thoroughly depraved."

She stopped laughing when she breathed in and smelled fresh gardenias, and saw the faint marks on her breasts and thighs.

Jema walked naked into the bathroom and switched on all the lights to examine herself in the mirror. What appeared to be light pink and lavender smudges circled both of her breasts. There were five on each side. Three more, darker purple marks like bruises marred the inside of her right thigh. She turned and found four more marks just like them on her left buttock.

"I've heard of convincing yourself that you're pregnant, but convincing yourself that you've been manhandled?" Jema had had one brief romance with a boy who had loved to nibble and suck on her neck, and she remembered how her easily bruised skin reacted to that. Daniel had nearly had a heart attack, thinking that she was showing symptoms of a secondary blood disorder, until she'd stuttered out an explanation. To make matters worse, that particular boyfriend had dumped her the very next day.

She touched one of the marks on her breast gently, testing it. They didn't hurt, and there wasn't any abrasion to the skin itself. It was the sort of mark left when someone took hold of a person and squeezed.

The way he squeezed me. Jema's face burned as that portion of the dream suddenly came back to her with vivid, intimate detail. The way he touched her; it had been embarrassing and thrilling and totally outside her fairly dismal experiences in bed with men. *Either I have a wonderful imagination, or I miss sex more than I thought.*

Jema started to make a hideous face at her reflection and stopped cold when that, too, struck her. She rarely looked at herself in the mirror. Now, because of some silly female version of a wet dream, she was feeling up her own breasts and clowning around in front of one, as if she did it every day.

Mirrors are not my friends.

With wary steps, she retreated back into the bedroom and took one of her work outfits from the closet. One of the maids must have sprayed some sort of concentrated air freshener in her room; the air was thick with the scent of gardenias.

Jema took an appreciative sniff. *Good thing I like the smell.* It made her feel great, for some reason. She'd have to ask Micki what it was so she could take some in to the museum. Her office could use some serious freshening treatment.

She hated going into work late—everyone took extra pains to ignore her for acting like the boss's daughter—but it was better than sitting around the house listening to her mother describe the depth and breadth of her imaginary chest pains. That she could listen to anytime. Plus she wanted to see Luisa before the weekend. Since she was already late, she could stop by the hospital on the way to work.

If she tried very hard, she could probably forget all about the marks and the fact that her room smelled like a hothouse.

She did hear Daniel and her mother in the library, and stopped there on her way to pick up something to take with her for breakfast. She was tempted to assume her usual listening post, to gauge how things were going inside, but suddenly she was tired of eavesdropping for mood swings. She knocked once and walked in.

"Good morning. I overslept a little." She glanced from Daniel to her mother. "Hey. You two look nice."

Meryl wore what Jema recognized as her favorite outfit, a ruffled skirt and lace blouse in a pearly cream shade that didn't leach all the color from her skin the way her other Snow Queen white outfits did. Daniel was his usual tidy self in his tweed jacket and pressed navy trousers, but he'd put on a good tie with a small gold caduceus tie pin.

"Are you feeling ill?" her mother asked at once. "It's not like you to leave so late. You should stay home today."

"I'm terrific. I can't wait to get to work; I have a mystery to solve. Then again, that's my job." Jema grinned as she noticed a large pile of legal documents sitting on her mother's desk. "Speaking of which—you never told me why you two were out on the town so late the other night. Everything okay with the family fortune?"

Meryl drew back as if Jema had spit in her face, while

Daniel avoided her gaze. It was such an unexpected reaction that Jema laughed.

"Everything *is* okay, right?" she asked, more tentatively now.

"Of course it is." Meryl recovered first, with a vengeance. "Daniel took me to see a heart specialist, and the tests took longer than we had expected."

Daniel cleared his throat and shuffled his feet. "We should have the results in next week."

Were these two acting *guilty?* Jema almost asked, but then remembered that her birthday was next week. Her mother had never celebrated it in a big way, but it was a landmark date—she'd always been told she'd be lucky to live to thirty. *Well, I made it, and if I keep hitting the bran muffins and the sugar-free, lactose-free yogurt, I might even make it to thirty-five.* "Let me know how it turns out. See you tonight. I shouldn't be late."

Jema liked visiting Luisa in the mornings. At night the hospital could be a little creepy, especially when they turned down the lights in the hallways. Today she stopped by the gift shop to pick up a small flower arrangement for Luisa's room. She made sure to pick flowers that had a nice scent, as her friend wouldn't be able to see them.

"I brought you a present," she said as soon as she came into the room.

Dr. Keller, who was standing at the window, glanced back at her. "Oh, you shouldn't have."

Jema put the arrangement within Luisa's reach—she felt sure that when she was alone, the girl liked to touch the soft petals—and squared her shoulders to face the doctor. She didn't like Alexandra Keller, but she could try to be polite to her. "I didn't think I'd see you here again, Dr. Keller."

"I try to be unpredictable, Miss Shaw." Alex gestured to Luisa. "Our mutual friend doesn't want me around, but I came today hoping to change her mind."

"You shouldn't upset her." Jema didn't feel like verbally sparring with Alex, and went to sit by the bed. "Did the eye doctor come by to check on you? It should be time to take the bandages off soon."

"Yeah, he did." Luisa reached for the flowers and caressed them with her fingertips. "What you buy me these for? It ain't my birthday."

"It's almost mine." Jema chuckled. "I thought you might like to smell something besides Nurse Kohler."

"The one that leaves a trail like a skunk?" Luisa shook her head. "My mama say she uglier than roadkill. Smell like it, too."

Jema thought of Nurse Kohler's trademark bright blue eye shadow. "Let's say she's cosmetically challenged." She saw Alex watching them, and then she saw two Alexes. With all her bouncing around this morning, she'd forgotten to take her morning injection. "Uh-oh." Fighting off the weakness, she groped for her purse. She could feel all the color fading from her skin, and Alex was staring at her. "May I use your bathroom, Luisa?"

"If Nurse Kohler ain't in there. She go a lot."

Jema walked carefully to the small lavatory and put her purse on the sink. She considered shutting the door, but the dizziness was getting worse, and she didn't want to pass out and scare Luisa.

"Need a hand?" Alex came in after her.

"With this, no, thank you." Daniel gave her prefilled syringes to carry in her purse kit, so all she had to do was strap up and raise a vein, which was never a problem. "I'm a diabetic, in case you're wondering."

"I heard that you were." Alex's reflection frowned at her. "You take your insulin intravenously."

"I'm a *bad* diabetic." She tied off her arm, flicked a likely spot with her fingernail, and then prepared the syringe. She felt self-conscious about injecting herself in front of Alex, but it couldn't be helped. "I was born this way."

The dizziness receded a few seconds later. She applied a small round Band-Aid to cover the injection spot and looked around for the biohazardous waste container, but saw none.

"Who manages your case, Miss Shaw?" Alex asked.

"Dr. Daniel Bradford. He's our family physician." She packed up her kit and washed her hands at the sink. "He lives at Shaw House with me and my mother. We both require a lot of monitoring. He's taken care of me almost from the day I was born."

"Sounds like a very dedicated guy." Alex handed her a paper towel. "Have you seen anyone else about your condition?"

"Dr. Bradford takes great care of me and my mother." Jema knew that Alex was simply being a good doctor, but she didn't like her insinuations. "He's become an expert on diabetes over the years, of course, and he's also done all sorts of research into treatments for lower spine trauma and paralysis. He has a full lab set up at our home. Unfortunately my mother will never recover, and neither will I." She gave her a cool smile. "We've never felt the need to go looking for a second opinion."

"That's great. You're lucky. And you look much better." Alex reached out and pressed the back of her hand against Jema's cheek. "A little flushed, but that's probably my fault for poking my nose in your medical business."

"Did you have to walk out on Luisa the way you did?" Jema asked on impulse. "Couldn't you have stayed in Chicago until she was stable?"

Now it was Alex's turn to pale. "I had no choice. I can't get into the details, but believe me, Miss Shaw, I wanted to be here."

Jema could hear the sincerity in her voice. "It was very generous of you to give her mother all that money. I know it's made a big difference in the quality of her care and recovery." She looked down at the used syringe and capped the needle. "I'd better take this out to the nurses' station. I think they have a needle box out there."

"Let me. I've got to get going anyway." Alex held out her hand, and when Jema gave her the syringe she tucked it in her pocket. "One more sort of nosy question before I go. Do you have any other family besides your mother?"

Jema frowned. "Well, my mother's family, but they disowned her for marrying my dad and they've never had any contact with me. My dad was an orphan."

"Your mother owns your father's estate, and I assume you're her heir," Alex stated. "Who inherits from you?"

"My mother," Jema said. "We set up our wills so that if one of us dies, the other inherits. If we both die at the same time, or close to each other, everything goes to fund the museum and about a hundred charities. One of them is this burn ward. Why?"

"Eventually the money I gave Mrs. Lopez will run out. I'm going to arrange a life trust fund to pay for Luisa's medical care, and I thought you might like to mention her in your will." Alex glanced out at the girl, who was holding the flower arrangement Jema had brought and was exploring the petals with her fingers. "Not that I'm wishing you an early death, but she'll need certain treatments and physical therapy for the rest of her life."

"That's a marvelous idea," Jema said, liking Alex a little more. "I'll speak to my mother about it."

Things did not go so well for Jema when she got to the museum. The doors had not yet opened to the public, thanks to a staff scheduling problem, which had administration in something of a muddle.

"I need three guards on the floor, not two," the head curator was telling the events coordinator.

"You can't use my tour manager for security," the coordinator argued. "She isn't trained for it."

Jema never interfered with the daily management of the museum, but as she needed help bringing up crates, she was obliged to get involved. With a little creative juggling of the staff, she was able to help the head curator get the museum open, and find a tour guide for the events coordinator to help her with a middle school class scheduled that day. That allowed her to borrow Thomas for an hour of work downstairs.

"I don't know what the deal is with Roy," Tom told her as they went into the storage area. "He's never missed more than one shift, and only when he's really sick. I even tried to call him, but he doesn't answer his phone."

"People have problems that are more important than work sometimes. Roy's a good employee; I'm sure he'll turn up." Jema went to the storage shelves designated for the Athos dig, but one of the crates for lot two-forty was missing. "Okay. Now I know this was right here last week. I did a count for the inventory program and I had to requisition more sample containers to send to the Wisconsin lab."

"You know, Roy was down here a couple of nights back, arranging things," Thomas told her as he helped her look. "He does that for Dr. Shaw now and then."

"Arranging things how?"

"I'm not sure. He gets a call from her, and he has me take over upstairs while he checks things for her. Once he had to take something over to your house after his shift. I saw him loading it into his car."

"My house." Jema glanced at him. "Tom, we don't keep any of the museum's property at home. It's against our insurance company's policy, for one thing, and we don't have reason to have them there."

"All I can tell you is that he took a crate out of here one morning," Tom insisted. "He didn't say it was for Dr. Shaw, but he'd had a phone call from her, and he took the lake road out of here. Roy doesn't live anywhere near the lake." He sniffed the air. "Have you been eating apples? I've been smelling them all morning."

"No, sorry, it's not me." She smelled the fruity scent, too, but dismissed it. "Bring the rest of lot two-forty into the lab now, Tom." Jema went to her office and called Shaw House.

Meryl took her call immediately. "What is it, Jema? Are you sick? I told you to stay home today."

"I'm fine, Mother. We're missing a crate from lot two-forty, and if I can't find it, I have to make a police report." Jema looked up at the painting over her desk. "One of the guards seems to think Roy might have brought it over to the house for you."

"Yes, I had a number of things brought to the house so I could examine them," her mother said, astonishing her. "I do have the missing crate here now, and it will be returned to the museum as soon as I'm through with it."

"Why are you examining things?" That was Jema's job.

"James was interested in an old legend he thought might be a true story," Meryl told her. "I'm still pursuing the proof he never found."

Jema felt troubled by the confirmation. They had always

handled the museum's collection with the utmost care and precautions. What Meryl was doing was highly irregular and unethical. "Does the head curator know about this?"

"Of course he does. What did you think I was doing, Jema?" Her mother's voice grew shrill. "Stealing from my own husband's museum?"

"No, of course not." She winced. "I will need that crate back so I can catalog the items and include them in the final inventory."

"I'll need them for only a few more days," Meryl told her. "Then it will be finished."

As Jema hung up the phone, she felt puzzled. What was her mother doing, and why was she trying to hide it from her? She took a deep breath and frowned. Tom was right: Her office did smell like apples—a whole barrel of them—but there was something else under the scent.

Gardenias.

Michael had run out of time, and so had John Keller. If he was going to keep Alexandra's brother alive, he would have to bargain with Tremayne, which required careful thought and planning. The high lord was within his rights to demand Keller's execution. He could also ignore whatever Michael wanted and send his own team of assassins to America to manage the task for him.

Somehow Michael had to make letting Keller live more attractive than killing him.

"You've got that someone's-going-to-suffer-for-this look in your eyes." Alexandra came into the bathroom and put her arms around him from behind. "If it's me, we'd better put away the breakable stuff in the bedroom. I'm not afraid to bite back now."

Michael still could not believe Alex was his *sygkenis*. She was so petite and vibrant and sizzling with unseen energy. He wanted to take her away to a remote island where they could be alone and he could paint her and walk with her and love her without the rest of the world trying to tear her from his arms.

"Suffer?" He turned around and hauled her off her feet, holding her in a tight embrace. "Is that what I make you do?"

"Not a good question, considering our history." She wrapped her arms around his neck. "It's okay. I like how you make me suffer now as opposed to then. How about we take a walk down by the water first?"

"You saw Jema Shaw at the hospital?" She nodded, and he set her down to put on his shirt. "Should Valentin hear this?"

"Not right now." Alex took a clip and used it to pull her hair back from her face. "He's in love with her. She doesn't know. You are not to say a word."

"I will not." Michael frowned. "How did you discover this?"

"He needed a sympathetic ear, and mine was available. Why don't you guys fall in love with lady vampires?" Alex asked him. "Not that I believe in that whole arranged-marriage crap they used to do in your day, but at least if you did your relationships would last a little longer."

Michael thought of Angelica, but decided not to mention her. Alexandra still had nightmares about killing Thierry's wife. "There aren't very many women who rise to walk as Darkyn. At the most, only one for every fifty men."

He checked to see that the sun had set before walking out of their room and down to the back entrance of the house. On the way he dismissed his guards and left word with Falco for Valentin, so he would know where they were. The lakeshore was not as beautiful to him as Lake Pontchartrain, but the stark appeal of Lake Michigan suited Valentin.

"Fifty to one," he heard Alex muttering.

"It was rare for a woman to rise from the grave. Most were turned by male Darkyn in the early days, when that was still possible." Michael took her hand in his. "You don't realize how special you truly are."

"I'll try to act snottier," Alex said. "You've got women in your *jardin,* right?"

"Only two. Liliette, Thierry's aunt, and Marcella, Arnaud Evareaux's cousin." He smiled down at her. She always had to collect facts and statistics about everything. "You must meet Cella when we return. She sculpts in stone and metal. You would like her."

"Maybe we could introduce her to Val. He's going to need

someone a little healthier in his life." Alex frowned and looked up at the house. "I saw Jema Shaw at the hospital today. She's not in good shape, although she seemed pretty happy. There's something very wrong with her. . . ." Alex's eyes widened, and a moment later she pushed him with both hands, knocking him down to the sand.

Michael heard a whisper of wind, felt it pass his neck, and watched in horror as a long copper bolt divided the air between them before it struck Alex in the chest.

"Alexandra." He was up and caught her in his arms, lifting her off her feet and running for cover. Two of Valentin's guards came to flank him. "Over there," he snarled, jerking his head in the direction the bolt had come. "Bring him to me alive."

The guards took off, while more came to help Michael with his burden. He wouldn't let them touch Alex, and carried her into Derabend Hall, shouting as he ran for Valentin.

The suzerain appeared and sized up the situation in a glance. He directed Michael to a small bedchamber on the first floor.

"Who shot her?" he demanded as he stripped the bed linens out of the way.

"Someone in the trees beyond the house. He was aiming for me; she pushed me out of the way at the last second." Michael placed her carefully on the bed and examined the wound. The copper shaft had buried itself in her shoulder, a few inches above her heart. "I want him."

"You will have him." Jaus touched the blood on Alex's shirt. "She yet bleeds, Michael."

"She doesn't heal as quickly as we do." He used his dagger to cut her shirt away from the wound and gently tested the set of the shaft in her flesh. "It is barbed copper. God *damn* him."

Alex opened her eyes. "Mike."

"Shhhh." He forced himself to smile down at her. "I am here, *ma belle.* Don't move."

"Not so *belle* now." She looked him over, checking him for wounds before tucking her chin to look at the shaft. "It wasn't the same one who tried at the hospital. This guy was . . ." A groan escaped her, and her body arched. "God this fucking thing *burns.*"

"We have to get it out of her," Valentin told him. "The copper is too close to her heart."

Michael knew, just as Jaus did, of Kyn who had been killed by the presence of the poisonous metal in their bodies, especially in close vicinity to the heart. Through movies, Hollywood had generated the myth that a stake through the heart would kill a vampire. In truth it took only a sliver of copper.

Sacher came in carrying Alex's medical bag. The old man looked ill but his voice was steady when he said, "Master, I have sent for Garomen."

"Garomen has some experience with treating the wounded in battle," Valentin explained. He turned to his *tresora*. "Did he go on the hunt tonight?"

"Yes, but we should be able to find him soon."

"No one else from the *jardin*," Alex said, her voice thin with pain. "I didn't see this guy's face, but I heard him in my head before he shot me." She looked directly at Jaus. "I only pushed Mike out of the way when I saw the crossbow through this jerk's eyes. I couldn't understand his thoughts because he was thinking in German."

Valentin swore in the same language. Cyprien uttered his own thoughts in French.

"Hold it together, now, boys," she warned them. "I've still got this thing in my chest. We need to get it out."

"It will not be easy, Alexandra," Cyprien told her. "The shaft is copper, and it is barbed on the end that is lodged inside you. It cannot be pulled out."

"Terrific." She shifted, trying to elevate her upper body. "I need some pillows to prop me up and some towels to soak up the blood. There's going to be a lot of it."

"The anesthetic you created," Michael said. "We can give it to you so you will feel no pain."

"No. I need to supervise, and I can't do that if I'm doped." She glanced at Valentin. "You're my surgeon tonight."

Michael wasn't letting anyone else touch her. "I will do what needs to be done."

"You? You are shaking too much." She flinched as Valentin placed two more pillows behind her. "Sacher, we need a scalpel and some antiseptic. You know the bottle."

"Indeed, I do." The *tresora* brought them to the bed.

She glanced at the scalpel. "Val, sterilize the blade by pouring some of the antiseptic over it. Soak it good. Michael, you have to turn me on my right side now."

Once Alex was lying as she directed, Val picked up the scalpel and looked at the smooth curve of her shoulder. "Tell me what to do, Alexandra."

She swallowed and gripped the bed with her hands. "Make a three-inch lateral incision in my shoulder, directly parallel to the tip of the bolt."

"No," Michael said at once. "You will not cut her."

"Babe, it's the only way we're going to get this thing out of me with minimum damage. Come here and hold my hands." When he did, she gave him an encouraging smile. "This is going to hurt and I'm going to get noisy. Don't panic. We've been through worse."

She was worried about him. She was lying there with a shaft through her body, the body she had used to shield him from it, and still she cared more for what he felt.

He was a Darkyn seigneur, master of seventy-nine *jardins,* thousands of immortals, and presently was as helpless and terrified as a child. "I love you."

"Say it in French. I love when you talk Euro to me." She took in a deep breath. "You ready to do this, Valentin?"

"You have but to give me the word, my lady."

"Now would be fine." Alex's smile became strained, and her eyes closed briefly as Valentin used the scalpel. "That's it. Now cut sideways—through the muscle you see—yes, like that." She bit her lip, and hung on to Michael's hands as if they were her lifeline.

"I have cut through, Alexandra."

"Good," she said on a burst of released breath. "Do you see the end of it yet?"

"Not yet."

Her fingernails stabbed into Michael's flesh. "Cut deeper."

Valentin plied the scalpel again. "A little more, my lady. A little . . . there." He lifted his head and met Michael's gaze. "I see it."

"Here comes the part where you want to cover your eyes

with your hands. Just don't." She looked up at Michael. "Take the shaft and push through me to Val. Val, you pull it out through the back. When it's out, douse the whole thing with antiseptic, and bandage me. I'll probably be out of it."

Cyprien put a hand on the shaft. For a terrible moment he didn't think he could do it. Then he saw her eyes, and the trust in them.

"Be strong," she whispered, "and fast, please."

He bent down to kiss her, and gripped the shaft and her shoulder with firm hands. As her lips clung to his, he pushed the bolt through. He caught her scream in his mouth as Valentin pulled the bolt out through the incision he had made.

"It is done." Val threw the bolt away, and it clattered on the tile floor.

"Great." Alex closed her eyes and went limp.

Cyprien used a towel to stanch the blood pouring from both sides of the wound before cleaning her torn flesh. "She will need blood when she wakes."

"I will have it ready."

Falco came to join them. "Master, I have found a trail. The assassin has fled on foot." He looked at Alexandra and his expression hardened. "Someone betrayed us. No human could have come here unless—"

"The assassin is one of our men," Valentin told his seneschal. "A native German."

"I want him," Cyprien said. "He belongs to me."

Jaus nodded. "I will care for her, Michael. Go with Falco."

Chapter 14

Jema made a point of arriving home in time for dinner, so that she could talk to her mother about the crate of artifacts she had taken from the museum. It seemed out of character for her to be working on some secret project; her mother had always been very proud and public about the museum and James Shaw's work. Jema was also curious about the legend Meryl had mentioned.

"I didn't know you were still actively researching, Mother," she said after the maid served Meryl and Daniel dessert and brought Jema's herbal tea. "Is this something new?"

"It's nothing. I'm only attempting to finish something your father was working on just before he died," Meryl said.

"Why? I mean, it's been thirty years. I don't think there's any rush."

"Who said I've been hurrying?" Her mother stabbed a piece of fruit from her dish of trifle. "I organized his papers on Athos many years ago, so that they might one day be published in recognition of his work. Unfortunately he never finished the dig, and his findings were incomplete, so I decided to finish the work for him."

"This legend is related to the Athos dig." Jema noticed her mother's agitation—her hands were trembling—and frowned. "If this is upsetting you, we don't have to talk about it."

"Did anyone watch the forecast?" Daniel asked. "I was wondering which way that blizzard out west is moving."

"West, I think," Jema said. "It's over Iowa."

"Please, God, not another riveting dissection of the atmospheric conditions." Meryl sighed and set down her fork. "If you must know, Jema, your father went to Greece to find a ceremonial object called the Homage of Athos."

"The Homage." A spasm of nausea made Jema swallow quickly.

"Yes. The peasants who lived near the Athos mountain in Greece apparently climbed it every year to present this homage to the gods. No one has any idea of what it was, precisely, but James said it was of great importance to the local population. We found a building that may have been the temple they built around it at the base of Athos. That was the first dig your father conducted there."

"Homage." Jema turned the word over in her head. "Could it have been a burned offering or a libation ceremony of some sort?" Both had been popular in ancient polytheist sacrificial rituals.

"James thought it could be an object with a map that showed the old pathways around the mountain, and the location of certain caves. The locals used the caves as natural temples." She moved her shoulders. "There is no description of the homage anywhere, except by name or unspecific reference, so that was purely speculation on his part."

The Homage of Athos. It sounded tantalizingly familiar. It also made Jema's stomach curl, or perhaps she'd eaten too much starch for dinner. Rice never did sit well on her stomach at night. "I think I've read about it somewhere, but I can't remember in what."

"It's in a few of the scholarly texts on early Greek mythology," Meryl said. "Some of the more contemporary texts refer to it as the 'Image of Athos.'"

"That would explain Father's map angle."

"Whether it was homage or an image, it was lost eight thousand years ago." The lines around her mother's mouth deepened. "Your father believed the people of Athos sealed it away in a ritual cave so no one could take advantage of it. The scroll refers to the hiding place only as 'the Well of Life.'"

"A cave that's also a well." Jema raised her eyebrows as she took a sip of tea. "Generally it's either one or the other, not both."

"I know how preposterous it sounds. I tried to persuade

your father to abandon the dig, many times. I never liked it."
Meryl's gaze grew shuttered. "He wouldn't listen to me. It was
the one time I couldn't persuade him to reason. He was ob-
sessed with finding it."

With a little more coaxing from Jema, Meryl related the details of the legend.

"That's just the Prometheus story, with a few of the partic-
ulars changed," Jema said after her mother finished. "You do
know that."

"That was exactly what I told your father. But he had an
Egyptian scroll that substantiated the legend, and some obscure passages from Hesiod he was convinced indicated otherwise. He wouldn't listen to me. That's why he's dead." Her
hand tugged at the lace collar of her blouse. "I knew it would
end badly. I knew it the moment I saw that cave that something
terrible would happen to anyone who went in it. I simply never
thought it would be . . ." She trailed off. "I almost died there.
That was the cave that collapsed on me and broke my back."

"This Well of Life," Jema said, trying to change the subject,
"was it only a hiding place, or did it have a part in the legend?"

"Hesiod referred to it as the source of immortality. James's
theory was that the one chosen by the gods after the homage
was presented would be led to the Well of Life and permitted
to drink. The water was supposed to heal all wounds, cure all
ills, and bestow immortality." Meryl made a bitter sound. "The
Greeks' eternal fountain of youth."

"You don't have to go to Athos for that," Daniel said, his
tone jovial. "Lourdes is much closer."

"James went back." Meryl's voice hardened. "He brought
me and Jema to the States as soon as he could bribe the Greek
doctors to release us. He left me here with a broken back and
a newborn, and went straight to Athos, and got himself killed
on that mountain."

Jema couldn't quite believe that her father had put so much
faith in an ancient legend. By all accounts, James Shaw had
been a very pragmatic man, focused on uncovering and preserving tangible proof of past civilizations. This sort of thing
sounded more like a plot for an Indiana Jones movie.

"Is there anything I can do to help with the project, Mother?" Jema asked.

"I'm nearly finished with it," Meryl told her.

"Whatever your father thought, I'm sure that the homage is only a legend," Daniel said gently. "There is no miracle water that can cure us, or keep us from dying."

"Who wants to live forever anyway?" Jema said, trying to sound lighthearted. "The taxes alone would be outrageous. The Social Security people would get very cranky."

"I wouldn't mind," Daniel joked. "I could end up with the world's best tee shot. I'd make Tiger Woods look like Wrong-Way Jones."

Meryl refused to be cheered, and pushed her dessert aside. "Take me upstairs now, Daniel. I'm tired." She wheeled out of the room before either of them could speak.

Daniel put his napkin on the table as he rose to follow her. "Night, Jem."

Her mother's depression tagged after Jema for the rest of the evening, until she gave in and went upstairs herself. After she took her evening injection, she changed into a nightgown and settled in with a volume of Mark Twain.

The Connecticut Yankee couldn't hold Jema's attention, however, not with the new worry over her mother. Why was Meryl trying to finish her father's work, and why did she need to take things from the museum to do that? It didn't make sense. The Athos artifacts had already been checked and dated; there weren't any that Jema could remember as even particularly remarkable.

Frustrated with having more questions than answers, she put away the book, turned out the light, and tried to sleep.

Sleep didn't want to have anything to do with Jema at first. Just as she thought she might toss and turn for the rest of the night, the scent of gardenias filled her head, and she drifted off.

The round-roofed white building was three stories tall, surrounded by rolling green grass and enclosed with channels of simple post-and-rail fencing. Jema dropped down in front of it, all floaty and nice, Glinda the Good Witch minus the Lollipop Guild. She couldn't see inside the structure, as there were only a couple of small windows near the roof eaves. She knew it was a barn even before she smelled the hay, manure, and animals.

Wherever she was, it wasn't Connecticut, or King Arthur's court.

The sun had sunk below the horizon, but threw out enough rays for Jema to get her bearings. There were no other buildings, just endless rolling green pastureland, the barn, and the big double doors handing wide open. The night closed around her, slowly but insistently urging her toward the open doors. A bored cop supervising a fender bender would have done it the same way. *Let's go, keep moving, lady; c'mon, c'mon, nuthin' to see here . . .*

"Cows." She could hear them chewing. "Why am I dreaming about cows?"

Maybe it was her way of dealing with being lactose intolerant.

She didn't walk through the door quickly, but crept in like a thief. Her caution seemed silly once she was inside, as it was nothing more than a barn: trampled straw speckled with bits of soil, manure, and feed covering a packed dirt floor. Some well-used tack and equipment hung from post pegs; a pitchfork was stuck in a pile of clean hay. Ten stanchions for milk cows, a couple of horse stalls, and a stock pen, all empty.

No cows. What was making that chewing sound?

Bemused, Jema took off her robe and hung it on an empty peg before she moved toward the center of the barn. It was so obviously a dream, and yet it felt real—as if this farm actually existed somewhere.

But I've never been to a farm, or walked inside a barn.

The light shifted, and she saw that she wasn't alone anymore. At the far end of the barn, a blond woman sat on a three-legged stool next to a fat black-and-white Holstein, her arms moving rhythmically. Jema could smell milk and hear squirts of liquid hitting the tin.

She glanced inside the empty stalls before she started toward the woman. "I beg your pardon. Can you tell me where I am?"

The cow ignored her and kept chewing its cud, but the

woman's arms stopped moving and she turned her head to peek at Jema. The woman's chunky golden braids, rosy cheeks, and bright blue eyes were milkmaid pretty.

"Guten abend, fraulein." She smiled, showing even, white teeth, and then went back to work.

Jema waited for her golden-eyed demon to appear. He didn't. The milkmaid continued to work, and the cow kept chewing. "I'm sorry, I don't speak German, but I need help. I'm looking for a man."

The milkmaid pulled a tin pail out from under the cow and got up from her stool. *"Wie bitte?"* She looked down at Jema's nightgown, and her smile wavered.

"What is this place?" Behind the cow was another open door, but Jema couldn't see what was beyond it. "Why am I here?"

The milkmaid smiled again.

Jema looked all around her. The dream made no sense. The milkmaid was simply a German woman, the cow was just a cow, and the stuff in the pail was . . . milk. A little foamy around the edges, and definitely not pasteurized, but certainly not acid or nitroglycerin.

Am I really this *boring?*

She looked up at a nest in the rafters. A swallow poked its head out, wasn't impressed, and went back to sleep. The German woman stood there smiling, the cow stood there chewing, and the milk in the pail stayed milk.

Jema tried to communicate again. "You don't speak any English?"

The other woman made the pained little face that was the universal polite substitute for *Obviously not, genius.*

Taking that Spanish class in high school didn't seem so bright now, Jema thought as she passed the woman to go around the cow.

The pail dropped and milk splashed out and went everywhere. *"Gefahr!"* She threw out her plump arms. *"Warten Sie hier!"*

Jema threw her hands up, but the milkmaid didn't strike her. They stood there another couple of seconds, Jema waiting, the milkmaid with her arms thrown wide and her expression one of horror and fear.

"You"—Jema pointed to the milk maid—"don't want me"—she pointed to her own chest and shook her head—"to go in there"—she walked two of her fingers toward the door behind the cow—"right?"

The milkmaid nodded so hard that the ends of her braids bounced off her generously filled work apron.

"I'm sorry, but I think that's the point." Jema went around the cow, stepped through the door into the darkness, and felt something squish under her shoes. The smell of raw meat filled her nostrils and turned her stomach. "Hello?"

Her voice made torches flare to life above her head. The flames illuminated fresh beef carcasses suspended by huge steel hooks on thick, crude chains. Innards and pools of blood covered ten big stone tables; blood and piles of raw fat flooded what looked like river weeds laid out on the floor. The stench enhanced the atmosphere.

The place wasn't just plain disgusting, Jema decided. It was fancy disgusting. It was disgusting with a wine waiter and no prices on the menu.

To one side was a cramped pen with nine dirty, skinny, miserable-looking cows in it. They didn't make a sound, and their eyes were sunk into their skulls so far they looked like black holes. The one closest to the gate had a withered bag with scabby, dried-up teats dangling so low they dragged on the manure-stained, trampled straw of the pen.

"You should not have come here," a deep, familiar voice said.

The quick, sharp breath Jema took in was so cold it numbed her teeth. "Any particular reason why?"

The cows shuffled around in the pen, carcasses started to sway, and the floor rumbled. No sign of her golden-eyed demon, however.

"I'm going to remember this," Jema warned him, turning around and peering into the shadows. "Better be nice to me so I don't hate you in the morning."

Jema's demon jumped down from the rafters and landed to stand in front of her. He wore a white tunic with an enormous red X across the chest, and carried a sword with a five-foot-long blade.

This was a much bigger, meaner version of the demon who had been haunting her dreams, one who evidently didn't care if she was impressed by his personal hygiene. He was filthy, his hair a matted, tangled mane, his eyes hostile slits. Drying blood spatters covered his arms, hands, and chest, and yet he still smelled of gardenias.

"What happened to you?" Without thinking, she reached for him, but he took a step back. "What's the matter? You're not afraid of me."

"Non." He leaned the sword against one of the butchering tables, took off the tunic, and tossed it next to a mound of organs. *"Allez-vous-en."*

French. She didn't remember him being French. "What does that mean?"

"Go away."

"If you come with me, I will." Jema wasn't sure how to leave this place. "Can you take me somewhere else? Netherfield?"

"Netherfield exists only in a book. This is real." The gauntlets he wore came off and landed on top of the fur with a muffled thump. His hands looked terribly raw, as if he'd pounded the sense out of someone. "You have a life, Jema. Why do you spend it reading love stories and only dreaming of better?"

"I don't know. There was nothing good on TV?" It was a pathetic joke, and so cold in this place that she could see her own breath as she spoke.

The demon removed the chain mail he had worn under the white tunic, which had been tied and strapped onto him in an archaic fashion. Beneath it he wore a loose-woven tunic and baggy trousers that hadn't been sewn together very well.

"If you need to change, I can wait outside." She gestured toward a glistening brain and some eyeballs with the ganglia still attached. "Happily."

"You come naked." Once he'd stripped to the waist, he walked toward her. "Naked to my charnel house."

Jema glanced down, indignant as soon as she saw she still had on clothes. "I did not—"

He clamped his hands on her waist and lifted her until her feet left the floor. "Naked as you are defenseless. I could do anything to you in your dreams, little cat, and no one could stop me." He brought her up to his eye level. "Is that what you wanted?"

She was in trouble. She would have tried the *Purpose-Driven Life* approach, but she was the only person in the country who hadn't read the damn book. "Is that what you want?"

He dropped her onto one of the tables. Jema's backside hit the stone edge, and something soft and wet splattered all over her back. She looked down and thought a replay of the morning at Wendy's was plausible.

"I don't like this, um, charnel house very much." She wanted to go back to another place, one where he did other, nicer things to her. "Do you?"

"No." He came to her, and braced his arms on either side of her, uncaring of what his hands squashed. "I never did. Even when I swore I would stay to defend the last man. Never did I enjoy what I had to do. Do you believe me?"

She blocked out their revolting surroundings and remembered how good it had felt to kiss him, to have his hands on her. His eyes burned with golden flame, and he spoke with his lips peeled back from his teeth, but she could feel something else.

He wants me to hit him. He wants me to fight him and hate him. To be disgusted by him. The way I behaved in the dream at the tavern.

"Why are you doing this?" she demanded, gripping bloody stone so she wouldn't slide off.

"You showed me your secrets. This is mine. This is what I was." He looked around them, as if he wasn't sure. Then, with more assurance, he said, "I lived a lifetime in this place. Killing for them. For God."

"It's not such a bad place." No, it was, but this didn't seem the time to get girly about it. She had blood from the table on her hands, and the cut she'd made across her palm stung. "Do you have to stay here?"

He stepped back, stunned. "Of course."

"But you could walk out anytime you want."

"Walk out? When Shujai and al-Ashraf had caught us in their trap, squeezing us to death between Beirut and Haifa?" He spoke as if it were something happening this moment, just on the other side of the walls.

"You were in Desert Storm?" He didn't look that old.

"Only two strongholds remained, Tortosa to the north, and Castle Pilgrim at Athlit, to the south. I was at Castle Pilgrim, sent there to safeguard the Christian pilgrims come to the Holy Land. Only none dared to come. There were only Saracens." Hatred and sorrow wove tight threads through his voice. "I wanted to go home, but I honored my vows."

"Tortosa? Castle Pilgrim . . ." Jema shook her head, completely confused now. "Those were Templar castles. What are you talking about?"

"Tortosa was abandoned first, and then ten days later the order came. We were to retreat to Ruad, where ships were waiting to take us home." He looked around him. "Someone had to stay behind until the last man left. I volunteered to stand watch against the Saracens."

"There aren't any Saracens here." She nodded toward the door. "The only person out there is a milkmaid. I think you could probably take her."

"Angelica." His mouth thinned. "She betrayed me. She sold me and our son and my family to the devil."

"I didn't know you were involved."

"You don't know anything about me. I was a Templar. I became a monster." He opened his mouth, and two long, sharp-looking white fangs appeared. "I have walked the earth for more than seven hundred years. I feed on the blood of the living."

She had to say something. "Have you read *The Purpose-Driven Life?*"

"Do not jest about this. I am a demon, Jema, simply not the one you've imagined. And I will never leave this place." He turned away from her, and his voice changed. "I can't. I've been here too long."

"That is such *crap*." Jema picked up something wet and

dripping and threw it at his back, smacking him in between the shoulder blades. Anger became horror as he looked at her. "I'm sorry. I shouldn't have done that."

He strode to the table, grabbed her by the calves, and yanked them, laying her out flat on her back.

Under him.

Not where Jema wanted to be. Not on a rock bed awash with cow tartare. Not when she had a pretty good idea of what he was going to do with those fangs.

She rolled, but not in time to avoid being pinned between his thighs. He brought his full weight down and flattened her against the stone. Things squished under her front and she fought to keep her face out of the gore. Behind her, his hands manacled her wrists and stretched out her arms so she couldn't use either elbow. His heavy legs were locked on the outsides of hers.

So, this wasn't good, Jema thought. At all.

His badly tailored pants were on the thin side, and her nightgown had ridden up, exposing her legs. She could feel just about every inch of what he had shoved against the curve of her butt. He wasn't having a problem with the ambience of the setting.

The problem was, neither was she. She was buried in gore, but she was smothering in the scent of gardenias. Everything below her collarbone wanted her to flip over and spread her legs and shove him into her. The heat and ache were so bad she nearly screamed for him to do it.

Not that he was going to do anything of the sort. Jema couldn't wriggle or breathe or make a sound, and he wasn't lifting up to let her. Darkness grew obese in front of her eyes, so she let herself go gradually limp and didn't move.

He fell for it and rose up.

Jema jerked her head back, driving it into his face, stunning him enough to wrench one arm free. She grabbed the edge of the table and used the wet surface to slide out from under him. His hands snatched at her back, but the gore had left her slippery. She was over the edge of the table and had her feet on the floor again before he scrambled off.

She was closer to his sword than he was, and she could

have grabbed it, but something made her hesitate. As if putting one hand on it would be worse than rolling around with him in all the blood and guts.

"What do you want from me?" she shouted.

"I want to save you." He looked at his bloodstained hands. "I cannot, Jema. I cannot even save myself."

"I'm not a damsel in distress." She stepped around a carcass, feeling behind her with her hands so she could keep her eyes on him. "I don't need saving."

"I could kill you." Not a threat, but a fact, presented with fangs and eyes that were cat-slitted and glowing.

"Really. You couldn't even keep me on the slaughtering table." Finally she felt a doorknob, and although it was as fun as peeling off her own skin with a dull butter knife, she turned, pulled it open, and ran through it.

No, Jema. No.

A huge hand yanked her back and into the dark, and for a moment she floated, a rag doll suspended from that hand, until her feet found solid ground.

Jema was standing on a silver-wooded pier that led to an old-looking boat tied to the end of it. The ocean around it was dark blue, the sky was a slate gray, and the salty air felt ice cold against her face.

She whirled around, but the farm and the slaughterhouse were gone, and only her demon stood behind her, his white tunic back in place and looking as pristine as if the wrestling match in the slaughterhouse had never happened. Her nightgown was clean, too.

"I like this better," she thought she should mention, "and I'll *really* like this if it's tonight's wrap-up."

He stared past her at the boat. "It will not end. Not for me." He looked into her eyes, and for a second she saw something too awful for words. Not tears, not fear, not anger. Despair. The bottomless, abandon-hope-all-ye-who-enter-here variety. "I would trade my life for yours."

"I don't like where you work, and my mother can be a handful." She was going to wake up soon, and she didn't want the slaughterhouse to be the only thing she remembered. They had so little time together as it was. "What's your name?"

When he started to answer, she shook her head. "Your real name, not the ones you make up for me."

"I am nothing, no one. Everything I had is gone." He seized her by the arms and shook her. "I am Death."

"You evidently have issues I don't know about," she said, trying to sound reasonable, "but I'd still like to know your name."

All the anger seemed to evaporate out of him. "Thierry. My name is Thierry."

"Thierry." She liked it, and smiled. "Was that so terrible?"

He let her go. He wasn't looking at her anymore, either; he was staring past her at the boat. "It is too late for me, little cat."

She turned to see what had his attention. The sky had turned black, and the sea a choppy, angry yellow-green. The boat had changed into a silvery, unearthly clipper ship with sails so crisp and white they seemed cut out of paper. Eerie blue light streamed through square holes in the railing around the deck. Planks exploded into the air as the boat's metallic hull slammed into the pier; then the snowy sails fluttered, and it swung away into the swelling waves.

A woman, dressed in a black robe and standing on the upper deck lifted a black-gloved hand. It wasn't a wave, but it was definitely a gesture of good-bye. Then the wind caught her hood and flung it back, exposing a beautiful face.

"Ex-girlfriend?" Jema guessed.

"My wife." In a toneless voice he began telling her about the woman, whose name was Angelica.

Jema could hardly stand to listen, for the story of what his wife had done to him was far worse than anything in the slaughterhouse. When he was finished telling it, they stood side by side and watched the boat sail off into the storm. The wind howled around them, and sleet and rain hurled down from the sky, but it didn't touch either of them.

When the ship finally disappeared, Thierry put his arm around her, and turned her to face him. It was almost a hug, only without the nice body-to-body-pressing part.

When she looked into his eyes she knew they weren't going to kiss, or pet, or do anything as before. There was death in his eyes, the pupils two vertical slivers of obsidian, the golden irises paling out until they matched the whites, and then they glittered with death, a flat, frozen void beyond white that was filled with bleached bones, drained flesh, and grinning skulls.

Jema could see her reflection in his eyes. Her eyes were so dark they looked black, and they glowed with heat. If there was such a thing as black fire, it burned in them.

Thierry lifted his free hand up and held it palm out. She folded her fingers through his, and felt something gentle and terrifying wrap around her heart.

He didn't say anything, and she didn't expect him to. The silence between them was a minefield. If they had been anywhere else, Jema would have expected to hear a minister say, "If anyone knows of a reason why these two people should not be joined in holy matrimony . . ."

Warm wetness distracted Jema from his eyes. Blood welled from between the intersections of their fingers to trickle down the backs of their hands. Nothing hurt, but it didn't stop. She didn't feel alarmed, but watched the two of them bleed together as if that, too, was meant to be.

They were joined now, in some way she couldn't fathom.

Thierry seemed to be waiting for her to say something. "What happens now?"

He leaned forward, not to kiss or hug, but to whisper against her ear, "You will not go into the dark alone. When it is time, I will take you. I will go with you."

"No." She twisted against him. "I won't let you." The night constricted around them, blanking out everything but his touch. "You don't die for me or with me. You stay alive. You go on without me."

He was trying to kill her now, taking the air from her lungs and changing it into gardenias.

"We'll go together," he promised, just before he kissed her. "Tonight."

His mouth touched hers, and she went with him.

Chapter 15

Jema?
  Something thudded.
  Jema.
  Another, harder series of thumps. "Jema."

It was the jangle of keys that tore Thierry out of the dream and back to reality. He was kneeling in the center of Jema's bed, her limp body in his arms. Her mouth and his were bloodied. *L'attrait* permeated the air in her room, made icy by the balcony window he'd left open.

How had he come in here? What had he done to her?

Thierry had been in thrall more than once and recognized the deep, aching pull of the blood dreams to which he had nearly succumbed. He felt for a pulse at her throat and nearly collapsed in relief when he found one. She was still alive, and not in rapture.

The keys. Someone was opening the door.

Thierry laid Jema on the bed and jumped from there to the balcony. Outside, he vaulted over the edge, where he hung from the frost-covered stone by one hand.

"Jema, it's freezing in here." The old doctor coughed as he turned on the light. "Did you break a bottle of perfume?"

Thierry kept his head down as he heard Bradford walk over to shut the balcony window and pull the curtains closed. Ice and stone cracked as he dug his fingers in, praying the edge would hold. When Bradford's footsteps moved across the floor, Thierry pulled himself back up and looked through a gap in the curtains on the other side of the window.

Dr. Bradford was covering Jema with her quilt and calling

to her. He took her pulse, frowned, and turned away, moving out of Thierry's sight. When he returned, he held a needle in his hand, which he used to inject Jema. Then he sat with his fingers pressed to her wrist, looking down at her face. He sat in that manner for five minutes, and then nodded and gently placed her hand on the bed before turning out the light and departing.

Thierry waited a long time before he went back into the room. He had to be sure he hadn't harmed her and performed his own examination. Jema was in a deep sleep, but her pulse was strong, and she moved restlessly when he said her name. Had she been enraptured, she would not have had the ability to move at all.

He hadn't killed her. She would live another day.

Leaving her tore at him, but Thierry moved back out onto the balcony, where he watched the snow fall around him. He had not fed before coming to Shaw House. She had been awake and reading when he had arrived, and so he had stayed in the shadows, waiting for her to fall asleep.

The long hours, the cold, and lack of blood had instead sent Thierry into a troubled sleep.

How had she slipped into his nightmare? Humans did not have talent; she could not enter the dream realm by her own will. Yet somehow she had—or he had lured her in. He had been a fool not to realize it was Jema's mind, not his fantasy of Jema, in the charnel-house nightmare. No, he had been too busy relishing the chance to tell her everything.

So he had told her. He'd told her of his dead wife, his ruined faith, the Kyn curse under which he lived—his name; he had told her his name. Everything that she was not to know about him had come out of his mouth. Thierry was surprised he hadn't given her the numbers to all the bank accounts he kept around the world.

Sometime during the dream his sleeping body had left the balcony and gone into her room. That was when the dream changed, and the feeding lust came over him. He had taken her blood again, almost draining her. It was only blind luck that Bradford had come in when he had.

Thierry left the balcony the usual way and went back to the

Nelsons' home, but only to gather his weapons and belongings. He had gone too far with Jema this time, and he could not go back. He could not trust himself anymore. Not when his feelings for her had nearly resulted in her death.

He had fallen in love with her. So much so that it had nearly put him in thrall to her.

Five hundred years ago, these feelings would have tempted Thierry to change Jema with his blood into his *sygkenis*—something he had never been able to do with Angelica, as she had risen to walk as Kyn, as he had—but the curse only killed humans now.

How had she done this? Jema had won his heart in the strangest fashion. Not in the midst of passion, but in the face of his anger, when he had displayed every secret, revolting part of himself in the blood dreams, and she had not turned away. She had embraced him. She had offered herself to him. She had even laughed at him. Yet when he had tried to give her some comfort in return, when he had told her that he wouldn't let her die alone, only then had she rejected him.

If that was not love, then Thierry did not want to know what it was.

Their hands, entwined, bleeding together. He looked down at his fingers, turning his hand over, expecting to see the mark of her blood on it. He didn't understand what it meant—it may have meant nothing at all—but it had felt like sanctification. As if something greater than him and Jema had given a blessing to their love.

What sort of God gave a dying woman to a cursed demon? Was it punishment for him, or for her? That God would do such a thing to her made him wish he could challenge the Almighty himself. Whatever Thierry had earned for his mortal sins, Jema Shaw was an innocent. She had not earned him.

There was a certain irony to it. Thierry had always wanted love. Within the heart of the warrior was a desperate need for peace, and gentleness, and kindness. A life lived to its fullest, with a lady at his side. A lady like Jema. He had wasted his love on a woman who had used it to destroy him, to drive him mad. He had nearly destroyed the woman who had brought him out of madness, who would have kept his love safe.

Thierry had no answers, no thought of how to cope with this new torment. He knew only that he could not stay away from her. He could protect Jema and follow her, and watch over her, and assure that nothing and no one harmed her.

He could not stay away from her, but last night would have to last him a lifetime. The risk of thrall and rapture was too great; he might not be able to leave the blood dreams a second time.

He could never permit himself to touch her again.

"The trail ends here." Falco rose from his crouch and looked down both sides of the street. "He is not Kyn, not from his scent. He is human, in one of these buildings."

Cyprien regarded the row houses, tenements, and condemned buildings that made up the neighborhood. Unlike Falco, he had been unable to pick up any scent, Kyn or human. Tracking was not something Michael did well when there were too many other odors to distract him. Here trash peppered the walks and gutters. A cat wandered out of a garbage can on its side, the head of a rat in its mouth. It reminded him of a district in London where Tremayne liked to hunt. The hopeless were here; the only thing missing was the whores.

A faded sign above the largest building read THE HAVEN. Cyprien remembered what Tremayne had said about John Keller, but it seemed far too convenient.

"What do you know about that place?" He pointed to the Haven's sign.

"Young ones who have no family or home go there," Jaus's seneschal told him. "The man who runs it is troublesome. The Kyn avoid it."

"Alexandra's brother works there now," he told Falco. "Can we enter the building without being seen?"

The seneschal gave the entrance a negligent glance. "Does it matter if we are?"

Cyprien wanted the man who had hurt Alexandra more than he desired absolute discretion. "No. Come."

The Haven's front doors were secured from the inside, but posed no challenge to Falco, who with one jerk tore the door panel off its hinges. He set it aside and strode in, his hand on the hilt of the sword under his coat. Cyprien followed, trying to catch the scent of Kyn on the air. The smell of body odor, waste, cleaner, and cigarette smoke was decades old in this place, along with a more acrid, less definable scent.

Human sweat, Cyprien decided as they swept through the rooms on the first floor. *Tainted with fear and anguish.* Tremayne would have inhaled it like the bouquet of a fine wine. *But no scent of Kyn.*

The administration offices were empty, but they heard voices in the kitchen and followed them.

"You have to use a medium-low heat," John Keller said. "Or the marshmallow burns."

A young female voice answered him. "That's why mine never turned out so good."

"Did your mother teach you how to cook?"

"No. She didn't know how to cook. I read the directions on the side of the box."

Cyprien motioned for Falco to stay in the corridor and walked in. A warm, sugary odor scented the outdated kitchen. "May I have a word with you?"

John looked up from the pot in which he was cooking, and handed the wooden spoon to the tall, fair-haired girl hovering beside him.

"Keep stirring it until the marshmallow is completely melted," he said, his tone void of emotion, "and then add the cereal."

"Might we have a word?" Cyprien asked.

The girl looked up, surprised. "Who are you?"

"Friends of mine, Pure." John pointed to a door on the other side of the kitchen. "We'll talk in there."

Cyprien followed him into the room, which was a large storage room being used as a pantry. He closed the door behind him. "Pure?"

"The opposite of Kyn." Keller positioned himself with his back to a wall. "Why are you here, Cyprien?"

"Someone tried to kill me tonight. Your sister pushed me out of the way and took a crossbow bolt in the chest." He watched the other man's shoulders jerk, as if his words had had the same effect on him. "Should I thank your friends, the

Brethren, or will you do the honors the next time you see Archbishop Hightower?"

"Is Alexandra alive?" John demanded.

"She is Darkyn," Cyprien reminded him. "She cannot be
killed so easily. Although if the bolt had pierced her heart . . ."
He picked up a meat cleaver that had been left on a shelf. "Was
it you, Keller? Did you harm her, trying to kill me? Was my
life the price the Brethren demanded in exchange for yours?"

"No. I didn't do this. I'm not involved with the Brethren
any longer. I've left the priesthood." John eyed the cleaver.
"Are you planning to use that on me?"

"Your demise would solve many problems for me and your
sister." Cyprien twirled the heavy blade through his fingers,
making a show of it.

"Most of the children in this place have seen enough ugli-
ness for five lifetimes," Keller said. He sounded afraid but resolved. "If you're going to kill me, take me away from here
first."

"I would enjoy that." Cyprien threw the cleaver, the blade
burying itself in the nearest wall. He noted the flinch Keller
gave at the sound. "Regrettably, I have promised Alexandra
that I would not harm you."

"I'm not interested in any favors, Cyprien." Still afraid,
Alexandra's brother was, but more resolved now than when he
faced death. "From you, my sister, or the Darkyn."

"You shouldn't expect any." Before Cyprien could say
more, Falco came through the door with his sword drawn.
"What is it?"

"I recognize this one." Falco started across the room for
John. "The high lord wants his head."

Cyprien grabbed Jaus's seneschal from behind just as he
was lifting his sword to decapitate Keller. "No. You are not to
harm him."

"He betrayed you." Falco gave Cyprien an incredulous
look. "He exposed your men, your *jardin.* Your *sygkenis.*
Tremayne has sent word to all Darkyn. This man cannot live."

"John." A thin man with hair that resembled a bunch of
thin, gnarled carrots came in through the door. He was holding
a scarred baseball bat. "Why are there are a frog and a Nazi in

my pantry, and"—his eyes widened as he saw Falco's sword—
"why does one think he's Highlander?"

John, who had been braced against the wall, straightened.
"Dougall, go back in the kitchen."

"I know I said you could have personal visitors after
hours," Dougall said, swinging the baseball bat back and forth,
"but I gotta say, John, I don't much like your friends." He
turned to Cyprien. "You look pretty smart. Do you know how
long it takes the Chicago police to get here after a nine-one-
one call about a homicide in progress? I made it two minutes
ago."

"Falco." Cyprien caught John's gaze. "We will meet again."

"Not on these premises, you won't, you French-fried fuck,"
Dougall called after Cyprien as he and Falco left the storage
room.

Cyprien and Falco chose a convenient lookout spot on one
of the roofs nearby, and waited there while the police arrived.
Five minutes after the four responding patrol officers went into
the Haven, they emerged with John Keller and the carrot-
headed man. The latter was still holding his baseball bat, and
was arguing with Keller.

"You didn't know those guys," Cyprien heard Dougall say,
"but they sure as shit seemed to know you."

"Mr. Keller, they could come back another night," one of
the cops warned him. "If you can identify them, we can pick
them up for questioning."

"Shove the questioning," Dougall said. "One of those guys
was carrying a sword, and the other one buried a meat cleaver
in my wall. I'm pressing charges."

"I don't know who they were; I've never seen those men
before tonight," Keller lied. "I'm sorry I can't help you. They
must have mistaken me for someone else."

Cyprien frowned. Why was Keller trying to protect them?
For Alexandra's sake, or his own?

"Seigneur, the trail ends in this place," Falco said as they
watched the police finish interviewing the two men. "The assassin must be here."

"We cannot search for him now." Cyprien watched the police cars drive off, and Dougall give John's shoulder a push

and demand in a loud voice to know what the hell was going on. "We will return tomorrow night."

John spread out his hands, then turned his back on Dougall and walked away down the street.

"I could take him now," Falco said, soft and persuasive. "It would look as if he ran afoul of street criminals. I will keep my silence on it. She need never know, seigneur."

Cyprien shook his head. A boy wearing a baseball cap and jacket slipped out of the shelter and walked in the same direction Keller had gone. "Put out the word among the other men. No one is to harm John Keller."

Michael wanted to follow Alexandra's brother. If he had been telling the truth, he still might know who the assassin was. But Keller would tell him nothing if he were dead. First he would return to Derabend, and make his bargain with Tremayne. There was one thing Richard wanted more than John Keller dead, and Michael would see that he got it.

Then there would be time for everything else. Time to find the Brethren who had compromised Jaus's security, and reveal the traitor within his *jardin*. Time to take John Keller, and convince him to tell Michael everything he wanted to know.

When they descended from the rooftop, Falco paused and turned his face into the cold wind. "There." He pointed to the side of a tenement across the street. "Human blood."

They went together around the building. Michael saw the body hanging upside down from the fire escape at the same time he heard Jaus's seneschal draw his sword.

"Put it away." He walked around the pool of blood on the ground and looked up into the face of the dead man. Because he had been hung by his feet, blood from his slit throat coated his face. There was only a strip of pale flesh where it had parted in two streams—just below the diamond-studded arrow piercing his right eyebrow. "Help me cut down the body."

"You'll have to help me do this, Val."

Recovering from the crossbow wound was taking more time than Alex had expected, and the sling she had to wear to keep her arm from moving was simply irritating. So was being able to do things with only one hand.

"I am still not certain of the reason why you need a sample of my blood," Jaus said as he tied the strap around his upper arm for her. "Mine will be as Michael's is, I should think."

"All my Kyn samples were destroyed in a fire in New Orleans, so I need to collect a few more. Analyzing them will help me nail the specific pathogens involved. This will sting." She inserted the copper-tipped needle into his arm and popped the collection vial on the other end. The vial's empty glass tube slowly filled with blood. "Back when you could change humans without killing them, how long did it take for them to switch over?"

He seemed amused by her wording. "A few days. Two or three in most cases." He shrugged. "I did not turn many humans. I never felt at ease with subjecting them to a life wrought by my curse."

"You are not—"

"Cursed. As you have said before. I hope you are correct." He watched her remove the vial and needle, and swab the tiny dot of remnant blood from his arm. "I have persuaded some of the men to provide more samples for you. Have you everything here that you need?"

"I think so." She gazed around at the laboratory Jaus had set up for her. It duplicated most of the hospital Cyprien had once provided for her in the basement of his New Orleans mansion. "I did remember to say thank-you for all this stuff, didn't I?"

"Your reaction was most adequate. I cannot recall the last time I heard that many colorful epithets. I am making a list of them for the next time I am surprised. I will send in the volunteers now." Jaus bowed and retreated from the lab.

Alex collected a few more samples from Jaus's cooperative, if somewhat surly, men, and spent the next several hours analyzing them. She was so engrossed in the testing that she didn't realize Cyprien was standing beside her until he put a hand on her good arm.

Even then she didn't look way from the test slide she was examining. "Is it important, or something that is going to give me a shrieking orgasm?"

"You have been locked in here half the night," he said. "You should feed and rest. The orgasm is, of course, optional."

"Later." She lifted her eyes from the scope lenses and sighed. "I don't get it."

"Orgasms?" He bent to kiss her with slow, devastating thoroughness. "You have been faking? All this time?"

"Smart-ass. Have a look." She pointed to the scope, and he peered into the lenses.

"What am I looking at?" he asked.

"My blood smear. Take a mental snapshot." She removed the slide and replaced it with another. "This is your blood smear. See the difference?"

"Yes, but you will have to explain what the difference is. Please use small words."

"My blood is more human than yours. It's more human than any of the samples I've taken from Jaus and the boys." She picked up the slide with her blood and held it up to the light. "No matches."

His hand did something gentle and arousing to the back of her neck. "Your blood may take time to change, as you did."

"True, or my blood isn't changing the same way. Kind of like my mutation isn't going the same way yours did." She placed the slide in a protective case. "I don't have any samples of my blood as it was prior to infection, or just before the change. That's what I really need to see to determine how this thing is moving along. Maybe the hospital kept some from when I was in ICU."

"Those samples were removed from the hospital and destroyed." He returned her outraged look blandly. "We could not risk the exposure, Alexandra. We never allow our blood to be taken by humans. That is why Jaus's men are so unhappy about donating samples for you. Among the Kyn, such things are not done."

She considered arguing the point, but he was right about the exposure. A hematologist would have a field day with Kyn blood. "Well, without them I can't go any further with this." She thought for a minute, laughed at herself for the idea that popped into her mind, and shook her head. "No, that'll never work."

"You said the same thing about us."

"If I obtained a sample of blood genetically close to my

own, that would help," she told him. "But to my knowledge, there's only one person in the world who can give me that, and we aren't speaking."

"Your brother."

"Who Valentin thinks is trying to kill you," she added. "He told me about your little hunting trip last night with Falco. It wasn't John, you know. He's a world-class prick sometimes, but he doesn't have it in him. Also, he doesn't know German, which was what Crossbow Killer was thinking in."

Cyprien didn't say anything.

"I mean it, Michael. It wasn't him. As for the blood, I'll put it on hold for now." She picked up a used syringe. "I'm just going run a test on this needle and then I'll go drink dinner. I hope Jaus has restocked his O positive."

He frowned. "Why are you testing needles?"

"I swiped this one from Jema Shaw at the hospital. I wanted to see what sort of insulin her doctor is using to control her diabetes." She carefully extracted a trace of residue from the syringe and transferred it to a paper test strip. "Synthetic insulin isn't as effective as the real human variety, and some of the stuff we import from overseas is downright dangerous. She also acted a little weird after she gave herself a shot." She glanced at him. "Lately you seem awfully interested in everything I'm doing."

"It is the modern way," he said. "To take an interest in your work is to show support, yes?"

"You support me plenty." Alex added a drop of chemical to the paper strip and waited. The treated paper should have changed color, but it remained clear. "This can't be right." She waved Cyprien away. "This is going to take more time. Go play swords with Val."

He smiled and kissed the top of her head. "Don't be in here all night. I should like a shrieking orgasm myself."

Two hours later, Alexandra marched out of the lab and found Valentin and Michael sitting in his office, going over maps of the city.

"Val, I need some more equipment." She handed him the list. "As soon as possible. I also need to find out everything we can on Dr. Daniel Bradford."

Valentin read from the list. "A genetic analyzer, DNA sorting and matching software—Alexandra, what is all this for, if I may ask?"

"I tested the 'insulin' Jema Shaw has been using. Guess what? It's not insulin." She tossed a lab report on his desk. "It's plasma, two different sedatives, and what I think is a synthetic hormone. I don't know what the hell to call it. Personally I've never seen anything like it before."

Now Valentin looked completely dumbfounded. "What does this mean?"

"I don't know, but I can tell you this much," Alex said. "If Jema Shaw has been injecting herself with the same concoction every day, then she isn't being treated for diabetes. And since she'd be dead without insulin therapy, that would mean—"

The report slipped out of Jaus's hands. "She doesn't *have* diabetes."

"Good morning."

Jema blinked a few times to clear her eyes, and saw Daniel Bradford smiling at her. "Hi." She yawned and stretched. "Lord, did I oversleep again? This is becoming a terrible habit."

"No, honey, you didn't oversleep. You had a bad night." He checked her pulse. "I heard you moaning from the hall and I came to check on you. You left the window open and the room was like a refrigerator. I couldn't wake you up, either, so I had to give you a shot." His pleasant face filled with sorrow. "I know I said you were taking too many shots, Jem, but I didn't mean for you to start skipping them."

"I didn't." Jema felt confused. The mugginess in her head wasn't helping clarify things, either. "At least, I don't think I did." Her memory was crowded with confusing images from the long dream she'd had.

"I'm not going to say anything to your mother," he told her. "She's been feeling very low the last couple of weeks. I know—how can I tell—but low for Meryl is devastated for the rest of us. Now, keep those peepers open for a second." Bradford leaned forward to check her eyes with a penlight. "Do you want me to give you your morning?"

"No, I can do it." She didn't feel sick or weak, just tired and very thirsty. The fact that Daniel was talking to her as if she were a three-year-old made her feel irritable, too.

"I'll see you downstairs." Daniel rose and stared down at her. "You're sure there's nothing you want to tell me about last night?"

"I . . . fell asleep." She worked up a passably puzzled smile. "That's all I remember."

"If you say so." With one last, troubled look, Daniel left her.

"Except for the visit from the golden-eyed demon, who yelled at me and pushed me around the most disgusting place I've ever seen in my life." Jema pulled up her knees and rested her forehead against them. "Thierry."

Until last night, the dreams she remembered had been like a naughty little secret. What woman wouldn't want to go to sleep each night to be seduced by a demon who would shape himself to be whatever she desired in a man?

Until last night.

Jema clearly remembered every moment of the dream. It was not like any of the others. Everything had felt wrong. The colors, the smells, the places—none of it was anything she could have imagined. It had felt too real. He had been too real.

Thierry was her demon, of course. Same golden eyes, same dark, brooding looks, that air of edgy sensuality. But he had been different. There wasn't any of that demon-lover facade as there had been in the other dreams. Last night he had been a person. Someone as sad and lonely as she was. Even as disgusting as most of the dream had been, Jema wanted to go out and search the world until she found him. A man who was fantasy, who didn't exist.

A man who was more important than anything she had in reality.

"I'm not in love with him." She flung herself out of bed. "You can't fall in love with a dream man. Especially one who works in a slaughterhouse and says he's a seven-hundred-year-old vampire."

It was the pink foam she spit out after brushing her teeth that tried to convince her otherwise. The blood tinting her toothpaste wasn't coming from her gums. It was oozing from the inside of her lower lip.

From two brand-new, fang-shaped punctures.

Chapter 16

Thierry stayed away from Jema for the length of one day, unable to rest, unable to cease tormenting himself, until his own company became unbearable to him. As soon as the sun set, he drove to the museum and parked on the street across from the back lot where her little convertible sat. There was no guard tonight, and the lot gates were left open.

He would wait, and he would watch for her.

The hours passed in silence as Thierry brooded, waiting for her to emerge so that he could follow her home. He had learned nothing from Jema to help him find the men who had attacked Luisa Lopez, and perhaps he had imagined her secret, hidden knowledge. He had certainly deluded himself about many things concerning Jema.

I should never have come here. What was he doing in Chicago? What redemption could be had from slaughtering more men, and using a frail, innocent human woman to get to them? *Where is the honor in this?*

It was very late when Jema finally left the museum. Thierry hunched down as he watched her walk to her car, her purse swinging, a stack of papers in her arms. Everything inside him cried out for her, for the sanity of her. Once he saw her safely home, he would return to the city and hunt. Perhaps he would return to the residences of the men thought to be responsible for the attack on Luisa Lopez and enter the dreams of their neighbors to glean information from their minds. The men had to be Brethren. Thierry knew there was no redemption for him now, but he could prevent them from harming another human. That much he owed to Alexandra.

Jema stopped a few feet from her car and turned around, as if startled. Glass shattered and the lamp providing light for the parking lot went dark. Three men ran out of the alley on the opposite side of the building directly for Jema. One grabbed her purse, another knocked the papers out of her arms, and the third flung his arm around her neck.

Thierry was out of the car and running for them before the first paper touched the ground.

The men were not men, but animals. Then he saw that they were men wearing masks made to look like animals. They were shouting obscenities as they shoved Jema back and forth between them. Laughing, excited. Enjoying themselves.

Thierry jumped the fence and had his dagger in his hand as he saw the flash of a blade.

He hit the first from behind, pulling him back from Jema and slitting his throat in the same motion. The man ejected blood and his last breath at the same time before he toppled over.

One of the two left dragged Jema back toward the alley. "Get him!"

Thierry pivoted around to parry a small ax with his arm, squinting as the sharp head bit deep into his flesh. Behind the mask, flat eyes went wide with glee as the man hauled the ax backward and swung again.

Thierry caught his arm on the downswing and reversed it, shattering his elbow and driving the ax into the man's belly. Something came from the side and drove a thick bar of steel into his ribs. He wrenched the ax out of the sagging second man and drove the handle end between the legs of the third, who had come running back from the alley. He went down, squealing and clutching his crotch.

Thierry reached down with his bloody arm and pulled the last living man up by the collar. "Where is she?" He shook him, making his head jerk wildly. "What did you do to her?"

The man didn't answer, and his head drooped at an odd angle.

"*Connard.*" Thierry dropped the body and ran for the alley where he had seen the man dragging Jema. He tracked her by her scent, and found her lying on the ground just around the corner, in the dark, unconscious.

He was on his knees, holding her in his arms. The smell of warm, ripe apples rose from her body and blocked out the exhaust-tinged city air. There was blood on her forehead, and she was so still he feared the worst. But no, there was her pulse, beating at the base of her throat. He kept his hand there, fearful that it would stop the moment he lifted his fingers. She wasn't moving, but she was breathing.

The gash across his left forearm was not closed, and more blood spattered the ground as he stood up with her. He carried her to her car and laid her carefully in the passenger seat before retrieving her keys from where she had dropped them. He paused only long enough to spit on one of the bodies before he got behind the wheel of Jema's car and started the engine.

Thierry didn't know how badly Jema was hurt. He could not take her to a hospital; there would be too many questions. He could not leave her in front of one, either. *Bradford is a doctor. He will know what to do.*

Keeping one hand on the wheel and one pressed against Jema's throat to monitor her pulse, Thierry drove. He didn't dare try to enter her unconscious mind while he was driving—and she could hardly be dreaming, not with that knot on her head—so he spoke to her.

"How could you be so careless to walk out there alone, so late at night, without an escort? Who allows you to do such things? Do these people at the museum wish you dead?"

He took a sharp turn and stepped on the accelerator to pass a slow-moving taxi.

"I think it is you who wish yourself an early death, that is what it is," he muttered. "You go out to crime scenes and pick over corpses, and then you lock yourself in that house or in that museum, surrounded by beauty that doesn't live, doesn't breathe, only grows more mold or disintegrates into dust. What sort of life is that?"

They were only a few minutes away now. He would park at the gate and move her to the driver's seat.

"Why did you do this to yourself? Why didn't you marry? If your sickness prevented children, you could have adopted them. In this country? You could have purchased them. You should have a keeper. One who wouldn't permit you to do foolish things that could get you raped and murdered in an alley. If I were your husband, you wouldn't leave our bed-chamber. You'd be too tired to walk."

He was irrational, furious, ready to shake her back to consciousness. Then he looked down and saw her face, and he wanted to stop the car and gather her into his arms and cry against her hair.

"What do I do now, little cat?" All the hopeless love in the world, and here was his, and he was wasting these precious minutes shouting at her. "How can I leave you now, even when I know I must? Who will be there the next time someone tries to harm you?"

At the front gates of Shaw House, Thierry stopped the convertible and got out to lift Jema from the passenger seat. She stirred a little when he eased her into the driver's seat. He used his fist to sound the car horn, watching Jema's face as he hit the horn over and over, until he saw Bradford hurrying out of the front doors.

Thierry moved back from the car and stood in the shadow of the wall. The gates opened and Bradford rushed out.

"Jema? Jema!"

He watched the physician check her, and then move her to the passenger side of the car. Bradford got behind the wheel, but before he drove off he stared hard at the deep pool of shadow where Thierry was standing.

It was his scent, of course. Strong emotions and spilling blood always brought it to its greatest intensity, and it was pouring off him.

Bradford shook his head slightly, put the convertible in gear, and drove through the gates.

Alex watched from the sidelines in the lists as Valentin Jaus defeated his fourth consecutive opponent. She glanced up at Cyprien. "How many more asses is he going to kick before he gets tired?"

Michael rested his chin on the top of her head and closed his arms around her. "He doesn't get tired."

Jaus had been like a caged tiger ever since Alex had confirmed her initial findings on the witch's brew that Daniel Bradford had been giving to Jema Shaw. Further analysis of the "insulin" revealed that Jema was being heavily sedated and subjected to a hormone that retarded several natural functions, primarily menstruation.

"She's probably had very few periods, if any," Alex told Jaus and Cyprien as she explained the effects of the hormone. "This stuff was once manufactured in Eastern Bloc countries and given to certain athletes, like gymnasts."

"This cannot be right." Jaus shook his head. "Jema does not perform gymnastics. She never has."

"Well, if she had wanted to, she could have been Olympic material, because she likely heals just fine. In addition to suppressing the menstrual cycle, this hormone prevents a woman's body from developing normal breasts and hips and putting on fat. These are all things that keep older gymnasts small and light enough to compete with twelve-year-olds." She rubbed her eyes, tired from staring at so many screens. "One more thing: This hormone has been banned for thirty years, ever since a little Asian girl died in the middle of a gold medal–winning performance. During the investigation, the Olympic Committee discovered that the long-term side effects include serious heart and liver damage."

After hearing that, Jaus excused himself and went to the lists to begin plowing through his men.

Alex wasn't sure why Bradford had been trying to keep Jema in a perpetual state of prepuberty, and, from her own observations, she felt he had been only partially successful. Jema's growth and development may have been stunted, but she showed too many signs of physical maturity. Now the big questions were, how long had Bradford been dosing Jema, and how much permanent damage had the mixture caused?

"We've got to tell her, Michael," Alex informed Cyprien as she watched Jaus take on a fifth opponent. "She'll need to be weaned off it—the sedatives are narcotic, so she's definitely addicted to them—and put in the hospital for tests to see what else is going on inside her." She winced as Jaus knocked his larger opponent onto his back and stood over him with his sword at his throat. "You'd better go over there and try to talk some sense into him. All the blood is starting to make the other guys slip."

Before Cyprien could speak to Jaus, the suzerain stalked out of the lists.

"I cannot fathom the reason for his anger," Cyprien said after he helped one of Jaus's men from the blood-spattered floor. "He cares about her, and with this new information we can help Jema. You said she could live a more normal life."

"If her insides aren't all fucked-up from Bradford's drugs." Alex felt the weight of Jaus's confidences bearing down on her. "I think Val needs another sympathetic ear. Let me go talk to him."

Back at the main house, Sacher told her the suzerain had retired to his bedchamber to wash and dress. Alex went up to the room Sacher directed her to and knocked on his door. When there was no answer, she debated whether or not to intrude, and then used a little Kyn strength to force the lock.

Her first impression of the sitting room portion of Jaus's bedroom was that it was big and silent and very, very white. Like the camellia scent permeating the air.

"The Kyn don't hang out with the Klan, do they?" she asked, looking around at the walls, floor, and the single whopping-huge leather sofa, all of which were as pristine white as the new-arrivals rack at a bridal shop. "I don't want to know what your bills for bleach are."

The sounds of someone dressing came from the next room over. Alex followed the rustle and entered a bedroom done in dark midnight blue, where the scent of camellias grew stronger.

"I'd hate to have to pick one color and live with it like this. I like too many of them. Imagine, just pink." She shuddered as she turned to see the wall opposite the bed. Twenty-nine framed photos of Jema Shaw at various ages covered it. The images were all candid shots, evidently taken from a distance with a powerful lens. "Couldn't fit these on your desk with the other one?"

"Go away, Alexandra."

"I will, eventually." She picked up the sword he had left on the coverlet of his bed, only to find her hand covered with blood. "I hope you Scotchgarded the mattress."

Now she heard splashing sounds from the adjoining bathroom.

Alex looked in and saw Jaus standing in front of a sink and washing blood from his hands, arms, and chest. He might be a shrimp like her, but with all those muscles, who would notice? "Feel better, Conan?"

"No." Still wet, he strode past her and went into the white room, and came back a minute later carrying a full fifth of Stoli.

"That's going to make you very sick," she warned him. Straight liquor was one of the worst things a Darkyn could ingest.

Jaus glanced at her. "Do you wish to provide the mixer?"

She held up her hands. "Who am I to get between a vampire and his choice of emetic?"

"I don't drink it." He opened the bottle and poured the liquor onto a cloth, then used it to clean the blood from his sword.

"Does that work well?" Alex wondered if it was the same basic principal as soaking instruments in alcohol.

"Unlike you, it evaporates quickly." He crumpled up the cloth and placed the sword in a case on the wall that held several other weapons. "Why did you break the lock on my door, Alexandra? Have I not sufficiently entertained you this day?"

"I have a soft spot for lost causes." She smiled brightly. "And men who can beat five other men into the floor without breaking a sweat."

Jaus propped one arm on the wall by the case and leaned against it. "I fight them so I won't go over to Shaw House and kill Bradford."

"Maybe I should go beat the crap out of someone, then." She still couldn't quite believe what the doctor had been doing to Jema, or why.

Alex went into the bathroom to wash her hands. The bathroom was, like the front room, all white with antique-looking fixtures. The tub sat on brass claw feet, and the toilet flushed with a chain. The chunky bar of yellow-gray soap in the dish smelled of lye.

"Whew." She wrinkled her nose as she scrubbed. "Man, I have got to take you to Linens 'n Things."

"I will pay you to change her as you were."

Alex dropped the soap in the sink. Jaus stood in the doorway, wiping his chest, arms, and hands with a white towel. "*Pay* me."

He tossed the damp towel into the tub. "Whatever you wish. Money, jewels, property, anything. You have but to name your price, my lady."

She turned off the taps, put the soap back, and sluiced the water from her hands. "What if I want the city of Chicago?"

"I do not own Chicago."

"Oh, well." She shrugged.

"I own part of Chicago. A large part. It is yours."

He was serious. "A tempting counteroffer." She saw there was no getting through the doorway at the moment. "But, nope, I can't settle for *part* of a major metropolitan city. Me being Cyprien's girl and all; everyone would just snicker behind my back. You understand."

He folded his arms, making muscles bulge in all the right places. "I am not jesting with you."

"I didn't think you were." She moved to stand in front of him. That was the nice thing about him; she didn't have to stand on a stepladder to go eye-to-eye with him. "Valentin, I know you love her. I knew it before I came in and saw the creepy stalker wall. That's why I'm going to pretend we never had this conversation."

"I must have her. I will do anything."

"No, you won't." She gestured toward the bedroom. "Let's go crack open a unit of AB negative. Have you ever noticed how it has a bit more zing than plain old type A?"

"You smug bitch." He wasn't moving a centimeter. "You dare deny me. When you could save her. You have your love for eternity."

"She's not your love, Valentin. Love is reciprocal. Love is two consenting adults who meet, fall for each other, and can't imagine life without the other one around. Throw in lots of sex your mother didn't want you to have." She saw Cyprien appear behind him but didn't twitch an eyelash. This one was on her tab. "Jema Shaw doesn't love you. She doesn't know you love her. She probably thinks you're a nice man, but what else have you ever been to her? The neighbor with the funny accent who sends her homegrown flowers once a year, that's it."

For a moment it looked as if Jaus might do something to her that would make Cyprien go crazy. "*That* is what I am to her."

"That's what you are to her now." Alex felt as if she'd sucker punched him a few times. "I'll tell you something about me. Before I met the Prince of Darkness, I rarely got involved with men. An occasional roll in the hay, but that was all. I liked my life. No ties. No picking up someone else's socks off the floor. No fights, no faked orgasms, no regrets."

Jaus watched her and said nothing.

"Also, no friends, no family, nothing to show for my time but an office I closed in three days, a house I sold in a week, and a car that I returned to the leasing company—" She stopped and smacked herself in the forehead. "Oh, shit, I *knew* I forgot to do something."

He was not amused. "Your point?"

"My point: You know *why* it was so easy for me to walk away from my practice as a surgeon, and my life as a human? No one was really sorry to see me go. I wasn't important enough to anyone to be missed. If I had died instead of changing, no one would have cried." She pressed her hand to his lean cheek. "If one of those guys in the lists slips and accidentally makes you a head shorter, who's going to cry for you, Valentin? Besides me?"

"Alexandra." His hand brushed some hair back from her face. It was a gentle, affectionate gesture, the kind John used to make when they were kids. "Forgive me."

She didn't know how she ended up with the suzerain of Chicago in her arms, holding on to her like a lost little boy. She glanced over his shoulder and saw the look of love Cyprien gave her before he turned away and left them alone.

They weren't alone for very long. A throat being cleared a few times in the adjoining room made Jaus lift his head from

Alex's shoulder. "Sacher. He would not interrupt unless it was important."

They walked out together to find the elderly man so agitated he was practically wringing his hands.

"What is it?" Jaus went quickly to him. "Wilhelm?"

"No, master, he is fine. Dr. Keller, the seigneur wished me to tell you that he had to go into the city to speak to someone." The old man grasped Jaus's hand. "Master, Falco called just after the seigneur left. Miss Jema was attacked by three men at the museum. She is home now, but she was injured."

Jaus's face turned to stone. "The men?"

"All dead, Falco told me. A Kyn warrior saved her, and killed them." Sacher glanced at Alex before he added, "Master, it was Thierry Durand."

Jaus agreed to have Alexandra accompany him to call upon Jema. It was the quickest way to get out of Derabend Hall, and she would prevent him from gutting Dr. Daniel Bradford on the front steps of Shaw House.

He hoped.

"It's almost midnight," Alex said as she walked with him along the seawall. "We're going to wake up the whole house. People are going to yell."

"Sacher said Jema was found thirty minutes ago outside the front gates," Jaus told her. "The household is already awake. No one yells."

"What I don't get is why Thierry saved Jema," Alex said as she walked along the seawall with him. "How does Thierry *know* Jema?"

"He likely chanced upon her while she was being attacked." He opened the back gate for her. "Durand has always been protective of women." He had been prepared to do what he could to save Cyprien's friend, even after Lucan's brutal advice. Though Thierry had saved Jema through some happy act of fate, in his madness Jaus knew he could have just as easily killed her.

Alexandra rang the front doorbell twice before a tired-looking maid answered it. "We're terribly sorry to disturb you, but we heard about Miss Shaw and wanted to check on her. I'm Dr. Keller, and you probably already know Mr. Jaus."

"Yes, ma'am. Sir." The maid gave Jaus a wan smile. "Please come in. I'll let Mrs. Shaw know you're here."

They were shown into a parlor off the main entry, but before they could sit down a white-haired woman in an electric wheelchair came in.

"Mrs. Shaw. This is my friend Dr. Keller." Too agitated to engage in elaborate introductions, Valentin left it at that. "How is Jema?"

"She is recovering from a vicious assault and a severe head injury, Mr. Jaus. How do you think she is?" Meryl Shaw eyed Alex briefly. "It is after midnight, and the police have just left. Perhaps you and your lady friend could harass us another time."

Alexandra frowned but said nothing.

"I beg your pardon, madam." Jaus was taken aback by her manner as much as her rudeness. "I came to offer what help I can. Is Jema's condition serious? Should she be transported to the hospital?" He could have men guard her around the clock at any facility in the city.

"If you'd rather keep her at home tonight, Mrs. Shaw, I'd be happy to examine her," Alex offered. "I'm a reconstructive surgeon, so I'm very familiar with head trauma."

Meryl looked more insulted than impressed. "Our family physician, Dr. Bradford, is looking after her, thank you. Now, if that is all—"

"No, it is not," Jaus said. "Forgive me, but I am very fond of your daughter. I will not be able to rest until I . . . until I have assured myself that she is well cared for."

"Mrs. Shaw, there is something else you should know," Alex said before Meryl could reply. "I've tested one of Jema's syringes to check the type of insulin she's using. Dr. Bradford has not been honest with you or your daughter. The syringe was filled with a substance that only looks like insulin."

"Jema may not be as sick as you think," Jaus put in. "Her illness could actually be caused by Dr. Bradford's treatment."

"What are you talking about?" Meryl gripped the arms of her wheelchair. "Jema has suffered from juvenile diabetes since birth. Her condition has seriously deteriorated, and we've all accepted that the end is near. There is nothing anyone can do for her. Tonight's incident was bad enough, but now you barge in here to make such ridiculous accusations? I should have you thrown out. I think I will." She wheeled over to pick up the house phone.

"I will bring the lab reports to you, Mrs. Shaw, so you may see the evidence for yourself." Jaus nodded to Alex. "Dr. Keller has spent a great deal of time testing Jema's medication. Dr. Bradford is not helping your daughter. He could be killing her."

"Enough of this." Meryl put down the phone and turned to Alex. "I don't what your motives are, young woman, but you're grossly mistaken. I've known Daniel Bradford for thirty years. He has done everything he could to keep Jema's diabetes under control." She glared at Jaus. "He's the reason she's alive."

"On the contrary, Mrs. Shaw. I'll bet that Jema doesn't even have diabetes," Alex said. "If you don't want to believe me, then have Jema's 'insulin' tested at an independent lab. They will confirm everything I've told you."

Alex's words pounded inside Jaus's skull, and the arctic fury that had driven him in the lists closed around him. "Where *is* Dr. Bradford?" he asked softly.

"He is with Jema, naturally," Meryl said. Disgust contorted her face. "I've heard enough of this nonsense. Please leave my home at once."

Jaus had never cared for Jema's mother. She was a hateful, bitter old woman who clung to her daughter like a leech. How much joy had she sucked out of his lady's life with her constant nagging and complaining? His men had reported that Meryl was a hypochondriac, and fancied herself to have a bad heart. It would be nothing to slip into Shaw House one night and put an end to her imagined suffering. Then Jema would be free.

"Val. *Val.*" Alex was tugging on his arm. "Time to go home."

"I have to see her." He looked blindly at Alex. "I can't leave like this."

"We'll come back tomorrow." She met Meryl's furious gaze. "Jema should feel up to having visitors tomorrow evening, shouldn't she, Mrs. Shaw?"

"I couldn't say, Dr. Keller. Jema hasn't regained consciousness yet." Meryl wheeled out of the room.

"He walked in here as if he owned the place." If Meryl could have risen from her wheelchair one time in her life, she would have done so tonight, to slap Valentin Jaus's face. "You should have heard him issuing orders. To *me*. The snide midget. Who does he think he is?"

"I'm glad you were firm with him. You'll also be happy to know that Jema is resting comfortably and in no danger," Daniel told her as he poured himself a drink. "In the event you were actually worried about her."

"That's your job, Daniel. Not mine." Meryl rolled over and took the glass he had poured for himself. "You'll have to burn her clothes and clean up the car. I don't want anyone to connect her with the murders. I told Jaus that the police had already been here. If anyone asks, you say it's been reported."

"Since we haven't actually reported it, I wonder precisely how your neighbor heard about it," he said. "How are you going to keep this quiet? Jema will want to make a statement to the police."

"We only need a few more days. Leave Jema to me. Why does this Keller woman think Jema isn't diabetic? How did she get one of her needles?"

"I have no idea. The syringes go into the incinerator every month, as usual. They burn better than Roy did." He made another drink for himself. "What did she say about Jema?"

"Some nonsense about her insulin. It was probably just an excuse to get Jaus up to see her; his father used to try sending doctors over here when she was little, remember? I can't have all this attention on us now." Meryl twisted the glass between her hands. "Not when we're so close."

"I could arrange to admit Jema early," Daniel offered. "In fact, we could use this mugging as an excuse to do it. The hospital has been keeping her bed ready. All I have to do is arrange the transport and take her up there."

"What I can't understand is why Jaus is so interested in her. The man is handsome, even if he is a foreigner. He's rumored to own half the city, so he couldn't want her for her inheritance." Meryl concentrated. "What did Jema tell the upstairs maid again about his party? Something about a gift."

Every conversation Jema had with the household staff was reported back to Meryl and Daniel.

"Jaus told her that he has a special gift for her. Something that he's been saving for a long time." Daniel sat down and rested his forearms on his knees. "It could just be a vase for the flowers he keeps sending her."

"I wonder if it could be something his father was saving." Meryl searched her memory for what her husband had told her about Valentin Sr. "James and Jaus's father were good friends. He always went to visit him whenever we were in town. I never cared for him, so I stayed home. In fact, James encouraged me to stay home. Said all they did was sit around and talk about weapons. Jaus apparently collected swords."

"I don't see the connection."

"James didn't have casual friends." She tapped her lips with a thin finger. "We socialized when we had to with people from the university, mostly to get grants and funding, but Jaus's father was the only man I can recall James ever making time to see." Had she been looking in the wrong direction all this time? "What if James took the Homage to Jaus's father thirty years ago and asked him to keep it for him? Without ever bringing it to the museum."

"That's quite a stretch. James came back to the States only to bring you and Jema home," he reminded her. "You told me that he left for Athos the very next day."

"He did, but I was sedated for the trip, so I didn't wake up until after he'd left for Rome." She felt a cautious excitement. "He could have walked over to Jaus's house anytime that night."

"But why would he?" Daniel laughed. "Meryl, the Homage was his obsession. He wouldn't have handed it over to your next-door neighbor."

"He would have handed Jema over to him, you idiot. Why didn't I think of it before now?" She wheeled herself over to the filing cabinet where she kept the legal papers, unlocked it, and took out a copy of James's will. She had been so angry when the lawyer had told her the terms of it that she had completely forgotten about the custody clause. "It's right here." She flipped through the legal document until she found the section on guardianship. "If I had died while Jema was a minor, Valentin Jaus Sr. would have been appointed her legal guardian."

"That's not proof that he has the Homage," Daniel said.

"Why leave Jema in the custody of Jaus's father? There were a dozen people we knew better who were younger and better capable of taking care of a child." She dropped the file in her lap and stared at nothing. "It would be just like James to give Jaus the Homage."

"If he gave it to anyone, it would have been to you."

"No. He was furious with me for causing the cave to collapse." Meryl remembered the only thing James had said to her after the accident. *I'd throttle you, you bitch, but she needs a mother.* "Jaus has never invited Jema to any of his parties. Why this one, on the night before her thirtieth birthday, if it doesn't have anything to do with his legacy? Jaus wouldn't have to know what the Homage was. James could have told him anything." She stared at him, aghast at her own suggestion. "He could have told the old man what else would happen on her thirtieth birthday."

"I still think this is very far-fetched, Meryl, but I suppose you could ask Jaus if he has it," Daniel suggested. "Perhaps tomorrow. You should also tell him that Jema will be in no condition to attend his party."

"I will do no such thing," Meryl told him. "We'll have to go with her to the party, and search Jaus's house. I can't allow him to give her the Homage. She'd start talking about it, and the press would get involved, and then it would ruin everything."

"Yes," Daniel said, looking sad now. "I suppose it would."

Chapter 17

John Keller had nearly quit his job at the Haven a dozen times since Dougall Hurley had hired him. This morning resignation number thirteen wrote itself inside his head.

It was rather like a confession, beginning with *To Whom It May Concern* instead of *Father, forgive me, for I have sinned.* It might sound better, in fact, if it did.

Father, forgive me, for I have sinned. It has been seven months since I left the priesthood to become a private citizen. Despite my wishes, I am incapable of meeting the challenge of providing quality counseling for the Haven's clients. This could be due to the fact that I am a) a failed priest; b) a former homeless child who never effectively transitioned into a productive adult life; or c) at odds with two dark forces, both of whom know where I live and work now. P.S. I can't sleep. Amen. Yours sincerely, John Patrick.

John thought the wording needed a little work, especially the part about the dark forces. He doubted he could think up any acceptable business euphemisms for vampiric immortal demons and sadistic zealot inquisitors. Also, it was extremely apologetic. He was tired of apologizing to people for failing them. Hurley had known John was a failure from the beginning; he should have hired someone with more promising personal dynamics.

Working at the Haven was not that much different from the homeless mission John had managed as a priest at St. Luke's.

The clients were younger, but in most cases no different from the bums, drunks, prostitutes, and addicts who had lined up outside St. Luke's satellite soup kitchen for hot meals three times each week.

> *I accepted this position because I felt I could help many of the Haven's clients with the myriad emotional problems that evolved from being young, homeless, and alone in the world. Having personally experienced life on the streets, I also have the unique perspective of having survived it. I would have used this to relate to the children and gain their trust; however, I have been unsuccessful in finding an avenue of communication—*

No, that wasn't the truth. He'd tried everything he could think of. Individual and group counseling, formal and informal. Food was always an attention getter, so he tried snacks. He was getting to be a whiz with homemade cereal bars, but the kids at the Haven weren't letting him in. They didn't want to hear his unique perspective. They wanted Cocoa Krispies treats. They couldn't care less what he wanted to do about their myriad emotional problems.

One client had summed it up with devastating succinctness: *Who the fuck are you to be getting in my shit, man?*

John had sensed the futility of his efforts from the beginning. The older kids would simply walk away. Pure and occasionally some of the younger children would pretend to listen, but they were more interested in getting a handle on him, or getting something out of him. The younger kids wanted protection; Pure wanted John to help her keep her baby, about which she still hadn't told Brian.

The fact that both the Brethren and the Darkyn knew where he was didn't help John settle in at the Haven. He had hardly slept since Cyprien and his man had paid him a visit, and Hurley still made sarcastic remarks about the men he called John's friends.

Are your friends coming over tonight? I'll call the National Guard. Your friends owe me a new meat cleaver; they broke the tip of the blade on my old one when they threw it at you. Hear any death threats from your friends lately?

He hadn't heard anything from the Darkyn, Hightower, or Alexandra, and that was another lead weight around his neck. He wanted to know if his sister had recovered from the attempt on her life, but he couldn't bring himself to find a way to contact her. She was part of Cyprien's world now, as lost to him as he had been to her during the long months he'd spent in prison.

John mentally ripped up resignation number thirteen. He couldn't afford to quit his job at the Haven, for obvious reasons. For many reasons, including Pure and her baby.

He was going to save someone, somehow, even if it was simply that single unborn child.

He went to the kitchen, where he had unearthed one of Hurley's old coffeemakers. It was incredible how many layers of brown sludge stains Dougall had built up on the inside of the glass carafe. John was trying to scrub them away when Sandy, one of the long-term residents, came in to warn him that two cops had arrived and were in the office questioning Hurley.

"Three Bones got cut up downtown," the girl told him. "I bet that's why they're hassling him. Anyway, they want to talk to you too."

"Three Bones?"

"Skins. You know, skinheads? 'White is right,' all that shit? Crazed and confused." Sandy twirled a finger by her temple as a visual aid. "Hurley used to run the Bones."

"Hurley was a gang leader?" John was stunned. The archbishop had said Dougall had been a priest. How could he have possibly been ordained if he'd been a street thug? Even before the present focus on priests' criminal behavior, the Catholic Church had maintained some standards. "You must be mistaken, Sandy."

Sandy snorted. "Why you think he's always going on about sticking with your own color?" She picked at a pimple on the side of her mouth. "Pure's gone, at least."

"Pure left the shelter?"

"Yeah, Decree came last night and took her. They never came back. Maybe they got into it with the boys." The girl examined the dot of pus on her fingernail. "Decree belongs to the Bones. He's, like, second in command now."

John rinsed out the carafe and dried his hands before he walked over to Hurley's office. The shelter manager had his door open and waved John in to join him and the two plainclothes detectives sitting inside.

"John Keller, my resident counselor," he told the cops. "John, the police would like to know if we have any information or leads on three kids who were knifed to death downtown last night. I was just telling them that we aren't missing any of our gangsters."

One of the detective took out a notepad. "Keller, John. Any middle name?"

"Patrick."

He nodded and scribbled that down. "Where were you between the hours of ten and eleven P.M. last night?"

"I was sleeping in my room. It's in the back of the kitchen." The room Hurley had allocated for John was roughly the same size as his quarters at the rectory at St. Luke's, but it was clean and the kids hadn't yet figured out how to pick the new lock that John had installed on the door.

"Alone?" the other detective asked, his expression bored.

"Yes, alone." John frowned. "May I ask to what these questions pertain?"

"Doesn't he talk beautiful?" Hurley asked one of the cops. "He can do it all fucking day, too."

"We're trying to establish where everyone was that night, Mr. Keller." The first cop nodded toward Hurley. "Your boss was also sleeping, alone, in his room."

"It was nighttime," Hurley said. "People do sleep at night."

The questions continued, with the detectives asking for information on known gang members staying at the Haven. Hurley joked and shrugged when they asked for names. John didn't know the residents well enough to contribute any useful information.

The bored detective caught a yawn with his hand. "You're sure you have no records on Roland Riegler, Gary O'Donnell, or Lawrence Kunde?"

"I'll check my files again, Officer," Hurley offered, "but they still won't be there."

"Call us if they materialize unexpectedly," the first cop said, handing Hurley a business card. He glanced up at John. "Have you anything to add?"

John shook his head.

After the detectives left, Hurley dropped the cop's card into his trash can. "Assholes."

"Why did they come here?" John went over to help himself to Hurley's coffee while it was still in liquid form. After the questioning, he felt he deserved it.

"Sandy didn't tell all?" Hurley clucked his tongue. "The kids who got stabbed are members of my old street gang, the Bones."

John turned around. "*You* were a skinhead? Before or after you became a priest?"

"Before." The shelter manager laughed. "Man, I couldn't *wait* to be a skinhead. Anything to give me an excuse to shave this shit off." He shook back his dreadlocks with the practiced aplomb of a bombshell blonde. "I'm not saying it was a good choice. I had the usual shitty childhood. My mom took off, and my dad took it out on me. I started living wherever I could, and fell in with the Bones. They didn't care about my hair or clothes, and they made me proud to be poor, white, and stupid. Took a couple of years of ducking drive-bys, getting Nazi tattoos and marching with the tri-Ks, but I outgrew the Bones and the movement. Same thing with the priesthood. I'm more into Pilates now."

"I can't imagine you as a priest, but I have no problem picturing you as a white supremacist," John said blandly. "I don't know why. Perhaps it's the holdover vocabulary."

Hurley's grin faded. "I take in little shits like the Bones seven days a week, Oreo, but in case you haven't noticed, I take the rest of the rainbow too. Sure, I used to *Sieg Heil* with the best of them, but I got over it."

"You still don't think the races should mix," John pointed out. "And you're very forthright with your attitude."

"That's because the mixed kids are the ones who suffer. They don't know what they are; they don't belong anywhere, and no one wants them. So yeah, I don't think we should fuck around with Nature's palette. I thought the Catholics would understand, but they didn't. That doesn't make me a Nazi, you know, and at least I can sleep at night."

John stiffened. "Meaning?"

"How long you been passing yourself off as lily white, man? Not going out in the sun so you don't get too dark, am I right? Keep your hair short so no one spots the kink? Talking like you eat Shakespeare and shit Susanna Clarke?" Hurley made a disgusted sound. "You might think you're better than me because you keep your prejudice inside, but we're the same." He produced a nasty smile. "The only difference is, I'm white on both sides, in and out."

John started composing resignation number fourteen as he left Hurley's office. *To Whom It May Concern. A racist Irishman has just made me aware that I am as bigoted as he is. Please excuse me from working with people of different skin colors until I can achieve an attitude adjustment. I do not wish to be a Nazi.*

"Entschuldigen Sie."

John looked up at into the dark eyes of the man who had come to the shelter with Cyprien. He backed up slowly.

"Einen moment, bitte." The man drew a knife and let John see it. Then he pointed toward the front of the building. "Come with me. To the car. Now, please, and quiet."

John couldn't risk having the man chase him or cut him up inside the building. Not in front of the children. Once he was on the street he could run, lure him away from the Haven.

"Yes." He walked like a robot toward his imminent death.

The vampire didn't turn to ash when they walked outside into the bright sunlight, but he did don a pair of trendy sunglasses. He sheathed his knife and pointed to a long, dark limousine waiting at the end of the street. "Go to the car."

"Go to hell." John took off in the opposite direction.

He'd always been a good runner. Carrying things up and down the Haven's stairs had toned his legs, and fear provided excellent impetus. John hadn't hit his top speed, though, when a big hand grabbed him by the back of the neck and spun him around.

"The car is this way," the vampire said through clenched teeth. "You will go now, please."

John went, marched to the limousine by the bigger man as if he were a truant child. The vampire didn't let go of him even when he opened the door to the back of the limo.

Alexandra Keller, her left arm in a sling, leaned out. "It's me, big brother. Get in."

The vampire helped John with the latter, a little too forcefully, and he ended up sprawled facedown on the leather seat opposite Alex.

"Thank you, Falco," she said to the vampire before he closed the door and went to the driver's seat. "Sorry about that. He's, um, enthusiastic."

John pushed himself up and looked at his sister. "Why didn't you just call?"

"I tried. The line's always busy. I didn't think you wanted me to show up asking for you at your job."

There were definite changes in the six months since he'd last spoken to her. Alexandra's hair, a curly mane of dark brown, was pulled up and away from her face and twisted in an elegant style. She wore a dress, something he couldn't remember her doing since high school, and the understated burgundy silk made the solid gold chain around her throat gleam. No makeup, not that Alexandra had ever needed any. She looked better, happier.

John let the indignation and pleasure over what he saw fight inside him until she said, "You look like shit, John. What's with this beard?"

He touched the short hair covering the lower half of his face before he remembered that he and his sister weren't on the same side any longer. They weren't even the same species. "What's with sending the Terminator to abduct me?" he countered.

"This isn't an abduction. We use drugs when we kidnap people." She used one hand to fasten her seat belt. "This is just a ride around the block and a chat."

"Cyprien told me that you'd been hurt." He nodded toward her shoulder. "Why is your arm in a sling? I thought you healed instantly."

"That's the reason for the chat." She gave her sling a wry look. "All things dark and spooky aren't exactly going according to plan. My mutation is different than theirs was."

"Your mutation." John knew his sister had read a lot of comic books when she was younger, but he never expected to hear her talking as if she were part of one. "Did Professor X tell you that, or Batman?"

Alexandra laughed. "Good one, Johnny." She leaned over and pressed an intercom button. "Park it somewhere, will you, Falco? Thanks."

She waited until the vampire had stopped the limousine on a side street by an abandoned building before she picked up her medical case from the floor. "The main reason I came to see you, John, was to ask for a favor."

He eyed the case. He had never understood his sister's calling any more than she had understood his. "What is it?"

"I need a little blood from you."

He flinched, revolted. "You couldn't get it from someone else?"

She frowned and then it dawned on her. "I'm not going to drink it, John. For God's sake. You're my brother." She made it sound as if he'd asked her to have sex with him. "I need a blood sample to run some tests."

"Ask someone else."

"I'm researching the cause of the Kyn's condition, and since I'm the only one who's survived the contagion in five centuries, my blood is integral," she said. "I don't have any samples of my own prior to infection, so yours is the next best thing."

He imagined his sister turning other humans into vampires. "Is this so you can infect other people? Do you expect me to help you?"

"No. I'm going to find a cure. You can help with that."

"A cure. For vampirism."

"The Darkyn are vampires only in the sense that they have fangs, are nocturnal, and live on human blood," she told him. "They heal faster. They're stronger." She started to say something else, and then changed her mind. "That's about it."

He rolled a hand over the sore spot on the back of his neck

where Falco had grabbed it. "That is the textbook definition of a vampire, Alexandra."

"Look, big brother." Her voice acquired an edge. "All I'm asking for is a sample. One vial of blood. Then I'll go away and you can go back and save kiddie souls and make excuses to God."

"I'm not a priest any longer." He looked down at his hands. They were rough and red from the hours he'd spent on his knees, scrubbing floors instead of praying. "I only made it official when I came back into town, but I left the church seven months ago."

"I'm sorry." And she was, when John had expected her to cheer. "I wish I could go back and change what happened in New Orleans. There are so many things I would do differently. So many bodyguards I would hire. Only time travel isn't one of the perks."

John studied her face, and then began slowly rolling up his sleeve.

A smile curved her lips. "Thank you."

He looked away again as she inserted the needle into his vein. "Cyprien. Does he treat you well?"

"As well as your average goddess. Why, I don't know. The man could have anyone he wants. I think he's had anyone he wants for the last seven centuries. Christ, I hate being part of a trend." She removed the tube of blood and drew the needle from his arm.

"You love him."

She nodded. "Sometimes that's the hardest part of this thing. Loving him, trying to work it out. Having fangs and drinking blood is the no-brainer stuff. I know you won't believe this, but Michael is a good man." Alex pocketed the blood sample and smiled. "When we get back to New Orleans—"

John never heard Alex's plans. A ball of fire smashed through the side window, soaking the seats around him and Alexandra with gasoline, and then blanketing them in flames.

How could you be so careless?
Who allows you to do such things?

If I were your husband, you wouldn't leave our bedchamber. You'd be too tired to walk.

Jema opened her eyes. A dull pain throbbed on the side of her head. She reached up and felt a square of gauze taped over the spot. Another time she would have panicked, but now she lay quietly, assessing what she felt. Her memory began with being attacked and beaten in an alley by the museum. It ended with Dr. Bradford carrying her into the house. Daniel had not been her savior last night, however.

He saved me. Thierry. The golden-eyed demon.

He had shouted at her, too. Not as he had in the dream, but in a mixture of French and English. Loud, harsh, furious words. Things about her life and her work that were true. Mean, but true. She had felt the weight of his hand the whole way home.

The gardenias. They belonged to him. She brought her hand up to her face. She could smell him on her skin.

How many times had she woken up, smelling him in her room, on her body?

Jema got up slowly, carefully. The sore, battered feeling wasn't a product of her imagination on this occasion; under her nightgown she was covered with bruises. She went into the bathroom and braced herself as she looked in the mirror.

They'd hit her in the face more than once, the men who had jumped her outside the museum, and the evidence was all over her face: split lip, black eye, reddened nose. A graze on her cheek from when she'd been thrown to the ground. Being mugged didn't feel the way it looked on TV or in the movies. It had been real, excruciating pain, and the worst was not being able to stop it or the men beating her.

Jema remembered praying when the one of them dragged her back into the alley. She had prayed because she had known she was going to die there.

And here she was, alive. Saved from being murdered by a man who didn't exist.

What do I do now, little cat? How can I leave you now, even when I know I must? Who will be there the next time someone tries to harm you?

She went over and knelt before the toilet, lifting the seat, holding back her hair. Throwing up seemed like a privilege.

After she washed her face and brushed her teeth, she went back out into her room. Her alarm clock had not gone off with the usual buzz, and she checked it. Someone had turned it off. She switched on the clock radio and tuned it to a local all-news station.

The announcer confirmed everything she remembered. Her attackers were the top story of the morning.

"The three youths, identified as Gary O'Donnell, Lawrence Kunde, and Roland Riegler, were found stabbed to death in the parking lot behind the Shaw Museum. Police are investigating other members of the 'Bones' white supremacist gang, who they believe may have information about last night's triple murder. In sports, the Bears suffered a setback when . . ."

She went to the window and stepped out onto the balcony. New snowfall enfolded Shaw House in white; the naked trees were dressed in glassy icicles. She could smell gardenias— Thierry—all over herself, on her skin, in her hair. *He's real. Everything we did together was real.*

Jema thought of one dream she'd had as a little girl, when she saw herself running out of Shaw House and willing herself to fly away. She didn't flap her arms and take off, as a bird did, but instead she had known how to make her body lighter than air. In the dream, she had floated up, gently, slowly, a leaf floating on a river of warm air. It had felt so real to her that the next day she had walked out to stand on the lawn and tried to do the same thing consciously. Her feet had stayed on the ground, and as every child must, she understood that what happened in her sleep was not real, could never be real.

Where was the ground now? She looked over the edge. If she dared step out, would she fall to her death? Or would she float, a brittle leaf, curling in on herself, able to fly? Or would she be too afraid?

"Jema?"

She turned and walked back into the room. Daniel Bradford was there, his medical case in hand. He looked upset and relieved.

"You should be in bed." He drew back the quilt for her.

Jema climbed in, too astounded by what she was thinking and feeling to protest. Daniel examined her thoroughly and changed the bandage on her head before he spoke again.

"Do you remember what happened to you last night?"

She folded her hands. "Some men came after me when I left work. They were going to kill me. Then I was here." She gazed up at him, willing him to explain what had happened in the time between the events.

"You have a mild concussion and some scrapes and bruises, but I think with a few days of bedrest you'll be as good as new. I keep saying that, don't I?" He grimaced and prepared a syringe. "You can imagine the state your mother is in."

Yes, she could. "She knows I'm all right?"

He nodded. "I think it would help if you stayed close to home for a bit. I know your work is important, but Meryl is terrified by what happened to you." He administered the injection. "I also think it would be a good idea if you wouldn't mention your friend or have any contact with him for the present."

"My friend."

"The man who drove you home from the museum last night." He misread her expression. "Your love life is your business, but it would just add too much strain to the situation. Once Meryl calms down, you can tell her about him. Invite him over for a meal, if you think he can stand the interrogation over dessert." He packed up his case and checked his watch. "If you feel up to coming down for breakfast, I know it would do great things for your mother's ulcer."

Jema didn't notice Daniel leaving her room. She felt disconnected from everything around her; breakfast and her mother were a million miles away. She pressed a hand to her mouth as it flooded over her. The only way Daniel could have known about Thierry was if he had seen him driving her home last night. The last fear that she was hallucinating or losing her mind disappeared, and she was left standing in a world where the man of her dreams existed.

Thierry was real.

"Oh, my God." There was so much she had to do. So much she had to know. Where he was, what he was doing, how he had done this thing, come into her dreams, shared them with her. She would know him if she were blindfolded, caught in the middle of a crowd of strangers, but she didn't know his address or phone number. She didn't know where he worked, if he lived in the city or at the lakefront.

Was what he had told her in the dreams true as well? Was he something other than a human being? Wouldn't he have to be, to do the things that he had done?

Jema's heart turned over in her chest. She had to get out of here. She had to find him, today, *immediately,* before another hour passed. She had to touch him and kiss him and slap him silly for what he'd done to her, and then throw herself in his arms and thank him for her life.

Thierry had saved her.

It took a little time and a lot of makeup to conceal the bruises and cuts on her face. When she went downstairs, Jema considered bypassing Meryl and going directly to her car. It would save precious time she could spend looking for her golden-eyed demon. She couldn't waste an ounce of energy on guilt or pandering to her mother's fears. As she walked past the dining room, she hesitated. The attack last night had been serious. The police were going to want a statement on what had happened. Jema knew she hadn't talked to them last night. She couldn't leave her mother to deal with them alone; Meryl would end up having a real heart attack from the hysterics.

Jema walked in and found her mother sitting by herself at the table. "I have to talk to you," she said, and saw her mother jerk in her chair.

"You startled me." Meryl's face had a gray tinge, and she pressed a hand under her breasts. "I told Daniel to keep you in bed."

"I'm fine. I have to go in to work. I'll call the police from my office and have them come by the museum to take my statement." She had no idea of how to tell her mother about Thierry. "There are other things that can't wait—"

"Sit down for a minute." Her mother gestured to the chair beside her. "Please. There's something I have to tell you."

Jema shook her head. "When I get home tonight—"

"You can't go to the museum. If they find out . . . with the

Chapter 18

Things only went from bad to worse when Jema arrived at the museum.

"Detective Newberry." Jema stopped in the hall leading to the basement, where the detective was leaning against one wall and reading over some handwritten notes.

"Morning, Miss Shaw." Stephen Newberry straightened and pocketed the notepad. "You've heard about the murders outside the museum last night?"

"I . . . yes, I did." Jema didn't know what to tell him. Her mother's revelations had her feeling as if she had to hide everything from the police. Then there was Thierry—had he killed those men, protecting her? Jema could remember seeing a large, dark shadow rushing at the men just before one of them had dragged her into the alley. If Thierry had killed them, he might be charged with murder. Aware the detective was staring at her, she said, "Sorry, I haven't had my coffee yet. Have you been assigned to this case?"

"The three guys who were killed were my primary suspects in a couple of assaults and murders, including the Fong case." Newberry scratched the back of his head. "The weird thing is, we found more of those hairs on the bodies. I was hoping your expert might have turned up something on them."

That was why he was here—not to question her, but to consult with her.

"Come down to my office," she said, keeping her expression controlled. "I'll call Dr. Tucker right now and see if she's made any progress."

Sophie Tucker was happy to hear from Jema. "I tried to fax

this report to you last night, but for some reason my machine didn't want to talk to your machine. The hair was identified by a faunal expert from Rio. It's from a hybrid type of llama in Argentina."

"A llama. Don't we have them here in the U.S.?"

"Not this kind. They're a hybrid, farmed for their wool—and get this. The Argentineans use it primarily to make theatrical masks." Sophie chuckled. "Just when you think you've heard everything, right?"

The men who had attacked her last night had been wearing masks. Masks that made them look like animals—with real hair, the same color as the hair that had been found on the body of the young Asian man.

Pull yourself together. Jema managed to thank her and ask her to send the report over as soon as possible, and then relayed the information to Newberry.

He was perplexed by Dr. Tucker's identification. "If they were wearing masks last night, who took them off the bodies? And how did they get from Argentina to Chicago?"

"I wish I could tell you. You might check with some of the local costume shops; they might be importing them," Jema suggested. If she had to keep up this act much longer, she was going to having shrieking hysterics. "Maybe they were wearing their Halloween costumes a little early."

He nodded, and then peered at her. "That's one heck of a black eye you have under all that concealer."

"This?" Jema resisted the urge to cover her face with one hand. "I was hurrying and tripped and fell down the stairs at home. I sort of landed on my face. Now everyone thinks my nice little old mother, who's in a wheelchair, is knocking me around."

"People watch too much Lifetime." Newberry chuckled as he stood up and shook her hand. "Thanks for all your help on this, Miss Shaw."

Jema thought of what he had said earlier. "Detective, just out of curiosity, what other cases do you have that are linked to these three men who were killed last night?"

"Well, the Fong murder that we worked together, a couple of beatings at a hip-hop club on the east side, and the Lopez case." His eyes narrowed. "Wait a minute. Luisa Lopez worked here at the museum, didn't she?"

"Yes, she did." Jema froze. "How is her case connected?"

"Only by the fiber evidence. The doctors recovered some of that llama hair from her." Newberry looked grim. "They found it lodged under her fingernails."

Cyprien hated being separated from Alexandra during the daylight hours. Although she tolerated the sunlight far better than he and the other Kyn did, he never felt safe letting her go out during the day. Now, with the knowledge that someone was actively trying to kill her, or him, or both of them, he paced and brooded every moment she was gone.

She is fine. She is lying dead in the gutter. She is safe. She is chained in a torture chamber.

He cursed himself for not accompanying her. Alex had insisted on going alone; she felt her brother would respond better to her request for a blood sample if he were not present. Jaus had sent Falco to drive her, so there was really no need to worry. The bargain Cyprien had made with Tremayne had lifted John Keller's death sentence.

"I am quite shocked that you dare call my attention to this," Tremayne had said when Michael had called Ireland to make his offer. "I could now demand it from you without sparing the priest."

"Such is your right, my lord," Cyprien said. "However, it is within my power to make it disappear before your men arrive to take possession. Rather like John Keller."

The silence that followed was brief. "You are annoying me, Michael."

One did not annoy Richard Tremayne and expect to live long afterward, but Michael thought it worth the risk. "It must feel the same as having one's authority tested, my lord. As you did mine by sending out the order to kill Keller."

Richard laughed. "So I did. Very well, Michael. I will permit Father Keller to live, so long as he does not interfere in Kyn business or return to the good Brothers. Should he do so, our bargain ends, as does his life."

Cyprien still had his own reservations about allowing

Alexandra's brother to live, but they were not as important as preserving his relationship with his *sygkenis*. If it became clear that he'd been wrong about Keller, he could use Falco to make the resolution swift and anonymous.

Cyprien waited until an hour had passed, and he no longer wanted to listen to his voice of reason. *This is taking too long.* He went to the window to look down at the circular drive in front of the house. If Alexandra did not return in ten minutes, he would go out and find her.

"An assassin would appreciate this," Jaus said, directly behind him. "Your back to an open door, your mind in another place."

Michael turned his head. "I trust you to at least keep the assassins out of the house." He looked at the file Jaus was holding. "You have identified him?"

"David Montague," Jaus said. "A former contract killer. He stopped working for hire some months ago, evidently to indulge his personal predilections. My hunters found traces of six private kills at his residence, but no evidence as to why he tried to murder Jema Shaw or you. I had them leave the body in the house. It is not over, however."

Cyprien listened as Jaus told him about the attack on Jema Shaw at the museum, and how Thierry Durand had killed the three men involved.

"Thierry saved Miss Shaw?" It could not be a coincidence. "How did he come to be there?"

"I cannot explain his presence at the museum," Jaus admitted. "Perhaps he came upon them purely out of chance."

Cyprien wasn't so sure of that. "He might have gone to the museum to find out something about Ms. Lopez."

"Yes, I remember now. She once worked there."

"At least we know Thierry is not responsible for killing Montague. He was on the other side of town at the museum." Something occurred to Michael. "There should be a connection between Montague and the three men whom Thierry killed. It will identify the Kyn behind these attacks."

"If there is, my men will find it." Jaus sighed. "Michael, I have enough men in the police department to protect Jema and remove the evidence that might expose the Kyn's involvement in these murders, but we cannot permit Thierry to go on killing humans. I believe he may be too dangerous now for us to try to capture alive."

"This is how you would reward him for saving Jema?"

"This is how I protect my city from a madman who is chopping up humans and leaving the pieces in his wake," Jaus replied evenly. "Even one to whom I owe a debt I can never repay."

Cyprien rubbed his eyes. "Very well. Give the order to your men. What will I tell Alexandra? Jamys?"

"It is better to say nothing of this," Jaus suggested. "Let the boy believe that his father was lost in a fair battle, not . . . " A commotion downstairs distracted him. "An assassination."

Michael followed him to the door in time to hear Alexandra shouting his name.

Jaus ran, but Cyprien didn't bother with the stairs. He jumped over the balcony and dropped thirty feet to the floor below. Alexandra and Falco were carrying Jamys Durand between them. Their garments were scorched and Alex's and Jamys's faces were covered with soot. The smell of gasoline was thick and sickening.

Jaus intercepted them as Cyprien took the boy in his arms. "*Mein Gott,* what happened?"

"They firebombed the limo," she told them as Michael carried the boy into the lab Jaus had set up for her. "Jamys pulled us out in time, but while he was saving us, they hauled John right out of the car. They took him."

Jaus shouted for his guards as Cyprien placed Jamys on the exam table. It was then that Michael saw the boy's hands were burned black. "How serious is it?"

"Hang on." Alex thrust a steel instrument into the boy's mouth and checked inside. "Okay. I need saline solution and two basins. Fast." She used a scalpel to cut open Jamys's shirt and checked his chest and abdomen while Cyprien and Jaus brought her the supplies she needed. "Empty the saline in the basins and put one under each hand."

Once they had the basins prepared, Alex carefully immersed Jamys's burned hands in them. Soot and dead tissue immediately floated to the top of the solution, blackening it.

Alex broke an ammonia ampoule and held it under the boy's nose. "Come on, Sleeping Beauty. Open those pretty dark eyes for me so I can yell at you."

Jamys jerked and opened his eyes, staring at them in shock before he coughed violently. Soot came out of his mouth, a small cloud of black dust.

"It's okay, let it out." When the boy had stopped coughing, Alex brought over an oxygen tank and fixed a mask over his face.

"Why are you doing that?" Jaus asked.

"Oxygen helps the internal healing." She checked his eyes with a penlight. "Looks like your brains are still working okay." She straightened and looked down at him. "I should whip your ass, Jamie. What were you thinking, diving into a car on fire?"

Jamys blinked and coughed again, then shrugged.

"Well, thank you for saving my life, you little shit." She turned her head. "We'll need two units of whole blood for our hero." When Cyprien brought them to her, Alex started an IV line and hooked both bags of blood to it so that both fed directly into his veins. Jamys's body began rapidly absorbing the fluid.

"How did this happen?" Jaus asked Falco.

"The doctor asked me to park the car so she could take the blood from her brother. While we were parked, someone threw a firebomb through the back window. The boy dragged me and your *sygkenis* out of the flames, but other men were there. They took the brother from the car, threw him in the back of a truck, and drove off with him." Falco looked at the floor. "I would have followed, but your lady insisted we return to Derabend Hall."

Cyprien glanced at Jamys. "Who were the men? Brethren?" He thought of the medical office in New Orleans. "Did they look like professionals?"

Falco looked uncertain. "I do not think so, seigneur. They were young men, with smooth-shaven skulls. I have seen them before, in the city. They are like dogs; they hunt in packs and attack the weak and the different."

"Skinheads." Jaus turned and issued terse orders to his

guards. To Cyprien he said, "I know these jackals. I will bring them here for questioning."

"I want to talk to them." Alexandra was sponging dead tissue from the back of one of Jamys's hands. New, healthy flesh was already forming.

Michael saw the urgency in the boy's eyes. "He can identify the men who did this?"

"Not now. He won't be writing any messages for a few hours, will you, kiddo?" Alex turned to the boy. "By tonight you should be healed, though, and then I'm going to make you write, 'I will never run away to Chicago and scare the wits out of Alex and Michael and my family again.' Five hundred times should do it."

Jamys gave her a frustrated glance before he gave Cyprien a heartrending look of entreaty.

"I understand how you feel," he said to Thierry's son. "Have you seen your father?"

Jamys's mouth turned down, and he shook his head.

"Jaus told you how Thierry saved Jema, didn't he?" Alex asked Cyprien. "I think that's a good sign of his state of mind."

"Yes." Cyprien looked away from the woman he loved, and the boy whose father he was going to have killed. "I think so, too."

Once Jamys's hands were cleaned of the burned tissue, Alex gave him a small dose of the sedative she had created for the Kyn.

"He'll heal faster if he sleeps," she explained as she took a blood sample from Jamys.

"Why are you taking his blood? More tests?"

"I think it might help to take a look at it. Jamys was seventeen when he made the change, right?" At Cyprien's nod, she said, "Forever a teenager, poor kid. Anyway, he's the youngest Kyn I've met so far, in a manner of speaking, so I'd like to see if there are any differences in the mutation of an adolescent versus an adult human."

"I was not so old when I changed," Cyprien told her. "Only twenty-two."

"You mean I'm robbing the cradle?" She chuckled, and then noticed a report that her printer had produced. "That was fast." She took out the paper and read it. "This thing must have a glitch in it."

Cyprien glanced at the computer analysis equipment. "What is it?"

"This thing is a prototype blood analyzer. Val was nice enough to bully it out of a medical researcher he has on the Kyn payroll. It performs hematological, biochemical, and microbiological tests on any blood sample, and the computer software program linked to it generates a comprehensive report and profile. I've been using it to compare the pathogens and anomalies in Kyn blood. I found a little blood in that syringe Jema used, so I figured I'd run hers, to serve as a human baseline." She stared at the paper again. "But this can't be right. Her results are way off."

"Is it caused by the combination of drugs she has been taking?"

"No, this is different." She shook her head. "It's got to be a software glitch."

"What do her readings indicate?" Cyprien asked.

"That she's something she's not, Michael." Alex reached in her pocket and took out a vial of blood. "Let me show you how this is supposed to work."

She put a drop of blood in another vial, which she then placed into a complicated-looking machine.

"This is John's blood. Certified human." As the machine began to process the sample, she went to the computer and pulled up a stored profile. "These are my readings." She turned so Cyprien could see the line graph. "John's will not be the same."

A few minutes later, John Keller's blood profile appeared on the screen and, as Alexandra had predicted, displayed dissimilar readings.

"Now I'll do Jema's over." Alex replaced the vial in the machine with another and processed it. The third screen that came up was closer to her own readings than John's. She made a frustrated sound. "I'll run Jamys's blood; I've tested him before. If that shows up wrong, we're going to make Jaus take this piece of junk back where he got it and ask for a refund."

She ran the fourth sample. Jamys's profile made her mutter, "You have got to be kidding me."

"Does this mean the machine is working, or not?"

"I must have contaminated Jema's needle." She rested her head against her hands. "I stuck myself, and my blood got on it and mixed with hers."

"Do you remember doing so?" He watched her shake her head. "The blood must be Jema's."

"It can't be." She looked up at him. "If that is her blood, then Jema is carrying the same pathogens in her blood that you and I and every other vamp in this place have. Michael, if this test is correct, Jema Shaw is in the process of becoming Kyn."

Thierry went back to the Nelsons' to check the house and assure himself that in his haste he had not left behind any traces of his presence. He walked through the rooms, inspecting them, welcoming the sense of emptiness.

He had no place in the home of a human. He could be only an intruder, unwelcome, unwanted. Never a part of their lives. He could not even find the men who had tortured Luisa Lopez. He was beyond worthless.

"I will leave," he told his reflection as he checked the master bathroom a third time. "I will go back to Cyprien. He will know what to do with me."

If his friend was smart, he would kill him. If he did not, Thierry thought he might be up to the task himself. The bitterness inside him was like drinking the blood of the dead. He would rather go quickly than die of despair.

He left the Nelsons' home, and stood in the snow for a time. The lights of Shaw House came over the wall and made patterns on it. He walked around them, reluctant even to touch the light coming from her windows. He was finished now, and he would stop behaving like a madman. He would contact Valentin Jaus and ask him to watch over Jema. Jaus had fought with him in many battles. He was an honorable man, and—

Thierry frowned as he saw the subject of his thoughts walking up the back lawn of Jema's property. He thought he must be mistaken, but then he heard Jaus's voice as he spoke to the maid at the door.

What was the suzerain of Chicago doing here?

Thierry jumped the wall and crept along the side of the house. From the sounds of the voices, Jema, Bradford, the mother, and Jaus were gathered in the front sitting room. Thierry went to the window and stood beside it, listening.

"I thank you for the invitation, but I have already . . . dined," Jaus was saying. "I came merely to deliver your costume for the masque tomorrow night."

"You didn't have to bring it over yourself." That was Jema. There was a small stretch of silence. "Oh, Mr. Jaus. It's beautiful."

Why was Jaus giving his Jema beautiful things?

"I had hoped you would find it so." Jaus sounded pleased.

As Jaus and Jema exchanged pleasantries, Thierry's bewilderment turned to suspicion. He knew the Austrian well. Jaus would never meddle with a human woman unless it served some ulterior motive. Why would he invite Jema to a masque? Why would he provide a costume? How did they know each other?

Thierry tracked Jaus from the house as soon as he left it, and discovered that Jaus occupied the house on the other side of the Shaw property. He assessed the compound, noted the Kyn guards stationed at every possible entrance and exit, and then slipped away before he was spotted.

Incredible as it seemed, Valentin Jaus appeared to be Jema's neighbor.

Thierry was bleakly amused to learn this. Here he had come to escape detection and capture by the Kyn, and the whole time the Kyn had been within a stone's throw of his hiding place.

The lights from Shaw House slowly went out, one by one. Thierry stayed in the shadows by the wall and paced, sorting out what he had discovered. With Jaus so near, Jema would be safe. He had only to call the suzerain and warn him about the attempt on her life.

When he saw the light disappear from Jema's bedroom window, Thierry knew it was a sign for him to go. She was in bed now, safe, soon to sleep and dream. Would it be a relief for her not to dream of him tonight?

He was climbing up to her balcony before he could think of what he was doing.

I will go to say good-bye, he promised himself as he swung up onto the balcony. *I will not disturb her or touch her. I will only look upon her.* He could leave, he thought, if he could see her one more time. One more image to carry with him, to last on the journey back to New Orleans, and what waited for him there.

He did not dare reach into her sleeping mind to see if she was asleep, but looked through the window. The light was out, but he could still see her form under the quilt. She did not move.

He waited, counting the minutes as he watched. Five minutes. Ten. She never moved once. She had to be asleep.

Go, quickly.

Thierry slipped the lock on her window with his dagger and stepped inside. The familiar scent of her drifted around him, stronger than it had been on the other nights. He closed the window behind him and breathed in, filling himself with her warm, sweet smell. He wished he could wear this on his skin, like his lady's colors, but it could only be another memory to cherish.

The light in the room snapped on.

Thierry looked at Jema, who was still sleeping. The door was closed.

"I'm over here."

He turned to see Jema standing by the wall switch on the opposite side of the room. At once he whirled around.

"Stay. Please."

His hand shook, and he pressed it against the glass. "I cannot."

"You stayed before when you came to see me, didn't you?" Now she was coming to him. Walking slowly toward him. Real. Awake. Aware. "Don't be afraid."

Afraid? Of her? He turned to look at her, and saw the bruises and cuts on her face. They looked a little better than they had last night, but the sight of them defeated his every resolve.

"They hurt you." He lifted his cold hand and touched the cut on her cheek. He met her gaze. "I killed them."

"I know." She closed her eyes and pressed her cheek against his hand, warming it.

Thierry would have stood there, willing and motionless, until the house fell down around them, just to feel that soft cheek upon his hand.

The knock at the door was another shock, one that made both of them jump.

"Jema?" It was the doctor's voice. "Are you awake?"

Jema was pulling Thierry toward her bathroom, pushing him inside. The door closed in his face, and then he heard her speaking to Bradford. He leaned his forehead against the door. What was she doing? There was no way for him to get out of the bath, no other doors, no windows. If Bradford discovered him here, in her room like this—

Thierry nearly stumbled as the door opened. The bedroom was dark now.

"It's okay," she said, taking his hand in hers and drawing him back into her bedchamber. "He's gone."

"I must go. I only came to say good-bye." He looked over at the bed. "How . . . ?"

She went to the bed and drew back the quilt. What he had thought was Jema's sleeping form was only a couple of pillows. Her eyes crinkled with amusement. "I fooled you."

He wanted to laugh. He thought he might weep. He would go. "Good-bye, my lady."

She darted around him, blocking his path to the window. "Why do you have to leave? Can't you stay and talk to me?"

"I think I have done enough to you." And it shamed him to admit it to her like this. He had never regretted his talent, but it had been wrong to use it on her as he had. He had violated her mind, and had almost done the same with her body. "I am sorry."

Her expression turned sad. "Didn't you like what we did together in my dreams? That's what happened, wasn't it? You came into my dreams."

"Yes. Sharing them made everything . . . more bearable." If

he were to be damned in her eyes, let it be for the truth. "I couldn't stop. I couldn't stay away."

"I'm glad you didn't." She took a deep breath. "Thierry. God, I didn't know if you were real, and then when I knew you were, I still couldn't believe it." She brushed at her eyes and laughed a little. "It sounds crazy, but I'd rather be in a dream with you than live in the real world."

"We cannot live in a dream," he told her. Something like the old madness was swelling inside him, but he didn't fear it. "Reality is better."

"I wouldn't know." She stepped up to him and placed one hand in the center of his chest. If he closed his eyes, he could imagine himself standing with her like this, in a grove of apple trees, sunlight all around them. "Would you show me?"

It was her touch that brought his arms around her; that made him lift her up and carry her to her empty bed. He bent down, holding her as he nudged the pillows out of the way, and then set her down. His hands were too big as he put them on her, her clothes too thin and insubstantial. He heard something tearing and realized he was responsible.

But his eyes were locked on her face, and Jema was not afraid of him. She was staring up at him, eyelids half-closed, lips parted. She needed him, wanted him.

Thierry let go of the last of his restraint. In some dim part of his head he knew he was being too rough with her. He tore her clothes from her body, and then helped her rid him of his own. The moment they were bare to each other, their skin touching, their hands moving over each other, he knew madness.

Jema was naked under his hands and he hadn't yet kissed her. His fangs made him hold back, until she curled an arm around his neck and put her lips to his.

Honey and almonds.

He cradled her bottom with one hand and lifted her from the bed, kneeling down on the mattress, holding her over and above him. She laughed and he took in the sound as he took her mouth, kissing her as deeply as he could. The glide of her tongue over his made his hands clench. His shaft throbbed, full and hard, eager for her.

She lifted her head and brushed her mouth against his ear. "Thierry."

In her dreams he had been gentle, erotic, everything she had wanted. It had delighted him to shape and bend himself to please her. From her dreams, he knew her as he had known no other woman. Now she would know him, his desires, his whims.

If only for this night.

Thierry lifted her higher so he could rub his face against her breasts and suck at them. It made her tremble and writhe between his hands, and when he brought her down she spread her thighs and met him, just as she had when she had given him the blood that had saved him.

There was nothing to keep them apart this time.

Jema braced her hands on his shoulders, and he reached between their bodies, grasping the head of his cock and working it between those full, slick lips opening for it. He pressed in, pushing her down, drawing back as he did so he could watch her face.

"Oh." Her eyelashes fluttered and her thighs tightened.

His back teeth met as liquid heat enveloped him. He kept her from impaling herself on him, wanting to fill the silky vise slowly, easily. She fit him as if fashioned exclusively for his pleasure, tight enough to squeeze the length of him, wet enough to make him groan.

Her bottom quivered as it touched his thighs. Her teeth were buried in her bottom lip, and Thierry's fangs ached as he smelled fresh blood. He held on to the other side of his hunger with a death grip as he moved in and licked the blood from her lip. Jema arched against his arm, her hips working, her breasts pressing against his chest.

Thierry rolled with her, off the bed, onto his feet, into the wall. He kept her on him and drew back only to drive into her again, hard and fast. A picture frame fell and landed on the bed. Jema's fingernails dug into his shoulders as she shuddered. Every time he shoved into her, her hips lifted and pushed back.

He sealed his mouth over hers and fucked her there against the wall, and then down to the floor, atop the pillows that had fallen there. He lifted her only to position one hand beneath her hips and then pressed her knees up and apart, opening her so he could use the deepest strokes, kissing her when she found her pleasure again.

His own would no longer be ignored, and Thierry groaned, afraid he would drive her through the floor. Jema brought one of her legs down and pushed, trying to flip over on top of him but unable to shift his weight. He remained buried deep inside her body as he let her turn him.

As soon as he was on his back she wrenched their bodies apart, sliding down him like a wraith, ignoring his hands as she caught him in her fingers and enveloped the head of his cock in her mouth. Thierry didn't dare move, and felt her hand tighten to a fist around him as she lifted her face.

"Let me," was all she said, but that was all it took. When her breath touched him he bowed, and when her mouth sucked at his cock again he became an arrow. Through slitted eyes he saw her head move, felt the scrape of her teeth, the velvet of her tongue.

She was going to kill him with her mouth. He would die a happy man.

The pleasure that had hovered, patient and then impatient, waiting for him to be satisfied with making her come, demanding its own moment, finally broke through the steel cage of his restraint. Thierry surged between her soft lips, shaking as his seed jetted into her mouth, destroyed by the low sounds she made as she sucked him dry.

He fell back, unsure he would ever move again. He could only lift one pathetic, weak arm to hold her as she slid up to lie against his chest. Her hand moved to his mouth, and he knew what she wanted. He opened his lips, and tasted the strangeness of himself on her fingertips.

"Real," she whispered, "is better."

Chapter 19

This ex-priest, Hurley, he will know where they are keeping Keller," Falco said. He was sharpening his dagger with a stone notched by decades of daily application. "You should let them have him."

"No." Jaus already felt guilty enough about persuading Cyprien to have Thierry killed. He would not deprive Alexandra of her brother, no matter how convenient it would be for the Kyn. "Go to Hurley; see what he knows. We must find Keller."

Falco looked exasperated. "As you say, master."

Jaus looked in on Alex, who was keeping watch over Jamys as he slept. He returned the smile she gave him. "Sacher said you were having a problem with the blood machine. Should I have it replaced?"

"I think I need to take some new samples before you do that. I may have accidentally contaminated one of them." She glanced at Jamys. "Do you think Jema's mother would let me see her if I go over to Shaw House? There's some questions I need to ask her about her condition."

He saw the fine tension in her body, and knew she was deeply concerned about her brother. How like Alexandra to hide it. "Jema will be coming here tonight, for the masque. It would be better to speak to her then, when I can distract her mother."

"Yeah, that lady is better than an attack dog," she said. "We didn't bring any costumes, though."

"I can arrange that with a phone call." He measured her with a glance. "You would be a petite size five."

"Size six," she said, and sighed. "I'd make a great jumbo shrimp."

He nodded at Jamys. "Would he be all right by himself for a moment? I have a catalog in my office, and you can pick out what you like."

"The sedative should have worn off by now, but I think he's just worn out, poor kid." Alex got up. "What kind of costumes are we wearing, anyway?"

As they left the room, Jamys opened his eyes, scanned the room, and then pulled the IV line out of his arm.

"Hey, you're waking up."

John opened his eyes to find himself in another unfamiliar place. He was sitting in a plaid armchair, to which he had been bound with yards of duct tape. Discarded drive-through bags and crushed beer cans littered the floor. Two open commercial paint containers overflowed with more cans. The smell of the place was Eau de Miller Time. From the look of the narrow, windowless concrete box and the roll-down door in front of him, he was in some sort of garage or warehouse.

Pure appeared in front of him. "I was so worried you'd be burned," she told him as she pulled down his gag and held a straw to his mouth. "It's okay. It's only water."

John took a cautious sip, and then another before he moved his head away. "Where is my sister?"

"She got away with the other guys," Pure told him. "I don't think Decree wanted them."

"Why kidnap me?"

She shrugged. "He didn't say. Decree pretty much does what he wants."

As she reached to pull the gag back over his mouth, John said quickly, "I won't shout or make any noise."

"Promise?" She looked over her shoulder. "Decree went to get us something to eat. Nobody can hear you out here, but if he finds out I let you yell, he'll be mad."

"I won't yell," John promised. "I only want to talk to you."

John couldn't quite believe Pure was involved in this. To know that she would participate in a kidnapping made him wonder if he could ever trust his judgment again.

"Why did Decree kidnap me?" he asked her.

"Raze told him to; that's all I know. He wanted you here while the Bones crash this big party at midnight." Pure sat cross-legged at his feet. "You don't understand, John. Raze has been so decent to Decree. He got jobs for all the guys, and now no one has to worry about money. Me and Decree, we're gonna have enough for our place soon." She lowered her voice to a whisper. "I'll be able to keep my baby, see?"

"I told you to keep him gagged." Decree ducked under the roll-down door and pulled it shut behind him. He handed Pure the bags of fast food he was carrying before he came over to look at John. "I guess this ruins me being your next altar boy, huh, Father?"

He'd obviously rehearsed that, to shock John. "I'm not a priest anymore," John reminded him, trying to keep the tired defeat out of his tone. "I don't know why you did this, Brian, but if you turn me loose, I won't press charges."

"Are you kidding, man? You are my cash cow. Raze is gonna pay five grand for you." Decree smiled as Pure handed him a burrito. "You like Mexican food?"

"Who is Raze, and why would he pay five thousand dollars for me?" John asked. "I don't even have five hundred dollars to my name."

"Don't know why." Decree took a bite of the burrito and chewed. "Raze is number one. Leader of the Bones. Don't you know anything?"

"Evidently not." John tried to shift, but the duct tape was wrapped too tightly around his chest and legs. "Listen to me, Brian. What you're doing is going to get you sent to prison. If you stop now, I promise I'll do everything I can to help you."

"Good old Father John." Decree tossed the rest of the burrito into a bag and crumpled it. "You always wanted to help Chris. Talking to him and shit like you do around the Haven. Only you're a big fucking fraud. Did you talk to my old man? Ever ask him to stop kicking the shit out of me and my brother?"

"I didn't know you were being abused."

"How many bloody noses and black eyes does it take?" Decree stalked away and took a beer from a paper sack on the floor. "You keep him gagged," he told Pure. "Cops drive by to check the place at midnight; I don't want them finding him. Raze won't come for him until after we do the French dude."

"What is Raze paying you to do, Brian?" John called to him. "Why are you risking prison to do what he wants? You never seemed that stupid to me."

Decree turned around and threw the can of beer at John. It hit the side of his head, a glancing blow, splattering him with the warm liquid inside.

"You don't say shit about Raze," the boy shouted. "You don't know nothing about Raze and what he's done for us."

"Tell me," John said.

"The Bones were small-time before he came," Decree said. "Little petty shit jobs, barely enough to keep us in beer. Then Raze took over. He got rid of everybody who hassled us. He even took out some cops that were gunning for us, you know? Then he hooks us up with the mad monks. Guys thinking the world's full of vampires." Decree shook his hands beside his head, making a ghostly sound, and then he laughed.

Mad monks. The Brethren. Now things made more sense. "What do they pay you to do? Kidnap people? Beat them up? Or are you just the delivery service?"

"We do all that, but we're moving up the fee scale. We got ten thousand for dusting a gink." Decree ignored Pure's shocked cry. "Man's gotta make a living. You know what the best part is? I used to paint swastikas on people's front doors and run away. Now, thanks to Raze, I get to carve them into some gink fuck's face, and people run away from me."

A drop of beer trickled into John's eye, making it burn. "You could still pull out of this, Brian. You're better than this."

"No, man. That's what's so sad about you. You don't get that this is exactly what I am." He smiled. "And I like it."

After repeating his instructions to Pure, who was pale and silent, Decree yanked the gag back over John's mouth and left. Pure started to cry a few seconds after the roll-down door slammed shut. She dropped into a miserable huddle on the floor and sobbed into her hands.

John closed his eyes. He didn't know how much time he

had left before Decree's leader—probably one of the Brethren—came for him.

"How could he?" Pure wailed. She was clutching her stomach with both hands. "What am I gonna do if they bust him for murder? I can't have this baby by myself."

John looked at her steadily, hoping she would come over and pull down the gag again. After several minutes she came to sit by the chair. He made a series of insistent sounds behind the gag until she reached up and pulled it down.

"Pure, I want to help you and Decree and your baby, but I can't do it like this."

"He'll kill me if I let you go." She sobbed out the words. "Or he'll give me to Raze. Do you know what Raze thinks he is? A vampire." That made her cry harder.

The door rolled up, and she screamed.

Jamys Durand and Dougall Hurley came in. Hurley closed the door quickly, and Jamys drew a dagger. He walked past the cringing Pure and used the dagger to cut John free of the duct tape binding him to the chair. Then he handed John the dagger and bent down to touch Pure's neck. The girl's eyes rolled back in her head and she slumped over on her side.

"What did you do to her?" John demanded.

"About what he did to me," Hurley said. He was pale and wide-eyed, a man who had received a healthy shock. "You know this kid has fangs?"

John flinched as Jamys reached out to him, and then felt an instant warmth where the boy touched him on the arm.

I only told her to go to sleep, a young male voice said inside John's head. *Alexandra is all right; she wasn't burned in the fire, but she and Michael and Valentin are in great danger. I can't speak and they can't hear me in their minds like this. Only humans can. Dougall will go with us, but he cannot tolerate my talent. I need your help.*

"Help to do what?" John felt dizzy.

"Stop the Bones," Hurley said. "Crazy little fuckers are going to commit mass murder. Or so Fang here says."

Inside John's head, Jamys said, *They're going to kill Michael and your sister for the Brethren. Tonight, at the lake.*

*   *   *

Jema didn't fall asleep until Thierry left her, just before dawn. She remembered telling him about Valentin Jaus's masque, and his promise to meet her there.

"We have much to discuss," he said as he bent down to kiss her good-bye. "I will see you tonight."

She had meant to ask him exactly where he would meet her, and if he'd wear a costume, but she was exhausted, and he was already at the window. He looked back at her, his golden eyes filled with love.

She fell asleep looking into them, but she didn't dream. She didn't have to.

Daniel came three hours later to wake her, and scolded her, but she barely paid any attention to him or the two injections he gave her. She only glanced down, frowning when he gave her the second.

"Another vitamin shot," he explained. "I think it'll be the last one you need. You look much better this morning."

She ate breakfast alone, and decided not to go in to work. She had to meet Thierry at the masque tonight, and she wanted to look her best. So Jema went back to bed, sleeping away the afternoon until it was time for dinner. Micki, the upstairs maid, brought her a tray before she could go down.

"Your mother thought you might like to have this in bed," Micki explained. "She also said you should be ready to leave with her and Dr. Bradford for the party at Mr. Jaus's in an hour."

"Were they invited, too?" Jema couldn't remember Valentin Jaus asking her mother or the doctor to attend.

"Yes, ma'am," Micki said. "I brought up your costume and hung it in the closet, so it's there when you're ready to dress."

Jema picked at her dinner, forcing down enough to balance her evening injection, and then took a long, leisurely shower. She took time with her hair and makeup—the cuts and bruises looked better today, but still needed covering up—before she dressed in the midnight-blue costume Jaus had hired for her.

It was a gorgeous ball gown made of stiff satin with a cobweb of matching lace over the full skirt. Tiny, teardrop-shaped crystals spangled the entire dress, which glittered subtly with her every movement. It was a little big at the waist and hips, but not enough to be noticed.

Jema left her hair loose and wore only a pair of small diamond studs in her ears. The gown came with elbow-length midnight-blue gloves, which she tried on and decided she liked, as they disguised the thinness of her arms.

Will Thierry think I'm pretty? She braved her reflection to study it. The blue did great things for her skin, and the makeup lent more color to her face. The red on her cheeks deepened as she remembered how he had loved her that last time, just before he left.

Earlier Thierry had carried her into the bathroom, but instead of turning on the shower he had filled the tub with warm water and some of her herbal bath salts.

"Don't you want to take a shower?" she asked. "It's faster."

"Let me do this. I wanted to one night when I saw you getting ready for bed," he told her as he picked her up and stepped into the tub, easing down into the water with her on top of him.

"You Peeping Tom." She braced herself against his chest with her arms and sat up, pretending to be indignant. "You saw me undress."

"I did not peep. I watched. I watched everything you did, as often as I could." He stroked her breast with the backs of his fingers. "It was a shameful thing, but I could not look away. My eyes wanted nothing more than to be filled with you."

She bent down to whisk a kiss across his mouth. "Before you filled my dreams."

He held her there, washing her first, and then tossing aside the cloth to use his hands on her. His slick fingers cupped her above and below, one thumb working over her nipple while the other exposed her clit. "I want more things. I wanted to take you while you slept."

"Thierry." Her breath caught in her throat.

"It would have been so easy to pull up your nightgown, spread your thighs, and put myself in you." He made the water splash around them as he lifted her up. "I wanted you to wake up while I was deep inside you, stroking you." He brought her down, impaling her with his thick, rigid penis until she took every inch of him. "The night I found you naked," he murmured as she trembled with a fast, helpless climax, "I almost did."

That memory made her thighs clench. It made her think of the things she wanted to do to him the next time she had him naked. Like taking him in her mouth again. Having him wake up while she was sucking him.

Jema looked down, and saw she had a death grip on the edge of the counter. She'd have to change her panties now; they were soaked through. *Stop thinking about sex.*

She knew there were other, equally important things that they would need to talk about. How he had entered her dreams, for one thing. Also, the fact that he thought he was a vampire, and that she had a terminal condition. The latter worried her the most. She didn't care if he really was a seven-hundred-year-old demon, or a Templar under a curse, or only a slightly delusional man who thought he was. Thierry could be anything, and she'd love him. But would he still love her if he knew that she was dying?

Yes. He would, her heart answered.

Just before it was time to leave for the masque, Jema walked downstairs and went into the sitting room where Meryl and Daniel were waiting.

"You look gorgeous, Mother." She admired Meryl's all-white Snow Queen ensemble. She laughed out loud when she saw Daniel Bradford, who was dressed as a mad scientist. "What's this? You look like Dr. Frankenstein."

"How do you know I'm not?" Daniel said, waggling his hairy false gray eyebrows.

Meryl made an irritable sound. "Can we go now, please? I'd rather not be late."

Valentin Jaus's mansion was a beacon of light on the lakefront. Jema caught her breath as she saw that the walks and drives were illuminated by thousands of dark blue candles in crystal holders. Overhead, silvery blue metallic streamers hung from the trees, dangling crystal spiders, ghosts, and bats.

"What a strange choice of colors for Halloween," Daniel said as he escorted Meryl and Jema up the walk to the front of Derabend Hall. "I don't think I've ever seen anyone go with an all-blue theme."

Other guests were arriving for the masque, and Jema patted herself on the back for asking Jaus to find a costume for her when she saw how beautifully dressed his friends were.

One couple wore Renaissance Italian-aristocrat costumes, heavily embroidered with dark metallic threads and bloodred faux gemstones. The woman's curly raven hair had been piled high in a tower of glossy ringlets, while the man had his brown hair in a short, intricate braid. Both wore stiff black satin masks outlined in golden and crimson thread.

Everyone wore a mask, which reminded Jema to put on the little blue satin strip of cloth that had come with the dress. Tying it over her eyes made her feel a bit like Zorro, but she was glad it covered her bruises. Makeup didn't hide everything.

"Mademoiselle," someone said, and she looked up to see a dark-haired giant dressed in a merchant's costume bow to her. "We are humbled by your beauty." His German accent emphasized the deep bass of his voice. "Suzerain Jaus could not have chosen a lovelier lady to grace his garden."

"Hello." Before she could introduce herself and correct his assumption, the man bowed and walked ahead of them. A petite redheaded woman dressed as a Harlequin looked back at Jema with open curiosity before she hurried to catch up to the dark merchant.

"What's a suzerain?" Daniel asked her.

"It's an old word that means 'lord,' " she said, frowning. "It hasn't been used since medieval times. Maybe it has something to do with the masque."

Meryl's mouth twisted as she eyed two men dressed in light armor, who were carrying authentic-looking sheathed swords at their sides. "All these costumes are ridiculous. Don't these Europeans know anything about Halloween?"

"I believe they invented it," was Daniel's tongue-in-cheek reply.

Valentin Jaus came to greet them at the door. He wore the costume of a prince, in the same shade of midnight blue as Jema's, with glittering silver epaulets and mock medals and ribbons fashioned out of crystal. His fair hair had been tied back in an old-fashioned queue that made the strong lines of his face seem more majestic than ever. He bowed to Meryl and Daniel, and then smiled and kissed the back of Jema's hand.

"Miss Shaw," he said, beaming at her. "You look like a dream."

"I feel like Holiday Barbie," she murmured to him, making him laugh. "But thank you." She noticed the white feathers embroidered down the length of one of his sleeves to make it appear more like a bird's wing. "Are you the Swan Prince?"

"You are very perceptive." He offered her his arm. "Come, let me introduce you to my friends. I have been bragging about how lovely the neighborhood is; you will be proof of it."

Jema glanced over at her mother and Daniel, but they were already moving into the room and greeting the other guests.

"I don't see anyone I know," she said as she took his arm, "so you may end up introducing me to everyone."

He gave her a rather mysterious smile. "I live for nothing else, my lady."

Jaus was the perfect host, and made the rounds of the room with ease. Jema found his friends to be very polite, if somewhat formal, and noticed that, like the man who had spoken to her outside, most had accents similar to Valentin's.

"Are most of your friends from Austria, like you?" she asked after meeting a tall, fair-haired man dressed like the composer of some grand orchestra of the past. The composer had actually clicked his heels while bowing to her.

"They are from Austria, Germany, and Switzerland," he said. "A few misfits from Spain and France. We are a very European group, I fear, Miss Shaw."

"I love their costumes." She had noticed a certain uniformity among them, as if everyone had rented their gowns to date to a specific time period. "You know, if you sent everyone in this room back in time to the fourteenth century, they'd be right at home."

"Indeed." He gave her a worried look. "Why do you say that?"

"Just look at them." She gestured at the other guests. "Don't you think they look like one of those marvelous medieval paintings brought to life?"

He chuckled. "I fear we are an old-fashioned group as well."

"Very polite, too." Jema noticed that no one had yet touched a single crumb on the beautiful buffet table or filled a flute at the enormous champagne fountain set up in the center of the room.

Jaus noticed her interest and asked if she wished some refreshments, but Jema felt too self-conscious to eat or drink when no one else was. "I really don't drink much," she told him as he guided her through an open doorway into a ballroom. "I don't tolerate alcohol too well."

"Nor do I," Jaus said. "I do miss going out to taste the first new wines of the year. It is a tradition in my homeland to do so."

Guests stood on either side, but no one was dancing yet. There were so many candles burning in the wall sconces and the three crystal chandeliers that Jema imagined she could feel the heat of them on her face.

"I hope your smoke alarms aren't too sensitive," Jema said.

Jaus lifted a hand, and a small orchestra set up in one corner began tuning up their instruments. He turned and bowed to her. "Would you honor me with the first dance of the night, my lady?"

He wanted to dance with her? First? "Oh." She looked down at his boots, which had a glassy polish to them. "You don't have sensitive toes, do you? I haven't danced in years."

Instead of replying, he led her out onto the floor and, as a waltz began to play, took her in his arms.

"Mr. Jaus," she whispered as he moved her into the first steps. "No one else is dancing."

"They are shy," he whispered back. "We will show them how it is done, *ja?*"

Jaus proved to be a wonderful dancer, and whirled Jema around the floor effortlessly. She grew breathless from the quick turns, and laughed at herself when she missed a step now and then. She managed not to step on his boots. By the middle of the waltz other guests were finally joining them, and she didn't feel quite so on display.

Everyone was still watching them, though. Everywhere

Jema looked, a pair of eyes returned her gaze. That was when she realized that she, not Jaus, was attracting all the attention. As if she had come to the party in a ship from another planet.

"Is there some dirt on my face?" she asked Jaus after being subjected to another, thorough study by an older man and woman dressed in the gold-and-white costumes of French aristocrats.

Jaus regarded her. "Not a speck. Why do you ask?"

"No reason." Obviously all these people knew each other, but they didn't know her, so they were curious. That had to be the reason she was getting so much attention.

"You have lied to me," Jaus said as he kept her dancing in the center of the floor, where they remained the center of attention. "You are an excellent dancer. You must have practiced for years in secret."

She grinned. "You caught me. I sneak out to ballrooms five, six nights a week."

"You must permit me to escort you one night." He pulled her a little closer during the next turn. He smelled of camellias, but then, he worked in his gardens so often he almost always did. "I get so tired of watching the History Channel. I feel as if I know the script for every program."

"You should try the Sci-Fi Channel. They have some great miniseries, like the *Children of Dune*. I loved that one." Jema didn't watch much television, so she groped for another topic. "Did your friends expect you to bring one of your girlfriends tonight?"

"I will tell you a secret," he said, leaning closer, his hand moving to the small of her back. "I have no girlfriends. I am all alone in the world, Miss Shaw."

"Oh." Jema wondered if all the women in Chicago had suddenly gone blind. Then a reason for so many different women in his life occurred to her. "You're not gay, are you?"

"I am feeling quite happy." He caught her expression. "Gay . . . ah, you mean it as a lover of other men. No, I am not."

"Thank heavens. I mean, not that it would be terrible if you were, just a terrible waste." She groaned. "Please step on my toes anytime now."

"It is difficult to guess what impression you make upon another person," he said softly. "I am not offended." He lifted his hand and brushed a piece of hair from her cheek, and then rested his hand against the side of her neck. "I would very much like to know your opinion of me."

She didn't want to hurt his feelings, but she felt a strange compulsion rising inside her—as if there were nothing more important now than to be completely honest with him. The next thing she knew, the truth was coming out of her mouth. "You're very handsome, of course, and in great shape. You're one of the nicest men I know. I don't know anyone who grows such beautiful flowers as you do."

"I see." He stared past her face and moved his hand back to the side of her waist.

"You know, if you're not dating anyone, maybe I could introduce you to someone I know." She thought of Sophie Tucker, who was a gorgeous redhead. *She is also five-foot-ten.* "Do you like tall women, or are you uncomfortable with that?"

Jaus muttered something in his native language as the musicians ended the waltz, and took her firmly by the hand. "I thank you for the dance, Miss Shaw. Would you excuse me, please?"

Worried that her suggestion had been insulting, Jema followed him off the dance floor. His guests stepped out of his way, but crowded in to speak to her.

"Guten abend, fraulein." A man dressed as a hunter bowed. The silver fox fur collar of his cloak matched the wintry color of his narrow eyes and short-trimmed hair.

"How are you?" Jema said, smiling as she eased past his quiver, which was filled with realistic-looking arrows.

A slim Latin man in a matador's costume caught her arm. "You dance divinely, Señorita Shaw. May I have the next?"

"Thank you, but I'm not dancing right now," she said awkwardly. How did he know her name? "I have to catch up with Mr. Jaus."

That seemed to have a magical effect on the people around her, who then parted as quickly and silently as they had for their host. Jema smiled again and hurried out to the front room, but by that time Jaus had disappeared.

In the front room the guests were talking and mixing, some in groups as large as ten to twelve. Five different languages buzzed around Jema as she stood looking around for the deep blue of Jaus's costume. Strange that she and her host were the only ones wearing blue tonight, but at least she stood out in the crowd.

Is Thierry here? She took off her mask, drawing more stares, but at least with her face exposed he would recognize her. *I wonder if I should tell Mr. Jaus that I invited him to come.* She turned to a heavyset man dressed in a burgher's costume. "Have you seen a tall, dark Frenchman come in? He would have been looking around; we were supposed to meet here."

"Ich verstehe nicht," the man said, regret obvious in his tone. *"Es tut mir leid."*

Jema repeated the question, only to discover that no one around her spoke English with any degree of fluency. Most of them would say only, *"Freut mich,"* or, *"ich verstehe nicht,"* as the first man had.

"I don't want to waltz," a familiar woman's voice said somewhere nearby. It was easy to pick up her words because she was the only person speaking in English. "I don't know how to say that in German. I mean it. Hands off, Hans; I'm taken. You—yes, Princess Buttercup, I'm talking to you—you speak any English? Wonderful. Where the hell is Val?"

Jema looked around, trying to fathom which woman was Alexandra Keller. The problem was that every other woman was a petite, dark-haired beauty in a mask that completely disguised her face.

"Alexandra?" she called out, as loudly as she dared, but there was no answer, and she didn't hear Alex's voice again.

The only person at the party dressed in a doctor's costume—something Alexandra might have worn—appeared to be Daniel. His white lab coat made him easy enough to spot, but he and her mother went out of the room and disappeared down a corridor before Jema could catch up to them.

Please don't start having chest pains, Mother, Jema thought as she followed them. *I have to stay long enough to apologize to Mr. Jaus and find Thierry.*

*   *   *

Thierry found Jaus's personal guard impressive, but not impassable. He used the trees to cross over the high security walls and jumped down to the roof, where he entered the house through an open window. He looked around the guest room, where several costume boxes had been left on the bed. Jaus always had been a fanatic about being well prepared for any calamity. It was too bad he didn't know Jema belonged to Thierry.

Tonight he would.

After sorting through the boxes, Thierry found a demonic lord costume large enough for him to wear, with a matching mask. He was here for Jema, not to be caught by Jaus's hunters, so he changed into the garish garments before he went downstairs to join the party.

Thierry picked up Jema's scent in the front room, and followed it into the ballroom. There he saw a couple dressed in dark blue waltzing in the center of the room.

It was Jaus, and he had Jema in his arms. He was dancing with her. Laughing with her. Thierry saw the way the Austrian was staring down the front of her gown as well, and giving off *l'attrait* so intense the room could have been packed from floor to ceiling with camellias. When Jaus touched Jema's throat with his hand, a slow, incredulous anger began to burn inside Thierry.

Jaus hadn't invited her to a Kyn masque out of neighborly kindness. Jaus wanted her. He intended to seduce her. He wanted to use her for sex. He was using his talent on her right this moment.

Use Jema. Take Jema. While she still had Thierry's seed in her body. *Not if he breathes through his neck.*

Thierry's dagger was in his hand as he stepped out onto the dance floor. So many of the guests were armed that no one paid him any notice. He wove through the whirling couples, intent on his target, and was only a few yards from Jema when two men stepped in front of him. One wore the costume of a mime, the other a priest's robes.

"Mr. Durand," the priest said as Thierry pushed him aside, "you must come with us."

Thierry swung around and looked down into the priest's smiling mask. The reminder of the Brethren brought something feral back to life inside him. "Why?" He brought the dagger up under the man's chin. "You think to take me again?" He leaned closer, enjoying the fear in the dark eyes staring up at him. "You should not have crawled out of your cell, priest."

"I am not Brethren. I'm John Keller, Alexandra's brother." When Thierry would have moved away, he seized his arm. "Mr. Durand, listen to me. Everyone here, including Miss Shaw, is in danger."

"Miss Shaw will not be in another minute," Thierry said. He glanced over at the man dressed as a mime, who lifted the white mask that covered his face. That was when Thierry got the second jolt of the night and nearly let his dagger fall from his hand. "Jamys? *Mon Dieu,* what is this? How are you here?"

His son, who was supposed to be a thousand miles away in New Orleans, reached across him and gripped the priest's arm.

"Please come with us right now, and I'll explain everything," the priest said. "Your son says that we don't have much time."

"My son cannot speak," Thierry snarled. "*Your* kind did that to him."

"He can speak through me," John Keller said, swallowing. "I can hear his voice inside my head. I'll tell you everything he says."

Thierry glanced at his son, who nodded. "You have been busy, boy." He looked at the dancing couple in blue, and reluctantly sheathed his dagger. "We do this quickly."

He followed Jamys and the human out of the ballroom and down a hall to a room where Jaus's collection of battle swords was displayed.

The priest closed the door and locked it. "Mr. Durand, members of a street gang were hired to infiltrate this party and assassinate Michael Cyprien and my sister, Alexandra. Your son rescued me from them. We came here to warn Cyprien, but it appears that they're already here, hiding among the guests."

"Now I remember you." Thierry went to the human and tore off his saintly mask. "You were the priest I almost killed in New Orleans." He turned to his son. "Why are you with him? Why did you not stay with Marcel and Liliette, where you would be safe?"

Jamys also removed his mask and came over to grip John's forearm with his hand.

"Your son came to Chicago to find you," Keller told him. "He was afraid for you. He knew Cyprien had issued orders that you were to be captured. He feared that one of the Kyn might kill you."

Thierry reached out to touch his son's face, but Jamys flinched away. That small rejection hurt him more than any wound he had ever received. "I have controlled this thing inside me. I will not harm you, boy."

Sweat began running down John Keller's face. "He's not afraid of you. He's ashamed."

"What?"

"Jamys wants you to know that he's sorry for what his mother did." The priest panted for a moment. "He should have told you, but he was afraid of her, and thought you wouldn't believe him. He thinks what happened to you is his fault." He looked up at Thierry's son. "I don't think I can take much more of this. I feel as if I'm going to pass out."

With a nod, Jamys took his hand away from Keller's arm. He went to inspect the swords Jaus had displayed on the wall, as if deciding which one to take.

Thierry removed his mask and went to join his son by the wall. Jamys had not changed for hundreds of years—would never change—but if he had grown to full maturity, he would have been his grandfather's twin. Thierry could see some of old Jean-Vayle Durand's fierceness in Jamys's eyes as he watched him.

What could Thierry say to heal the wounds that still bled inside his son? Perhaps it was time to show Jamys that he was not the only Durand still bleeding.

"Your mother brought this evil into our house, but it was always inside her," Thierry said. "I loved her too much to permit myself to see it. I think that is what drove me mad. Not the things they did to my body. My blindness to her, my failure to protect you and our family from her."

Jamys shook his head violently and moved away, going to the next case of swords.

"I understand how you can blame yourself," Thierry said, following him. "It is all that I have done since she died. It is part of what drove me away from you. I believe your mother wished for that. In her hatred she could not understand love. She could only destroy it. Now she is gone, but her evil lingers. Must it be forever between us? Her hatred, turning us away from each other? Have we not suffered enough?"

The boy covered his face with his hands.

Thierry went to him and put a hand on his shoulder. "I should not have left you behind with Michael. I did not think of how it would make you feel, that you would blame yourself, as I did. I could not think, Jamys. The madness consumed me. When I had a lucid moment, I was terrified. I feared that I would harm you, or Marcel, or Liliette, and I would not be able to stop myself." He pulled the trembling boy into his arms and held him close. "I could not take that chance. Forgive me, my son."

They stood together like that for several minutes, holding on to each other.

"Mr. Durand," the priest said, sounding exhausted now, "I don't want to interrupt, but there was something else that your son told me. This assassination attempt is planned for midnight." As Thierry looked over at him, Keller pointed to a large, polished oak-and-brass grandfather clock standing in the corner of the room. "We have only ten minutes left."

Michael Cyprien finished copying the last of the data from Alexandra's medical computer and removed the CD copy from the burner. For the last half hour he had listened to Valentin Jaus pour out his frustrations with Jema Shaw and his anger at himself. He kept his silence until the Austrian finally requested permission to resign from his position and return to his homeland.

"You cannot step down as suzerain." As he slipped the CD into a protective case, he turned toward Jaus. "I need all the men I can trust in this country. You are one of them."

"I contacted Lucan to ask his advice on how to handle

Thierry Durand," Jaus said. "He told me the only way to stop him was to kill him."

Cyprien knew his friend was deliberately trying to goad him into losing his temper. "That was probably wise. Lucan did capture him in Dublin." He glanced up from the files he was sorting through. "I would prefer you limit your contact with Lucan. He will use you to get to me."

"That is just another reason to let me go. I cannot do this anymore, Michael." Jaus's shoulders sagged. "I would put an end to it, now, before my humiliation destroys me."

"What shall I tell Tremayne?" he asked, letting some of his own frustration color his voice. "That the man he handpicked to serve as suzerain of Chicago is running away from his responsibilities? Because some human female rejected him?"

Jaus's expression turned remote and arrogant. "Whatever the reason, it is my right."

"Do you know what I am doing? I am making copies of Alexandra's research so I may send them off to Tremayne." Michael removed the duplicates he had made of the blood-profile printouts from the copy machine bin. "Without her knowledge or consent."

"You are braver than I," Jaus said.

"Courage has nothing to do with it. She wants her brother alive, and this is the price I pay for that." Michael tucked the report copies into a document wallet and sealed it. "I love her, but I am stealing from her. I wish it could be another way, but I have responsibilities to more than my love. Tremayne wants this information. As long as I feed it to him, I will be able to keep her with me, and her brother alive."

"So I must compromise." Jaus rubbed a hand over his face. "Settle for what I can have. Is this your sage advice, seigneur?"

"I would never advise anyone to love a woman whom he may have to kill someday," Michael told him. "As I may Alexandra."

Jaus looked appalled. "You cannot mean that. I have seen your love for her. You would rather suffer yourself than harm her."

"This is not about harming her. It's about saving her. You think you know Richard, but I am the only one who has been close enough to know him completely. I know exactly what he would do to Alexandra. I will never permit her to suffer that fate, even if it means killing her." He handed the files and the disks to Jaus. "You may send this by private courier to Dundellan Castle. Mark them for Richard's eyes only."

"If Alexandra discovers you are doing this, she will leave you," Jaus warned.

"If she did, she would not remember it," Cyprien said. He met Jaus's narrow gaze. "Alexandra is still human enough to be affected by any Kyn talent. With mine, I can make her forget anything I wish."

Jema wandered down the hall and checked through each open door she passed, but she couldn't find her mother and Daniel. She was about to give up and return to the party when she saw a closed door and heard her mother complaining.

There she is. She opened the door to look in, and saw her mother and Daniel with their backs toward her. They were looking through the shelves of what appeared to be Jaus's library. She opened her mouth to ask them what they were doing.

"I don't want to put her in your private hospital," Meryl said. "People will ask too many questions. I've told you, the only way to be sure is to kill her."

As if she were sleepwalking, Jema slipped inside the room.

"I never agreed to murder, Meryl." Daniel took down a heavy volume to look behind it. "Our arrangement won't hurt anyone. Jema will be locked away, safe and sound, and you'll have her millions to spend."

"They're not her millions; they're *mine*," her mother snapped.

The doctor sighed. "Once Jema turns thirty, there's no more risk of the estate going to charity. She inherits everything James had placed in trust for her. We've done the paperwork; you're her legal guardian. The board of trustees will no longer have any say as to what you do with the money."

Jema pressed herself back against a wall, but neither her mother nor Bradford noticed her.

"It still won't be mine until she's dead," Meryl told him.

"I don't know how you can be so callous," Daniel complained. "Jema is your daughter. She's all you have left of James, for God's sake."

"James hated me because of her. He blamed me for almost killing her in the cave-in. Did he care that *I* nearly died? That it turned me into a cripple? No. All he wanted was his precious daughter." Meryl wheeled over to begin searching a desk.

"James was upset over what you did," Daniel said. "If he had lived, he would have forgiven you."

"He would have divorced me, you idiot. Why do you think he changed his will before he left for Greece? It was as if he knew I'd spend the next thirty years keeping the sickly little bitch alive just so I could get what I was due." Meryl looked over at her reflection in the floor-length mirror. "I can't stand another minute of it. Do you know what it's like, watching her walk around and smile and do everything I can't? She should be in this chair. No. She should have died in that godforsaken cave. Then James wouldn't have stopped loving me."

Jema looked across the room, aware that in a moment Meryl would move close enough to see Jema's reflection in the mirror. Jema in the mirror . . . Jema in the mirror . . . the conversation she'd had with Luisa, the one she'd forgotten.

The one I refused to think about. It all came back to Jema, who stood paralyzed and lost in the memory.

Roy's looking for something for your mama. Luisa had stopped by Jema's office after she had finished her shift. *You know if we got an ah-midge, Miz Jem?*

She had smiled. *What's an ah-midge?*

Don't you make fun, now, Luisa said, lifting her nose and posing in a deadly imitation of the events coordinator in a huff. *I'm going to night school. I get my diploma; I'm gonna start college courses. Then you'll see—I'll talk as nice as you, and so will my baby.*

I know you will. Jema admired Luisa and how hard she worked, not only to support herself and the baby she was expecting, but to improve her situation in life. She made a silent promise to do what she could to help the girl.

Luisa had looked out of Jema's office and frowned. *Maybe*

it's Roy you looking for, Miz Jem. See your nameplate in the mirror over there?

Jema had gotten up to look. The sign on her office door, JEMA SHAW, was reflected in a display mirror that had been temporarily moved downstairs, and read WAHS AMEJ.

See? Jema backward spell ah-midge. Don't worry, Ms. Jema. I won't tell no one. I know how to keep a secret.

Luisa had left, giggling over the joke. The next day her mother had called, choking out the news through her sobs that Luisa had been attacked and burned, and was not expected to survive the night.

The words pounded inside her head.

Jema. Amej. Image. Homage.

Meryl went past the mirror and began poking through books on another shelf. Jema looked into the mirror, where she had no reflection, and went cold. The same thing had happened that night, at the museum, after Luisa had left. When she had stood looking at the reflection of her name. She had been thinking about Meryl. Thinking about how her mother looked at her sometimes, as if she wished Jema would just disappear. Then it happened, just as it did now. She had turned transparent, and then invisible.

Her image slowly appeared in the mirror, and then faded away again.

The museum had not been the first time. There had been other times she had forgotten, when she was a little girl. It had taken an hour of staring into the mirror at the museum before she could make herself reappear. That was what had frightened her so much that she refused to remember it. She'd hated mirrors ever since she was a child, and now she knew why.

Jema stared at her reflection. *If I can control it . . .*

Daniel Bradford walked right past Jema without seeing her. "I wonder if this is something special," he said, opening a glass display case and taking out a long, folded length of ancient linen. "Look at this." He showed Meryl one side of the cloth, upon which was the image of a Christlike face.

"It's a cheap reproduction of the Mandylion," she snapped. "Claimed to be one of the possible burial shrouds of Christ— and a piece of religious nonsense. The Homage would be something Greek. Something older, perhaps a pot or a carved chest."

"I've sometimes wondered if Jema wasn't the real Homage of Athos James brought back from Greece," Daniel said, his eyes crinkling with amusement. "After all, he did find her in the cave, where you gave birth to her. He certainly treated her as if she were some rare and priceless object. And he left all his money to her, and not a penny to you. Maybe it was his little joke."

"Only you would think of something that dim-witted, Daniel."

"Someone has to, I suppose." Daniel turned and looked directly at Jema. He walked over and took a book out of a shelf not six inches from her trembling shoulder. He sniffed. "Smells like Jaus is having his friends bob for apples out there."

Jema waited until Daniel walked away before she silently opened the door and fled.

Frantically Jema searched the masks of the guests, looking for anyone who might be Alexandra or Thierry. She saw a group of late arrivals walking in and hurried over to them. They were dressed in medieval animal costumes, with very realistic-looking masks.

She stopped a few feet from a man in a hyena mask. She didn't have to pull any hairs from the mask to recognize the fiber. It was the same hair she had found on the hate-crime murder victim. It was also the same type of mask the men who attacked her had worn.

Daniel Bradford considered himself a patient man. He'd had to be, working for Meryl Shaw. It was strange that after three decades of planning, waiting, researching, and doing what he was told—or, at least, acting as if he were—that he discovered that his infinite patience had suddenly come to an end.

"It's not here." Meryl slumped in her wheelchair. "Can we get into any other rooms?"

He set aside the shroud and put on a pair of latex gloves before he opened the medical case he was never without. Tonight he had tucked inside it a silver flask filled with Meryl's favorite brand of bourbon and a crystal glass.

"With all these people, it's going to look very strange." Daniel filled the glass from the flask and brought it to her. "Here, my dear. Have a drink."

"How thoughtful." Meryl sounded sarcastic, but she drank down half the glass with two swallows. "Oh, this is useless. Once I have the money, I can hire people to search this place. Find Jema, and let's go home. You can call the hospital and cancel the arrangements when we get back to the house."

"As I've told you repeatedly, Meryl, I'm not going to kill her." Daniel picked up the shroud and tugged at the material. Bits of ancient spun flax flaked from the linen onto his gloves, but the material was still remarkably strong. He wondered if it truly might be the burial shroud of Christ. *Wouldn't that be appropriate?*

"You'll do as you're told." She drained the glass and dropped it on the carpet. "Or would you like me to call the police and tell them how you've been practicing medicine illegally for the last thirty years?"

"I've done nothing but help you and Jema." That was mostly true. He had taken some steps to assure that Meryl would never leave her wheelchair, and he had burned the journal he had found among James Shaw's personal effects when they were sent from Athos to the States.

"They won't care, and this time they won't simply bankrupt you and take your license. They'll see to it that you'll go to prison." Meryl smiled. "Especially when I tell them how you're implicated in two murders: Roy's and Jema's."

Anger, something Daniel rarely felt, finally reared its small, ugly head. "I couldn't stop you from killing Roy, but I won't allow you to hurt Jema. She really is the Homage of Athos, you know."

"She's worthless, and you can't stop me, you pathetic weakling." Meryl shoved aside a stack of books, uncaring of the noise they made as they landed on the floor. "Who do you think they're going to believe is the murderer? The doctor convicted of experimenting on mindless old people at his nursing home, or a bereaved, helpless woman in a wheelchair who took him into her home and trusted him?"

"Jem should have been my daughter." Daniel shook out the shroud and wound each end around his hands. "You have no idea how precious she is. She was always the reason I stayed. It was never the money you promised me."

"Oh, God." Meryl rolled her eyes. "Spare me the devoted-doctor routine. It stopped being convincing years ago. You'll give her an overdose of insulin tomorrow morning, and it will all be over."

Daniel came up behind her. "There's something I haven't told you, Meryl. Dr. Keller was quite right." Quickly he looped the shroud around her neck and twisted the ends, pulling on them. By her ear, he whispered, "Jema's diabetes went away. She hasn't had it since she was a year old."

While she choked and fought, Daniel kept a firm hold on the shroud and told her everything she didn't know about her daughter. How James Shaw had referred to her in his journal as the Homage of Athos, both for the cave in which she had been born, and because she was the only real treasure he had ever found in his life.

The stink of urine rose as Meryl's bladder emptied.

Daniel continued, releasing a little on the shroud now and then to allow Meryl a breath, only to cut it off before she took another. He described how amazed he had been to discover the strange pathogens in Jema's blood, and how they had not only cured her diabetes, but began changing the toddler. How difficult it had been to find the right combination of drugs to keep her alive, and her bizarre symptoms in remission.

Sometime during Daniel's description of how he had scared off Jema's first lover, just as he had paid off all the others she had become involved with, Meryl died.

Daniel looked down at his employer. Her upper torso sagged, twisted halfway around in her chair, and her tongue hung out of her gaping mouth.

"Don't worry, my dear." He smiled down into her bulging eyes and crimson face before he pressed his lips to the top of her white hair and kissed her good-bye. "I'll take good care of our little girl. The way I always have."

Chapter 20

Alex staggered through the Kyn, unable to make herself understood, now unable to speak, bombarded from all directions.

Gun's loaded in my pocket, safety off—

Can't wait to shoot some of these rich fucks—

Raze gonna love this—

Guy in the red mask—pop him first—Cyprien—

Head or heart, head or heart—

There were more thoughts, thoughts in French and German, roaring behind the others, as savage and lethal as the killers who were thinking in English. Images of swords and copper bullets and death imagined.

Too many to block. Too loud and vicious to endure.

"Michael," Alex shrieked, but the guests were all talking, and music was spilling out of the ballroom, and her voice alone could not compete.

Alex almost went down on her knees before she was caught up in strong, familiar hands.

"I know you," Thierry Durand's golden eyes glittered from behind a demon lord's mask. "You gave me back my legs. You made my feet smaller. None of my boots will fit now."

"Thierry." She grabbed onto him. A few dozen yards away she saw Valentin turn his head sharply toward them. "There are about ten guys in this room who are going to start shooting people with copper bullets any second—"

Any second turned out to be the next.

Gunfire broke out, rapid explosions, metal whining as it sped through the air. Bullets sprayed the guests from all angles of the room. Blood sprayed in wide, crimson swaths across the white walls.

"Au secours," Thierry shouted. *"Ayuda, Hilfe."*

He shouted for help again, this time in English, before he dragged Alex toward the nearest cover, the entry to one of the corridors, shielding her with his larger frame until they got there. He shoved her into the hands of a man with orange dreadlocks streaked with black paint hiding behind the corner.

The smell of burned gunpowder and wilting flowers became choking.

"They're giving the women away?" the man said as he hauled her behind him. "Hey, John, she's a babe. Can I have three more?"

"Shut up, Hurley. She's my sister." John, who was wearing a priest's costume, put his arms around Alex. "Did they shoot you?"

She shook her head, and then pressed her hands over her ears. The killers' thoughts were rising, an evil tide that dragged at her mind as it swelled higher.

"They're going to keep shooting until they find Michael and kill him," she said, panting out the words as the hatred tore at her from the inside. "You have to get him out of here."

Another shot rang out, very close. Hurley stumbled back against Alex, falling to his knees. He looked down at the blood pouring down his presidential DON'T SCREW WITH THIS BUSH T-shirt with mild surprise. "Son of a bitch. It *is* red." He fell over.

Alex focused on Hurley and found doing so blocked some of the killing thoughts. She checked his neck and found no pulse. "He's dead." There were Kyn falling all around them, but unlike Hurley, some of them she might be able to save. "Johnny, give me a hand." She crawled out to pull the nearest body back behind the wall.

Thierry waded through the press of bodies as the Kyn tried to escape the rain of deadly bullets, his dagger in his left hand, a sword stolen from Jaus's collection in his right. "Jema? Jema."

He came to where the gunmen were standing and firing at the guests. The first man he cut down was shooting wildly, laughing and whipping from right to left as he did. As he turned to find the next, a Kyn wearing a Grim Reaper costume brought a long sword down to split his head.

Metal screeched as Thierry parried the strike and thrust his own sword into the Reaper's robes. The man staggered back and pushed away from him, holding his side. He shouted something filthy in German before he hobbled off.

"Why ain't they screaming?" someone shouted over the gunfire. "Why they so—"

Thierry spotted the man who was shouting, and saw the gun leap out of his hand. It flew across the room to land in a pile of fallen Kyn. The invisible force swept around the room, jerking weapons out of the killers' hands and tossing them out windows, doors, and into the champagne fountain.

Thierry took advantage of the sudden stillness and turned toward that presence that no one could see, but that had left a scent path that smelled of apples. "Jema. To me, now."

The Kyn who were unharmed or not seriously injured turned en masse and formed a quick circle around the disarmed gunmen. They ripped the hyena and jackal masks from their face, and pushed them back into the center of the circle when the gunman tried to break free. As the Kyn smiled, fangs flashed and the room filled with scents of a hundred different flowers. None of these smelled as if they were wilting.

They smelled of flowers burning.

"What are you freaks?" one of the Bones shrieked.

The circle slowly closed in on them.

Thierry could not see anyone in a blue gown in the room. He saw the Grim Reaper, however, trying to edge down one wall toward the door, and began wading through the fallen bodies after him.

"Durand." Valentin Jaus stepped into his path. He raised his battle sword.

"Get out of my way, Jaus." Thierry looked over him to see the Reaper stumble outside. *Let him go; Jaus's guards can butcher him.* He turned, seeking the faint trace of apples he had picked up before. "Jema. Where are you? Come to me, now."

The Austrian didn't move. "You cannot have her."

"She's already mine." Thierry lifted his sword. "Can't you smell her on me?"

Jaus's face emptied of all emotion. "No." He lunged.

There was no madness left in Thierry, but the rage of seeing Jema in Jaus's arms came back, and he drew on it, crossing swords with the Austrian so viciously that sparks flew from the metal.

There was no time to think or calculate his attack; Jaus was a whirlwind, coming at him with huge, whistling strokes of his sword that, with his disadvantage in size, should have been impossible for him to make.

Jaus had improved greatly, Thierry thought with grudging admiration as he kept the Austrian from decapitating him by a single parry.

The only thing Jaus had forgotten was that he fought the man who had been left behind to hold Castle Pilgrim until the last Templar had escaped. The man who alone had fought his way through a gauntlet of five hundred Saracens to reach freedom. The man who had left five hundred headless, armless, and lifeless bodies in his wake. The man who had spilled enough blood and bowels in his years as a warrior priest to quench even the merciless thirst of the desert sand.

Durand does not dominate on the battlefield, the Kyn would say of him in years to come after the Holy Land was lost. *He makes it his charnel house.*

"Jaus. Durand." Michael Cyprien stepped into the room, the Grim Reaper in his hands. "Lower your swords. Now."

Cyprien's order was ignored. Jaus was in a cold, killing rage, and Thierry was happy to match it. Their swords clashed, slid, and danced, moving in patterns too swift at times for the blade to be clearly seen. They circled and sidestepped, gradually working their way into the ballroom, until they were battling in the center of the floor.

"Thierry, please, stop this."

Jema's voice, so close to him, proved the one distraction he could not resist. His eyes moved toward her instead of following Jaus's attack, and the bright flash of steel came out of nowhere.

"No!"

So, too, did Jema appear, out of thin air, directly between him and Jaus's sword. There was simply no time or space to prevent what happened next. Jaus's expression changed at the last second from fury to horror as he saw her, but it was too late.

The blade pierced Jema's abdomen and came out the other side.

Thierry bellowed his rage and brought his sword down on Jaus's arm above the elbow, cutting it off. The Austrian staggered back as Thierry caught Jema's waist and pulled the sword out of her body. It fell to rest beside Jaus's severed arm.

He snatched his love up into his arms and carried her out of the ballroom. "Cyprien! Alexandra!"

Jamys was beside him, directing him. Thierry carried Jema into a room filled with medical equipment. This, he knew, would be Alex's place. She could save Jema here, as she had saved him in New Orleans. Thierry looked up when someone appeared in the doorway, but it was Daniel Bradford, not Alexandra, and his blank eyes were fixed on Jema.

"Jem?" he called, his voice hollow as he shuffled into the room. "Jem, it's Daniel. Wake up, honey; it's time for your shot." He looked at Thierry and down at his case. "I'm her doctor. Please step back; I'll handle this."

Thierry saw blood dripping from under Jema's body to spill onto the floor at his feet. He turned to his son. "Find Alexandra."

Jamys ran out.

He ignored Bradford and held on to Jema's cold hand. "Little cat," he murmured, brushing her hair back from her face. "Open your eyes for me."

Jema stirred and her lashes fluttered. "Thierry?"

"I said, please step back from my patient," Bradford said as he came up on the opposite side of the table. He had a syringe in his hand.

Thierry would have lunged across the table and broken the man's neck in that instant, but he couldn't let go of her. "She's not yours; she was never yours," he snarled, baring his fangs. "Get away from her."

Bradford took a small pistol out of his pocket and pointed

it at Thierry, then changed his mind and pressed it against Jema's head. "Step back now," he said, almost pleasantly.

Thierry saw Cyprien and Alexandra enter the room with Jamys, but so did Bradford.

"Don't come any closer," he told them. "I will pull the trigger, and I believe she's still human enough to die."

"What have you done, Bradford?" Alex demanded.

The doctor ignored her and took a syringe from his pocket. Thierry hissed as Bradford stabbed it directly into Jema's neck. "Here you are, honey," he crooned to Jema as he depressed the plunger. "This will make it all better."

"Thierry," Michael said.

"I know." He faced the madman across the table from him. If his own derangement had taught him nothing else, it had made him able to understand an irrational obsession. "How will it make her better, Doctor?"

Bradford smiled down at Jema. "You have nothing to worry about now, Jem. Your mother died a little earlier this evening. I know you'll feel sad at first, but she was a terrible woman. She wanted me to kill you so that she could have the money James left you."

Jema's eyes opened, and she stared up at Daniel. "Mother?"

"She didn't understand," Daniel said. "Part of that was my fault. You see, I never told her how special you were. That little trick you have with turning invisible? You did it so much when you were a baby I put bells on your shoes so I could find you.

"I had to keep pretending you had diabetes, of course, but that was to explain the injections. It took time to find the right drugs to keep you from changing." He gave her a fond smile. "You can now that she's dead, you know. You'll have all the money you need, and we don't have to tell anyone what you are."

Jema glanced at Thierry. "Daniel," she said, her voice a thread of pain, "why did you do this to me?"

"You're going to be an immortal, honey," he said. "I only slowed it down so it wouldn't burn up your body. It did almost kill you before I got it under control. The good news is, once you finish changing into your final form? You'll never die. I'm going to study you and test you until we can figure out how to make me like you." He frowned. "It's your blood, sweetheart. All the secrets of life are in your blood. Your father was right about you."

Thierry had the reflexes of a swordsman with seven hundred years' experience. He knew that if Bradford could be distracted for even a fraction of a second, he could disarm him.

Jema looked up at Thierry, squeezing his hand and moving her head slightly. He tensed, and when he returned the nod, she vanished.

"Jem, please don't do that. Please." Bradford put a hand out to grab what he couldn't see.

Thierry's dagger knocked the gun from Bradford's hand. Michael was there, hauling the doctor back from the table, while Alex came around the other side to rip open Jema's gown and examine the sword wound.

Jema reappeared and smiled at Thierry. "Worked."

"Miss Shaw is *my* patient," Bradford said, holding his bleeding hand.

"No," Alex said to Thierry as he started around the table. "I need him alive so I can find out what he's done to her." She bent over Jema. "Open your mouth for me, Jem." She looked inside, swore, and straightened. "You *removed* them, you sick bastard?" she shouted at Daniel.

"I had to," Bradford said, looking sulky now. "She couldn't use them. She couldn't know she had them. I drugged her and extracted them as soon as the recesses formed. They keep growing back anyway. I've taken them out seven times since she was born."

"Taken out what?" Thierry demanded.

"Her fangs," Alex said. "He extracted them and he sutured the abscesses shut." She glared up at him. "Have you two been swapping large amounts of body fluid?"

It took a moment for him to understand what she was asking. "Yes."

"That might be what accelerated things. Or saved her. I don't know, and Christ, I hate it when I don't know." She turned to Jema, who had fallen unconscious. "Jema." She shook her slightly and checked her pulse. "Nonexistent.

Thierry, I hate to spring a *sygkenis* on you, but Jema is making the change, and she's doing it right now."

"How can this be?" Cyprien asked, astounded.

"My guess? She was infected with Kyn blood when she was a child. Why she didn't die is anybody's guess." Alex stared at Bradford. "He's been using the drugs and hormones to suppress the change, and the plasma to keep her alive."

"You can't take over my case," Bradford told her, indignant now. "I have a history with this patient."

"Alexandra, what about the sword wound?" Thierry said. "Will it stop her from making the change?"

"Take a look." She gestured toward Jema's abdomen.

Thierry parted the torn material of the gown. An angry-looking red scar marred Jema's flesh. "She healed." He smiled, touching the closed wound. "My *sygkenis*. God, can it be true? I am not mad?"

"You're not mad," Alex said. "I am."

Bradford drove a syringe into Cyprien's arm and twisted free, diving to grab the gun from the floor.

"You can't have her," he babbled. "I won't let you." He lifted the gun and pointed it at Jema's face. His hand was shaking badly. "Jem? Get up. We're going home now."

Thierry seized an IV pole and threw it. The metal rod pierced Bradford's chest and drove him into the wall. The gun went off, the bullet lodging into the wall behind Jema's head. Bradford hung skewered, dead.

"There goes thirty years of experience treating vampirism." Alex sounded more resigned than angry. She went over to Cyprien, who was extracting the syringe from his arm. "You okay?"

"I should have held him tighter." Michael looked at Bradford. "He was insane, wasn't he?"

"We can hope," Alex said.

"I will stay with her while she makes the change." Thierry picked Jema up in his arms. "I need a room where we will not be disturbed."

"You'd better take her back to Shaw House," Alex suggested. "We're going to need all the beds here for the wounded."

* * *

John disappeared while Alex had been treating the injured. She called the shelter where he had been working, but the temporary manager there claimed her brother had packed his belongings and left.

"I work over at the state shelter, but he insisted I come here and take over for Dougall Hurley until he gets back," the man complained. "You have any idea where Hurley is?"

Hurley's body had been transported to the city and left in a place where it would be found. Alexandra had hated that, but understood the need to avoid exposing the Kyn. "No, sorry, I don't. Did my brother say where he was going?"

"He said something about getting out of the city," the man told her. "That's all."

Once Alexandra had finished patching up the last Kyn, she went to see Jaus, and found him sitting on the seawall. He had covered his arm stump with a white jacket, and from a distance she could easily imagine it as a swan's wing.

"Hey." She pushed aside her annoyance with her brother. "Some party. I was wondering, why didn't the police ever show up? All that gunfire should have scared the neighbors."

"The house is soundproofed. No one heard anything." He looked up. "Tell Thierry I am here. I will not fight him."

"Jema's not dead." She gave him a minute to absorb the shock, and then told him what she knew about Jema, Bradford, and her change into Kyn. "Valentin, when you found her in your garden, all those years ago, did you cut yourself when you picked her up out of the broken glass?"

"Yes. I took a sliver out of her hand, and it lodged in my palm." He stared at his hand. "It was nothing. We heal at once."

"I have a very shaky theory," Alex said, sitting on the wall beside him. "Let's say some of your blood got on Jema's hands. She sucked her thumb, and ingested it. For whatever reason, it didn't kill her. It cured her diabetes, and then it began to slowly change her into Kyn. Bradford was able to arrest the progress of the change with his hormones and sedatives. As her digestive system deteriorated, she'd have passed blood; I showed it in my urine, but he could have made that look like a kidney infection. He added the plasma, probably to keep her from starving to death."

"What are you saying?" Jaus looked as if he had become part of the stone seawall.

"It's the only explanation that makes sense. Jema's diabetes disappeared when she was a year old. You were the only Kyn she came in contact with at that specific time in her life." She looked out at the black water of Lake Michigan. "Bradford found out, and began experimenting on her. All he had to do was make everyone think she still had the disease. For a doctor, it wouldn't be difficult." She exhaled. "I just wish I knew why your blood didn't kill her when she was a baby, and why Michael's didn't kill me when he attacked me. There has to be a connection between Jema and me."

"Where is she now?"

"Thierry took her over to Shaw House. He's going to stay with her until she finishes the change." This was the part Alex didn't want to handle, but felt she should try. "Val, I'm sorry—"

"Yes. So am I." Valentin rose, awkward and slow. "She loves him, Alexandra. She belongs with him."

"I do get the feeling they've been an item for a while." She gestured toward his missing arm. "You like the folded-sleeve look?"

"It doesn't matter." He walked past her.

"The reason I ask is that I think I can reattach it." That stopped him in his tracks. She smiled as he turned around to stare at her. "Kyn spontaneous healing plus my dazzling reconstructive surgical skills. I've got your arm on ice up at the house. No guarantees, but want to give it a try?"

"When we were dancing, I asked her opinion of me," Jaus told her. "You were right. She thinks exactly as your said."

"Maybe she was just being polite—"

"Not this time." He looked up at the stars. "She was still human enough for it to affect her. You see, it is my talent. When I touch humans, they cannot lie to me."

"Really." She thought about it. "That must more than occasionally suck."

"It is why I have never touched her." He smiled briefly. "I think a part of me knew what the truth would be. That to Jema, all that I am, all that I will ever be, is a nice man who grows beautiful flowers."

"You are more than that, Val, and if I weren't in love with Cyprien, you'd be too damn busy to have a broken heart." She held out her arm. "Life goes on, pal. Or, in our case, on and on and on and on and on."

He took her hand.

"How many dead?" he asked her as they walked up to the lists, which Alex was using as a temporary hospital for the wounded Kyn.

"Fifteen, counting the gunmen. Twenty-three wounded but recovering quickly. I should be able to clear everyone out of here by tomorrow." She smiled at him. "Do your people carry major medical insurance, or am I going to have to bill the hell out of the *jardin?*"

Cyprien met them as they entered the lists. "I know you must do this surgery soon, but Valentin has to decide what to do with the ringleader. He is the only survivor."

Val and Alex followed Cyprien through the hospital to one of the storage rooms. There the man dressed as the Grim Reaper was being held by two of Jaus's guards. Cyprien reached down and removed the Reaper's mask, revealing Falco's face.

Alex rubbed her brow. "Terrific. The guy who was driving us around town."

"I have nothing to say to you," Falco told her. He turned to face Jaus and spoke in rapid German.

"He seems to have a lot to say to Val," Alex told Cyprien in a conversational tone.

"My seneschal confesses to making private pacts with the Brethren," Jaus said. "In English, Falco. The seigneur will hear this."

"The seigneur." The big man sneered at Michael. "He is nothing but Richard's pretty boy. Yes, I went to the brothers and bargained with them. They had targets they wished eliminated. I went to the streets, found the stupid human boys, and trained them to kill. Every job we did bought more protection for the *jardin.*"

"Montague? Was he part of this?" Cyprien asked.

Falco spit on the floor in front of Michael's shoes. "He was only to kill the Shaw woman. I used the crossbow that day by the lake. You would be dead if not for your yellow bitch."

Jaus stared down at Falco sadly. "He wanted to assassinate you, Michael, so I could succeed you as seigneur. He is an Aryan, Alexandra, so your racial background makes you unacceptable in his eyes."

"Oh, so he's a Nazi," Alex said. "I get it. But I'm not yellow. I think of myself as sort of a light caramel." She leaned over and smiled in Falco's face. "Remember that the next time you insult me, you racist jerk-off."

Cyprien crouched down in front of the seneschal. "Falco, how much did you tell the Brethren about us?"

"Nothing." Falco looked at Jaus. "I swear this to you, master."

"I don't think your word holds much weight with the master anymore," Alex advised him. "I wonder how many other people he has killed over the years?"

Jaus suddenly straightened. "Kurt."

"He got in my way too many times," Falco said, looking righteous. "He came into the city and saw me when I was meeting with the monks. He would have told you. He never could keep his mouth shut."

Val's eyes glittered. "So you killed him."

"He had to die, like the Shaw woman." Falco shook his head. "You spend too much time obsessing over her. She made you weak, but you would have chosen her over everything. After all I did to make you strong, to keep you safe."

"Michael," Jaus said, "lend me your sword. Alexandra, please step back three paces." When Cyprien handed Jaus his sword, he lifted it. "Do you have anything else you wish to tell me, seneschal?"

Falco swallowed, his eyes locked on the sword. "I want to fight you. It is the only way to die with honor."

"You gave your honor to the Brethren." Jaus brought down the blade, and with a single stroke decapitated Falco.

Alex watched the severed head fall and the body slump over. "I'm not reattaching that. Just FYI."

*   *   *

Jema wasn't afraid of what was happening to her body. Deep in the comatose sleep of change, she was still aware of Thierry beside her. He stayed there, a constant presence until she opened her eyes three days later.

They were in her bed, covered with her grandmother's old quilt. Thierry was dozing, his big naked body wrapped around hers. Jema stayed where she was, enjoying the novelty of waking up in the arms of the man she loved. Then she thought of what her mother and Daniel Bradford had done to her, and her happiness ebbed.

Thierry's eyes opened. "Jema?"

"Still here." She snuggled up against him. "I guess I made it."

"Stay in bed." He didn't, and after pulling on his pants hurried out of the room. He returned a few minutes later with Alexandra Keller.

While Thierry paced the room, Alex gave Jema a complete physical and explained the changes that had taken place in her body. "You can't eat solid food anymore, and most liquids are out. I'm going to keep you on intravenous blood until your fangs regenerate. I've opened the apertures, so it should take only a week or two."

"I can't believe I'm a vampire," she murmured. "A real vampire. And you think I've been one for how long?"

"I can tell you what I've pieced together from what Bradford said, and what we know about you and your life." Alex explained her theory about Jaus's blood infecting her and how Bradford had taken advantage of it. "Your mutation is just as strange as mine is. Like your ability to disappear; that's a Darkyn talent, but it should work only on humans. Instead it works on everybody, the way my talent does."

"Did Dr. Bradford do anything else to me?" Alex had already told her Daniel was dead.

"I'm not sure," Alex admitted. "We're going to search his lab, see if we can find any notes."

Thierry insisted on carrying Jema downstairs. "You are still weak, and you need blood," he said, overriding her objections. "I will tell you when you can walk."

She smiled. "You said I'd be too tired to walk." She giggled as he whispered against her ear what he intended to do to her when she was feeling better.

"Am I going to have to make you two get a room?" Alex complained. "Again?"

All they found in Daniel's lab were twenty-nine years of charts, falsified to make it appear as if Jema were being treated for diabetes.

"He must have kept it all in his head," Alex said as she thumbed through the charts. "I'll go through everything, in case he encoded something. You're sure he didn't use a computer?"

"He hated them." Jema went over to Daniel's desk, where there was a framed photo. It was a picture of Jema at her college graduation. Daniel had been so proud of her for obtaining her degree. "Do you think he loved me?"

"I guess. In a sick, psychopath kind of way." Alex shut the filing cabinet drawer. "Sweetie, I need to run more tests on you, but chances are there won't be any lasting effects. Kyn changeover heals everything."

"I'm just sorry I was so rude to you about Luisa," Jema said. "I hope we can be friends."

"You're an heiress, you own a museum, you have a huge mansion on Lake Michigan, and you're the only other Kyn in the world like me. That automatically makes you my best friend." Alex laughed as Jema hugged her. "I expect great Christmas presents, by the way."

After Alex went back to Derabend Hall, Thierry seemed restless. Jema had sent the household staff on a monthlong vacation, to give her time to adjust to her new life, but she didn't want to stay at Shaw House. She told him that later in the evening when they went for a walk by the lake.

"I want you to meet my family." Thierry said after he told her about Marcel and Liliette.

"Are you sure you want me to?" Jema stopped and looked up at him. "I feel as if I know you better than anyone in the world, but in reality we met only a few days ago." She hesitated before she added, "Your wife, Angelica, how long did you know her?"

"We grew up together."

"Maybe we should take more time to—*Thierry*." Her feet left the ground as he hoisted her up in his arms. "You can't carry me off like a caveman."

"It tempts me." He held her so that their faces were close. "It is true that we have shared only a few days together in this world. But think of all we shared in the dream realm. We saw the best and worst of each other, Jema, and it did not change how I felt. It made my love stronger. You made me stronger. In all the years I spent with Angelica, she never did that. She never shared herself with me as you have."

"So we take a chance together?"

"I am willing, if you are." He kissed her. "Would you come back to New Orleans with me? Jamys wishes to become acquainted with you, and so do my brother and my aunt. I can teach you how to hunt, and to live as Kyn. I will not allow Alexandra to poke you with too many needles."

Jema wanted to go at once, wherever Thierry wanted to take her, but there was one person holding her back. Valentin Jaus. She had so many questions about his involvement in her life. The way he had spoken to her and held her while they were dancing at the masque . . . he had acted like a man in love.

Was he?

"Before I say yes," Jema said, "and it's going to be yes, Thierry, I need to do something."

Thierry walked her over to Jaus's house, but stayed outside. "I will wait here. It is best."

Alex and Michael were staying with Jaus until he recovered from the surgery Alex had performed to reattach his arm. Jema saw that Alex had some reservations about letting her see him, but assured her she wouldn't be long.

"He's taken some hard knocks in the last couple of days," Alex said. "Thierry cut off his sword arm, and while I've got it back together, it's never going work the way it did."

"Is he in love with me, Alex?" Jema asked.

She shrugged. "You need to ask him that question."

Valentin was in his bed reading a report when Jema went in. "Miss Shaw. How kind of you to visit me."

"I don't think we can be Mr. Jaus and Miss Shaw anymore,

Valentin." She went over and sat on the side of his bed. Could this man really have secretly loved her all these years? Why hadn't he said anything to her? "I'm so sorry about what happened at your party."

"I thought it was one of my better ones," he joked.

How could she put it without embarrassing him? "I meant, I'm sorry I didn't realize how you felt about me. I should have guessed."

"How I feel about you as my neighbor?" When she shook her head, he frowned. "Then I am confused."

"I'm in love with Thierry Durand," she said, not to hurt him, but to make the point. "Suddenly I'm noticing a lot of things I never have in the past."

She glanced over at the wall, where it appeared he had taken down a great many paintings recently. The only photo left in the room was that of Jaus holding a dark-haired baby. The baby's face was turned away from the camera, but Jaus was looking down on the child in a way that made Jema shiver.

"My godchild," Jaus said when he followed the direction of her gaze. "You know that we cannot have children. Alex has told you?"

She nodded. "I never expected to, so it wasn't a big disappointment. I just . . ." She made a frustrated gesture.

"Alex believes I infected you with my blood," he continued. "If I did so, I assure you it was not deliberate. I hope you will forgive me someday for my part in this."

"Forgive you? What about me? I feel as if I've done something terrible to you by falling in love with Thierry." She gave him an uncertain look. "Does that sound completely conceited?"

"My dear Jema." He took her hand in his. "You are a beautiful young woman. Were you not attached, I would gladly take you out dancing whenever you wished. But that is all it would have been."

She bit her lower lip. "Really?"

"It has been a pleasure to know you as my neighbor." He bent over to kiss the back of her hand. Even lying in bed, Jaus made the gesture seem completely natural. "Go back to the man you love, and be happy."

She searched his face for some indication that he was lying to her. All she saw was a distant affection and sincerity.

"I guess I was reading into things too much." On impulse, she bent over and kissed his cheek. "I hope you feel better soon. Thierry and I are going to New Orleans. I'll write and let you know how it goes, if that's okay?"

"I would like nothing better," he assured her.

Alexandra watched Jema Shaw walk out of Jaus's house. She stood at the window long enough to see Thierry pick up his *sygkenis* and whirl her around in the snowy air before carrying her off. It was a terribly romantic moment, one that panged even Alex's decidedly unromantic soul.

"I'm going to check on Val," she told Cyprien, who was working on his laptop.

"Do not be long." He gave her a direct look. "I have found a bedroom we have not slept in yet, and there is the matter of the shrieking orgasm you owe me."

Alex went to Jaus's room. He was sitting up in bed now, and she felt sure he would be back on his feet in another day. When she looked in, Jaus wasn't in bed, but standing by his window, watching the snowfall.

He'd taken off the sling and the dressings, leaving his arm bare. The moonlight poured silver over him, created a thin line of shadow on the surgical site. Despite Kyn healing, Valentin would always carry a scar from having his arm severed. The limb had been separated too long from his body, Alex thought, to regenerate completely. He might never use a sword again.

She didn't want to guess what sort of scar losing Jema had left on his heart.

He wasn't looking at the snowfall, Alex realized. He was looking down at the seawall, where Jema and Thierry had been walking.

Alex started to say something, and then she saw the moonlight silver a tear slowly winding down Valentin's face.

She turned away and quietly left him there, as Jema had, alone in the moonlight.

Read on for a preview of
Lynn Viehl's next novel of the Darkyn

DARK NEED

Coming from Signet Eclipse
in June 2006

Despite the ninety degree heat and soup-thick humidity, a long line of patrons were waiting outside *Infusion*. Sam found an empty space halfway up the block, parked, and flipped down the visor to display the unit ID card. Harry was busy staring back at the club line.

"What is this place, like that Rocky Horror movie?" he asked, disbelief escalating his bushy eyebrows.

"You're stuck in the seventies, pal." Sam noted a couple passing by them: a young man who had tricked himself out to clone Marilyn Manson; his sulky companion, a Cuban girl, had affected more of a Daisy Fuentes on Acid look. "This is beach goth." And not the kind of people or place she'd have expected a class act like Lena Caprell to frequent.

Harry grumbled all the way from the car to the front entrance of the nightclub, where a sign by the door indicated the cover was twenty bucks. The door man, a muscular tank in a surprisingly nice tux, stood up as Sam and Harry cut the line.

"Turn it around." A meaty hand came up to make a stop sign. "You have to wait like the rest of them."

"But we have special invitations from the city." Sam flashed her shield, and the bouncer rolled his eyes before he jerked open the club's steel front door. "Thanks."

It took a moment for Sam's eyes to adjust to the near total darkness inside, and then she took in the basic layout. *Infusion* was cavernous for a beach club, lighting and sound equipment hanging from a flat black ceiling thirty feet above her head. There were plenty of tiny tables and stools crowded around a huge gray slate dance floor, and polished chrome-and-glass bars that stretched the length of three walls. Bunches of red, oval-shaped lights glittered from the shadows, giving the impression of hundreds of watchful, vicious eyes.

"Welcome to my nightmare," Harry muttered.

Like the bouncer, the bartenders also wore beautifully tailored tuxes, and had their hair slicked back from handsome, bored faces. The waitresses sported abbreviated black French maid outfits, but without the usual mini white aprons and mob caps. No, the decor was definitely red and black—heavy on the black.

Music started up unexpectedly, and Harry flinched as Nirvana's "Smells Like Teen Spirit" came screeching out of the oversized speakers above their heads.

"See the office?" he shouted to be heard over Kurt Cobain.

Sam spotted a plain door off to one side. "Over there, I think," she yelled back.

They found the door locked, and a shouted inquiry at one of the bartenders nearby revealed that the owner had not yet arrived.

"I don't know when Mr. Hell will be in," the young man bellowed at Sam.

She frowned. "Mr. Hell?"

"Ell," the bartender repeated, emphasizing it. "Ell for Lucan."

"Christ, he only has one name?" When the bartender nodded, Harry made a disgusted sound and jerked his head toward the entrance. "Sam, this shit is gonna blow out my ear drums. I'll go canvas the line."

She nodded and caught the arm of a passing waitress, showing her and the bartender Lena's photo. "Either of you recognize this woman?"

The bartender shook his head and went to deliver two screwdrivers to a couple of middle-aged women at the end of the bar.

"Sorry, no," the waitress said before she hurried off with a tray heavily loaded with Mai Tais.

That was the same answer Sam got from everyone, and after an hour of coming up empty, she was ready to leave. The pounding music and clouds of cigarette smoke had given her a brutal headache, and if Lena Caprell had ever come to *Infusion*, she'd apparently done it invisibly.

"Sam." Harry appeared and watched the gyrating bodies on the dance floor for a moment. "No luck outside. You?"

"Manager still hasn't shown up. I think we'd better—" A huddle in one corner caught her eye. "We got a deal going down over there."

Harry squinted. "Yeah. Take two o'clock, I'll come up from nine."

The five men and women grouped together in the corner stood shoulder-to-shoulder, half-hidden between a square column and one wall of the club. Sam strolled up, peered over one shoulder and saw a woman in the center. Ten hands were doing various intimate things to the woman's body.

"Hey." Sam prodded a back. "Time for a cigarette."

"I don't smoke." The thirties-something man glanced over his shoulder and bared some fake plastic fangs. "Would you care to join us?"

"You talking up my date?" Harry asked as he came up on the man's other side. He peered at the guy's mouth with mocking astonishment. "Halloween was over in October, buddy."

One thing Sam hadn't been seeing was any sign of drunkenness or drug use, two favorite activities at the downtown beach clubs.

"Let me talk to her." She pushed two shoulders apart and stepped into the huddle. "You okay here, lady?"

The woman's hair was a tangle, and her button-up dress was open to the waist, but nothing was hanging out. Her eyes focused on Sam after a couple of seconds.

"I'm fine." She leaned back against one of the men, who cupped her breasts. "So fine."

Everyone smiled at Sam and Harry. Everyone wore plastic fangs.

Swingers playing oversexed vampires. It took all kinds. "Look," Sam said, "why don't you folks find a nice hotel?"

"Is there a problem here, officer?"

Sam swiveled and nearly slammed into a broad chest. She looked up into ghost-gray eyes. "Who are you?"

The man took her hand in his, the touch of the black velvet

gloves he wore shocking her. "I'm Lucan, the owner of the club. You wanted to speak to me."

What kind of man wears velvet? In July? Sam tugged her hand from his. "Detective Brown, Fort Lauderdale homicide. My partner, Detective Quinn. We need to ask you a couple of questions, Mr. Lucan."

"It's simply Lucan." His thin lips curled into something between a sneer and a smile. "Shall we go to my office?" His pale eyes briefly flashed up at the speakers. "It's the only place you'll hear my answers."

Sam heard Harry wheeze and saw more people lighting up cigarettes around them. She leaned close to him. "Let me handle this; you go outside before you have an attack."

Harry scowled but trudged off.

Lucan waited until she looked at him, turned, and walked through the crowd to the office. Sam followed, studying him from behind. He didn't match the description of the suspect; he was too big. She figured him to be at least six-four and two-twenty. He wore his silver-blond hair like a lion's mane, which should have come off stupid but didn't. Even the silly velvet gloves didn't seem prissy, but he had huge hands.

How would it feel . . . Sam shoved aside the mental image of black velvet on her breasts. *Quit thinking with your crotch.*

The interior of Lucan's office matched the club in style, decor, and darkness. He removed his jacket, turned on a small desk lamp, and offered Sam a drink, which she refused. She inspected him up close as he poured some wine for himself. The full-sleeved, white poet's shirt and plain black trousers were retro nineteenth century, but it was a goth club; he probably considered it a uniform. He wasn't Cuban, not with the corn-silk hair and spooky eyes. His voice sounded British, but only vaguely.

"How did you know we were cops?" she asked him as he came to stand with her in front of his wide, spotless chrome and slate desk.

"You're not wearing black lipstick." He sipped his wine before returning her inspection. "Judging by your suits, you were either bill collectors or police officers. How may I be of service, detective?"

"We're investigating an incident that happened nearby." She showed him Lena's photo. "Do you recognize this woman?"

Lucan studied the image. "Yes, but I don't know her name."

"How do you know her?"

"I had sex with her several weeks ago." He sat back on the edge of the desk.

"You were lovers?"

He smiled. "We were strangers."

Sam tried not to jump on that, but it was irresistible. "Do you often have one night stands with strange, nameless women, Mr. Lucan?"

"Three nights." He drained his wine glass and straightened, moving a step closer.

Sam smelled night-blooming jasmine, but couldn't identify the source. "What was that?"

"It was a three-night stand. I kept her in my bed for three nights." He bent closer, and his voice dropped to a bedroom murmur. "How many nights would you last, Detective?"

Was he hitting on her? "None." Sam felt strange, rooted to the floor. "I don't have sex with strangers."

One velvet-covered finger touched her dry lips. "Then let's get better acquainted, shall we?"